RAGNAROK

Baen Books by Patrick A. Vanner

THE XAN-SSKARN WAR

Ragnarok

Niflheim*

Valhalla*

*forthcoming

RAGNAROK

PATRICK A. VANNER

BAEN

Ragnarok

A Baen Books Original

Baen Publishing Enterprises
P.O. Box 1188
Wake Forest, NC 27588
www.baen.com

ISBN: 978-1-4391-3384-2

Cover art by Kurt Miller

First printing, September 2010

Distributed by Simon & Schuster
1230 Avenue of the Americas
New York, NY 10020

Library of Congress Cataloging-in-Publication Data

Vanner, Patrick A.
  Ragnarok / Patrick A. Vanner.
      p. cm.
  ISBN 978-1-4391-3384-2 (trade pbk.)
  1. Space warfare—Fiction. 2. Human-alien encounters—Fiction. I. Title.
  PS3618.A673R34 2010
  813'.6—dc22
                                             2010020470

10 9 8 7 6 5 4 3 2 1

Pages by Joy Freeman (www.pagesbyjoy.com)
Printed in the United States of America

To my father, without whose love and support
I would not be the man I am today.
I love and miss you, Dad.
This one is for you.
Semper Fidelis

Acknowledgments

My thanks to everyone who made this book possible by supporting me over the years. There are too many of you to count, but you all know who you are.

Patrick

Chapter One

USS *FENRIS*
JULY 20, 2197
0342Z
LACAILLE 9352

"BRACE FOR IMPACT!"

The light cruiser rocked violently as missiles tore a wound in her flank; the debris, air, and water vapor were lost in the steady stream already hemorrhaging from the ship.

The mauled and wounded light cruiser *Gna*, named for the handmaiden of Frigga who was the messenger of the Norse gods, valiantly tried to live up to her name, racing toward the hyperlimit and escape. Escape to not only save herself and her crew, but to warn the rest of humanity of the horrors and dangers she was desperately trying to outdistance.

"Damage report!" Commander Alexandra McLaughlin, captain of the *Gna*, shouted into the smoke-filled command deck.

"Hull breach, port-side aft," a voice yelled back to her. "And we have—" the voice cut off in mid-sentence as the *Gna* heaved again.

Alex tore her eyes from the panels on her command chair to look at the speaker, Lieutenant Commander Hatty, her XO. She watched as he stared helplessly back at her, his mouth working silently and his uniform jacket glistening in the dim red emergency lighting, blood flowing from around the jagged piece of metal embedded in his throat. Alex forced herself to turn away.

"Tactical, report!"

"A quartet of Xan-Sskarn fighters. And it looks like they're lining up for another attack run," Lieutenant Commander Greg Higgins called back to her. His soot-streaked face watched her until she nodded her acknowledgment. Then the man quickly returned his attention to his console. The battle net was nothing but a memory now, the static hissing from her headset a constant reminder of the young ensign still strapped into his chair, hands blackened, burned, and melted into his console by the same electrical surge that had stopped his heart.

"Yes!" Greg shouted. "Splash one Sally fighter and . . . Shit!" Alex watched as he spun around to face her. "Incoming missiles!"

Gripping the arms of her command chair, Alex braced for the impact. There was no need for her to call out a warning. Greg's shout had alerted anyone who could worry about such things anymore, and she could no longer warn the rest of her crew. Once more, a swarm of missiles ripped apart the *Gna*'s armor.

"God damn it, Guns, clear those fucking fighters from my sky!" Alex shouted. "NOW!"

"I'm trying, Skipper, but we just lost primary point defense. What's left of the net is in auxiliary local control, and with the main sensors down, the Sally's ECM is washing out the target locks at anything beyond one hundred kilometers." Responsibility for the sensors had become Greg's when a wet, meaty-sounding impact had come from the location of the sensor station directly behind her. The agonized gurgling had been mercifully short and had ended over an hour ago.

Greg was doing his best. Alex knew that, but he was doing his job, his assistant's, and running what was left of the *Gna*'s sensors. Unfortunately, she could not spare anyone to take some of the burden off him. Turning to get an update from the navigation officer, Alex twitched in shock as her headset suddenly burst back into life. The *Gna*'s damage-control teams were still alive and performing miracles.

"—defense envelope depth." The static and interference was bad, but Alex could still make out what the voice was saying. "I say again, this is Lieutenant Bandit of Valkyrie Flight 225. We're coming in off your starboard bow, requesting verification of your point-defense envelope depth."

"Bandit, this is the *Gna*." Alex didn't waste any time expressing the relief she felt. "Depth is one hundred kilometers. I say again, one hundred kilometers. We've got three bogies that need your attention."

"Roger that, *Gna*. That's what we're here for. Be aware, you have another seven bogies closing from astern, but don't worry, we've got them." Bandit's voice was light and cheerful despite the fact that he had to know that he and his fellow pilots would never leave the system. Even if the *Gna* could reduce her speed enough to allow those Valkyries to land, her landing deck and hanger bays were no longer operational. "Bobbie, Psycho, close up on me—we're going in. Godspeed, *Gna*."

"Good hunting, Bandit." Alex cut the connection.

"Sweet Jesus," Greg hissed over the now-restored command net. The battle net was still inoperable, leaving the command deck cut off from the rest of the ship. "There are only three of them. And where the hell did Valkyries come from, anyway? We're too far out for them to have made it here on their own."

"I don't know, and it really doesn't matter. All that matters is they're here, and they're buying us some breathing room."

The flashing light of an incoming communication drew her attention to one of her panels.

"This is the *Gna*," Alex said, opening the channel. "Go ahead."

"Oh, thank God," a hysterical-sounding voice came back to her. "This is the *Hervor*. We need help! The captain's dead, and we lost our broadsides, and people are dead all over the ship, and—"

"Calm down. This is no time to panic," she snapped into her mike.

"Yeah, right," Greg's voice muttered in her earpiece. Alex couldn't bring herself to comment on that.

"Now, let's start over. Who is this?"

"Lieutenant Maloy, ma'am."

"Okay. Now, Lieutenant, who is in command over there?"

"I think I am, ma'am. The captain's dead, and I can't get hold of anyone else." The panic was beginning to rise in his voice again.

"That's fine, Lieutenant," Alex soothed, trying to head off another round of hysterics. "Are you in contact with any other ships at this time?"

"Ah, yes, ma'am. The *Sunna*."

"Good. Do you know who is in command over there?"

"I spoke with an Ensign Effant, but I don't know if she was in charge or not." Maloy's voice was becoming more level as he seemed to be getting hold of himself.

"Okay. Here's what we are going to do. First, I want you to slave the *Hervor*'s sensors to the *Gna*. Then I want you to contact the *Sunna*, find out who is in command, and get them on the line with us," Alex ordered, giving out simple commands that would help to calm the lieutenant even more. Muting her connection with Maloy, she turned to Higgins.

"As soon as you get the feed from the *Hervor* I want you to get their positions relative to ours. Lieutenant Donahue." Addressing the *Gna*'s navigation officer, Alex continued. "When you have that information, plot us an intercept course. Let's get those ships in close."

Both officers voiced their assent, and while they were turning to their tasks, Alex reestablished her connection to Lieutenant Maloy.

"Okay, Lieutenant, what have you got for me?"

"Ma'am, I have Ensign Effant on the line with us. She is the ranking command officer of the *Sunna*."

"Very well. Status report, Ensign."

"Ninety percent casualties, two laser mounts and one torpedo tube operational on the starboard broadside, one missile tube and one torpedo tube operational on the port. We have exactly seventeen missiles left for our remaining launcher." The ensign's voice was a wooden monotone, a clear sign she was in shock, but at least she seemed to be tracking well enough to provide what Alex hoped was accurate information. "Point defense is off-line, and there are multiple hull breaches throughout the ship."

"Thank you, Ensign. Lieutenant?"

As the lieutenant began his report, Alex watched the nav plot update with their new course to rendezvous with the two frigates. She was relieved to see that the *Hervor* and the *Sunna* were already close enough to support one another, though as damaged as both ships were, there was not much each could do for itself, let alone its mate.

"Status change," Greg's voice called out across the command deck just as the navigational plot updated to include another ship. "New contact. Looks to be a Xan-Sskarn destroyer. I'm not reading any plumes or energy fluctuations, and she's headed our way."

The destroyer that Greg just picked up was undamaged and fresh, ready for a fight. Which in turn meant that the two heavily damaged frigates would be easy meat for her guns. The thought that the *Gna* was just as heavily damaged and in no shape to tangle with a fully operational and battle-ready destroyer never entered Alex's mind.

"Helm, bring us about. New heading, zero nine one mark three one eight, best possible speed," Alex ordered without hesitation. "Lieutenant Maloy, the *Hervor* and the *Sunna* will head for the hyperlimit. We'll slow them down long enough for you to clear their engagement envelope before you begin your turnover."

"But ma'am," Maloy began.

"You have your orders, Lieutenant. Carry them out."

"Yes, ma'am. Thank you, Captain, and good luck."

"You, too, Captain. *Gna* out."

"Course laid in, ma'am," Donahue informed her.

"Very good, Lieutenant," Alex stated formally. "Execute."

The shrilling alarm of an incoming communication filled the darkened cabin. Captain Alexandra McLaughlin, commanding officer of the heavy cruiser *Fenris*, rolled over in bed, groaning.

It's been almost two years since Ross 128. Why the hell would I be dreaming of it now? I put those ghosts to rest a long time ago.

Her hand slapped blindly for the accept button. Silencing the alarm, she flopped back onto the bed.

"McLaughlin."

"Sorry to disturb you, ma'am, but long-range sensors have picked up a translation at the hyperlimit," the caller said.

Of course a ship translated in at the hyperlimit. That would be why it's called the hyperlimit. Keeping her sarcastic reply to herself, Alex also refrained from giving the caller a basic outline on why the hyperlimit was just that as her mind drifted back to a lecture she had attended years ago.

"Jumping a ship across or into a planetary system's gravitational forces is a recipe for disaster," the wizened old man in a suit two sizes too big for him lectured. *"The multitude of gravitational fields and their varying strengths play merry hell with ships in fold space. If a person is crazy enough, or just plain stupid enough, and if that person is very, very lucky, they will only end up off course.*

If not, well, some people looked forward to becoming one with the universe."

Taking a deep breath and closing her eyes for a moment, Alex divested herself of the memory, forcing her sleep-addled mind back to the task at hand.

"Understood. I'll be up there in fifteen minutes." She was just about to close the channel when she thought, *What the hell— misery loves company.* "Wake the XO and have him report to the command deck as well."

"Yes, ma'am."

"McLaughlin out." As the channel went dead, Alex sat up in bed, and reaching out with one hand, turned up the lights in her cabin while running the other hand through her tangled mass of red hair. The dream still lingering in the back of her mind, Alex's thoughts turned to the ghosts of her past. She could not shake the feeling that they had been trying to tell her something or, worse, do something to her. Alex shivered at that thought. Standing up and shaking her head to clear the last vestiges of sleep and dreams from her mind, she headed toward the shower.

Stripping off her nightclothes, Alex stepped into the shower stall and turned on the water. *Besides*, she thought, leaning back into the spray, *what harm can ghosts do?*

Commander Greg Higgins, Executive Officer of the heavy cruiser *Fenris*, stood next to the captain's chair on the command deck, sipping a cup of coffee while holding a second cup in his free hand. The soft hiss of the lift hatch opening announced the arrival of the captain.

"Captain on deck," Greg said in a bright, cheery voice, with a beaming smile directed at his captain.

"As you were," Alex ground out, staring daggers at her XO.

"Good morning, Captain. How are you this fine morning?" he asked, handing over the second cup of coffee after she settled into her command chair. While Greg had never been a fan of early mornings, over the years he had come to realize that if there was one thing in the universe that Alexandra McLaughlin hated, it was early mornings. And he took every opportunity he could get to tweak her about it. In return, she would do the very same thing next time they had to leave the ship. His hatred of flying was on par with her attitude toward mornings. Smiling at her as she took a sip of coffee, he could have sworn he heard her mutter something about "evil" and "unnatural."

"Okay, XO, what have you got for me?"

"Well, we've got a pair of destroyers that jumped in about three hours ago, so any communications or messages should clear translational distortions in another ten minutes or so."

Greg knew that despite her distaste for mornings, it only took her a moment or two to wake up; the rest was really just for show, her trying to maintain her reputation.

Alex let her eyes wander over the command deck as she drank her coffee. The glossy black consoles with their multicolored lights and the constant murmur of voices and humming of equipment were soothing after her violent nightmare. She felt safe and satisfied watching the dozen-plus men and women sitting and standing around her, quietly going about their various duties.

Several minutes passed before a voice came from behind them.

"Incoming communications."

They both continued to drink their coffee while the comm officer on duty copied the incoming message traffic and sorted out the priority messages from the routine.

Looking at the pad the ensign handed him, Greg smiled.

"Well, anything that was worth getting up this early for?" Alex asked, finishing off her coffee and holding out her hand for the pad.

"I'd say so, ma'am. Looks like we're done with our patrol of Lacaille 9352. We have orders to join Admiral Stevens' fleet at Groombridge 34," he said, handing the pad over.

"Groombridge 34. That's the front lines."

"Yes, ma'am, it sure is."

Greg watched as Alex leaned back into her chair, scrolling through the rest of the message traffic, and he didn't miss her quiet response.

"Good. It's about time we got back into the fight."

Chapter Two

CAMP LEJEUNE, NORTH CAROLINA, TERRA
JULY 20, 2197
0930Z
SOL

"Battalion!" cried a voice.

"Company!" several voices shouted.

"Platoon!" even more voices called out.

"Atten-hut!" the first voice bellowed, and several hundred heels snapped together in unison, generating a loud pop. "Dis-missed!"

With that final command, the whole of Third Battalion, Second Marine Division, took one step backward, performed a parade ground–perfect about-face, then erupted into cheers. The neat and orderly lines of the formation dissolved into chaos in a matter of seconds.

Lance Corporal Alan Lewis joined his platoon in their cheering. At one hundred seventy centimeters and eighty kilos of solid muscle, with close-cropped light brown hair and hazel eyes, he normally looked as if he had just stepped out of a recruiting poster. However, at the current moment he appeared to be nothing more than an exuberant young man looking forward to a long weekend of fun and relaxation.

The Old Man had just given them a positive review for the field evolution they had been on for the past two weeks. Even better, he had granted them a seventy-two-hour liberty. Not including the rest of today, they had three full days to do as they wanted, with nothing to worry about until Monday morning.

Better yet, he had been ordered to accompany the headquarters platoon on their return to the base last night to service and secure the classified equipment he and his fellow Intel specialists had used during the exercise. So he had already squared away his gear and had had the chance to clean up.

Laughing and joking along with the rest of his friends, he filed into the barracks, heading for his room. Though he had returned last night, it had been late when he had arrived, and the maintenance on the comms and encryption equipment had taken most of the remainder of the night. Feeling the lack of sleep catching up with him now that he had no pressing duties, Alan lay back on his bunk and relaxed.

Awakened by a pounding on his door, Alan swung his still-booted feet onto the floor and answered it. Opening the door, he was surprised to see the company gunnery sergeant standing there.

"Gunny Bliss?" Still shaking off the last vestiges of sleep, he tried to think of a reason for the company gunny to be standing in front of him.

"Good evening, Lance Corporal Lewis," Gunny Bliss started off with an overly friendly smile and tone that had Alan instantly wary. "Sorry to wake you, but the captain would like a word with you."

Captain Bellefontaine, company commander of First Company, was a man you did *not* want to get on the wrong side of, and lance corporals were normally not summoned into his presence unless they were on the wrong side of something.

"Me, Gunny?"

"Yes, you. Now, come on." Gunny Bliss put his hand on Alan's shoulder and practically dragged him out of his room and into the passageway.

"Am I in trouble?" Not wanting to sound as if he had a guilty conscience, he tried to keep the question in, but he blurted it out as they walked. The passageway was eerily silent. The rest of the barracks' residents, having been released for a long weekend, had apparently vacated the building without delay.

"Did you do something wrong?"

"No, Gunny."

"Then you're not in trouble." The gunny's simple logic did nothing to quell the uneasiness churning Alan's stomach.

Finally, they reached the company commander's office. Gunny Bliss walked directly in, telling Alan to wait outside. Several minutes later, Lieutenant Marshall, his platoon commander, arrived, pausing in front of him.

"Lance Corporal Lewis, why am I not surprised to see you here?" Lieutenant Marshall grinned at him. "Wrong place and wrong time yet again, and this time it's going to cost you." Patting him on the shoulder, she stepped past him, knocked once on the door, then walked into the captain's office, closing the door behind her and leaving Alan alone with his thoughts once again.

Alan Lewis swallowed hard. He wanted to pretend that he didn't know what the lieutenant had been talking about, but that wasn't possible.

For some reason, whenever something really interesting or spectacularly unlikely was taking place, he could be found in close proximity. Most of these occurrences weren't bad things, and a majority of them weren't his fault; he just seemed to be a magnet for unusual circumstances.

Gunny Bliss suddenly appeared, beckoning him to enter the captain's office. Stepping forward, he felt the gunny's hand on his shoulder again, guiding him toward a position directly in front of Captain Bellefontaine's desk.

The captain's office was like any other military office to be found on the base, with awards and commendations decorating the drab-colored walls, a file cabinet in the corner, and several chairs in various locations. The desk was unadorned and functional, the paperwork and data pads stacked neatly on its surface illuminated by the holo display built into the desk top.

Seeing Captain Bellefontaine seated behind his desk, flanked on one side by Lieutenant Marshall and on the other by Battalion Sergeant Major Tiwari, the uneasiness in his stomach increased tenfold. If it had not been for Gunny Bliss behind him, Alan would have stopped dead in his tracks. As it was, the gunny's presence forced him to keep moving, leaving him standing before the captain.

"Lance Corporal Lewis, reporting as ordered, sir!" Alan half shouted, nerves getting the better of him.

"At ease, Lewis. Relax—we're not on the parade field." Smiling, the captain took any possible sting out of his response. "Please, have a seat. I wanted to have a word with you."

Alan looked around behind him and saw a chair; he didn't remember seeing it on his way into the office, but then again, his eyes had been locked on the two men and woman behind the desk. Keeping his back ramrod straight, feet together, and hands resting on his thighs, Alan sat at attention. The two officers and two senior NCOs seemed to approve of this, as all of them had a small smile on their lips.

"Lewis, I've just had a short conversation with Lieutenant Marshall about you."

"Yes, sir?" Alan said, not knowing what else to say but not wanting to just sit there staring at the captain.

"Yes, and from what she has said, and from what I have read in your file, it is apparent to me that you are one outstanding marine. That being the case, I need your help."

"My help, sir?"

"Correct." Still smiling at him, Captain Bellefontaine explained the situation. "As you may or may not be aware, Corporal Veach of Second Platoon was scheduled to rotate out tomorrow for Recon School. His unfortunate accident yesterday will keep him out of action for at least a week as the QuickKnit takes care of his broken leg. That kills his chance of making this evolution, as class starts 0500 sharp, Saturday morning."

"Saturday?" Alan asked without thinking, then flushed scarlet, realizing that he had just interrupted the captain. Not seeming to mind the interruption, Bellefontaine answered.

"Yeah, Saturday. Don't ask me why—I haven't been able to figure that one out."

"If I may, sir?" Sergeant Major Tiwari interjected.

"Of course, Sergeant Major."

"It's simple, sir. Classes start first thing Saturday mornings so the instructors can be sure to have students that are not hung-over. Everyone reports in on Friday and is confined to barracks for the evening, no exceptions. If we started first thing Monday, you'd have students who were out all weekend celebrating with their friends and in no shape to begin training right away." His explanation finished, the short NCO leaned back against the wall, folding his arms.

"How disappointingly logical," chuckled Gunny Bliss. "And here I was hoping for some big secret." Everyone laughed at this. Even Alan managed a weak chuckle.

"As I was saying," Captain Bellefontaine continued after everyone had settled back down, "the colonel wants Veach's slot filled, and he wants it filled tonight. If we don't, Third Battalion may not get one next time. So, after speaking with Lieutenant Marshall, Sergeant Major Tiwari, and Gunny Bliss, I've decided you're the man for the job. Interested?"

Alan could do nothing but stare at the captain.

"Time is short, Lewis. I kind of need your answer now," Bellefontaine prompted him.

"Me, sir?"

"Yes, you," the captain said patiently, realizing that he might have overwhelmed the marine sitting in front of him. "I can't order you to take this, so it's up to you to decide whether you think you have what it takes to go Recon."

"But I'm not infantry, sir."

"You don't have to be. Besides, you've been attached to an infantry unit for the past eight months. You'll do fine."

"I don't know anyone in Recon. How am I supposed to get a recommendation before Saturday?"

"That's not true. You know the sergeant major here, and not only is he former Force Recon, he is also a former instructor. He has graciously consented to write you a sterling recommendation should you accept."

"Ma'am?"

"Take it, Alan," his platoon commander said, surprising him with how soft her voice was, as he normally only heard it shouting orders during field exercises or on the PT field. "You'll be fine. Besides, 'the wrong place at the wrong time' seems to be Recon's unofficial motto. You'll fit right in." Smiling at the vote of confidence, he turned back to the captain. "I'll take it, sir."

"Excellent. We'll have your orders cut by the morning. You go pack." Alan took the sheet of paper the captain extended toward him. "That's a list of what you are required to bring with you. If you are missing anything from that list, let Lieutenant Marshall know in the morning, and we'll get it rectified."

"Yes, sir." Alan stood up, bracing to attention before heading for the door. Gunny Bliss followed him out.

"Excited?" the gunny asked as they walked back toward his room.

"Terrified might be a better term, Gunny." Alan saw no reason not to be honest about it.

"I don't doubt it. Just remember—you wouldn't be going if the captain and lieutenant didn't think you were qualified. Keep that in mind."

"I will, Gunny. Thanks." They reached his room, and as he opened his door he turned to face the gunnery sergeant. "Can I ask you something, Gunny?"

"Sure."

"What made you decide to pick me?" Puzzled by the guilty expression that flashed across the gunny's face, Alan waited for his answer.

"Honestly, Lewis, you were the only one I could find."

Friday afternoon was just as hot and humid as it had been the day before, and Alan was equal parts nervous and excited. But regardless of whatever he was feeling moment to moment, one thing remained constant: he was not looking forward to what he knew was going to be some of the most difficult training he had ever gone through, and doing it in this stifling heat.

Well, it's better than being cold. I HATE being cold.

Following the directions he received at the admin office, Alan found his way to the barracks. Opening the door and entering, he saw two long rows of beds. He had not been in an open squad bay since boot camp, but he was not surprised by the setup. Open bays let the training instructors keep an eye on everyone at once, and it also let the trainees form camaraderie and unit cohesion. Case in point, there was a friendly discussion taking place at the far end of the bay. Walking in that direction, Alan set his duffels down on the floor and stood quietly behind the group of marines as they gave him nods of greeting but continued their conversation.

"I'm telling you, that vid was the worst piece of trash I've seen in years." The speaker was a sergeant leaning up against the wall, and Alan could see that he had his supporters as several heads nodded their agreement. "I mean, come on, it was not even remotely believable."

"That's the point," the corporal that seemed to be leading the opposition said. "It's a vid, and it's only there for entertainment, not education."

"Yeah, but you and I both know how many people out there take what they see in vids as the truth." The corporal opened his mouth to respond, but the sergeant cut him off. "Wait, let's get a fresh opinion."

Alan watched as the ring of marines expanded to include him, and everyone turned their attention to him.

"Uh, I really don't have any idea what you are talking about."

"The vid they showed last week. It was on all the major networks," the sergeant explained. "I mean, they hyped it for weeks before showing it. How could you have missed it?"

"Well, I was in the field for the last two weeks and just got back yesterday."

"Wow, two weeks in the field then right to Recon school. Sucks to be you." The corporal gave him a pitying look. "Anyway, the vid was about the Xan-Sskarns and why we're fighting the war. I don't want to ruin it for you, but the basics were that they were coming to eat us and strip the planet of its natural resources. Not the most original of plot ideas, I'll grant you, but still it was exciting."

The sergeant pushed away from the wall, beginning to speak, but the corporal stopped him.

"Now, just wait. You said you wanted to get another opinion, so give the guy a chance to say something first, even if he hasn't seen it."

Leaning back against the wall again, the sergeant watched Alan expectantly.

"Okay, as I said, I've not seen it, but from what I know of the plot I can give you my opinion of it," Alan started hesitantly, waiting to see if they still wanted to hear what he had to say. As the group continued to watch him, clearly waiting for him to continue, he began to warm up to the topic. *I guess I'll fit in here, after all.* "The idea that the Xan-Sskarns are here to eat us and strip the planet is just ludicrous. Everyone knows that the Xan-Sskarns come from a draconian and militaristic, patriarchal society that is formed around a strict caste system. This system of government has led to rampant expansionism, and as a result, they have polluted the three habitable planets of their home system. Polluted them so badly that they've lost a great many of their spawning grounds. Those spawning grounds are found along coastal waterlines, and that's what makes our planet so attractive to them. Our oceans are nowhere near as polluted as theirs, and they want them. Captured records show that they intend to reduce the human race to a manageable level and subjugate us in order to use us as laborers. I've never seen any evidence that they have any intention of exterminating us or using us as a food source. So..."

Alan stopped as he noticed the vacant expressions on the faces around him.

So much for fitting in.

Chapter Three

DEEP WATERS
OCTOBER 5, 2197
2219Z
STRUVE 2398

Bright actinic energy blossomed in space, immediately followed by an even larger pulse of electromagnetic energy and gravitational distortions as a ship appeared at the edge of the system. Resembling a smooth stone pulled from the bottom of some stygian sea, the ship was oblong, colored in putrid browns and fungal greens of no discernable pattern. The Ssi-Nan sped forward at maximum acceleration as a hatch along its spine opened and the long-range communications array emerged. As the ship cleared the distortion area generated by its space fold, the array came to life and began transmitting.

Summoned by an urgent message from the staff within, Vice Commander Si'Lasa stepped into the *Deep Waters*' communications center. Si'Lasa, at two point five meters, was large, even for a Xan-Sskarn, but was a perfectly representative specimen of his race in every other respect: amphibianlike, with an iridescent skin

17

of browns and reds, standing on heavily muscled legs ending in webbed feet, with a long, powerful tail extending behind him, its tip twitching. His long and lean torso heaved as he breathed heavily. His long arms remained at his sides as he stalked to the center of the room, the razor-sharp talons at the end of his hands clacking together in rhythm with his steps. A long, sibilant hiss preceded Si'Lasa's angry demand as his powerful neck muscles swung his head toward the issuer of the message.

"What reason do you have for interrupting my planning session and summoning me here?"

"Vice Commander, I offer my most abject and humblest apologies for the summons, but a Ssi-Nan that just translated in-system will speak to none other than yourself or the high commander, and I thought not to bother the high commander," the communications tech replied in a servile manner, careful not to look directly at the face of the irate Xan-Sskarn in front of him.

"You did wise not to disturb the high commander, but should this Ssi-Nan not have a *lashana* good reason for disturbing me, you will both pay. Him for this nonsense, and you for not insisting that he transmit his information to you as protocol demands."

The communications tech looked down at his instruments. Si'Lasa, smelling his fear pheromones, smiled, exposing rows of razor-sharp teeth.

"Yes, Vice Commander."

"Very well. Put this Ssi-Nan on line, and I will speak with him. Now."

The tech moved his shaking hands across his controls, and an image appeared in a crystalline display mounted on the bulkhead directly in front of Si'Lasa. A Xan-Sskarn in a mottled gray-and-black uniform displaying the rank tabs of a junior officer coalesced into view.

"Vice Commander, I am Tesh Na'Leash. I beg your forgiveness for this breach of protocol, but you must have this information at once," the Ssi-Nan commander began without preamble.

"I shall be the judge of what I must and must not have, Tesh; you would do well to remember that. Now, tell me, where have you returned from, bearing such *important information*?" Si'Lasa's mocking tone was not missed by either the tesh or the communications tech. Their worried expressions broadened the smile on his face.

"Vice Commander, I have just returned from my surveillance

of the hhhumannss's"—he dragged out the word in a complicated hiss—"advance fleet."

"Tesh, you may have just ended your life with that admission, as you are not due to finish that mission for many more tides. You are aware of the penalty for disobedience, are you not?"

"Yes, Vice Commander, I am, and I will submit to that punishment with a glad heart, for I deem this information worth more than my life or my honor, as it will ensure our victory over the Dry-Skins."

Si'Lasa pondered this last statement from the tesh. For a junior officer to disobey or disregard orders was very rare. For one to openly admit to it, and just as openly accept the punishment dictated by this action, was practically unheard of. His anger forgotten and his curiosity aroused, Si'Lasa stared directly at his subordinate on the display.

"Very well, tesh. Tell me of this information, and we shall see if it is indeed worth your life."

The hatch in the front corner of the command deck irised open. The guards flanking the command throne turned toward the sound. Two pairs of death-black eyes tracked the entrance of the newcomer onto the command deck.

Looking up from a display built into the arm of the command throne, the high commander could see the hazy outline of the newcomer through the translucent display located atop the forward station. Recognizing the visitor, the high commander was glad not only of the location of the hatchway but of the displays as well. This, of course, is why they were where they were.

The displays, constructed of a translucent crystalline material standing one meter above each of the stations, served a dual purpose. The first and most obvious purpose allowed the operators to monitor the flowing and constantly updating information, vital to both the functioning and controlling of the ship, projected within it. The second wasn't so obvious. Their synthetic crystalline matrix was highly impact-resistant as well as being capable of both dissipating and reflecting high-power, focused-energy bursts—such as those produced by an assassin's micro-laser.

The high commander closed his display and leaned back into the command throne, thoughtful. Xan-Sskarn battle doctrine dictated that Le-Kisnan, or carrier class vessels, were targeted first and eliminated, then the next smaller class of vessel, then the next, and so on. It appeared that human doctrine was similar, as Le-Kisnan were also being targeted and destroyed before lesser vessels. Whether by original design or adaptation did not matter, as with each Le-Kisnan or other senior-class vessel lost, the loss of those of the higher blood lines increased. Xan-Sskarn ships could only be commanded by those of noble blood, and the closer to the True Blood, as the nobility called it, an officer was, the larger, more powerful class of ship one could command. However, the expansion that the Swarm had experienced, along with the losses it had suffered since the war's onset, had subsequently generated the need for more commanders and officers, and lessened the need for such elaborate security measures. In most cases, with those new positions now available to those of lesser bloodlines, assassination had not been needed to advance in rank and status quickly anymore—a development the Swarm Masters were relieved to see. Though assassination, common during times of peace, was frowned upon but not outlawed during war, the disruptions caused by inexperienced officers could lead to disastrous results in battle. However, some Xan-Sskarn were not willing to wait for these opportunities to present themselves, choosing instead to create their own.

The newcomer rounded the console in front of the hatch and approached the command dais in an open and yet guarded manner. The two pairs of eyes ever left their target, and while they judged the newcomer as unarmed and having no duplicitous intentions, they did not relax their vigilance—not with whom the newcomer was and certainly not with whom their master was.

Vice Commander Si'Lasa stopped a meter from the command dais and, with the rasp of tail and scratch of hind claws, knelt on one knee.

The high commander looked down at his second-in-command. As hatchlings, all Xan-Sskarns were screened to determine genetic purity and then marked accordingly. The number of stripes corresponded to the number of relations removed from the True Blood. Si'Lasa was from a family but two relations away from the True Blood, as denoted by the twin tattoos sweeping from his muzzle and trailing down his neck. Xanle-Kisnan, formerly the sole dominion of one-stripes such as himself, were now being commanded by those with two. His vice commander was a friend, very capable, and very, very ambitious. Si'Lasa had risen through the ranks quickly during the war and would do well with a command of his own. With assassination being an acceptable tool of advancement, assuming one could get away with it, he would have to keep his guard up around Si'Lasa now, which brought the high commander a faint feeling of regret.

"By your leave, High Commander," Si'Lasa intoned in a deep, guttural voice.

"You may rise, Vice Commander," he said, finishing the ritual.

As the vice commander rose to his full two and a half meters and looked directly into his friend and commander's eyes, the high commander could see and smell the conflicting emotions emanating from him. He could sense the vice commander's fear—not fear for himself, but for his commander, and for the Battle Swarm should something happen to him. Underlying this fear, far fainter, as if hidden, the high commander sensed something far more powerful: pleasure and pride. The high commander could see his subordinate's joy at the prospect of his possible ascension to the command throne and feel his pleasure at causing worry and uncertainty in the Xan-Sskarn who sat on that throne now, even though it would mean betraying and murdering his friend and mentor.

"What do you wish to see me about, Vice Commander?"

"I have"—he paused, searching for the right words—"odd news, High Commander."

"What kind of 'odd' news? Do we have new orders? Have we been recalled? Is the strike delayed yet again?" The worry left him as he turned his full attention to the possibilities that this news might bring.

"No, nothing like that, High Commander. In fact, it is not from the Swarm Masters. This news comes from our Ssi-Nan stalking the Dry-Skins."

"*What?*" the high commander roared. "What do you mean it is from our Ssi-Nan? They are not due back for"—he opened his display—"another twenty tides."

"I am aware of our timetable, High Commander, and informed the tesh commanding the Ssi-Nan that he violated his duties, but nevertheless the Ssi-Nan is back and has transmitted data to us that you will want to see."

"That ship was to stalk the Dry-Skins," the high commander

hissed, "and gather all information possible about their ships and how they are deployed. What information could be so vital that this tesh would risk detection to bring it back? We will not be able to get another Ssi-Nan into that system undetected before we attack, and if the Dry-Skins send more ships into that system and we do not know how they are deployed, we will not be assured of our victory."

"I understand your anger, High Commander. However, when the tesh transmitted what he had seen and recorded, I congratulated him on his quick thinking and decisive action. He is a tesh who bears watching."

"Very well, Vice Commander Si'Lasa," the high commander said, getting himself under control again. "What is this news?"

"The Ssi-Nan detected a signal hidden in the lower spectrum of the Dry-Skins' navigational sensor sweeps of the system. This hidden signal contained information about the deployment of all of the Dry-Skins' assets. Not just the current deployment information, but all future deployment plans for the next thirty tides." Si'Lasa extended a data chip to his commander and waited as he took it and placed it into the reader built into his command throne.

"The next thirty tides?" The high commander began to read the scrolling information on his display. "Is this right?"

"I believe so. Their way of keeping time is strange, but not overly complicated. The Ssi-Nan confirmed that the current information was correct before translating out of the system."

"Yes," he said, beginning to understand, "I can see why this tesh thought to return to us immediately with this information. You are correct; he is to be commended for his action."

"So, do you believe that this information is reliable? If so, why would the Dry-Skins send this information to us? How could it possibly serve them?" the vice commander asked. Even after two cycles of battle, the Dry-Skins still confused him.

"I do not think that the Dry-Skins sent this message, but only one of them. Possibly even a small group working against their leaders," mused the high commander quietly as he continued to read the displayed information.

"But why?" Si'Lasa asked, exasperated. "How could the destruction of their fleet serve them? They would be killed along with the rest of their fleet. I do not think that this message can be trusted. It has to be a trap—"

The high commander's head came up quickly at his subordinate's questioning.

"If this is meant to be a trap, it would be the poorest way to set one up. They would not know if and when we planned to act upon this information, so they would have to be at combat stations constantly for the next thirty tides. These Dry-Skins are weak and would not be able to maintain that level of readiness for that length of time. No, Vice Commander, this is no trap," the high commander stated decisively. "I'm certain."

"Yes, High Commander." Si'Lasa came to attention. He still had doubts, but the decision was not his to make, nor was it his place to question, and as his nostrils picked up the shift in his commander's pheromones to anger at having his judgment questioned, Si'Lasa knew this conversation was over. "In twenty tides, we shall destroy the Dry-Skins completely."

"No. Send a message to the Swarm Masters," came the high commander's soft reply, his lips pulling back to expose rows of razor-sharp teeth. "This Battle Swarm will attack within the next two tides."

Chapter Four

USS *ASGARD*
OCTOBER 7, 2197
1643Z
GROOMBRIDGE 34

"Attention on deck!"

In an instant, the wardroom snapped to attention, the occupants so rigid they appeared as if in stasis. Those officers facing the direction of the command witnessed the admiral's arrival, as the lieutenant junior grade who had shouted the command stepped aside and the admiral stepped through the hatch.

"As you were." The admiral's voice resonated with quiet authority throughout the wardroom.

Reanimated at those words, the wardroom occupants resumed their conversations, but at a more subdued level.

Admiral Adam "Steely" Stevens approached a small group of his senior officers, where a heated debate was taking place.

"If we can take Epsilon Eridani and hold *this* system, we'll be in a position to strike both Sirius and Procyon, as well as take the Sallys' forward base of operation," stated Captain Beckham with the conviction of someone who assumed he was one hundred percent correct and therefore there should be no further conversation

on the matter. Beckham, a tall man, thin to the point of appearing emaciated, and with thick blond hair bordering on the very
edge of regulation length, leveled his gaze at the shorter officer
he addressed. He constantly moved as he spoke, as if filled with a
boundless energy, as fast and fluid as the light cruiser squadron he
commanded. He was just as well known throughout the fleet as his
opponent, Captain Zimmer, but for entirely different reasons. Being
on the defensive for the last year had caused more of his aggressive
and impulsive personality to be displayed; this argument between
him and Captain Zimmer was a prime example.

"It would be a mistake to attack Eridani at this time," Captain
Zimmer disagreed, matching Beckham's conviction. Zimmer, a
stocky woman with her brown hair in a style that most marines
would find severe, commanded the battleship *Mjölner* and its
screening ships.

As Beckham was bold and daring, desirous to be on the offensive
and in the thick of battle, Alice Zimmer was known throughout
the fleet as a reliable, dedicated, and relentless commander. A bit
on the predictable side and not given to recklessness or brash
action, she was nevertheless one of the best battleship commanders in the fleet.

"We have no firm intelligence on the location of the Sallys'
base of operations." She briefly glanced at the four people standing around her before continuing. "For all we know, it could be
in Kapteyn's Star, and they're just using Eridani as a jump point
to make us believe that they're staging there. Yes"—she pushed
forward, seeing Beckham prepare to respond—"they could be, and
probably are, there in Eridani, but it'll be several more weeks before
our recon ships will be able to confirm or deny the presence of
a base there. It would be unwise to extend our remaining forces
so thinly without solid intel. We cannot afford another Ross 128."

At her last statement, the officers lowered their eyes for a
moment and remembered Ross 128. Zimmer stole a glance over at
Captain McLaughlin and Commander Higgins, who were tucked
in the corner sharing a private laugh.

Lieutenant Rogers spoke for the first time since announcing
the admiral.

"Absent friends," he intoned solemnly, raising his glass.

The admiral nodded his approval as he and the rest of the small group echoed the lieutenant, raising their glasses in the traditional toast to fallen comrades.

Captain Zimmer glanced at Rogers with a look as if to say, *What does someone as wet behind the ears as you know about a loss like that?*

Admiral Stevens, at first just as curious at the serious tone of the lieutenant's voice, recalled that a significant portion of Rogers' academy class, including his fiancée, had been assigned to that ill-fated task force.

As the members of the group returned from their silent introspection, the debate continued.

"I have to agree with Captain Beckham," Commander Marks spoke up, which wasn't surprising, Marks being Beckham's XO, after all. William Marks, a man of average height and build, his black hair shot through with gray, was not physically imposing but possessed piercing green eyes that appeared to stare directly through whomever he spoke to.

"We should jump this fleet into Eridani and take it," he continued. "After that, we consolidate our position there and have Earth send part of Admiral Tanner's Home Fleet to hold here and cover our asses."

"You can't be serious," was Captain Zimmer's incredulous reply. "Attacking Eridani with our forces here is one thing, but stripping Sol's defenses to hold a position we are assigned to is not only tactically unsound, but a very dangerous gamble. Earth needs Tanner right where he is while the yards rebuild the fleet."

"From the last reports I saw, the yards were ahead of schedule with construction," Marks countered. "Besides, I'm not proposing we strip the whole system, just a small fraction of Home Fleet to hold this position, and those ships will be replaced on an almost daily basis as the yards complete construction."

"I've seen the same reports, and the first of those ships aren't scheduled for launch for another four weeks, even with the advanced timetable. Then there are the acceptance trials, and only a fool would think that ships thrown together so quickly wouldn't have their share of problems that can only be found during normal operations. No, we have incomplete intelligence on Eridani, we cannot marshal the forces necessary to take that system without exposing another system, and, on top of all that, both the fleet and marines have taken a hell of a lot of pounding and punishment in the last eighteen months. We need this time to not only rebuild our forces, but our strength as well."

"Captain Zimmer, what you say makes sense in the logical, statistical aspect of things, but sometimes in war, chances—" Marks began.

"I tell you again, Commander"—Zimmer overrode him—"we cannot afford another Ross 128. A gamble like the one both you and Captain Beckham are proposing could, mind you, *could* give us the advantage and breathing room we so desperately need. However, if it goes even partially wrong, we'll be decimated, and there will be no coming back from that. We wait for the recon ships, we rebuild our forces, and we get our spirit back. Then we go into Eridani, take it, stand on it, and move on, pushing the Sallys back into their oceans."

"I agree with you, Captain," said Beckham, startling Zimmer into silence with his acceptance of her argument. "We can ill afford another Ross 128. However, even that mess had its silver lining. Obviously, that fleet was on its way to Sol. Had Wentworth not gone in, incomplete intelligence or no, and destroyed or damaged a significant part of that fleet, it would've jumped into Sol, and where would we be now? We wouldn't be here having this conversation, that I can tell you."

"No, we wouldn't, but not because of the reasons you're alluding to. Think of the strength of the fleet when Wentworth jumped out. Not his fleet, but the entire fleet that was in Sol at that time. We would've had the advantage not only in numbers, but the home-field advantage as well. The mines, the stations, the satellites, the fixed defenses." Zimmer ticked off points on her fingers. "Yes, we would've taken more than our fair share of damage, but we would've held."

Recognizing that he wasn't going to sway Zimmer to his point of view, nor willing to relinquish his own position, Beckham turned to the admiral, who had remained silent throughout the entire debate.

"What's your opinion, sir? Should we go now, or wait? I can see where Captain Zimmer's arguments have *some* merit"—he nodded toward Zimm—"but as my XO was starting to say, sometimes in war one has to take chances. We cannot fight a purely defensive war and win. Nor can we hope to maintain a status quo. The balance must be changed, and it should be us, not the Sallys, that tip the scales."

Admiral Stevens cleared his throat and took a drink.

"You do have a point, Captain." He could see that Zimmer was preparing to launch another verbal attack and forestalled it. "However, Captain Zimmer has made some very valid points as well."

Captain Zimmer looked pleased with herself now that it sounded as if Admiral Stevens supported her position.

"Both you and Commander Marks are correct as well," he continued, noting the fall of Zimmer's face. "All three of you are voicing what every other person in this room is or has discussed time and time again in the last few months. Indeed, the senior fleet commanders were, and still are, having the same argument. I am not going to discuss my opinion here, at this time. This is a night for addressing at least one of Captain Zimmer's points— rebuilding the fleet's morale. I am sure you can agree with the necessity of that, can't you, Captain Beckham?"

"Yes, sir, I can." His tone made it clear that accepting one point did not mean accepting the others.

"Good. Very good." He smiled at all of them over the rim of his glass as he finished off his drink. "Now, if you will excuse me, I must find myself another drink and mingle with some more of my guests. I hope you enjoy the rest of the evening."

Admiral Stevens nodded at the group, and both he and his shadow, Lieutenant Rogers, turned and headed toward the bar. He smiled as he heard the debate picking up again. He had been honest with his officers when he said that the same debate was going on at the highest level of the fleet. He was always honest with those under his command. He could not tell them everything he knew, of course—there would always be an issue of "need to know"—but what he could pass on, he did. He did not like to keep secrets from his people as others in his position did. There was nothing to be gained from secrecy and far too much that could be lost.

The admiral's thoughts stayed with the group he had just left as he moved toward the bar, shaking the hands of some of those he passed, nodding to others.

He reached the bar and claimed the glass of whiskey waiting for him. Turning around, he leaned back against the bar and surveyed his other officers in the wardroom. There were senior ship commanders and their executive officers in attendance, squadron and wing commanders in their white dress uniforms, and senior officers from the marines embarked with the fleet in their black. The atmosphere was starting to lighten within the room—he could feel it. Spirits were lifting; moods were changing for the better. His gaze drifted to the far corner, and he saw one of the few people whose accomplishments made him feel like a junior officer again.

Alexandra McLaughlin, captain of the independent heavy cruiser *Fenris*, was not an imposing figure at one hundred and fifty-two centimeters, and he had almost missed her in the crowd of people. Slight of build, with a long braid of red hair and deep blue eyes, she appeared to be in her early twenties—unless one looked directly into those deep blue eyes and saw the pain and anguish residing there. The admiral chuckled to himself, thinking of her and her XO, Commander Higgins. Again, it was a study in opposites. Higgins, tall, heavily muscled, and looking every day of his forty-three years, was nothing short of painfully handsome, whereas she could only be described as cute. While many of the other officers in this room thought that the two of them were lovers, he knew for a fact that no relationship beyond the bonds of close friendship formed over many years existed between the two. The one piece of evidence that the others overlooked was that Commander Higgins was completely dedicated to his wife and family. The admiral tried to quash any rumors he heard, but they persisted. As Higgins didn't seem to be bothered by them, the admiral didn't concern himself with such scuttlebutt beyond what he came directly in contact with.

Now that he had a clear line of sight on McLaughlin, he saw one of the most competent officers in the fleet, though she did not look it. She usually didn't like to be the center of attention, though he knew from Commander Higgins that she did enjoy functions such as this one. She and Higgins were having a spirited conversation and enjoying themselves; he could see two pairs of empty tumblers on the table next to them, and each was holding a fresh one. Seeing her standing there smoking, drinking, and laughing with Higgins, it was hard to picture them both as having seen the worst parts of this war and having been in the most dire of situations. Even though this was an occasion for full-dress uniform, she wore only ribbons, not medals. At this distance, while difficult to distinguish between awards, two items stood out on her uniform. The first was the black skull and wings of a Loki pilot, and the second was a single sky-blue ribbon with five small white stars on it that occupied the top row of her awards in solitary splendor. As Commander Higgins moved to the side to allow someone to pass, Admiral Stevens saw that he, too, wore only ribbons so as not to draw attention to his captain. She had an independent command, not tied to any particular squadron but free to maneuver and fight as she willed, within the scope of an overall battle plan. He thought about how she had earned the honor and privilege of an independent command many times over: Ross 128.

As commanding officer of the light cruiser *Gna*, Commander Alexandra McLaughlin had followed Admiral Wentworth into Ross 128. Unlike the admiral, she had managed to exit the system, but had paid a terrible price for that escape. Her after action report, however, did not do justice to the real story of her escape from that killing field known as the Ross system. Her tactical officer at the time, Lieutenant Commander Higgins, had been more detailed about what his captain had done to save her ship, her crew, and the surviving crews of two other ships. Greg's report, and those of the surviving officers of the other ships she had rallied, had earned her that sky-blue ribbon. Admiral Wentworth may have brought the *Gna* and her crew to the gates of hell, but it was Commander Alexandra McLaughlin, with most of her crew killed or wounded and her ship falling apart around her, who had brought the *Gna* home again, where so many others had not.

The *Gna* herself had lived up to her name and had been the swift messenger that carried the first news of what had happened at Ross 128, and what the cost had been. She had taken everything that the Xan-Sskarns could throw at her, and kept most of her crew alive. There was not a man or woman of the surviving crew who had not wept when the *Gna* had been consigned to the breakers.

Admiral Stevens, realizing he was still staring at Captain McLaughlin's sky-blue ribbon, allowed his gaze to roam around the room. As he turned his head back to McLaughlin and Higgins, he noticed something was out of place. While he could hear subdued chuckles and see small smiles among the other officers, very few people in the room were openly smiling and laughing. Only McLaughlin and Higgins seemed to be treating this as a party and not some sort of senior officers' conference. He continued to survey the crowd, amazed that it was those two who were the liveliest of the guests. The others, discussing the military situation here and at home, or politics and ships' duties, while just as animated as McLaughlin and Higgins, did so in a hot and almost combative way. He wanted them all to be like the pair sequestered in the corner—leaving those topics behind, if even for a few hours, and simply relaxing and enjoying themselves.

He had spoken with both of them on several occasions since they had been attached to his fleet and found himself with a slight case of hero worship, feeling like a midshipman on a training cruise when the conversation turned to Ross 128, as it inevitably did.

A peal of laughter rang out from the corner, and the admiral smiled. He didn't know what was so funny and entertaining over there, but he was sure as hell going to find out. Signaling to the bartender, he ordered.

"I would like a refill on this please," he indicated his nearly empty glass, "and a round for those two having the good time in the corner." The bartender nodded as the admiral stood back from the bar and headed over to the laughter in the corner, trusting the drinks to follow. As he neared the pair in the corner, he could hear Higgins chuckling at something McLaughlin said, but it was too low for him to make out over the buzz of conversation in the room.

"Okay, you two," he said, coming up behind Higgins and startling them both. "What's going on in this corner that's so damn funny? You don't see anyone else acting like this is some sort of party, do you?"

"Sir!" came the dual response as both captain and executive officer tried to come to attention with drinks—and, in the case of McLaughlin, a cigarette—in their hands.

"Damn, it was a joke, you two! At ease." The admiral sounded exasperated. "This *is* a party, and you both are supposed to be having a good time, which, from everything I've witnessed, you are. I just wish the rest of them were having as much fun."

They both visibly relaxed and smiled as a steward arrived with the admiral's ordered drinks. Stevens took one and waved a hand at the others in invitation. Both of them took a glass, and all three were raised in a silent toast to each other.

"So," Admiral Stevens began, "is either of you going to tell me what you've been talking about in this corner that has you both in such a good mood?"

"Well," Alex began, then looked at her XO. Greg waved her off, smiling.

"You're the captain."

"Very well, Commander Higgins, I'll remember this." Smiling, she turned to the admiral. "We were just discussing the, umm, discrepancies in our memories."

"Really? You?" The admiral sounded shocked. "Now, Greg here, I can understand. I mean, he is getting on up there in years, but I don't think you have anything to worry about."

"See, I told you, didn't I? Even the admiral can see that you're getting on up there in age." Her smile was wide and infectious.

All three of them started to laugh. More than a few heads turned at the sound of their laughter, and some of the faces wore frowns.

"You would think this was a funeral or church they way some of them are looking at us," McLaughlin commented. "I did read the invitation correctly, didn't I? This is a Dining-In, right?"

"Yes, it is, and unfortunately, Alex, you and Greg seem to be the only ones who realize that it is indeed supposed to be a party."

She blushed at his use of her first name. This was the first time he had addressed her as anything but Captain McLaughlin. He called Greg by his first name frequently, but he had a history with him that went back further than hers did.

"Now, tell me," he went on, ignoring her blush, "what brought on this conversation about age." He looked curious as he watched both of them over the rim of his glass, sipping at his drink.

"Well, it's kind of embarrassing, sir," began Higgins, and he faltered as he looked at his captain.

"Yes," she said and cleared her throat. "Well, we were discussing your aide, Lieutenant Rogers."

"Oh?" asked the admiral, cocking an eyebrow.

"We were just commenting that neither of us could remember being that young and eager. I told Greg here that of course he was that young, and I'm sure I was as well, but seeing as how he's more, ah, advanced in years than I am, he was having a more difficult time remembering that far back. That was how the topic of age came up." She finished and blushed more deeply than before.

"I see. And besides his age—and I admit to you that I can't remember being that young, either—is there anything else that came up on the topic of my aide?" He didn't appear angry, but as if he genuinely wanted to know their opinions.

"Nothing, sir," came the simultaneous reply from both of them. The admiral smiled at that.

"Nothing?"

"Well, there was one other thing," Higgins looked even more embarrassed to admit.

"And that was?"

"We both thought that we heard Lieutenant Rogers squeaking," McLaughlin answered, looking just as embarrassed as her XO.

"He is new, isn't he?" The admiral smiled.

"Just a bit, sir," she replied, smiling as well.

Lieutenant Rogers appeared out of the crowd as if summoned by his name. He stopped at the admiral's shoulder and spoke in a quiet voice that McLaughlin and Higgins could still hear even over the background conversations.

"Everything is ready, sir. We can start whenever you wish."

"Very well, Lieutenant, thank you. You're the Vice President of the Mess tonight, so you'll be directing the rest of this evening's activities. You may sound the chimes at your discretion, Mr. Vice President."

"Aye, aye, sir." He came to attention, turned, and disappeared back into the crowd.

Chapter Five

"So, Lieutenant Rogers is the Vice President of the Mess this evening, is he?" asked Commander Higgins.

"Yes, he is, and why shouldn't he be? Tradition dictates that the Vice be the lowest-ranking member of the Mess. In this case, that honor falls to Mr. Rogers," said the admiral.

"I believe that the regs state that the position can be delegated to a person of higher rank, should the occasion call for it." Captain McLaughlin entered into the conversation. "Nothing against the lieutenant. Both Greg and I know that to become and remain your aide, he has to have his shit wired right—unlike your last, what, two or three aides that suddenly found themselves with new orders almost before they finished processing in. But with this much heavy brass floating around, I would think that he might feel a bit overwhelmed by it is all."

"You've got that right. He definitely is on the ball, and as you said, unlike the last four, actually, who seemed to think their job was to kiss my ass and shield me from all the bad news that they could intercept." Nodding and agreeing with McLaughlin's assessment of both his current and past aides, the admiral continued. "Rogers will do fine, and the experience will serve him well. Besides, it's not like things can be changed now anyway."

"True," said Higgins, smiling.

"Unfortunately, I'm the President of the Mess, and as stimulating as this conversation has been, it looks like the Vice President is going to be sounding the chimes soon, so I had best move on and greet the rest of my guests."

"Yes, sir," McLaughlin answered.

"Good evening, Admiral," Higgins intoned.

With his final statement, and a slight inclination of his head to the both of them, Admiral Stevens turned to the next cluster of officers and moved off.

"That there is a great man, and one hell of an incredible commander." Higgins' tone was admiring, with none of the humor or sarcasm that had colored most of their conversations this evening.

"Yes, he is. We're damn lucky to have him in command out here at the front," McLaughlin agreed. She extracted her cigarette case and was about to open it, then looked at her watch. She slid the case back into her jacket pocket, realizing that the Mess would be convening in a few moments, and tradition did not allow lighted smoking material in the Mess.

"Amen to that." Higgins smiled and tossed back the rest of his drink. Tradition also dictated that drinks were not brought into the Mess, either.

Alex smiled back, lifted her glass in salute to her XO's statement, and downed the rest of her drink as well.

Three silvery chimes rang throughout the wardroom, and Lieutenant Rogers' voice could be heard over the freshly quieted room.

"Ladies and gentlemen, the Mess is now called to order. If you would please take your seats."

Drinks were finished and smoking material extinguished as the officers began to enter the dining room though the double doors the lieutenant had just opened.

"Well, now, you behave yourself, Captain McLaughlin, and play nice with the other captains," Higgins said.

"And you, Commander Higgins, I hope you remember how

to use tableware. Eating with your fingers is just not acceptable among the company of other officers."

Some of their fellow officers appeared shocked by the interplay going on between captain and executive officer. While some of the other captains and XOs shared a close rapport, a majority acted in a strictly professional manner toward each other, with only a hint of friendship. Most of them did not mind the tradition of seating COs and XOs apart from one another. While this had the benefit of allowing new relationships to form and new ideas to be explored, McLaughlin and Higgins were among the few officers who didn't approve of this tradition. Those who hadn't shared their experiences would never understand their bond, and Alex and Greg would prefer to work as a team to deflect those who wanted to pry into their already painful memories at these kinds of formal engagements. Unfortunately, the admiral's aides who laid out the seating arrangements were sometimes not privy to the machinations of the upper ranks, so they followed the manual and tradition.

"Enjoy your dinner, Captain."

"You do the same, Commander."

With those final words, the two walked past the admiral and the other members of the head table, who were waiting to be announced so they could parade in after the guests had assumed their seats. They passed through the double doors and went in opposite directions, checking place cards as they walked between tables.

McLaughlin continued moving between tables until she came to a table near the front of the room. Glancing down, she saw a place card with Capt. A. McLaughlin printed on it, and took her seat. She was feeling a bit warm from all the whiskey she'd had in the wardroom, so reached past the glass of wine at her place setting and grabbed the pitcher of water. Filling her glass, she took a deep drink and glanced around at the place cards to her sides. Her good spirits started to fade.

"Oh, great," she whispered to herself with a wry smile, "Captains Zimmer and Beckham. This should be fun. Maybe water is not the way to go." She finished her water and reached again for the pitcher. This evening's dinner conversation was more than likely going to be akin to juggling live grenades. No need to dull her wits and possibly let slip her "colorful" personality.

"Captain McLaughlin, nice to see you again." Beckham took

his seat and extended his hand. She took it and pumped it once before disengaging herself.

"Nice to see you as well, Captain Beckham." She pasted a false smile on her face.

"Good evening, Captain McLaughlin." Captain Zimmer had arrived. Looking at Beckham, she glowered and took her seat. *Yes, fun indeed.*

"Captain Zimmer."

"Well, Alexandra," began Beckham, "how have you been? We've not seen each other since you arrived in-system to join the fleet."

She could tell from his condescending tone that he was one of those officers who resented her independent command. Well, two could play at that game.

"I've been good, Richard. I'm sorry we haven't had time to socialize these past few months, but commanding a heavy cruiser like the *Fenris*," she said pleasantly, her false smile still in place, "keeps me occupied and limits my free time. It's a big job, with quite a bit of responsibility. Doubly so because I have an independent." She knew that he desired his own heavy cruiser, even a full squadron to let him get into the thickest parts of battle. She could see that reminding him of what he coveted stung, as his face fell into a frown.

"So," she said, turning to Zimmer, "Alice, it's been, what, seven years?"

"Yeah, I think that's about right." Zimmer was wearing a smile that Alex could see was sincere; clearly she was enjoying seeing Beckham put in his place. "Not since we were both on the *Odin*. That was a good tour, one of my best—that is, before fleet gave me the *Mjölner* and my squadron. It's like having my own personal fleet." She was getting her digs in against Beckham as well. Her battleships alone held more offensive and defensive capabilities than Beckham's entire squadron. And then there were the screening ships under her command to take into consideration.

Beckham's face was completely closed and hard. He looked from one woman to the other and, seeing that for the moment discretion was the better part of valor, turned to the captain seated on his other side and extended his hand in greeting. Alex and Alice watched him turn away from them and smiled at each other, Alex giving Alice a conspiratorial wink. But as she opened her mouth to speak, she was interrupted.

"Ladies and gentlemen," Lieutenant Rogers called, and the murmuring conversations died out. "I present to you the President of the Mess, Admiral Adam Stevens, and the members of the head table." The assembled officers stood and came to attention as "Ruffles and Flourishes" sounded from the overhead speakers while Admiral Stevens and the rest of the head table marched into position at the head table and stood behind their seats. As the music ended, the members of the head table took their seats. After settling in, the officers still standing at attention relaxed at a nod from the admiral and assumed their own seats once again.

The admiral picked up the gavel from its traditional position on the table to the right of his place settings and rapped it loudly, once.

"I now call this Mess to order," the admiral announced in a resounding voice. "Post the Colors."

At this command, the assembled officers, this time including the entire head table, came to attention facing the flag. The lights in the room dimmed, and a spot light illuminated the National Colors mounted to the right of the head table. A deep baritone began to sing the national anthem, *a cappella*. It took a moment for Alex to realize the voice was filling the whole room without the aid of a microphone or any other kind of electronic amplification. She was also shocked to recognize the voice of Lieutenant Rogers. As he finished singing, she found that she had been moved more by that single beautiful voice than she had ever been when it was performed by a full orchestra, broadcast and filtered through mixing boards and sophisticated speakers. Drama could be overdone, but this was a perfect blending of drama and simplicity, resulting in a powerfully emotional moment.

As silence fell in the room, the admiral cleared his throat quietly, overcome with emotion himself.

"Please bow your heads for the invocation."

Lieutenant Commander Yu, a short, slightly overweight man, shifted to face the assembled Mess as they bowed their heads. The soft light glinted off the silver crosses on either side of his collar, and the backlighting of the spotlight seemed to surround him with a heavenly glow that left no doubt as to the vocation of this man.

"Heavenly Father," he began in a soft, quiet voice that nevertheless carried great conviction behind it, "during this time of strife and battle, we commit our bodies and our souls to your keeping. When we are in peril of life, give us the courage to perform our duties. When we are tempted into sin, grant us the strength to resist. Should we fall sick or wounded, grant us healing. Should we fall in battle, we beg of your mercy to receive us to yourself, forgiving us our sins. We humbly beseech you to bless all who are near and dear to our hearts and keep them in your fatherly care. And through your good providence, out of these evil times, bring us to everlasting peace. In your name, O mighty Lord, we pray. Amen."

"Amen," came the quiet response from the bowed heads. The lights were brought back up and the spotlight extinguished.

The admiral spoke again as Father Yu raised his head and moved back behind his seat.

"Mr. Vice, I have a point of order," spoke a voice from one side of the room.

"Sir," replied Lieutenant Rogers' voice, "state your point of order."

The voice directed its next statement to the head table.

"Mr. President, I would propose a toast. To the Colors."

"To the Colors," came the response, and glasses were raised and sampled.

"Mr. Vice," called a voice from the opposite side of the room, "I have a point of order."

Again the lieutenant's response was just as formal.

"Madam, state your point of order."

"Mr. President, a toast, to the President."

The Mess responded as before. This toasting ceremony continued on as toasts were proposed for the Secretary of War, the Joint Chiefs of Staff, the Secretary of the Navy, and the Commandant of the Marine Corps. As the final toast was finished, the admiral spoke.

"Please be seated."

There was a quiet shuffling of chairs as seats were reclaimed. Alex adjusted the bulk under her jacket at the small of her back as she sat. Admiral Stevens, however, remained standing.

"Ladies and gentlemen, I would first like to thank you all for accepting my invitation to this Dining-In." The handful of chuckles from the audience brought a smile to his face. As if any of them would refuse an "invitation" from the fleet commander. Doubly so from "Steely" Stevens.

"There is a purpose for everything in the military, as I am sure you are all aware," the admiral continued in a pleasant yet firm voice. "The Dining-In ceremony is no different. The origins of the Dining-In are not clear, as with many of our traditions that come to us from ancient times. We do know, however, that formal dinners are rooted in antiquity, from the pre-Christian legions of the Roman Empire, Viking warlords of the second century, to the knights of King Arthur. Feasts to honor military victories and individual and unit achievements have been a custom. When the customs of the Dining-In were adopted by the military, they became more formalized and structured." He paused to let this sink in, and Alex saw him survey the room before continuing.

"The purpose of the Dining-In is to bring a unit together in an atmosphere of camaraderie, fellowship, and social rapport. While a Dining-In can be used as a way of bidding farewell to members of a command, or welcoming new arrivals, its main function is to allow its members to enjoy themselves and the company they find themselves in. It has the added feature of being a highly effective forum for building morale and esprit de corps. That is the purpose I wish to achieve tonight. As you are all aware, things have not been going well for us. While we are not on the brink of losing this war, the setbacks and defeats we have suffered have done more than deplete our physical strength. They have depleted our spiritual strength, our strength of conviction. We have lost our confidence in ourselves and our mission."

Alex joined the other seated officers in shifting uncomfortably at the admiral's words. Yes, they had suffered setbacks, but they had won some decisive victories as well. They had not lost anything.

"I know what you are thinking. We are still strong; we have not lost anything of ourselves. We've had losses, but we have had victories. Yes, that is true. We have had victories, and losses, but it is also true that we have lost something of ourselves. I have felt it for months, the slow downward spiral of our inner strength. The extinguishing of our inner fire. I could see it out there in the wardroom this evening. This is a time for relaxation, for letting our hair down and enjoying the company of our fellow officers. You are the commanders of the ships, the fighter squadrons, the marines of this fleet. The burden of this war lies heaviest on you. Your crews look to you not only for guidance but for assurance. Assurance that we are not only engaged in a just cause, but that we will be victorious! Yet when you are with your peers, when the burden of command is lifted from your shoulders for a few short hours, you do not take advantage of it."

As the officers sat shocked at what the admiral was saying, Alex could see that he had their attention. They each felt as if they were once again junior officers being chastized for not performing to expectations.

"You've wrapped the mantle of command around yourselves so tightly that you don't know when to let it drop. You've concentrated on being commanders, on setting an example for your crews, and make no mistake—you have been consummate officers. But in dedicating yourselves to your crews, you have neglected yourselves. You have forgotten the most important characteristic of leadership—be yourself. You are the finest group of officers it has ever been my privilege to command, and it pains me to see you ignore the part of yourselves that makes you the best commanders in the fleet."

She saw the others beginning to stir at the admiral's words. This was not a dressing down, but an assurance that they had not failed in the trust that he had in them.

"You must allow yourselves to see past what you are now, and to what you were, and to what you must become. You must attend to your own well-being, your own morale—you don't have to suppress your doubts but eliminate them. I should have addressed this problem when I first realized it, and I failed you when I did not. I am here now to rectify that mistake. I have already said that things have not gone well for us this last year, but that is going to change!" His exclamation brought Alex and the rest back from their inner reflections. Change. A change in the war, in their favor. The thought of this possibility started to fan the embers of their fire.

She could feel them begin to come around, to see that they, herself included, had been indeed neglecting their own well-being, had begun to lose confidence in what they were doing. The admiral smiled out at them.

"You all know what is going on here and at home. We are rebuilding and rearming. We will be going on the offensive once again, and we will not surrender that momentum. We will show the Xan-Sskarns that we are not a species to be provoked. They may have started this war, but, by God, we will finish it!"

The ember became a spark.

"We are going to build a pyre of their dead so large that not a single man or woman who has fallen in this war will fail to see it. Not a single soul will be denied entrance to the hallowed halls of those who have fallen in battle; we will buy their rest with Xan-Sskarn lives. With Xan-Sskarn blood. With Xan-Sskarn souls!"

The spark became a fire.

"The way forward will be difficult and dangerous, but I tell you now—we will prevail. We will make them pay for every cubic meter of space that they wish to take from us. We will fight, fight with everything that we are. We will show them that we can be even more vicious and deadly than they are. They will curse the day they decided to attack us, I promise you. I will not lie to you—there will be sacrifices, more losses of friends and comrades. But I am telling you now, we will fight to the last. We will not yield. We will never surrender. You all know the pain of loss and death. There is not one among us who has not been blooded in battle, who has not been on the front lines and fought the Xan-Sskarns face-to-face. We have all seen more than our share of this war, and we know that death may claim any of us at any time. Death, however, will come for us all some day. Death may come for us today, or tomorrow, or years from now. In the coming months, though, he will have ample opportunity to claim us. The battles ahead will be hard fought and hard won, and if, during those battles, Death should come for you, there is only one thing you can do."

The response from the assembled officers could be heard three decks away.

"Make the bastard work for it!"

The fire had become an inferno.

A different mood prevailed as dinner began. Conversation flowed more easily and freely, laughter and smiles in evidence at every table. The admiral, more than pleased with the change in his officers, sat back in his place at the head table and reflected on that change. His officers were a sharpened sword, ready for battle. Of course, he did not expect the edge he had honed this evening to last much more than a day or two, but he would not allow that edge to be dulled, not again. He would continue to hone it until he had a razor edge that would cut through any opposition. Yes, he would not let this sword be sheathed again. He intended to use it, and soon, to fulfill his promise.

∎ ∎ ∎

Captain McLaughlin enjoyed her meal almost as much as she had enjoyed the admiral's speech. His words had stirred something in her that she did not realize was dormant until it had been roused again. She could picture the battles ahead; she could see them with a clear vision, the admiral's words painting a picture inside her mind. She was even enjoying the company of Captains Beckham and Zimmer. Both officers now knew that what they wanted was there. Beckham's desire to attack and once more be in the thick of the fray was to come true soon enough, and Zimmer's desire to revitalize the fleet before committing it to a long and bloody campaign was also going to happen. Neither was getting what they wanted on the timetable they wished, but they were content with the compromise the admiral had alluded to. Each represented a significant number of the officers in the room. And like Beckham and Zimmer, those officers knew that the status quo was going to change and were excited by the prospect.

After dessert was finished and the dinner was coming to a close, a commander at McLaughlin's table stood and requested permission from the vice president to propose a toast. As he turned to face the Mess and present a toast to the marines, McLaughlin could see the gold wings of a Valkyrie pilot on his chest, which, coupled with his rank, indicated he was a senior wing commander. As the marines cheered his toast, a colonel— a regimental commander, Alex thought—stood and repeated the ritual that the wing commander had just gone through, the only difference being that he offered his toast to the fleet. As she applauded along with the rest of the members of the fleet in attendance, she found herself standing.

"Mr. Vice, I have a point of order," she called out over the applause.

"Madam, state your point of order." She could hear the rekindled passion in the lieutenant's voice.

"Mr. President, a toast to the air wing and their fallen comrades." She could hear a difference in her own voice as well.

The admiral nodded his approval, and she turned to face the Mess and began to recite a very old, traditional toast to airmen and their fallen comrades.

"We toast our hearty comrades who have fallen
from the skies,
and were gently caught by God's own hands to be
with him on high.

"To dwell among the soaring clouds they've known
so well before,
from victory roll to tail chase at heaven's very door.

"And as we fly among them there we're sure to hear
their plea,
'Take care, my friend, watch your six, and do one
more roll for me.'"

The members of the air wing exploded into applause. She sat back down, feeling her passions stirring. She knew—right then, at that very moment—there was not a man or woman in the room who would not lay down their lives for another. She also knew it would not last. Old rivalries would arise, and the power of impassioned speeches would wane. But for now, the air itself seemed to be charged with electricity and conviction.

As the room settled back down, all eyes turned to the head table and saw that the admiral also appeared to have changed. They could see that he believed every word he had said to them—it had not been just a speech to boost their spirits, though it was obvious that it had had that effect.

He stood, addressed the Mess, and picked up his gavel.

"Ladies and gentlemen." His voice was filled with energy. "I invite you all to join me in the wardroom for cigars and brandy." He rapped the gavel twice, signaling the closing of the Mess.

Lieutenant Rogers took his cue and called the room to attention. The head table stood and proceeded out of the main doors, led by the admiral. Once the admiral's party had exited and the doors were closed, Rogers dismissed the room and reopened the doors. Alex found the closing and almost immediate reopening of the doors amusing, but tradition was tradition, after all.

McLaughlin and Higgins met up again and reclaimed their corner, drinks in hand.

"Steely sure knows how to give a speech. I don't think I've seen a room so keyed up and ready for a fight since Ross 128." There was still some pain in her voice as she said this. The same pain flashed across Higgins' face for a brief moment.

"You can say that again." He looked even more roguish than usual with a cigar in his teeth, a smile across his face, and a snifter of brandy in his hand. "By the time he was finished, the major seated at my table looked like he was ready to take on a company of Sallys in nothing but his shorts and a vibro-knife."

"I know what you mean. I wanted to climb back into the cockpit of a Loki myself." She reached up and fingered the black wings on her chest absently, a wistful look on her face.

"I'd rather have the shorts and vibro-knife, myself."

"That's a sight I would like to see. It would make for one hell of a picture on the Officers' Club wall." She laughed heartily at the thought.

"You're evil, you know that?"

"What? This is a surprise to you?"

"No, not really."

"So"—she changed the subject—"it looks like the admiral accomplished his goal. Morale certainly seems to be improved. Passions are definitely running high."

"Speaking of passions"—his voice dropped to a whisper—"I've had two inquiries this evening as to your, um, shall we say, your social availability."

"Oh, Jesus!" she muttered, eyes rolling. "We're in the middle of a war, *and* I have an independent command. What the hell kind of relationship do they think I could have? Besides just sex, that is."

"And what's wrong with that?" he inquired innocently.

"You know I'm not like that. I'm no prude, but, damn, at least a few dates and maybe a dinner or two, and not in the Officers' Mess, would be nice. Besides, I'm also not oblivious to the fact that I look like a teenager." Exasperated, she continued. "I swear, sometimes it seems all I attract are perverts with a slight predilection for pedophilia." She looked sharply at her XO. "Okay, Commander Cupid, what did you tell them in regard to my 'social availability'?"

"Hey, I'm many things, but Cupid isn't one of them." He had his hand on his chest, sounding as if he were lecturing. "I told them that if they wanted to know the answer, they should ask you the question. I'm your executive officer, not your father."

"Thanks," came her sarcastic reply. "So, what you're saying is that I can probably expect at least one or more passes tonight." She arched her eyebrow and fixed her eyes on him. "You know, you could've just told them I was unavailable."

"I could've," he agreed, "but do you think that would stop them from trying?"

"No." She sounded resigned. "Well, at least tell me this—were they good-looking?" She finished half the brandy in her glass while waiting for his reply.

"She was," he said, smiling around his cigar again, "but he wasn't anything to write home about."

"Well, at least I'm forewarned."

"That's my job—keeping my captain updated with all the current intelligence."

"Somehow"—it was her turn to smile—"I don't think that extends to inquiries into my social availability. But I appreciate the intel nonetheless."

He nodded as she squared her shoulders as if preparing for an assault of proposals.

"Admiral on your six"—he indicated over her shoulder with his drink—"and closing fast."

"You sounded like a Valkyrie rider there for a minute." She grinned at him.

"Perish the thought." He shuddered.

Alex let out a little chuckle as she turned to face the approaching admiral.

"Nice speech, sir," Higgins said by way of greeting as the admiral joined them.

"Thanks, Greg." He took the cigar from his mouth and turned to Alex. "And what did you think of it, Captain?"

"I liked it. Very powerful, very inspiring," she replied honestly. "I was just telling Greg here that I have not seen anyone this keyed up since before Ross 128. I think we would jump to the Sally home world tonight if you asked."

"I'm flattered by your support, Captain, but I don't think we will be jumping that far anytime in the near future. In fact, I don't think we'll have to worry about tangling with the Sallys anytime soon."

Alex and Greg both looked at the admiral, perplexed.

"Inside information, Admiral, or a hunch?" asked Alex.

"A bit of both, to tell you the truth." He snagged another brandy from the steward who approached them. "From what I have seen, it looks like things will be quiet for a while, and I don't think that the Sallys are ready to try anything. They've been going pretty strong for the last year, and I would guess that they're taking this time to rest and rearm as well."

"From your mouth to God's ears, sir," Greg said. "Lord knows we could use the break."

"Yes, everyone has been wound a bit too tight lately." His mood was somber. "Just look at the two of you."

Again they exchanged questioning glances.

"Us, sir?" they both said as one.

"Yes, you." His smile was back. "Both of you. This is a Dining-In, a gathering of your fellow officers and friends, and yet here you are, Captain McLaughlin, in attendance, armed."

Alex put her hand to the small of her back, feeling the pistol in her belt, and blushed guiltily.

"Ah, y-yes, sir," she stammered. "Sorry, sir. The standing order on my ship is to be armed at all times, and, well, I've just gotten used to carrying it."

She was blushing darker than her hair now, and he could see Higgins starting to blush and fidget.

"You carrying, too, Greg?" It was more of a statement than a question.

"Yes, sir."

"I see." He looked from one officer to the other then back again. "May I ask why you have that order in effect on your ship? It's your prerogative, of course. You are the captain, and it is well within the regs, but I must admit that I'm curious as to why."

"The *Thor*, sir," came her immediate reply. She still looked embarrassed, but not apologetic. He was right; it was her ship, after all.

"The *Thor*?" Puzzled for a moment, he remembered. The carrier *Thor* had been lost to enemy action. Enemy boarding action. The reports from the survivors told the story of how the marines had put up a valiant defense, but there were too many areas of the ship to defend, too many Xan-Sskarns on board, and not enough bodies to do the job. If the rest of the crew had been able to mount even a minimal resistance, the *Thor* might not have been lost. He nodded his understanding.

"I would say that you were paranoid, Captain." He grinned at them both again. "You, too, Commander. But then again, in this case I suppose that there really are things out to get you."

They all laughed at that. Alex extracted her case and retrieved a cigarette. The admiral's expression changed from puzzled to quizzical.

"Cigarettes, Captain?" he asked. "From what I've seen of your proclivity for smoking, I would have thought that you would enjoy a good cigar. They are Cubans, after all."

"I do enjoy a good cigar, sir, and Cubans have always been, and are still, the best." She looked around at the room. "But with the fact that I look like a teenage schoolgirl, coupled with my knowledge of the personality of my comrades here, I'm of the mind that a cigar might be a tad too Freudian for them."

They all chuckled at that. A guilty look came over her face, and she leaned in close to the admiral.

"Besides, sir"—she patted her jacket, indicating the pocket inside—"I took a couple for the road."

"Good for you. I hope you get a chance to enjoy them later. Now, it's getting late, and we'll be wrapping the evening's ceremonies up soon, so I need to circulate a bit more before I retire." With that, he smiled at them both one last time and turned to leave.

"Good evening to you then, sir," Alex called to him as he turned, "and thank you."

He looked over his shoulder and saw that she was thanking him for more than just the party. Higgins nodded in assent with his captain.

"You're welcome. Captain. Commander." And with that he disappeared into the crowd and smoke.

Chapter Six

USS *ASGARD*
OCTOBER 7, 2197
2312Z
GROOMBRIDGE 34

"*Attention on the flight deck,*" rang out over the *Asgard*'s hangar bay. "Mjölner *shuttle preparing for launch. All passengers please report to number two lift.*"

"Well, Alex," Captain Zimmer said as she extended her hand, "it was great to see you again. Maybe next time we'll be able to spend more time catching up."

Alex took her hand and began to shake it.

"I hope so, Alice," came her sincere reply. "It was good to see you, too. You take care out there."

"I will, and you do the same." She turned to Commander Higgins, standing behind her. "You take care, too, Commander, and try to keep her out of trouble if you can." She was smiling, knowing that if Alex was intent on getting into trouble, no one would be able to keep her out of it.

"I'll try, ma'am," he replied straight-faced. "Have a safe trip back to the *Mjölner*, Captain Zimmer."

With the party over, Greg was back to being the highly competent officer that he was. They watched as Captain Zimmer threw them both a jaunty salute and jogged over to her waiting shuttle. She was followed by the flight engineer, and the hatch closed. The shuttle taxied forward into the lift alcove directly in front of it, and a hatch slid up from the deck behind it, sealing it in. The speakers came to life once more.

"Mjölner *shuttle in the bay.*"

Alex and Greg stepped over to the bulkhead and out of the way of the flight crews getting the visiting officers' shuttles prepped for launch.

"Mjölner *shuttle launching.*"

With the bay depressurized and open to vacuum during flight operations, the sound of the shuttle launching did not transmit down to them, but they did feel the vibration in the deck as the engines powered up to full throttle and shot the shuttle out into space.

Alex and Greg leaned against the bulkhead and enjoyed a companionable silence. While the flight crews were busy getting multiple shuttles ready for launch, and the hangar-bay speakers were announcing shuttle statuses every few minutes, there was no point in trying to have a conversation, so neither of them missed the hatch to their side opening and a seaman apprentice stepping into the bay. He looked around as if this was the first time he had ever been there. His eyes finally settled on the wall of equipment lockers that they were standing near, and he headed in their direction. As he approached, he noticed the two senior officers standing casually against the bulkhead and froze for a moment. They could see his discomfort around high-ranking officers and shared a small smile. Here was someone else who squeaked. By an unspoken agreement, they remained where they were but did not stare at him. He was going to have to get used to officers at some point in his career, and he might as well start now.

As he arrived at the first locker farthest from them, they could see why he looked so out of place on the flight deck: he wore the rating tab of a radar tech. He looked at the two officers again, squared his shoulders, came to attention, and saluted.

"Good evening, ma'am. Good evening, sir." He rendered the appropriate greeting of the day to each of them. A little overly formal, addressing them both individually, but correct all the same.

"Good evening, Seaman." Captain McLaughlin returned his

greeting just as formally, her hand rising to the brim of her beret sharply and quickly snapping back down. Greg gave him an appraising glance, then gave him a smile and a slight nod in the way of a greeting.

The seaman stood there at attention, seemingly not sure of what to do next. He could have continued on with whatever task had called him to the flight deck after greeting them, but he seemed not to know this. Higgins turned toward McLaughlin so his head was facing away from the stiff seaman. He smiled and mouthed the words "Squeak, squeak, squeak." She felt the corners of her mouth attempting to tug upward in a smile. She came to the seaman's rescue.

"Carry on, Seaman." Her voice held none of the humor that was evident on her face.

"Carry on, aye, aye, ma'am," the seaman barked out and then bent down to the first locker, looking relieved.

The two of them remained where they were, watching small groups of officers depart from one waiting area or another and board waiting shuttles as the overhead speaker announced them. As they quietly admired the well-choreographed moves of the crews on the flight deck, the seaman proceeded to open a locker and thoroughly search it before closing it, opening another, and beginning to search again. After the seaman was two-thirds of the way though the lockers, Captain McLaughlin looked quizzically at her XO. He raised a puzzled eyebrow as well. Curiosity overcame her, and she stood away from the wall and addressed the seaman.

"Excuse me, sailor, but what exactly are you looking for?" Her question startled the seaman into attention, facing the locker he was searching.

"Ma'am?" came his nervous and confused response.

"At ease," she said gently, trying to set his mood at ease as well. "I was just wondering what you were looking for."

He looked at her questioningly for a moment, and she could see him searching for the best way to answer her.

"Ma'am, I'm looking for five meters of flight line."

"Did you just say you were looking for five meters of *flight line?*" she asked incredulously. Alex did not know what kind of response she had expected, but that most certainly was not it.

"Yes, ma'am." The seaman was now back at attention, looking even more nervous.

"And can you tell me why you need five meters of flight line?" Her voice was tinged with amusement now.

"Ma'am, my section head said that we would need it to help recalibrate the point-defense radar to detect incoming ships." His tone was no longer nervous or questioning, but deadly serious. Here was a man on a mission of vital importance.

Commander Higgins began to shift away from the bulkhead and open his mouth. With a slight shake of her head, she stopped him. His brows furrowed in confusion, but he didn't argue and settled back against the bulkhead.

"Well, Seaman"—she sounded every inch a captain now—"I don't believe what you're looking for will be found in these lockers. I suggest you go ask one of the other seamen over by those Valkyries if they know where you could obtain five meters of flight line." He looked over at the crews she had pointed at, then turned back to face her as she continued to speak. "Besides, you wouldn't want to just walk off with something from another department. It's always wise to ask someone where something is located and if they can spare you any, understand?" Both her suggestion and explanation were gentle; she didn't want this sailor to think she was lecturing him, but merely providing friendly advice.

"Ah, yes, ma'am, I understand." For the first time, he did not seem overcome by nerves, and his answer was more relaxed.

"Now, carry on with your task and remember what I said." She gave him a friendly smile.

"Yes, ma'am. Thank you, ma'am." His voice came out in clipped tones again, but this time she could not hear any fear or wariness behind it. He stiffened to attention once more and saluted her again. She returned his salute just as crisply as before. He did a sharp about-face, then broke into a trot across the bay toward the Valkyries at the other end.

"Sharp kid. He'll do well once he gets a bit more experience under his belt," she said as she turned back to face her XO. Greg started to open his mouth to speak again when he was interrupted, this time by the overhead speakers.

"Attention on the flight deck. Fenris *shuttle preparing for launch. All passengers please report to lift number one."*

"That's us." She started to trot toward lift one. Greg pushed himself off of the bulkhead and headed toward the waiting assault shuttle. She slowed as she approached the shuttle so he could catch up, allowing them to arrive at the same time. Because military protocols called for the shuttle passengers to board in reverse order of seniority, she did not want to arrive at the shuttle first and have it seem that she was waiting on him. It was unnecessary and would be embarrassing for him as well, and they had been together too long and through too much for her to purposefully embarrass him, especially in front of strangers. He nodded his thanks to her, returned the flight engineer's salute, and boarded. She looked over to the other end of the bay and could just make out the seaman talking to several others clustered around one of the Valkyries and saw that several of them seemed to be laughing. She smiled.

Oh, well. He'll get over the embarrassment soon enough, she thought to herself. Facing the flight engineer, she returned his salute and boarded the shuttle.

"Ten!" the strained voice gasped out. A loud clang followed as a bar came to rest above the bench. Lieutenant Commander Elaine "Barbie" Grant, squadron leader, Valkyrie Flight 127, currently assigned to the USS *Fenris*, sat up on the weight bench and accepted the towel from her spotter.

"Thanks, Digger." She toweled her face then hung the towel around her neck. She stood and faced her RIO, Lieutenant Derrick "Digger" Rutherford. "How long have we been in here?" She looked around for the clock but could not see it past the exercise machines between her and the bulkhead.

"Almost two hours." He looked just as haggard and sweaty as she did. "We have just enough time to hit the showers and make it to the mess before it closes."

"Sounds like a plan," she grunted as she stretched her arms over her head. "Meet you back out here in fifteen." Digger nodded his head, and they both walked toward the locker rooms.

Twelve minutes later, Barbie was standing in front of the locker rooms waiting on her RIO. She ran her hand through her shoulder-length blond hair. It was still wet from the shower, so she had not braided it yet. She knew it was not regulation, but fighter pilots were known to be a *tad* on the eccentric side when it came to regulations.

"You know, you had another couple of minutes, you could've

tried to dry that mop of yours," Digger called to her as he walked out of the men's locker room.

"I don't think you're the person I should be taking hair-care tips from." She looked from his bald head down to his eyes and smiled.

"Ouch." He didn't sound hurt at all. He reached up and ran his hand over the top of his smooth head. Lieutenant Rutherford was an average-looking man of average height with plain brown eyes and a plain face. He did, however, have a charming smile and an impressive physique. Being partnered with Barbie, that last part was inevitable. He had never met anyone who was so fanatical about exercise. When he had begun to lose his hair at an early age, he decided to help Mother Nature along and shaved his head completely. He pulled the zipper of his flight suit halfway up and turned toward the hatch as Barbie finished adjusting the zipper on her flight suit as well. They were an identical black, the only difference between the two being the rank insignia on the shoulders and the fact that Barbie wore the gold wings of a pilot, while Digger wore the silver wings of a RIO.

"You're just lucky that you're in the fleet. Your choice of hairstyle is not exactly unique here, but out there"—she made a gesture out in front of her, indicating the rest of the universe outside of the military—"among the civilians you would stand out a bit." She followed him through the hatch and fell in beside him as they walked down the passageway.

At one hundred and seventy centimeters, she was on par with her RIO for height. Her physique was just as impressive for a woman as his was for a man, doubly so when her bust size was taken into account. To say that it was extraordinary would have been an understatement. That, in part, is what had earned her the call sign "Barbie." Her flight instructor, a collector of classic toys and memorabilia, had informed her that she looked as if one of the dolls from his prized collection had been modeled after her. When he showed her the doll in question, she could not help but laugh. Along with the impressive bust line, she had the same narrow waist, sunny blond hair, and bright blue eyes. There were, however, two glaring differences between reality and fantasy, the first being that she was extremely well-defined in regard to her musculature where as her diminutive counterpart, while still shapely, was smooth and devoid of definition. The second was the smile. While they both had the same beautiful facial structure, they did not share smiles. Whereas the doll had a large, toothy smile that extended from one side of her face to the other, Elaine Grant had a smile that consisted solely of the upturning of the corners of her mouth.

They kept up a running dialogue as they continued down the passageway toward the mess hall and entered to find the room almost empty. They had made it just in time, as the cooks and mess hands were starting to put the food away and clean up. Picking up trays, they headed for the serving line.

"I'm starved!" Barbie exclaimed as she passed down the line, piling her tray with food.

"I can't see why," laughed Digger. "You only burn off more calories in a day than most people do in a week. You're at the gym at least twice a day, and when you're not there, you're either flying, sleeping, or eating."

"Well, a girl has to have her hobbies." She winked at him and laughed. "And mine are better than some."

They turned from the serving line, trays laden with food, and headed to the drink carousel.

"I certainly hope you are not referring to my choice of hobby," he said innocently.

"You call poker in the squadron ready room a hobby?"

"Of course I do. I don't take it too seriously, and besides, it's not like there's anywhere else for me to spend my money out here." He stood next to the beverage station, looking around the mess for a table. The mess hall was mostly deserted, but most of the tables still needed to be cleaned.

She looked around as well, and her gaze fell upon a lone officer sitting at a table at the far end of the mess. Barbie indicated it with a tilt of her head, and they both walked over.

"Evening, Commander Heron," Barbie said cheerfully as they approached the table. "Mind if a pair of lowly riders joins you?"

A pair of jade-green eyes lifted from the text pad lying on the table and fixed upon the both of them. Commander Grace "Heron" Denton, chief engineer of the *Fenris,* was a tall, thin woman with short brown hair and a pug face covered in freckles. She had earned the nickname Heron during her midshipman cruise when she came up with the solution to a serious problem with the lift doors on the carrier *Odin*'s flight-deck elevators. The temporary pneumatic solution worked just as well as the original mag rails and had impressed the *Odin's* chief engineer, inspiring him to say her solution was worthy of the ancient Greek engineer and inventor Heron of Alexandria himself. Along with the commendation her solution had earned her, the chief engineer's comment was also added to her fitness report, so that when she returned to the Academy after her tour, her new name had not only preceded her, it had stuck. Addressed as Commander Heron more than as Commander Denton, she doubted that no more than a handful of the crew beyond her own engineering staff knew what her true name was. She didn't mind; at least it was better than a majority of the call signs and nicknames she had heard in her career. The woman standing in front of her was no exception, and she grinned at the thought.

"Commander Barbie, Lieutenant Digger, I would be honored by the company of the best flight team in the fleet," she said just as cheerfully.

The pair sat and smiled at her compliment.

"So, Commander, how go things in Down Below?" This from Digger; Barbie had already begun to eat.

"Everything down in engineering is five by five," she replied, using fighter-pilot terminology in response to his use of engineering's "Down Below."

Barbie looked up from her food and smiled at this exchange.

"Well, Commander," she said around a mouthful of steak and pointed at the text pad with her knife, "what've you got for reading material tonight? Whatever it is, it has to be better than what you had when I last saw you in the O Club. I know that waste-management systems are very important on a ship, but it's got to be a shitty read." She chuckled at her own pun.

"That was bad even for you, Barbie." Heron chuckled herself and shook her head. "But tonight I'm reading something that I'm sure you'll find of great interest. Actually, I'd be surprised if you haven't read it already."

Barbie's eyebrows rose. She wasn't the type to spend her time reading just any kind of engineering manual. This had to be something in reference to a Valkyrie's systems. She'd read about some new tech lately, weapons, armor, performance, and a few systems upgrades, and was curious as to which manual Heron was referring to. Heron's long, dexterous fingers spun the pad around and pushed it across the table to her. One quick glance down confirmed her suspicion, and Heron was correct; she'd read it already.

"I'd love to have those new I-Coms on my Valkyrie. It would make for one hell of a ride." She had an almost maniacal glint in her eyes and childlike glee in her voice.

Digger's head came up from his meal.

"What's this about new I-Coms?" He swallowed his food quickly and reached out for the pad. Barbie picked it up and handed it to him, but told him anyway as he paged through the manual.

"It seems that Fighter Command R & D has come up with a new inertial compensator that will allow a fifteen percent increase in turning velocity during ACM." She sounded ecstatic.

"Christ, that's all we need," he muttered.

"What was that, Lieutenant? You don't think that we can use every advantage we can get in this war?" Heron didn't sound angry, but there was a bite to her question. "Or don't you think that the ability to finally outfly Sally fighters is a worthwhile achievement?"

"Of course I do, ma'am!" His shocked voice carried across the room. "That's not what I meant." He looked surprised that she thought that of him. Barbie looked back and forth between the two of them. She, too, was shocked that the commander could possibly think Digger wouldn't welcome every advantage that they could get.

"What did you mean, then?"

"The 'we' I was referring to was Barbie and myself." He indicated his pilot and risked a wry smile. "She likes to ride not only the edge of the turning threshold, but beyond it. I'm sure that you've seen the maintenance reports on our ride. That's nothing compared to what she loves to do to me."

"I'm sorry, Digger." Heron's voice was apologetic. "I just get a bit jittery when the Skipper and the XO are both off the ship, riding around in a shuttle while on the front lines."

"Don't worry about it, Commander—there's nothing to forgive. We're all a bit jumpy with them off the ship." His voice was light and friendly.

Barbie took this opportunity to distance them from the moment.

"So, Digger, do enlighten me, and the commander as well," she began with a slight chuckle, "as to what it is that I love to do to you. I'm curious."

Heron looked at him with curiosity as well.

"Well, seated behind you, facing the rear as I do, your, ah, shall we say, exuberance during ACM is a bit punishing. Especially with the way you like to ride the threshold, boss. No matter how much the straps of the harness are padded, they still dig in and hurt like hell pulling the gees we do. I think you take some sort of perverse pleasure in it." His smile took away any possible recrimination from his statements.

"I'm shocked, Digger," Barbie said in mock outrage, "shocked that you would think that of me. Whereever would you get such an idea?"

"We do talk while we fly, Barbie. I can hear it in your voice every time you tell me we're about to maneuver." He laughed.

"Now you know why I make you work out with me. Just think of how much more it would suck if you weren't in such great shape." She winked. "There's a method to my madness, you know."

"Of course I know. You don't think I would let you punish me the way you do if I didn't see the reason for it, do you?"

"I knew you were smarter than you looked."

"He'd almost have to be," Commander Heron chimed in, smiling at their banter.

"Yeah, well, don't you have a manual to finish reading?" he retorted. "We're going to want those new I-Coms on our ride as soon as possible, you know."

"Oh, so now you want them, do you?" the engineer asked.

"Of course I do." He sounded as if he thought she was out of her mind. "I never said I didn't. I love riding the threshold, and I don't care how many bruises I get doing it."

"I knew there was a reason I kept you around!" Barbie said, slapping him on his back.

"Seeing as how the best flight team in the fleet wants these new I-Coms, I guess I had best get studying, so when they become available you can have them and ruin the maintenance cycle on your Valkyrie." She got up from the table, accepting the pad back from Digger as she clasped him on the shoulder in way of a final apology.

"Nice lady," Digger said as he leaned back from his now-empty tray. "A bit high-strung, though, if you ask me."

"Well, cut her some slack." She pushed her tray away as well. "You'd be more than a little stressed out, too, if you had her job. Between us we only have to worry about fourteen flight teams, including ourselves. We don't even have to worry about the whole flight—that's the CAG's responsibility. Now Heron, on the other hand, she has to know every single weld, circuit board, and piece of equipment on this tub inside and out. Including our Valkyries."

"I see your point, and you're right, I sure wouldn't want the job," Digger agreed and stood up. "But on the other hand, she isn't out there flying around in a tiny little fighter with a bunch of Salamanders trying their best to blow her out of space."

"Good point."

She stood as well, and they both headed toward the exit.

"Well, I'm going to head down to the simulator and program in the new I-Com parameters and see how it handles."

"Want some company?" he asked sincerely.

"Nah, I got it covered. It'll take hours to get a new simulator program up and running. Besides, I'm sure that there's something going on in the ready room that you'll want to sit in on." She smiled at him and made a shooing motion with her hands. "You go and enjoy yourself, and we'll catch up later and see how good my programming skills are."

"Aye, aye boss. Catch you later." With a wave, he turned into a side passage and disappeared.

She entered the lift at the end of the passageway and punched the button for the flight deck as the doors closed. Time to get to work.

Alex grinned when Greg gripped the side of his jump seat as their assault shuttle launched from the *Asgard*'s bay. Her grin widened as the force of their acceleration pressed them into their seats and he clamped his eyes shut, his knuckles going white.

"Problems, Greg?" she said conversationally as the force pushing against them lessened when the shuttle reached its cruising speed.

"Ugh," came his ineloquent response. After a few more moments, he opened his eyes and looked across at her. They were seated on opposite sides of the troop compartment. "I hate flying. Even more so in this bucket. At least the captain's launch is marginally more comfortable. You know, half the guests came in their launches." His tone was recriminatory.

"And the other half came in assault shuttles, just like we did. You did notice that we are on the front lines, didn't you?"

"Of course I noticed, and you'll notice that I didn't ask why we didn't take the launch, just noted that others did."

"Well, they have less distance to travel than the rest of us." She slapped the release on her restraining harness and stood, stretching her back. "I'll trade comfort for speed, armor, and weapons any day. Besides, assault-shuttle pilots need flight time, too."

"Captain," said the flight engineer as he came up to her, holding a bundle in each hand. He extended one to her.

"Thanks, Chief," she said, taking the proffered gun belt and holster. She pulled her pistol from her waist band, ejected the magazine, and checked to see that the weapon was clear. Satisfied that the weapon was safe, she handed the butt toward the chief. "Hold this for me for a sec, would you, Chief?"

"Sure thing, Cap'n." Taking the pistol, he let out an appreciative whistle. "Nice piece you have here."

Straightening up from securing the tie-down strap around her thigh, she adjusted the belt slightly until it felt comfortable.

"Thanks. It was a gift from my father. He figured since I couldn't hit the broadside of a barn at any kind of range, this would work for me. It doesn't have much range, and it won't punch through bulkheads, but let me tell you, with an eleven-millimeter round at close range, a person will definitely know that they've been kissed."

"They would at that." He returned her weapon, and she slipped the magazine back in and slapped it into place. Sliding it into the holster, she sat down into her seat and looked like she was feeling much better. Commander Higgins repeated her motions, though a bit more unsteadily than she did, uncomfortable at being out of his seat. As he placed his standard-issue flechette pistol into its holster, he faced her.

"Okay." He sounded a bit queasy as he resumed his seat. "Are you going to tell me why you let that seaman continue looking for five meters of flight line when you know damn well it was nothing more than petty hazing?"

The chief's head came around at that, and he chuckled.

"Five meters of flight line, huh? It is kind of comforting to know that some traditions die hard." The chief was referring to the practice of sending NUGs (new useless guys) out to find a piece of fictitious military hardware. Some of the more common important "items" included a box of LOBs (a line of bearing used for land navigation), a bucket of jet wash, or, as in this case, a length of flight line. None of these items actually existed in a form that could be retrieved but did serve the purpose of having the victim wandering around the ship looking into everything and generally looking lost.

"Yeah, Chief, that tradition is still alive and kicking." Higgins sounded slightly disappointed. He turned toward the captain. "Though I can't for the life of me figure out why you didn't let that kid off the hook when you had the chance."

There was a beeping at the rear of the compartment, and the chief left to investigate as the captain answered.

"I know it can be an embarrassing and sometimes annoying tradition, but I feel that it does serve a purpose."

"Oh, and what purpose would that be?"

"It makes people learn to think things through. Not necessarily to question orders, but to assess those orders and think them through to their conclusion. That way, someone will be able to think for himself and differentiate between moral orders and those rare occasions when he may be issued an immoral one."

"That's a lot to take away from a little joke, don't you think?"

"I don't think so." She seemed a bit defensive, and he didn't know why. "I know you're a Mustang, and were in the same position as that seaman at one point. Did you ever fall for that?"

"No, my section was a bunch of decent guys when I was first assigned to them," he explained. "They told me about that little tradition and several others, so I knew to look out for them when someone else tried to pull them on me."

"Well, you see, that's why you don't see the value in it as much as I do."

"I know you didn't go to the Academy, but went through ROTC, but we both know plenty of ring knockers and have heard the stories of some of the 'traditions' that take place there." He looked at her intently. "I wouldn't mind the loss of those few traditions you think serve a purpose, to be able to get rid of the dozens that only serve to embarrass and ridicule."

"I can see your point," she conceded, "but I still think that this particular tradition serves a purpose."

He thought she sounded as if she was trying to convince herself as well as him, and he shot her a quizzical glance.

"So, what was it you had to go and find?" His voice regained some of its mischievous tone from earlier in the evening.

"It doesn't matter." Her cheeks flushed a light pink.

"No, no. If it's *such*"—he emphasized the word, enjoying himself—"an important and educational tradition, I'm sure you can tell me what it was that you had to find."

She mumbled something, looking around the troop bay but not meeting his eyes.

"I'm sorry, I didn't quite catch that." He had his hand cupped to his ear.

"I said, 'A box of AC batteries,'" she looked at him and snapped, her face going even redder now.

"A box of AC batteries? Alternating-current batteries?" He laughed.

"Yes, that's right, and stop laughing." She was glaring at him. "After that, I learned to think about what it was I was told to do." It sounded as if she was making excuses, even to her.

"Uh-huh, right. You keep telling yourself that, Alex." He was laughing even harder now.

"It's not that damn funny, Greg."

"I'm sorry, it's just that I can't get the picture of Midshipman McLaughlin wandering around a ship, poking into every equipment locker she could find, looking for a box of AC batteries." He was laughing so hard tears ran down his face. Under her stern glare, he got himself under control and took a few deep breaths, calming himself.

They settled down into silence and relaxed after the long evening. They sat there like that for several hours, lightly dozing and just letting their minds wander toward what they would be facing in the coming months.

"Wait a minute!" Higgins burst out suddenly, causing Alex to jump. Startled to full wakefulness at his outburst, her hand groped at her holster.

"What?!" She looked around as if expecting to see some kind of danger approaching.

"A midshipman cruise takes place between the junior and senior year of college, right?" He started laughing again.

"Yeah." She sounded a bit leery. "That's right."

"And when you were in college," he began, but she interrupted him loudly.

"Drop it, Greg," she warned.

"No, wait a minute." He ignored her protest and continued on between gasps of laughter. "Your major—wasn't it—"

She interrupted him again.

"I'm warning you, Greg. Let it go." Her voice was laced with venom.

"Electrical Engineering?" he finished and howled with laughter, watching her face turn a deeper shade of red than her hair.

"I warned you, Greg," she said, chuckling as she stood, "and now you are going to pay."

"Huh? What?" He was holding his sides, still overcome with laughter.

"Hope it was worth it." Her grin was even more mischievous than his as she made her way forward to the hatch leading to the cockpit.

"Hey, wait." He straightened up, tears still running down his cheeks, but he looked concerned now. "What're you going to do?"

She palmed the hatch-release controls and looked over her shoulder. She winked at him and stepped though and disappeared as the hatch cycled closed behind her.

"Oh, shit, I am so screwed," he said resignedly as he shook his head and felt the shuttle start to accelerate. He grabbed wildly for his restraining harness and began to buckle it around him, cinching it down tight. Still smiling, he gripped the sides of his seat. It *had* been worth it.

Chapter Seven

USS *FENRIS*
OCTOBER 8, 2197
0430Z
GROOMBRIDGE 34

"What the hell is that jarhead doing!?" came a roaring voice.

Commander Ian "Hangman" Kaufman, commander of the air group, stepped up behind the tech in "the tower" overlooking the hangar bay. While it was actually just a room that overlooked the hangar bay where, from behind the transparent wall, one could observe the entire bay, long-standing naval tradition dictated that this control room be called "the tower" after its predecessors of the old wet navy, where the CAG lorded over his domain. Kaufman bent down over the shoulder of the tech and jabbed his finger at the tracking screen, pointing at the approaching assault shuttle.

"Commander," Petty Officer First Class Foster started, sounding clueless, "I have no idea. He didn't say anything before he started, and I don't see anything else within a hundred thousand kilometers of him."

"Are you sure?" he asked, looking up at the long-range sensor return. "That sure as hell looks like evasive maneuvers to me."

"Looked that way to me, too, sir. That's why when *he* started, *I* started running full sensor sweeps and informed the alert pilots to stand by." The petty officer was referring to the flight teams that were waiting on the flight deck next to their Valkyries, ready for launch within moments of getting the word of an attack. Their job was to intercept anything incoming and keep it busy long enough for the rest of the squadron to launch.

"Good man." He put his hand on the petty officer's shoulder in approval. He turned to another tech sitting at a communications terminal and called out to him. "Find Captain Mathews and let him know what his pilot is up to." Captain Mathews commanded the company of marines deployed aboard the *Fenris*.

"Sir, I have an incoming transmission from the shuttle," the com tech called back from his post. "The pilot reports that everything is fine and that he is merely practicing his evasive maneuver skills, per Captain McLaughlin's suggestion." He was grinning by the time he finished his report. The CAG and the sensor tech both chuckled.

"I bet the XO is loving that," Kaufman said sardonically.

"Should I inform the deck officer that he may want to have a maintenance crew standing by for a cleanup in the shuttle?" the petty officer at the communications station asked, amusement lacing his voice.

"No, contact the shuttle's crew chief. It's a marine boat—let the marines clean up any mess." He was grinning wickedly at the thought of being able to stick it to the marines.

"Yes, sir!" the com tech replied enthusiastically.

"What's their ETA?" Kaufman asked as he turned back to the sensor tech.

"Seven minutes, sir."

Once again, Kaufman spoke, this time with no trace of humor in his voice.

"Inform the deck officer that we have an incoming assault shuttle and to prep for retrieval."

"Aye, sir, inform the deck officer to prep for retrieval," the com tech repeated back to the CAG, then turned to his board and began speaking quietly into his headset.

"I'll be down in the bay to welcome the captain home," Kaufman called over his shoulder to the room as he walked out the hatch.

"Aye, sir." The response chased him down the passageway.

■   ■   ▮

"*Shuttle now on lift two and descending,*" a voice called out from the speakers in *Fenris'* hangar bay. Twenty seconds later, a low vibration could be felt in the front of the bay as the lift settled in the tube. After the pressure equalized, the lift-tube doors cycled open and the shuttle taxied out, following the hand signals of a deckhand, and into its designated space.

"*Shuttle has now arrived. The captain is now aboard,*" came the announcement as the shuttle settled on its landing gear and the passenger hatch opened.

Captain McLaughlin stepped down the access ladder and turned to see Commander Kaufman standing at attention, saluting.

"Welcome home, ma'am."

"Good to be home, CAG," she said warmly, returning his salute.

"We saw your final approach." Amusement colored his voice. "I told the shuttle crew chief to be ready for a possible cleanup."

"Good thinking, CAG." She smiled. "But that won't be necessary this time."

"Really?" He sounded shocked as she nodded her assent. "So, how's the XO?"

"The XO," came a weak voice from behind them, "is just fine, thank you very much. I just need something to settle my stomach." Commander Higgins worked his way down the access ladder unsteadily and walked toward them, swaying slightly. As he reached them, Commander Kaufman could see that he looked somewhat green.

"Well, it's zero four thirty, so the mess hall is just opening," Kaufman said as he turned and led them across the bay to a hatch leading to the lifts. Higgins groaned at the thought of breakfast.

"The mess hall it is, then, Ian," McLaughlin said cheerfully, eliciting another groan from Higgins.

"You don't have to eat, Greg. Just have some juice to settle your stomach," Ian said as they reached the lifts. "By the way, what'd you do to piss off the captain?"

"What makes you think that I did anything?" Greg asked, leaning against the side of the lift.

"Well, that marine flying the shuttle called in and said that he was practicing his evasive maneuvers per the captain's suggestion. So, if it wasn't his idea, and the captain is the one who told him to do it, that leaves only one suspect as to the reason why." Ian looked closely at Greg, waiting for an answer to assuage his curiosity.

Greg looked up at the captain and met her gaze as she stood there, smirking slightly. Ian looked back and forth between the two and saw that he was missing something very interesting.

"Oh, I bet this is good." He rubbed his hands together in anticipation.

Greg straightened and tugged his uniform jacket into place. He was about to speak when Alex beat him to it.

"CAG, who's scheduled for the next patrol?" she asked quickly.

"The next patrol?" He sounded confused at the sudden change of topic. He closed his eyes for a moment, pulling up the duty roster in his mind. "That would be Lieutenant Commander Grant and her wingman, Lieutenant Patterson, ma'am."

"Good." She turned her gaze back to her XO and smiled, her voice still sweet and innocent. "Commander Higgins, you may want to think long and hard before you answer Ian here. You wouldn't want to go for a ride with Barbie, now, would you?"

"You wouldn't!" He sounded scared, and she cocked her head at him. "You would." He sounded defeated and turned back to the now disappointed-looking CAG.

"Ian, the captain and I were merely discussing the deficiencies in the education system back on Earth, and how it can affect shipboard life."

"Riiiiiight." he knew it was the best explanation he was going to get. The captain and XO were too close for him to be able to worm it out of the XO later, especially with the captain's implied threat. From the way she looked, it had to be something embarrassing, which was reason enough not to push matters. He respected Alex McLaughlin too much as his captain and friend. "Well, if the captain doesn't want to talk about it, then we won't talk about it."

Alex nodded her thanks as they entered the mess hall and went directly to get their drinks. They filled their glasses and headed for a side table near the hatch. As they were settling in, Commander Heron entered, walking right past them with her face buried in her pad.

"'Evening, Heron," Alex called out.

Dropping her pad to her side and looking around, Heron's eyes found the three of them sitting in the booth. She looked down at her watch and then back up.

"Don't you mean 'good morning,' ma'am?"

"Maybe for you, Heron," put in Greg as he yawned, "but for some of us, this is still evening."

"I see. Just get back, did you?" she called back as she poured herself a drink.

"Yes, about fifteen minutes ago," said Alex. "The *Asgard*'s nice, but there is no place like home." She took out her cigarette case and opened it. She offered it to Commander Kaufman, and he smiled as he took one and lit it.

"Thanks, Cap'n." He exhaled a cloud of smoke. "Speaking of the *Asgard*," Ian went on, "How was the party?"

"It was nice. The admiral gave one hell of a speech," Alex said, lighting her own cigarette. "He passed on some very interesting info." She looked around the table for something to flick her ashes into. There were no ashtrays on the table, as smoking was not permitted in the mess under normal circumstances. While she would not have broken that particular reg had there been anyone in the mess, the compartment was deserted, and, well, it was good to be the captain. Kaufman downed his coffee and pushed the empty cup across to her.

"Really?" Heron asked. "Like what?"

"Well," Greg began, but was cut off by a high-pitched whistle emanating from the intercom built into the table. Reaching out, he keyed the mike open. "Commander Higgins," he said professionally.

"Commander, this is the Officer of the Watch, Lieutenant McKeenan. May I speak with the captain, please?"

"This is McLaughlin. Go ahead, Lieutenant." She, too, was all business.

"Ma'am, we're getting something very strange up here on the long-range sensors, and I thought you might want to know," Lieutenant McKeenan said. Of all the nearly eight hundred men and women on the *Fenris*, McKeenan was easily the most nononsense, straight-laced, and regulation-oriented. Despite this, he was a supremely competent junior officer who had a good reputation aboard ship, somehow not letting his dedication turn him into a martinet.

"What do you mean 'strange,' Lieutenant?" she asked.

"That's just it, ma'am. We're not sure. It looks like—" He stopped mid-sentence, then spoke to someone on the command deck. "I want confirmation on that, Ensign, now!" All four of the officers sitting around the table sat up a bit straighter. That outburst had been totally out of character for McKeenan.

"Lieutenant, what's going on up there?" Alex put her drink down and extinguished her cigarette inside it, not liking what she heard emanating from the speaker.

"Confirmed!" came a shout from someone on the command deck.

"Lieutenant McKeenan, report!" She was standing, and the rest of the officers were getting to their feet, not liking what they heard, either.

"Oh, shit!" they heard McKeenan exclaim. All four officers stood looking at one another, shocked at what they had heard from the prim and proper lieutenant.

Alarms began to howl throughout the ship. The four officers had already began sprinting for the hatch seconds before the lieutenant's voice, once more sounding like the voice of the highly competent junior officer that he was, exploded from speakers throughout the ship.

"General quarters, general quarters! All hands, man your battle stations!"

Chapter Eight

USS *FENRIS*
OCTOBER 8, 2197
0450Z
GROOMBRIDGE 34

"Read 'em and weep, boys and girls!" Lieutenant Digger grinned smugly as he laid his cards on the table.

"Are you kidding me?" came an incredulous voice from across the table. "You drew two cards into a straight flush?"

"Skill, my good woman, skill." Laughing now, he pulled the pile of chips across the table toward him as the other players tossed their cards into the middle of the table. He slid his head around the table and smiled at his fellow card players. They all wore identical black flight suits, displaying a variety of ranks and wings. They were in the pilots' ready room adjacent to the flight deck and had to pause in their conversation while a tender rumbled by, drowning out all possibility of speech below a shout.

"Skill my ass!" came another incredulous voice as the noise level returned to the steady hum of background noise associated with a busy hangar bay. "You've got to be the luckiest son of a bitch on the whole ship."

"Of course he is," a sultry feminine voice from the hatch called

73

out. "Why else do you think I let him fly with me, Cat?" They all turned to see Lieutenant Commander Barbie standing against the side of the hatch, suited up for flight, holding her helmet in her left hand as her right adjusted the holster strapped under her left arm.

"Ouch," said the first voice again, drolly.

"Well, I would rather be lucky than skilled," Digger said as he stood up from the table and indicated the pile of chips in front of his seat. "And tonight is my lucky night, as you can see."

"If you say so," shot back Barbie. "Now, Mr. Lucky, are you ready to ride?" She jerked her thumb over her shoulder toward the flight line.

"You know it, boss." He grinned back at her as he came back from his locker with helmet and flight gear in his hands. "Let's fly. I don't want to embarrass my fellow officers any further than I already have."

"From the beatings you've been taking over the last week, Digger," came a third voice, "you were due for a good night. You know—"

None of the assembled pilots and RIOs got the chance to hear what the voice was about to say as alarms began echoing throughout the hangar deck. The men and women seated around the table jumped up and bolted for the hatch, grabbing gear as they went. Chips and cards scattered across the deck from the overturned table as Lieutenant McKeenan's voice spoke to an empty room.

"General quarters, general quarters! All hands, man your battle stations!"

"Why the hell aren't my birds moving!?" Commander Kaufman bellowed as he ran into the tower.

"The alert fighters are moving into the launch tubes now, sir!" called a grizzled senior chief from across the room. He turned to a sailor seated at terminal beside him. "Run a diagnostic on tube four's catapult. We just replaced the mag coils, and I don't want any surprises when we've got a bird in the tube."

"Aye, Senior Chief," the seaman acknowledged as he turned to his console and ran his hands over the controls, checking readouts. After a few moments, he nodded to himself and turned back to the chief. "All systems are in the green, and the mag coils check out at one hundred percent. The catapult is good to go, Senior Chief."

The senior chief grunted in acknowledgment and walked over to stand beside Commander Kaufman.

"Sir, any idea what's going on? This just a drill or what?" He didn't sound worried in the least. It would take something much more serious than an emergency scramble to rattle a twenty-five-year veteran like the senior chief.

"No, Senior Chief, this is no drill," he said quietly so as not to be overheard by any of the techs working diligently at their posts. He looked down onto the bay and saw flight teams sprinting toward their waiting Valkyries as the flight crews prepped them for launch. He reached down and slapped an override button, silencing the alarms ringing throughout the bay, but those on the flight deck did not seem to notice as they continued their furious pace. A moment later, the alarm was replaced with Kaufman's booming voice. "Okay people, let's move! I want full load-outs on those Valkyries, I want them in the tubes, and I want it five minutes ago! This is no drill. Now move your asses and make it happen!" The activity on the bay floor increased as crews rushed to get the *Fenris'* Valkyries into space. They heard it in the CAG's voice: these birds were going to be needed, and they were going to be needed fast.

"Report!" McLaughlin barked as she bolted through the hatch while the door was still cycling open.

"Captain on deck!" announced the ensign sitting at a console adjacent to the lift.

"Belay that! And shut that damn noise off. Now, someone tell me what the hell's going on," she spat out at the members of the command deck. She accepted a headset from the ensign and pressed it into her right ear as the alarm klaxon died away. She adjusted the mike as she composed herself and stepped down toward her command chair. Commander Higgins had followed through the hatch right on her heels and rushed to his station, inserting his earpiece as he went. She reached up and touched the earbud and heard the chatter of background noise and conversations as she assumed her seat and began strapping herself in. McLaughlin dialed down the earpiece and spoke into the microphone over the open band of the battle net. "Lieutenant McKeenan, I have the con." She sounded calm and almost tranquil as she began strapping herself into the command chair.

A sandy-haired young man with wide eyes and a slight case of acne leaned back in his chair, obviously relieved.

"You have the con, aye, ma'am," McKeenan's voice came back just as professionally. He was seated at his normal station as junior tactical officer but was monitoring both his displays and those of the senior tactical officer. A slightly balding, overweight officer arrived on the command deck mere seconds after the captain, headed directly to the station beside Lieutenant McKeenan, sat down, and began to strap himself in. Lieutenant Commander Martin, *Fenris'* senior tactical officer, nodded to his subordinate and took charge of his own boards.

McLaughlin looked over at her communications officer and said brusquely, "Tactical."

"Tactical, aye, ma'am," came the smooth response from the comm officer as he pressed controls on his console without even looking at them, patching the captain through to the tactical group. He kept his eyes locked on the captain, not wanting to miss any command she might issue for battle-net access while she was strapping herself in and was not able to direct the net herself.

"Commander Martin, status?" she asked quietly, breaking into tactical's battle net as she proceeded to arrange the panels and displays around her chair, taking in the status of her ship in a brief glance.

"Just finished strapping in, ma'am, and my crews are buttoning up now." His reply was cool and dispassionate; the reality of the situation had not yet struck him.

"Very good. Now, Lieutenant McKeenan, would you mind telling me what the hell is going on and why you sounded general quarters?" Her tone was not accusatory but intently curious as she continued to look over her boards.

"Ma'am, I don't think you'll believe me. Hell, I don't believe me, and I saw it for myself." He sounded confused but determined to give his captain all the information he had. "Captain, an entire Sally fleet jumped in-system, right on top of us." He said it quickly and turned to see her expression at hearing this news.

"Well, that sucks," Commander Higgins muttered into his mike. He was automatically cut into whatever net the captain was in, for reason of continuity of command in the event of the captain being incapacitated or killed. "But at least we'll have time to get ourselves into position to intercept them."

"No, sir!" McKeenan half shouted into his mike, sounding nearly in tears. His exclamation could be heard around the command deck—even by those not tied into tactical's battle net, and heads turned to look at him. "Captain, Commander, you don't understand. They jumped in right on top of us. They jumped in, *in-system*. They're within engagement range of over ninety percent of the fleet, and their remaining ships are moving to engage now. Currently, we're outnumbered one point five to one, but that's just an estimate. I expect that count to be revised upward. The residual energy distortions from all those folds are playing havoc with long-range sensors." He slumped in his chair, looking spent from having passed on such unbelievable news. There was complete silence on tactical's net as the reality began to register.

"That's impossible. You would have to be completely out of your fucking mind to jump in-system like that." Greg sounded incredulous. Alex didn't blame him; she felt the shock and disbelief of such an unheard of, not to mention totally insane, action on the part of any fleet commander—whether human or Xan-Sskarn.

"Impossible or not, crazy or not, it looks like that is exactly what they did," McLaughlin said matter-of-factly, leaning back into her chair. She pulled up the sensor reports to see where the *Fenris* was, relative to the rest of the fleet, and to the Xan-Sskarns as well. "Status?"

"All departments report battle stations manned and ready, Captain," Higgins answered, looking at the status reports being displayed on his own consoles.

"Multiple contacts! We have fighters incoming—looks to be at least three squadrons!" shouted a new voice from the sensor consoles. The deep baritone voice booming across the command deck belonged to Ensign Green. A man of African heritage, Ensign Green had a proclivity for bodybuilding that gave him an intimidating physique. While his size was imposing, the bright cheerfulness dancing in his eyes and his jovial attitude put those around him at ease, but that brightness turned to hateful fire where the Xan-Sskarn were concerned. He had lost a father and a sister so far in this war and wanted nothing more than to kill every Xan-Sskarn who crossed his path. "And they're closing fast!"

McLaughlin's head snapped up at this shout, and, out of the corner of her eye, she caught the comm officer tapping on his panel, cutting scanning into tactical's net before she could do it herself.

"Time to missile range?"

"Missile range in twenty-one point seven five minutes at current velocity."

"Twenty-one point seven five minutes, understood," she shot back, her mind racing. "Guns."

"Yes, Captain?" Martin responded immediately.

"PDLs and PDGs set to five thousand kilometers, maximum coverage, fighter interception, until squadron launch. After launch, set PDLs to two thousand five hundred kilometers and PDGs to one thousand kilometers, maintain full coverage, fighter interception." She issued her orders coolly but rapidly.

Martin repeated the order back to her in a quick but calm voice, acknowledging his understanding. He turned to McKeenan, manning the point-defense station, and issued the same order. McLaughlin was peripherally aware of this, and of McKeenan's echo and acknowledgment, trusting in her XO to maintain his ever-vigilant watch, assuring her orders were carried out in the manner in which she wished. She cut herself out of the battle net and spared a brief glance at Lieutenant Bennard, her comms officer. Reaching up, she tapped her right ear and gave him the thumbs-up, indicating she had the net. The brown-haired, brown-eyed youth at the communications station dipped his head in acknowledgment and turned back to his panels, assuming full control of intership and ship-to-ship communications.

"Shit," muttered Alex as she looked down at her fighter-status screen. All fourteen silhouettes of the *Fenris*' Valkyries were still yellow. She punched a button on her armrest. "CAG!" she snapped into her mike.

"Kaufman," came a quick response, but the voice sounded harried and distracted.

"CAG, we have at least three squadrons of Sally fighters closing fast, and they'll be on top of us in twenty minutes. What the hell are those Valkyries still doing in the bay?" Her voice was demanding, but not angry. Yet.

"The alert fighters are dancing vac now, Captain," said Kaufman, still sounding distracted, obviously overseeing launch operations.

Alex looked down again and saw that two of the silhouettes had turned green. "The other tubes are loading as we speak. All of my birds will be out and dancing in less than three minutes."

"Very good, Commander. Carry on." She signed off from the CAG's battle net. She still needed to see the whole situation and deployment of forces in the immediate vicinity of her ship. Keying a control on the panel on the arm of her command chair directly beneath her right hand, she cut into scanning's battle net. "Give me a plot, two hundred fifty thousand kilometers radius, on the display."

"Plotting, two hundred fifty thousand K, main projector, aye." Petty Officer Michelle Conrad, senior sensor tech, spoke in a tiny voice trembling with fear as she complied. Conrad's classically beautiful face was twisted in fear, her pale blue eyes wide; she already knew what they were up against.

The projector sprang to life with a quiet hum as a holographic three-dimensional representation of space, centered on the *Fenris* and spreading out to two hundred fifty thousand kilometers, coalesced into view. Alex looked intently at the image slowly rotating directly in front of her. The projectors in a recessed circular section of the deck in front of her command chair projected an image slightly below eye level, making her look down on the display. She frowned, and lifted her left hand to her face and began to slowly stroke her chin thoughtfully.

"Extend range to five hundred thousand kilometers, please," she said after a moment.

Alex had the range extended to one million kilometers, and then once more, to two and a half million, which was the limit of their sensor resolution with both the Xan-Sskarn jamming and residual jump distortions. She looked at the projection for a moment longer.

The fingers of her right hand tapped on the console again, while her head was still propped up by her stroking hand. She had just cut her mike over to the private net she shared with the XO.

"Greg?" she asked quietly into her mike, not wanting to be overheard.

"Go ahead." His response was just as subdued as hers.

"Do you see what I see?" She looked up through the top of the projection to see her XO's eyes staring intently at her from across the command deck, then glanced back down to the display.

"Yes, I do." His voice sounded concerned. He dropped his eyes back down to the projection of the tactical situation as well, and he didn't like what he saw. The display was full of too many red enemy icons and not enough friendly green ones. The resolution wasn't fine enough at the current range to denote individual fighters, but a designation of ship type or fighter count was listed below each icon along with an annotation as to how long of a time lag there was between due to distance and light-speed restrictions. As they both watched, green became tinged with yellow as more and more of the fleet became engaged in combat.

"What do you think?" Alex asked softly.

"We're fucked. All of us. It's Ross 128 all over again." He didn't sound upset, but clinical.

"We're fucked," she agreed. "But it's not Ross. We at least know what we're up against, and while we may be spread out all over the system, so are they. We're not barreling down on them with no option but to go through them, hoping for the best. The situation is desperate, though," she said quietly to herself, then sat silently for a moment.

"Captain?" Higgins called softly, slightly concerned at her last comment and then her silence that followed it.

"Well, let's see what we can do about changing that, shall we?" Her voice resumed a normal tone as she came out of her introspection. "Or at least make them work for it. Reset to five hundred thousand kilometers," she said quickly. She didn't hear Conrad's response but saw the display dissolve then reform.

Higgins smiled grimly at her paraphrasing of the admiral's comment from earlier this evening.

"Yes, ma'am! So, what's the plan?"

"First," she began counting off to him, "we take care of our current situation. Second, while we're doing that, we try to get hold of the Flag and see where we are needed, if we can punch through the distortions. Third, after we get our orders from Steely, we haul ass and drop a world of hurt on whomever he points us at. Fourth, we try and get ourselves out of this mess as best we can, because make no mistake, this is going to get very bloody." She finished and looked up to see his reaction.

"Agreed." He met her gaze and nodded. There was a quiet determination in his voice.

She cut them both back into the shipwide battle net.

"Listen up people, this is the captain," she said crisply. The crew, listening intently, continued to work at their stations, getting ready for the battle to come. "By now you've all heard what we're up against, and I won't lie to you. Things are looking a bit on the bleak side right now." There were a few smiles at this. If the captain thought that what they were facing was only a bit "bleak," then there might be some hope for them getting out of this after all.

"Individually you are the finest men and women of the fleet. Together you are more than just the sum of your parts. To say that you're the best crew in the fleet would be not only an understatement, but an injustice. There's nothing you have not accomplished above and beyond what I have ever asked of you since I was given the honor of being your captain. I ask that you do this one more time. Not just for my sake, not just for the sake of your fellow crewmen, but for the sake of this entire fleet. We are one of the only ships that fell outside the Sally's trap and are therefore free to maneuver. I intend to use their mistake to our advantage. We are going to be the hammer to our trapped friends' anvil and smash the Sallys between us. I have no doubt that we may be called upon to swing that hammer many times before this day is done, but with you behind me, I know that we will not falter and we will not miss a stroke!" She finished triumphantly and closed the shipwide battle net.

Captain McLaughlin kept herself dialed into the shipwide net long enough to hear department heads and section chiefs hustle their people along. There was no mistaking the determination and confidence in their voices. They were ready for a fight, and they would give their ship and their captain everything they had or die trying. She looked around the command deck and could see the same sentiment reflected in everyone's faces and actions, and she caught sight of more than one feral smile as she scanned the crew. Whatever came their way, they were ready for it.

Chapter Nine

USS *FENRIS*
OCTOBER 8, 2197
0501Z
GROOMBRIDGE 34

"This is *Valkyrie One*. I am moving into number three tube and am requesting clearance to launch." Barbie spoke formally into her faceplate. Standard flight gear was composed of a G-suit worn beneath an insulated black flight suit, boots, gloves, helmet with a full transparent faceplate, and a tactical vest carrying a variety of survival materials, as well as a heavy pulse pistol. The suit had locks at the feet, hands, and neck, allowing it to be totally sealed when gloves, boots, and helmet were attached, providing full protection against hazardous environments, including vacuum, should the flight crew find a need to vacate their ride quickly and unexpectedly. There was a click as a comm channel opened.

"Stand by, *Valkyrie One*, number three tube is sealing now," said a brisk and businesslike voice. Launch operations, a daily occurrence, were well rehearsed and choreographed, and could be performed even under the most dire of circumstances without any loss of efficiency or apparent strain. There was no room for mistakes during a launch. A mistake almost always meant death. "Tube three sealed, depressurizing now."

Barbie could hear the hiss of air for a brief moment before a vacuum established. She double-checked that her engines were at standby and that she had a green light on the catapult lock indicator.

"How you doing back there, Digger?" she called over the net to her RIO sealed in the rear facing compartment behind her.

"Everything's good to go back here, Skipper. Diagnostics all come back in the green, I read a positive catapult lock, and all weapon systems are hot and ready," Digger replied. He, too, verified the catapult lock status from his board.

"*Valkyrie One*, tube three outer door opening. Prepare for launch."

"This is *Valkyrie One*. All systems are go, ready for launch."

"Good hunting, *Valkyrie One*. Launch in three. Two." The voice from the tower counted down. Both Barbie and Digger took deep breaths and tightened their muscles. "One."

At that, *Valkyrie One* raced down the tube, the acceleration slamming Barbie back into her seat. The fighter shot from the middle of the three tubes located on the port side of the *Fenris'* bow, her engines cutting on at one hundred meters from the ship. Barbie pulled the stick over and stepped on the foot pedals, causing her fighter to bank hard to starboard. Keeping her speed down, she rendezvoused, forward of the *Fenris,* with her wingman, who had just launched from the number four tube located directly opposite hers on the starboard side of the ship.

"*Valkyrie One* to *Valkyrie Eight*," she called to her wingman.

"*Valkyrie Eight* here. Go ahead, *Valkyrie One*," Lieutenant Junior Grade Carl "Cat" Patterson responded with a deep rumble.

"Cat, everything green?"

"Everything is five by five here, Barbie."

"Good. Form up and stay tight on me—this looks like it's going to be one hell of a knife fight." She heard his acknowledgment as she checked the status of her squadron. The alert fighters were out in front of her, screening the ship and the squadron as it finished launch operations. The next pair of Valkyries had launched from tubes five and six almost immediately following her launch. They were already forming up on her as she watched the rest of the squadron launch in pairs, staggered just far enough apart to allow the preceding fighters to maneuver out of the flight path of the ones following them. Within the next one hundred and twenty seconds, the rest of her squadron was in space and forming up. She opened up a comm channel to the CAG's net.

"CAG, this is *Valkyrie One*." She kept an eye on her squadron display as she awaited his reply.

"*Valkyrie One*, this is the CAG, go."

"*Valkyrie One* reports successful launch of Flight 127. We are formed up and are awaiting instructions." With a call to general quarters followed by an immediate launch, there had been no time for a mission brief. She glanced down at her sensor readout and could see the incoming fighters. She could guess what her orders were going to be—intercept and engage incoming enemy fighters— but she waited for verification from Hangman.

"*Valkyrie One*, your orders are as follows. Accelerate to full combat speed," Hangman said in a cool manner. So much for what she had thought her orders were going to be. At full combat speed, there would be no time for full engagement. They would blow right though the middle of the Sally formation and have to spend time bleeding off their forward momentum if they wanted to turn around and engage them again. She brought her mind back to the moment at hand as the CAG continued. "Engage the enemy as you close. Take as many of them out as you can. You are free to take evasive maneuvers on your forward vector, but you are to maintain full combat accel until you are through the enemy fighters." These orders sucked as far as she was concerned, and she had a feeling that they were about to get worse. She wasn't wrong.

"After you clear their formation," the CAG continued in the same dispassionate voice, reading orders that were going to be costly and bloody, "you are to turn and burn, past threshold and into the red, back at the enemy fighters. When you are on an intercept vector, decelerate to engagement speed, and, as you close with them, the squadron will engage as you see fit. Understood?" She almost told him that no, she did not understand. What he'd just ordered was going to cost over half, if not all, of Flight 127, most likely before they even passed through the Sally formation. The Sallys were in a staggered flight, with each twenty-fighter squadron overlapping the other. The formation was deep, and with no room to maneuver except up and down, and side to side, along with rolling, they were going to present a very pretty sight picture to the Sallys and their targeting systems. Assuming that any of them survived *that* bit of madness, turning and burning past threshold and into the red was risky. Very risky, especially with fighters that more than likely would have sustained battle damage.

Turns while in combat were very demanding on both the crew and the fighter. Newtonian physics stated that a body in motion tended to stay in motion unless acted upon by an outside source. Thus, while a fighter moved forward, it would stay moving in the same direction, no matter which way it was pointed. To overcome that forward momentum, force would need to be applied in the opposite direction. The more force applied, the faster the change could be effected. The power plant of the Valkyrie could easily provide all the power and force necessary to affect a rapid change in direction. The primary problem with executing rapid directional and speed changes came from the crews piloting the Valkyrie. Even with inertial compensators, G-suits designed for extreme high-speed maneuvers, and a degree of muscle control that most martial arts masters would find difficult to attain, the human body could withstand only so much pressure. Unfortunately, all attempts at A.I.-controlled fighters had ended in abysmal failure. Fighter combat was as much instinct and intuition as it was calculations. Because of this, a great deal of time and money had been invested in developing ways for the necessary human component to endure the rigors of ACM.

The second problem arose from the Valkyrie itself. While its airframe could withstand significantly more stress than its human pilots, it still had its limitations. Though the frame could be damaged by too tight of a turn at high speeds, this wasn't considered a problem, as the crew inside the fighter would be turned into so much red paste long before the airframe failed under the stress. No, the problem was not the airframe but the engine exhaust. The engine cowling and armor of the Valkyrie were designed to withstand limited exposure to the highly energized particles being expelled from the engines. This protection allowed the fighter to rapidly change direction while engaged in ACM at lower speeds. But at high speeds, a Valkyrie couldn't just reverse its direction and throttle up to change its vector. The power plant could provide the power for such a maneuver; however, not only would the crews not survive the stresses such a maneuver would generate, the Valkyrie itself would be consumed by its own exhaust.

To overcome the physical limitations of the flight team and to prevent the Valkyrie from self-immolation, changing vectors was accomplished by means of an exaggerated turn. While this maneuver would be slower than a tighter turn, the length of the arc would prevent the Valkyrie from passing though its own exhaust, as well as allowing for a more gradual change of vectors.

The turn could be executed at faster speeds while maintaining the arc, which would allow for a quicker change of direction. However, this put more stresses on the crew. While riding the threshold (the point where a crew would begin to be noticeably affected) could be dangerous, riding beyond the threshold presented its own set of dangers. Beyond the threshold, the crew was incapable of performing within acceptable margins. The Valkyrie's systems were programmed to take the ship through a turn beyond the threshold, performing evasive maneuvers during the turn and immediately afterward, while the crew recovered. Although the computer was highly effective, a Xan-Sskarn fighter could eventually discern the evasive-maneuver pattern the computer had selected and anticipate its moves, allowing them to destroy the Valkyrie while the crew was helpless to respond. Where many pilots enjoyed riding the threshold, as it allowed them to perform to the limits of their endurance, none liked riding beyond it. They preferred to trust their own instincts and reflexes rather than those of a computer program. Turning into the red meant the crews would begin to red-out from the forces exerted on their bodies, and would have to trust to the computer to bring them through the turn and back on course.

"Understood." she forced out through clenched teeth. *I understand you just ordered me to throw away fourteen flight teams for no discernable advantage. Closing at engagement speed and dancing with the Sallys would probably lead to the same result, but we would take a hell of a lot more Sallys with us before they took us down.* She swallowed the bile rising in her throat before confirming her orders.

"Barbie." Hangman's voice was a barely audible sympathetic whisper, seeming to read both her mind and her mood. "I'm sorry. I don't like these orders any more than you do. You and your squadron are going to have to be the beaters and drive them toward us. The captain has point defense configured for extreme short range, maximum fighter interception. They'll be at point-blank range by the time you come up behind them. When point defense opens up, keep pushing them toward us and take out what you can—let the guns get the rest. We need to take them out quick and get into the fight before there's no fleet left to help."

"Roger, Hangman." She let him hear the apology in her voice. "Valkyrie Flight 127 will comply." She cut out from the CAG's net. Before she could do anything else, Digger spoke up over their private com. He'd heard everything she had.

"You okay, boss?"

"Yeah." She exhaled loudly. "God, those orders suck."

"Yep, but it's the best way we're going to get those fighters out of our sky fast. Hangman was right—we need to be elsewhere."

"Yeah, I know, Digger. Doesn't mean I have to like it." She sounded resigned to her fate as she punched up the squadron's battle net. "Okay, boys and girls"—her voice now light and cheerful—"we got our orders, so listen up."

"Alright, that's the plan—any questions?" Barbie's voice came though Alex's earpiece. Valkyrie Flight 127 was instrumental to the first part of her plan, but she knew that her orders were going to devastate it, if not outright destroy it. Barbie and her squadron were far from stupid and had no doubt seen what the cost of following her orders would be. She'd dropped into the squadron's net to hear what they thought about the price they had just been asked to pay. What she heard filled her with shame. She should've known that there was no better Valkyrie squadron, no better pilots, in the fleet, and she was ashamed of herself for expecting to hear anything less than what she did. Her shame was quickly replaced with pride as she heard the acknowledgments.

"No questions here, Skipper."

"Let's ride."

"Sounds like fun."

"Who wants to live forever?"

This went on until everyone had their say. She wished she could be out there with those brave crews, laughing in the face of death. She looked to the monitor above her station, switched it to a forward view, and saw fourteen plumes of fire light up space as Valkyrie Flight 127, assigned USS *Fenris*, leapt forward and raced to face their destiny. She touched the panel and cut herself out of their net.

"Godspeed, 127," she said softly to herself. Shaking herself slightly, she turned back to the task at hand. "XO," she began but was interrupted as Ensign Green's voice shouted across the command deck.

"New contact, multiple incoming!"

Chapter Ten

USS *FENRIS*
OCTOBER 8, 2197
0507Z
GROOMBRIDGE 34

Alex punched up scanning's net almost as soon as Ensign Green finished his announcement, just in time to catch Greg muttering to himself about more good news.

She didn't see anything, so whatever was bearing down on them was beyond half a million kilometers.

"Conrad, extend range and replot to include new contacts. Green, what've you got?" she asked quickly as the display expanded to one and a half million kilometers and she saw the new red shapes moving toward them at high speed.

"Ma'am, looks like three fast attack frigates with two destroyers in support." His words confirmed what she saw on the display. "None of them appear to have sustained any damage, and they seem to be loaded for bear from what I could read of their weapons power-up signatures and targeting sensors before their ECM came on line."

"Thank you, Ensign," she said absently as she absorbed what he had said. She cut out of the net and muttered to herself. "Damn.

Damn!" Green had given her the information she'd asked for, but it wasn't what she'd wanted to hear. Five ships, closing in on her with three squadrons of fighters screening them. She had to get her fighters closer to her before the Sallys could accomplish what she was intending to do: clear the sky of fighters so that point defense could be set for maximum fire interdiction. But with that many fighters bearing down on her, she couldn't switch point defense over until they were taken care of. No doubt that was why the Xan-Sskarn ships were so far behind their screen; they were waiting for the *Fenris* and its fighters to be fully engaged with the fighters, giving the *Fenris* no chance to intercept their own missile fire.

She looked down and saw that two of the Valkyrie silhouettes were already red. Two fighters gone, and they still had twenty seconds to missile range. She knew that more of those silhouettes would be red before the *Fenris* was through the Xan-Sskarn fighters; she just hoped not too many more. The *Fenris* was not going to need a fighter screen while engaging the incoming ships. There were too many ships and not enough fighters for the Valkyries to make any difference, so she would not throw them away in a futile gesture. But she would still need to survive the incoming fighters relatively intact if she was going to get past those five ships advancing on them, and her Valkyries were going to be instrumental in that. She punched up the CAG.

"CAG, new orders," she said simply into the mike.

"Go ahead." The CAG sounded slightly subdued. She was sure he wasn't just watching the fighter displays, but listening to their battle chatter as well.

"CAG, the minute the Valkyries are through the Sallys, I want them to execute a turn and burn in the black and get on their asses. We'll be moving in to close the distance and bring the Sallys to us. It's imperative that we clear those fighters out of our way. I'm sure you see their friends behind them."

"Yes, I do, ma'am. They're no doubt trying to do what we are, but with three times as many fighters, they got a little too complacent and are hanging too far back."

"No doubt. Command, out." She signed off, letting Kaufman issue the new orders. She didn't have time to listen to Barbie's response to the new orders, but she knew that those twelve—she looked down at her fighter display, now eleven—Valkyries would take those orders in stride and would be there when they were needed. She keyed engineering.

"Heron," she called out, looking at her ship's status board.

"Heron here," the chief engineer called back after a brief moment.

"Contact in sixty seconds. Have your damage-control teams ready to go. As soon as we get through those fighters, we'll be tangling with five of their big brothers. Things are going to get ugly, fast."

"I saw it, Captain. We're as ready as we're ever going to be. Don't worry—we'll keep her together even if I have to send my teams out with duct tape." The last came across with a slight chuckle.

"Let's hope it doesn't come to that. Forty-five seconds until contact. Command, out." She signed off from engineering's net and punched up navigation. "Commander Samuels, are you ready for a little drive?"

"That I am, Captain." Lieutenant Commander Samuels, a tall, thin man with a shock of wavy chestnut hair, was the senior navigation officer, and he had a golden touch when it came to maneuvering the *Fenris*. "The drive envelope is fully formed and stable, and the P-Drive is on line. The *Fenris* is ready to run."

"Good job, Sam." She looked at her boards and at the main display while her left hand danced across a keypad, entering speeds, distance, and time. She got her answer and spoke into her mike. "Commander, bring the particle concentration up to thirteen percent and put us on the same course as our Valkyries."

"P-Drive to thirteen percent, match course to Valkyrie squadron, aye," Commander Samuels called back as his fingers began to caress his board. There was a brief wavering in the air as the ship's Particle Drive came to life.

Warships and larger commercial vessels maneuvered through normal space by means of a Particle Drive. These drives created what was known as a drive field around the ship, partially dropping that ship out of normal space. With this partial phasing out of normal space, a ship equipped with a Particle Drive could accelerate rapidly and to great speeds—speeds great enough to allow a ship to travel across a planetary system in as little as fifteen hours. An added advantage was that the field created around the ship not only partially removed it from normal space, it also provided partial protection from weapons fire, although kinetic weapons could do marginal damage, for while passing through the drive envelope objects lost a great deal of kinetic energy. The drive envelope also dampened laser weapon wavelengths.

The Particle Drive didn't allow for space travel in the same manner as a normal reaction drive. Rather, the drive was drawn toward a concentration of particles generated within the drive envelope. If that particle concentration was directed in a particular direction, the ship would be drawn toward the greater particle concentration. The larger the concentration generated, the greater the acceleration achieved. However, as with everything, there was a price to be paid. The higher the concentration of particles, the greater amount of time it would take to maneuver them within the drive envelope. Thus, the greater a ship's acceleration, the slower its ability to turn.

Alex's displays showed that the *Fenris* had shot forward and reached thirteen percent particle concentration in a matter of seconds. They began to close with the incoming fighters now and would quickly be on top of them. She punched up tactical's net.

"Commander Martin, bring ECM up on line," she said before the Xan-Sskarns came into range.

"ECM up and running, aye, ma'am." Martin's voice sounded tense as he began engaging his first ECM program and brought it on line.

The remaining forty-eight Sally fighters opened fire as one as they reached maximum effective range. Missiles shot out at the *Fenris*.

"Missiles impact in ten seconds," Ensign Green's voice boomed.

She spared a quick glance to her fighter display and saw that they had passed through the Xan-Sskarn fighters and were executing their black turn and burn. There were now five red silhouettes, which was better than she had expected. She could see holes in the enemy formation where twelve fighters once had been. The Xan-Sskarn fighters vomited fire at them again.

"Five seconds."

The Valkyries were exiting their computer-controlled turn now. She hoped that the pilots would recover from their blackouts quickly, or they were going to be easy targets as their onboard computers brought them back into the fray.

"Two seconds."

She flipped the cover up from over a large red button and pushed it, immediately connecting to the ship's public-address system. A third salvo of fire came at them.

"All hands," she began, looking at the display and watching the distance to the incoming Xan-Sskarn fighters count down. "Impact..." She let the word drag out as she watched the last kilometers counted down. "Now!"

With point defense set for fighter interception and not for fire interdiction, and only ECM being used to counter enemy missile fire, over sixty-five percent of the first salvo maintained target lock. That number would only increase with each successive salvo, for as the Xan-Sskarns closed, they would be able to refine their targeting solutions.

The *Fenris* shuddered as missiles impacted along the length of her hull, the damage negligible at first thanks to the drive envelope. The second wave of missiles capitalized on the first salvo, and the *Fenris* shuddered again. Damage was still slight, but began mounting. Armor plating had been reduced in several locations and had buckled in others. Wave three impacted with damaging accuracy, rupturing the outer hull in two different locations and scouring away armor plating in several others. Alarms began to wail in outer compartments as the final missiles of the third salvo impacted, causing damage to internal systems. Damage-control teams began to move throughout the ship. Lasers now flashed from the Sally fighters as they reached effective beam range. They impacted almost as soon as they were fired, boiling away armor and leaving dark scorch marks crisscrossed along the hull. A fourth wave of missiles followed the lasers in and dealt more damage. The outer hull was breached in three more locations, and sparks began to fly in outer compartments as systems overloaded. The inner hull had not been breached yet, but it was only a matter of time. The Xan-Sskarn's accuracy increased with every kilometer the distance between them and the *Fenris* shrank; if something wasn't done to change the situation, the *Fenris* wouldn't be in any kind of shape to come to anyone's aid. If she even survived this encounter.

The situation *was* about to change, however. As the distance between the two forces dropped to twenty-five hundred kilometers, it was the *Fenris'* turn, and she struck back with a vengeance as Lieutenant McKeenan's point-defense programs came to life. With the mistaken belief that the *Fenris* had configured her point defense for the coming engagement with their ships following them in, and the fact that the Valkyries had blown right through their formation without slowing to engage, the Xan-Sskarns continued to bear down on the *Fenris* without taking any evasive maneuvers.

Fire erupted from along the length of the *Fenris* as tri-barrel point-defense lasers spun to life and began to spit coherent death at the incoming Xan-Sskarn fighters. Overconfident at the lack of response as they closed, and feeling safe behind their ECM, the Xan-Sskarns had flown right into the teeth of *Fenris'* fire. At this range, ECM was next to useless, and without engaging in evasive maneuvers, the incoming Xan-Sskarn squadrons were perfect targets for the long-dormant point-defense stations. Within the first five seconds of the point-defense lasers announcing themselves, fully half of the remaining incoming fighters were transformed into rapidly expanding spheres of fire and debris.

Shocked out of their complacency, the remnants of the Xan-Sskarn squadrons scattered and tried to escape the trap they had flown directly into.

While the Xan-Sskarns were beginning their evasive maneuvers, the range closed to one thousand kilometers. The still-firing point-defense lasers were now joined by the point-defense guns, as six-barreled chain guns cycled up and hurled twenty-five-millimeter pieces of death into space. Another seven Xan-Sskarn fighters were flamed out of existence as lasers and shells found their marks. Scattering the way they were, the Xan-Sskarns couldn't maintain target lock on the *Fenris*, and their fire ceased as they pulled away from the engagement. Directly into the flight path of Valkyrie Flight 127.

"*Fenris*, this is *Valkyrie One*, request verification of point-defense envelope depth," came an anxious voice over the general battle net.

"Envelope depth set to two thousand five hundred kilometers," Commander Martin responded immediately, ready for the question.

"Barbie," said Captain McLaughlin, breaking into the conversation, "push them our way, and we'll mop up whatever you miss. Good luck, and good hunting."

"Thanks, Cap. We're starting our attack run now. We'll try and leave a few of them for you," she called back, the smile evident in her voice. "Okay, boys and girls, it's time for a knife fight." She was now speaking over the squadron net but had not dropped out of the general net. "Let's dance!" She cut her Valkyrie hard to the port and began to dive at the scattering Xan-Sskarns below her, letting out a bloodthirsty howl that made more than one person's hair stand on end. The rest of the squadron let out whoops of excitement and followed her down, guns blazing and missiles flashing out, letting the Xan-Sskarns know that they weren't out of the fight yet.

Alex watched as all of the remaining Valkyries of Flight 127 cut a swath of destruction through the fleeing Xan-Sskarn fighters. All but two of the remaining Valkyries, that was. She saw that those two were still on the heading they had assumed coming out of their turn and burn. She switched over to the CAG's battle net.

"Ian," she began quietly, but before she could voice her question, he answered.

"I see them, Captain. *Three*'s crew is still blacked out. *Eight*'s is dead." His voice was heavy with emotion at the loss of fifty percent of his flight teams, and he knew that this day wasn't over yet.

"Dead?" She was shocked at that. Usually anything that would kill a flight crew would destroy the Valkyrie as well. "How?"

"Battle damage. Diagnostics show that their I-Com failed during the turn and burn. At least they didn't suffer. They were blacked out before failure." His voice became toneless as both he and the captain watched another Valkyrie disappear from their displays.

"Understood. McLaughlin, out." She hated just cutting him off like that, but there would be time enough to grieve later. Right now, she had more immediate concerns. One of which was that Barbie's Valkyries had accomplished their mission, and the Xan-Sskarns were turning tail again—this time, right back at the *Fenris*. She keyed up Barbie.

"Break, break, break!" she shouted into her mike and watched her display as the Valkyries broke off engagement and got clear of the *Fenris*' point-defense envelope. While the guns would not track them thanks to their IFF transponders—assuming that they were fully functional and not a casualty of battle damage—it was still possible to fly into fire meant for a Xan-Sskarn fighter.

The *Fenris* barreled through the remaining enemy fighters trying to evade the vengeance of the Valkyries, leaving nine balls of fire and two fighters in her wake. The final two were running flat out to get clear of the murderously accurate point-defense fire. They'd cleared the twenty-five-hundred-kilometer point-defense envelope when they were intersected by bright blue laser fire from the aft point-defense stations. Alex turned her head to look at Lieutenant Commander Martin and saw he had his gaze locked on Lieutenant McKeenan, manning the point-defense station.

"Lieutenant?" Alex asked in a quizzical voice. "Is there some reason why our aft PDLs reached out and splashed those Sallys beyond the point-defense envelope?"

"Well, ma'am," he began in a guilty voice, "there were just the two of them left, and all of our Valkyries were clear of that fire zone, so I retasked the aft PDLs to four thousand kilometers as we were clearing them when I saw those final two." He looked from the captain to Commander Martin. He was surprised to see Martin smiling and nodding, then snapped his head back to look at McLaughlin.

"Quick thinking, Lieutenant. Good job." She sounded pleased, and her smile was approving. "Now, if you would be so kind as to reset PDLs and PDGs to maximum fire interdiction."

"Aye, aye, ma'am." His face flushed slightly from the captain's compliment.

While he turned to his station and began to retask the *Fenris'* point defense, Alex opened her command net, which included all of the members on the command deck, the CAG, Flight 127's squadron leader, engineering, medical, and the marine commander. She began immediately, without preamble.

"Barbie, good job. Now if *Valkyrie Three* is awake, collect him and form up five hundred kilometers behind us and stay at maximum combat speed. You are free to maneuver and engage as you see fit—just be sure to meet us on the other side of that formation in front of us." She was busy looking at her consoles and kept looking back down at the display projected in front of her.

"Aye, ma'am, five hundred K, and run full out. Valkyrie Flight 127 will comply," came a voice just coming down off an adrenaline high.

"Heron, damage looks like it was minimal"—Alex read the damage reports on one of her screens—"but keep an eye on propulsion. I'm going to want speed over everything else, understood?"

"Understood, Captain. The P-Drive is purring like a kitten, and we'll keep it that way," she responded confidently.

"Very good." She thanked her engineer and moved on to navigation. "Sam, bring us to maximum military power on a heading of three one five mark zero one seven."

"Roger that, ma'am, engaging now." Lieutenant Commander Samuels sounded relaxed, even though the heading he had just set put them on a course right through the center of the oncoming Xan-Sskarn ships.

"Scanning, time to maximum firing range and time to intersection, please."

"At current speeds, missile range in ten point three minutes, beam range in fourteen point seven five minutes after that. Time to intersect is nine minutes after entering beam range. Mark." Petty Officer Conrad's voice was still tinged with fear, and after hearing they were now on a course to deliberately intersect with the oncoming Xan-Sskarn ships, there was an edge of panic in it as well. Alex heard this, but didn't have time to put the petty officer at ease. She looked up and caught her XO's eye. His eyebrow went up questioningly, and she nodded in response. He dipped his head in acknowledgment and began to undo his safety harness. He would reassure Conrad and make sure that she was ready to do her duty.

"CAG, those distortions haven't completely dissipated yet, and it looks like at least some of the carriers got their Lokis off the deck. We can't get a good read on the situation, so I don't know how much time we'll have after we get past those ships, but I want you to land the Valkyries, get them rearmed and back into the tubes—fast."

"Roger that, Captain. We'll get it done." His confident tone reassured her.

"Doc, I see we didn't have any casualties during our little tussle." The relief in her voice was evident, but the relief changed to regret as she went on. "I'm sorry to say that our next engagement is going to be a bloody one. I want you to take over whatever space you need and prepare for incoming wounded. Is there anything you need now to get yourself ready in the next ten minutes?"

"Well, ma'am"—Dr. Swartz began thinking as she spoke—"if engineering could spare it, I could use emergency generators and power leads set up in the mess hall, and if I could borrow a few of Captain Mathews' marines from the damage-control teams to clear out the tables and chairs, it would free up my people to set up our equipment and prep for casualties."

"Very well." Alex didn't bother asking if it could be done. "Heron, get two generators down to the mess and a team to run the leads. Captain Mathews, send two fire teams to the mess to assist Dr. Swartz in setting up her stations."

"The generators and a team are already on their way to the mess now, Captain," Heron spoke up just as Alex finished issuing her orders.

"Aye, aye, ma'am," came the crisp voice of Captain Mathews. "Gunny Brock is cutting two fire teams loose now, and they'll be there before Dr. Swartz's teams arrive."

"Good." Alex was pleased with how efficiently her officers were handling the situation. "Captain Mathews, I don't know what we're going to be up against once we get out of our current situation, but once we're clear, I want you to get your assault shuttles prepped and loaded. We may find that you'll be needed to assist in repelling boarders, and I want to be able to board your marines and get you on your way with a minimum of delay."

"Roger that, Captain." He still sounded crisp and eager. "I'll have my birds ready for launch, should they be needed. I'll also have one platoon armor up as well, just in case we need to repel boarders ourselves. The rest of the company can stay with the damage-control teams, and if we have to deploy, they can suit up in the shuttles."

She didn't think that they would have to worry about repelling boarders themselves. Not with so many larger and more inviting targets in-system. The captain's armored marines would not be as useful as the rest of the damage-control teams in their hazard suits, but they could still help. Combat armor, after all, was not designed to mend, but to take things apart, brutally.

"Good thinking, Captain," she replied just as crisply as he had. She turned her attention to her tactical officer. "Okay, Guns, the bad news is that this is going to be a point-blank slugfest, as you're well aware. The good news is that the way they're deployed now, it should be relatively quiet once we get in their formation."

"Assuming of course the Sallys don't just fall in love with the sight picture of us right in the middle of them and decide to open up on us anyway, friendly fire or no," Higgins cut in over their private channel as he returned to his seat, earning a reproachful glare from Alex. She continued with her orders.

"You are free to engage as we range on them, but with beams and kinetics only, and maintain your fire until we're clear."

"Engage as we range on the Sallys and keep hammering at them till they're vapor or we're clear. Got it, ma'am," Martin growled as he began to enter attack parameters into his console, sending orders to his gun crews. The missile crews stood down and secured their payloads as the new engagement parameters were received. Gun crews moved into action at the same orders, and pulse-cannon mag coils drew power while laser batteries were charged.

"Very good, people. Any questions?" When none were forthcoming, Alex went on, glancing down at her console. "Conrad, count us down to missile range, thirty-second intervals and a final countdown from fifteen."

"Counting down, aye, ma'am." Thanks to whatever the XO had said to her, she appeared to have her fear under control. "Five minutes, mark."

"Now, let's get moving, people—we have a job to do." Alex's voice was brusque, and a chorus of affirmatives sounded in her earpiece as her crew snapped into action at her words. Watching the quiet, efficient movements of the crew around the command deck, she began to stroke her chin, waiting.

Chapter Eleven

USS *FENRIS*
OCTOBER 8, 2197
0532Z
GROOMBRIDGE 34

Five minutes had almost passed when Ensign Green shouted.

"Vampire, vampire, vampire! Reading multiple missile launch from the fast attacks, ma'am. It looks like they decided not to wait until they had the range. They'll be ballistic by the time we intercept them, so point defense should have no problem with them."

Alex saw Commander Martin glance at his console, then at Lieutenant McKeenan's. He seemed satisfied that the lieutenant had everything well in hand.

"Looks like we're going to be under fire the whole way in and probably on the way out, too," Greg said into his mike.

"What? You were expecting them to just let us fly right through their formation and blow the living hell out of them?" Alex replied absentmindedly, still stroking her chin.

"No, but I can always hope, can't I?"

"Don't let it ever be said that Greg Higgins isn't an optimist."

"Yeah, well, we all have our crosses to bear."

"Missile range in ten seconds." Petty Officer Conrad interrupted their quiet banter.

"Okay Greg, time to go to work." Alex sat up straight and gripped the arms of her command chair tightly.

"Five seconds."

On her repeater screens, the external view was faithfully represented, though Alex knew from experience it lacked the perfect clarity of vacuum. The forward view showed flashes of laser fire lancing out at the incoming missiles. The point-defense stations were intercepting everything at this range, but the *Fenris* was about to enter into the Sally's powered-missile envelope. The missiles coming in at them then would still have life in their drives; they could and would be performing evasive maneuvers, becoming that much harder for the point defense to target as they homed in on their target.

"Three, two, one. We are now within powered-missile range." Petty Officer Conrad finished her countdown in a steady voice. "Beam range in fourteen point seven five minutes, current speed and heading."

Though no physical change came about as the *Fenris* crossed this invisible line in space, the atmosphere on the command deck intensified. They were committed to their attack run. To try and disengage now would lengthen the Xan-Sskarn's engagement time, not lessen it. Alex could not help but think of Tennyson's immortal line, *Into the valley of death rode the six hundred*. While there may have been more than six hundred souls aboard the *Fenris,* the valley they were riding into was also significantly more deadly than the one the Light Brigade had charged into.

The *Fenris* sailed toward the Xan-Sskarn ships unhindered for another three minutes as the point defense picked off missile after incoming missile. The Xan-Sskarn fire became more intense, gaining more life on their drives with each passing moment as the ships closed on one another. Inevitably, a missile evaded the point-defense net and closed on the *Fenris*. Two hundred meters from the *Fenris'* drive envelope, it detonated. High-energy plasma blossomed from the detonation and washed over the hull, boiling away armor and vaporizing sensor and communications arrays.

"Damage report!" Alex barked.

"Detonation starboard, amidship. Armor integrity down fifteen percent, sensors down two percent, communications not affected,"

Greg read from his board. The list was short, but Alex knew it was going to grow much longer in a very short time.

"Time."

"Ten minutes until beam range, nineteen minutes to interception, mark."

"Thank you, Petty Officer. Helm, maintain current speed and heading. Tactical, you are free to sweep with the main mounts."

"Refocusing the lenses of the main mounts and preparing to sweep," Commander Martin called back to her as he began to retask the *Fenris*' main laser mounts to aid in missile defense.

"Barbie, how're you doing back there?" Alex called to the Valkyries trailing behind the *Fenris*.

"Nice and quiet, Skipper. *Valkyrie Three* is awake and with us, and we're maintaining full combat speed. You guys must really have your foot down, 'cause you sure as hell have us sucking contrails."

"Sorry, Barbie, but you know you won't be of any use in what's coming up. Plot a course to rendezvous with us once we clear their missile envelope on the other side." She smiled into her mike. "Don't be late—we won't be able to hang around for long, and if you miss the boat, it's a long way home."

"We'll be there, ma'am. Besides, if we miss our ride, well, I've heard the *Odin*'s officer's club is the best in the fleet." She sounded wistful at that comment.

"Cute. Be there. *Fenris* out." Alex cut out of the net and shook her head. She was still smiling as two more missiles found their way past point defense. The *Fenris* rocked as twin waves of plasma washed over the bow, and alarms wailed in the forward compartments of the ship, signaling a hull breach.

"We have a hull breach, port-side forward, sealing off that section," Higgins barked out as he continued scanning the latest damage report.

"Commander Martin?" Alex inquired.

"Reconfiguration and refocusing completed, ma'am. First sweep commencing now." He stabbed his finger down on the firing control for the *Fenris*' main laser batteries. The refocused lenses projected a conical beam in overlapping fields of fire. This refocusing severely reduced both the range and power of the beams. Yet while this configuration was of no use in ship-to-ship engagements, and very little help against enemy fighters, it did have its advantages. The power was sufficient to overload the missiles' onboard computers, causing detonation, and the range was great enough that the missiles could be enveloped in the cone and distant enough to remove the *Fenris* from the blast radius. Alex looked up at her repeater display and saw several brightly colored spheres appear as the lasers flashed out, and still more appeared as the point-defense net continued to reach out and touch the incoming missiles.

The volume of fire that the oncoming ships could launch with each salvo was not enough to saturate the point-defense net with the main batteries in support, but the laws of probability still had a say in the matter as missile after missile evaded the net and managed to find its target. Damage reports continued to pour in as the *Fenris'* armor was savaged and her systems began to feel the strain. Several point-defense stations were destroyed, opening gaps in the defense net, allowing more missiles in.

With the *Fenris* hemorrhaging atmosphere and water vapor, the distance closed to beam range. The Xan-Sskarns could only engage with their forward-mounted beam weapons, which in the case of the fast attack frigates meant one mount each, and they weren't very powerful. The destroyers following the frigates, while mounting a pair of more powerful forward-facing lasers, could not fire on the *Fenris* while screened by their own ships. They could still engage with their missiles, however, and would do just that as the range closed, making it imperative that the *Fenris* deal with the frigates quickly.

Lasers, being light-speed weapons, flashed by the *Fenris* almost as soon as the Xan-Sskarn had fired. The *Fenris'* point defense could do nothing to stop the incoming beams, and her frontal armor was already damaged. However, there were measures that could be taken.

"Guns, deploy your drones," Alex called out to Martin. "And reconfigure the forward mounts. I want you to concentrate all your fire on that frigate in the center of their formation."

"Aye, aye, ma'am." He issued his orders to the forward-battery crews as he began programming his drones. The *Fenris* carried six drones, and they could be configured to simulate the radar and sensor readings of a large range of targets. "Drones programmed and deploying now." Martin was an experienced-enough tactical officer to deploy the drones in a fashion that left the enemy wondering as to the position of their true target. Both drones sped forward of the ship and activated, remained in place for a moment, then spilt off into wildly different vectors. They moved some distance from the *Fenris* and then assumed the same heading—toward the Xan-Sskarn ships, but not on an interception course.

"Very good, Guns." Alex watched her own sensor display, tracking the drones as they moved away from them. She hoped these decoys could suck some of the ever-more-accurate missile fire away from them. They would only be of use for a short while longer, but every moment they could buy themselves a respite, they could use. "Status on the forward mounts?"

"Reconfiguration ninety-five percent complete, both mounts. I have the center frigate dialed in and am ready to engage."

"Engage when ready, Commander."

"Yes, ma'am." Martin locked his eyes on his display, waiting for the status light for the forward laser mounts to turn from yellow to green. The port-side mount light went green, and he jabbed his finger on the firing stud. "Port-side reconfig complete, firing." The second light winked to green, and he fired again. "Starboard side, firing."

"Mr. Green, damage assessment, please." She waited anxiously for the report; something had to break their way soon, or by her calculations they would pay too heavy a price to clear the Xan-Sskarn formation.

"Looks like we scored one hit. Not reading much debris—and no plumes." Green kept his eyes on his readout as he relayed his assessment. "Sorry, Commander, looks like all you did was scratch the paint." Alex grinned at this last comment. Martin was known for his pride in his gun crews as well as his own skill, and there was no better way to get him motivated than to make light of his or his crew's results.

"Just getting their range," he muttered. The status lights flashed green as the forward lasers signaled ready. Firing both mounts again, he turned his attention back to his drones and checked their status. They were still with them, and had pulled some of the fire away from the *Fenris*. It was only a matter of time before one of those errant missiles managed to reduce one of those drones to its constituent atoms. As if brought about by his thoughts, the port-side drone flashed out of existence. "Shit! Port-side drone off the grid." His board flashed green again, and he fired another salvo from the forward guns. "Lieutenant McKeenan, prepare another drone."

"Belay that!" Alex interrupted his dancing fingers. "We're going to need them later, and it won't do us any good for much longer anyway. Maintain your fire on the frigate."

The *Fenris* rocked again as yet another missile breached the defense net, followed by two more. Then laser fire washed over the bow, opening more of the ship to space. Sparks flew on the command deck as secondary systems overloaded and burnt out. The primary systems were still operational, but that could change very quickly.

"Sally frigate is trailing a large debris cloud, and I'm reading fluctuations in her power emissions. Looks like you got a piece of her drive, Commander," reported Green.

"What's the status on her firing, Ensign?" Alex said anxiously. She needed to remove some of the factors from this particular equation.

"Missile fire looks to be down forty percent, and laser fire has ceased." Green sounded pleased with his report.

"Guns, two more salvos at the center frigate, and make 'em count," Alex encouraged her tactical officer.

"Can do, ma'am."

Two more rapid pairs of shots flashed out from the *Fenris,* two of which connected with their target. Green reported the results immediately.

"Two hits, reading zero energy output. Looks like they're dead in space."

"Good shooting, Guns. Now alternate targeting port and starboard frigates. We only have a few more minutes until we're past them, and the destroyers are going to want to tangle with us. We won't want to be interrupted."

"Rotating fire, aye, ma'am." Martin programmed the new targeting parameters into his fire-control station and engaged the new firing solution. Lasers flashed out again.

Just then, both remaining frigates scored hits with their lasers on the already weakened bow, followed by a trio of missiles, the plasma capitalizing on the lasers' damage. Explosions rocked the *Fenris*, tossing to the deck anyone who wasn't strapped in and knocking the ship off course.

Someone in the background began swearing, and several more people were getting up from their stations to extinguish the fires that had sprung up around the command deck. Having just been slammed against her restraining harness, Alex settled back into her chair.

"Damage report!" She had to shout to be heard over the alarms. "And shut those damn things off!" The alarms were silenced once more.

"Port-side armor shot away from the bow back to frame thirty-three, and the whole section is open to space. CAG reports that port-side launch tubes are inoperable, and he has multiple fires in the bay. The forward laser, port side, is gone, and we've lost one laser mount and two missile tubes port side, and another is damaged and cut off from the firing computer. The missile crew reports they still have manual control," Higgins shouted to her from across the command deck. He'd lost his earpiece when his head had been forced back into his chair, and blood ran down the side of his face. "Casualties are being reported from all over the ship, and we've lost contact with five damage-control teams. We have a fluctuation in the drive envelope, but we still have full particle concentration, and we've been knocked four degrees to starboard. Point defense is either down or destroyed for the entire port-side quadrant back to midship."

"Sam, get us back on course. Now." *Jesus*, Alex thought, *they're beating the hell out of us, and we still have to get past them.* "Guns, new orders. Concentrate all forward fire on that port-side frigate."

"Ma'am, request permission to engage with missiles!" Martin's pained request rang across the command deck. He had just lost four of his gun crews and wanted to avenge them. Alex was about to deny his request when the *Fenris* shook again with fresh impacts on her lower hull. Damn, she had thought that they would be able to make it through the Xan-Sskarn formation without taking this much damage, but it seemed like the incoming missiles were ignoring the ECM and jamming the *Fenris* was broadcasting. She'd wanted to save as many missiles as she could for what she knew was going to be a hell of a lot worse than this engagement. But she needed to get *through* this engagement. Another laser washed across the hull, searing away more armor along with another point-defense emplacement.

"Permission granted, Commander," she snarled. "You're free to engage with all weapons. Clear them from my sky."

"Yes, ma'am!" He began punching new commands into his console, queuing up his missiles for return fire. Another blossom of plasma, and then his missiles were in the tubes. "All my fish are in the tubes, targeting port-side frigate, and firing." He viciously stabbed his finger down, as if he were trying to impart his fury to his missiles. Tubes along both sides of the *Fenris* came to life as a salvo of missiles erupted from them and began to track the oncoming frigate. A second wave of missiles raced after the first, and then a third. The starboard-bow laser mount added its fire to the attack, the beam burning into the frigate's hull, followed quickly by the first missile barrage. Explosions were still evident along the frigate's hull as the second wave impacted, followed closely by the third. The Xan-Sskarn's point defense had picked off many of the *Fenris'* missiles, but the surviving missiles of the first two salvos had washed the frigate with plasma, burning away armor and point-defense stations. The final flight of missiles closed virtually unopposed, losing only three of their number to defensive fire. As the fire cleared, the frigate could be seen spinning away from its companion, trailing atmosphere and half-melted armor plating.

"One minute to interception," Petty Officer Conrad called out.

"Good work, Guns. One more flight of missiles at the starboard frigate, and then prepare a full broadside, beams and kinetics."

"Roger that, ma'am. Missiles away, and broadside ready," Martin called out just as another round of fire from the remaining frigate impacted the *Fenris*. With only one ship left, the volume of fire was much reduced, and point defense was able to intercept most of the incoming missiles; the damage was light.

"Vampire, vampire, vampire!" Ensign Green shouted from his scanning station. "Full missile launch from the port-side destroyer." With the first of the destroyers adding its missiles to the remaining frigate's, and the main batteries not configured for sweeping, the volume of fire directed at the *Fenris* was once more capable of swamping her point defense.

"Commander Martin, hit that frigate hard—then all missiles engage the destroyers." The range closed, and the *Fenris* drew even with the last frigate.

"Broadside away!" Lasers flashed from the starboard mounts as the pulse cannons accelerated their ferrous rounds to a significant fraction of the speed of light. Armor plating vaporized as the lasers clawed along the hull, then shattered at the impact of the hypervelocity rounds. The *Fenris* sailed past the wounded frigate and began to fire on the rapidly approaching destroyers.

"Starboard frigate damaged but is still maneuvering. Port frigate is turning to reengage," Ensign Green reported. "Missiles incoming from both destroyers now." The ship shook once again as a beam from a destroyer bored into the *Fenris*. "And lasers."

"Martin, maintain fire on both destroyers. Port and starboard midship batteries only, prepare for another broadside."

"Midship batteries only, ma'am?" he asked, not understanding why she would want to use only a pair of lasers and pulse cannons, not the entire broadside. He launched another missile salvo.

"Midship batteries only, Commander." She assured him that he had indeed heard her correctly. "Navigation, prepare for maneuvering. At my mark, ninety degrees up on the bow, maintain current vector and acceleration." She watched the projection, seeing the distance between the *Fenris* and the destroyers closing. Laser and missile fire continued to lance back and forth between the ships. The distance continued to close, and as they passed an invisible point in space, Alex leaned forward in her chair and shouted, "Mark! Get her nose up, Sam." Lieutenant Commander Samuels began to swing the *Fenris*' bow upward. With the drive at one hundred percent, maneuvering the ship within the drive field while maintaining particle concentration and location was slower than at a lower concentration. Thus, while a simple reorientation of the ship was something that could be quickly accomplished, doing so while maintaining their current heading and speed required more time, as well as a delicate touch on the controls. After several long seconds, Commander Samuels' skill had the *Fenris* perpendicular to the Xan-Sskarn destroyers while maintaining their course between them.

"Bow up, ninety degrees," he called out. The *Fenris*, while still within their cross fire, now presented a much smaller profile to their line-of-sight weapons.

"Guns." She did not elaborate further.

"Firing." Lasers and hypervelocity rounds reached out from the *Fenris*' midship batteries and smashed into the destroyers, while a majority of the Xan-Sskarns' return fire missed *Fenris*. Some of that fire, however, still found a target, and explosions erupted along the length of both destroyers.

"Ensign, what's it look like?"

"Ma'am, I'm reading hull breaches along both destroyers. I don't think we got any critical systems, but I do read a slight power fluctuation in the starboard destroyer, and it looks like we got a couple missile batteries and laser mounts along the way." Green refined his scanning sweeps to see if there was any more information that could be garnered from them. Another wave of missiles was incoming, and point defense intercepted most of them. The few that did manage to evade the tracking guns expended their plasma along the top of the *Fenris'* hull where damage was minimal. The armor along the top side boiled under the intense fire, but held.

"Navigation, port-side spin, ten degrees per second. Guns, reengage with broadside missile batteries, both destroyers, as we present to them. Maintain fire until fifty percent losses to their point defense, then cease fire."

The dual affirmative responses reached her simultaneously.

"Good move. Looks like they couldn't pass up the chance to get us in a cross fire." Greg murmured into their private channel.

"Thanks, I really didn't think they would risk friendly fire, but there's no point in taking chances. And this time it paid off," she replied and refocused on the projection.

They were through them, but not yet past them. Ensign Green reported that both remaining frigates and the destroyers were changing their headings. Alex continued to gaze at the projection in front of her. She could see the Xan-Sskarn ships spinning themselves about, but it was a futile maneuver. By the time the Xan-Sskarns had shed their forward momentum and could begin to accelerate on another vector, the *Fenris* would have too much of a lead for them to have any hope of catching up, even with the *Fenris* braking to recover her Valkyries. The display was counting down the time until they were out of engagement range. Twelve more minutes and they would be safe, for a while. The *Fenris* had passed beyond effective beam range ninety seconds ago, but missiles continued to home in on them; however, the more distance they gained from the launchers, the more time the point-defense net had to target and eliminate them. Two minutes later, *Fenris'* missile tubes fell silent. The Xan-Sskarn's point defense had the same advantage they did. There was no point in spending missiles on an ever-diminishing chance of scoring a hit, not when they were going to be needed elsewhere, and soon. The final twelve minutes of the engagement dragged out for what seemed like hours. Five more Xan-Sskarn missiles managed to avoid the point-defense net and inflicted yet more damage on the already wounded *Fenris*.

"We are clear of engagement envelope," Ensign Green reported; the relief in his voice was pronounced.

"Thank you, Ensign." She, too, was relived that they could finally breathe easy. "Bow down ninety degrees and cease port-side spin. Level us out, please, Sam." The Xan-Sskarn's missile fire had been far too accurate to risk allowing only aft point defense and the single-chaser laser mount to provide defense. She had kept the *Fenris* perpendicular and rotating, relative to the Xan-Sskarns, even though it had presented a larger target, so that the entire ship's point defense could be utilized. It wasn't something she would have normally ordered during a battle, exposing the entire ship to fire, especially when they had already been hurt so badly, but she hadn't been able to see another way. She didn't think the *Fenris* would have cleared the engagement envelope in any shape to fight if she had remained with only her stern facing the enemy.

"And slow us to one-quarter speed."

As the *Fenris* adjusted to the new settings Samuels entered, Alex punched up flight operations on her net.

"CAG?"

"CAG here, ma'am."

"What's your status down there in the bay? Can we land the Valkyries?"

"Well, we have a few small fires to contain, but my crews are on that now. The landing bay is functional, though we're going to have to recover one at a time. Port-side launch tubes are out of commission this side of a shipyard, but the starboard tubes are all in the green. We can land them, Captain, but the bay is a mess, and with only three tubes operational, it's going to take that much longer to get them back out into space." Alex's left hand began entering numbers and equations again. With the current deceleration rate of the *Fenris* and the speed of the Valkyries, interception would be in nineteen minutes. "Ian, give me your best-guess estimate on turn around time for the whole squadron." She didn't want to say "the remaining squadron," but she knew that with only eight Valkyries left, recovery operation times were going to be reduced.

"I would have to say between twenty and twenty-five minutes from first recovery to last launch, ma'am." His reply came fast enough that Alex knew he had been waiting for the question.

She entered his high-end estimate into her calculations. Factoring in that, acceleration, and last known distance to the *Asgard*, she saw that they would have just enough time to accomplish the recovery operations before they were back in the thick of things.

"We'll begin Valkyrie recovery as soon as they are in range. Ian, you're not going to have much wiggle room on your turnaround time. Twenty-eight minutes after the first touchdown, we're going to be engaged again, if not sooner."

"Captain, my boys and girls will have those birds back in space before then, even if they have to throw them out of the ship with their bare hands." He sounded confident. He knew that launching fighters with fire incoming was extremely dangerous. It was too easy for a Valkyrie to be washed away by missile plasma before it could get clear of the blast radius.

"You're free to begin recovery as soon as possible. Contact Barbie and get 'em lined up and on the deck."

"Roger that, Captain." With that, Alex cut out from the net, punched up engineering, and listened as Heron began a litany of damage they had sustained in their brief engagement.

"Alex, port-side forward is a total write-off. I have the compartments sealed off, but we took too much damage there to do anything else. Hell, some places are still hot. I can get port-side missile-tube three back into the firing net, and we're reinforcing the areas behind the hull breaches now. The calibration on the drive envelope is out of alignment, and it's causing a slight fluctuation, but it's still within acceptable safety margins."

"What's the status of the in-system and FTL drives?" She was concerned that with the drive envelope fluctuating, the *Fenris* might suffer a drop in maximum speed.

"The P-Drive is at one hundred percent, as are the emitters, and the Humptys are just fine. We took a pounding, but we lucked out in that regard. I should also have some of the damaged point-defense stations back on line by the time we reengage." Alex smiled in relief: finally, some good news.

"Pass my compliments on to your damage-control teams and stay on top of things. McLaughlin, out." She was about to order that the plot be expanded when she was interrupted by Lieutenant Bennard.

"I am receiving message traffic now, ma'am. Mostly battle chatter at this time—nothing directed at us yet."

"Keep me informed of anything major, Lieutenant." She knew that Bennard would screen out what she needed from the flood of messages he was receiving and would update her accordingly. She checked her fighter display and was surprised to see that landing operations had already commenced.

"Navigation, be prepared to take us to maximum military power, heading zero four eight mark zero eight five, as soon the last Valkyrie touches down."

"Heading zero four eight by zero eight five max accel on completion of recovery operations, aye, ma'am."

"Scanning, give me a picture out to five light-minutes; I want to see what we're heading into." She waited as the projection distorted then rematerialized into view, showing a much larger view of the current conflict. From what she could see on the plot, there were still localized distortions more than likely caused by Lokis. Only two other ships besides the *Fenris* were currently unengaged, and all of them were pulsing, showing signs of battle damage. Even with the display set to a five-light-minute radius, there were too few green icons and far too many red. They were outnumbered almost two to one, and as she watched, the ratio increased as several icons representing screening ships increased the tempo of their pulsing, suffering more damage, then winked out of existence. She searched along the heading she had ordered and found the flagship. The *Asgard* icon was pulsing slowly; her remaining screening ships were shielding her, taking the brunt of the damage, but with the number of enemy ships closing in, it was only a matter of time before that screen was wiped away. Already she could see the icon of a light cruiser begin to pulse dangerously fast. By the number of ships surrounding the *Asgard*, there was no doubt in Alex's mind that the Xan-Sskarns knew exactly which ship in this fleet was the flagship. They needed to get in there and pull off some of that attacking force before it was too late. She saw that the last fighter was on approach and signaled Commander Samuels to stand by.

"Commander Samuels, go," she ordered as soon as she saw the status of *Valkyrie One* change from in-flight to recovered.

"Engaging new course and speed now, ma'am." As he executed the new flight plan, the *Fenris* leapt forward, racing into the fight.

Chapter Twelve

USS *FENRIS*
OCTOBER 8, 2197
0712Z
GROOMBRIDGE 34

It was beautiful. Painfully, hauntingly, disturbingly beautiful. It was all there in front of her, displayed for her viewing: the multicolor flashes of lasers, the expanding balls of fire that were once ships, and even the deadly dance of the fighters. Alex was mesmerized by the beauty of the delicate yet intense flames leaping from damaged ships, both friend and foe alike. As she watched the conflict unfold, another battle was playing across her mind. She saw ships weaving and spinning in a ballet of death, friends giving their all to no avail as, one after another, they fell to an overwhelming enemy. Voices yelling in confusion and fear as they passed on grim reports, others shouting her name, looking to her for answers.

"Captain," Greg called into his mike, wiping blood from his face as he watched her stare at the events unfolding in front of them. He knew what she was seeing; he was seeing it as well. Ross 128. The difference was that he had only been the *Gna*'s tactical officer, she had been the captain, ultimately responsible for her ship and crew, and she had lost most of one and, later, the other. Both losses weighed heavily on her.

"Alex!" he hissed intently, and relief washed over him as he saw her shake free of the past.

"Conrad, time to battle zone assuming we go for Valkyrie launch?" she snapped, coming out of her reverie.

"Ten point two five minutes to maximum engagement range of the closest Sally ship." Deflated at the sight of what they were speeding into, Petty Officer Conrad's voice was flat. Alex connected to the flight-operations net.

"CAG, what's the status of the Valkyries?"

"We're finishing rearming the first three now, Captain. They'll be in the tubes and ready for launch in two minutes. The next group will be ready three minutes after that, and as soon as they clear the tubes, group three will be ready for launch. Say eight minutes to full squadron launch." That was cutting it close, and she said so. "Well, we'll still have seventy-five seconds to engagement range, so they will have plenty of time to get clear once we slow to launch speed."

"I guess that'll have to do. Notify the helm when your birds are in the tube, and keep in mind we don't have much time for deceleration. We're going to be at maximum launch speed, so tell them it's going to be a rough one."

"They're ready for it, ma'am." She acknowledged him, and signed off.

"Captain," Lieutenant Bennard's hushed voice said in her earpiece. "I'm picking up specific comms traffic now."

"How bad is it, Lieutenant?" Alex's voice was soft.

"Bad, ma'am. The carriers *Aegir* and *Uller* and their entire battle groups are completely destroyed. Their remaining fighters are moving to support the rest of the fleet now. The *Mjölner*, *Vidar*, and *Hermod* are the only remaining battleships, and the *Vidar* and *Hermod* are each reporting heavy damage and the loss of most of their screening ships. The *Mjölner* has lost main power, but is still under attack. What's left of her squadron is attempting to shield her, but they're all reporting extensive damage as well. Ten percent of the Valkyries were lost upon launch or never made it out of the tubes. Overall, fighter strength is down to forty-seven percent, and falling fast. The carrier *Odin* reports fires out of control in both her bays and cannot land her fighters.

She is requesting—" He stopped his litany with a sharp intake of breath. "Correction, the *Odin* has been destroyed. The carriers *Sif* and *Asgard* are under heavy attack and are requesting assistance. Their screens are still relatively intact, but they are now heavily outnumbered. The *Sleipnir* and *Sigyn* destroyer squadrons are responding," he ended quietly.

"God in heaven," Greg breathed over the net. "This is not good." A sudden thought struck him. "What's the status of the troop transports?"

"Seventy-six percent of them and their screening frigates have been destroyed. From what I'm hearing, it sounds like the Sally bastards are using them for target practice, sir." The anger now lacing Bennard's voice was reflected in Higgins' face. Alex saw that the *Fenris* had slowed to launch speed and that the first of the Valkyries were launching. Eight more minutes to engagement range, and it looked as if the Xan-Sskarns were ignoring them, concentrating on the flagship and the remains of the fleet rather than worrying about a single damaged heavy cruiser closing in on them from behind. She intended to make them regret that decision.

"Ensign Green, status of the fleet?" she asked, though she knew that answer would be demoralizing to all those who heard it.

"Yes, ma'am. Sixty-three percent of the fleet is either destroyed or no longer combat capable, and all remaining ships show signs of battle damage. Fighter losses are now at seventy-eight percent. The enemy now outnumbers us two point seven five to one, though a majority of their ships are damaged as well. Currently, only the *Fenris*, the *Ran*, and the *Krulak* are not engaged at this time. However, two Xan-Sskarn destroyer squadrons are on an interception course with the *Ran*." Alex knew that the *Ran* was another heavy cruiser of the same class as the *Fenris*, but she was not familiar with the *Krulak*.

"XO, the *Krulak*?" she asked. He turned to his console and began to retrieve the information that she had requested.

"Yes, ma'am." He scanned the text. "The *Krulak* is a commandant class marine amphibious assault ship. Records indicate she has a full infantry battalion of the Fifth Marine Division on board."

"Thank you." The *Krulak* would not be of much use in this kind of ship to ship engagement, but between the *Ran* and the *Fenris*, they might be able to distract the Xan-Sskarns long enough for the remnants of the fleet to punch a hole in the enemy's formation and let them extradite themselves. Assuming, of course, that the *Ran* could avoid the destroyers closing on her, and that she was intact enough to go on the offensive. Alex spoke up, her confident voice carrying around the command deck, dispelling the growing air of despair. "Try and raise the flagship. We need to know where the admiral wants us to counterattack." She may have said *counterattack*, but the command crew heard it as *payback*. She checked the status of the Valkyrie launch and saw that another three fighters were speeding down the launch tubes now. The *Fenris* was now three minutes from extreme missile range, and the Xan-Sskarns still had not paid them any attention. The last two Valkyries shot from the launch tubes and joined the squadron holding position above the *Fenris*. Two minutes.

"Helm, maintain launch speed." They needed more time to execute any coordinated attack plan that the admiral might have planned.

"Captain, I've managed to get through the Sally jamming, and I have the admiral. Putting him on your screen now," Lieutenant Bennard reported as the *Fenris* closed to four minutes from engagement range. As the display screen began to resolve, Ensign Green called out.

"Status change! We have fighters incoming, ninety seconds out."

"How many?" Alex kept her eyes locked on the display and was not shocked at the ensign's report. The Xan-Sskarns were bound to notice the *Fenris* sooner or later.

"It looks like an entire wing, ma'am." She didn't have time to deal with that, as the admiral's image finally appeared.

"Greg, handle the fighters," she told her XO over the net, trusting him to take care of them just as well as she could.

"I've got them, Skipper."

"Captain McLaughlin." Admiral Stevens' transmission was distorted, but she could see smoke and flames in the background, and the admiral himself did not look much better than his command center. Alex could see that his left eye was swollen shut and his uniform jacket was singed. Blood stained his shoulder boards and medals, but he did not seem to be bleeding. The distance between the two ships was small enough that if there was any lag time, it was unnoticeable as the admiral continued speaking. "I have some unpleasant orders for you." Despite his injuries, the pain she saw in his expression was not from any physical injury.

"Admiral," Alex interrupted him. "My Valkyries are twenty

seconds from engagement, and the *Fenris* is right behind them. We are ready to hit the Sallys wherever you need us to. We'll get their attention, and you can punch your way out while they are concentrating on us. The *Ran* may be able do the same from the other side, giving you some more breathing room."

"Alex, that's not what I need from the *Fenris*. I need you to warn Earth." Shocked by what he had just said, she did not even notice that the *Fenris* was rocking under the impact of missiles.

"Sir, I don't understand. You want us to run?"

"No, Captain, I want you to escape. Escape and tell Earth what happened here." His voice was sympathetic, but firm.

"Admiral, we are engaged with a full wing of Sally fighters and are now within missile range of the outer ships of the attacking fleet. We can't just leave." She wanted him to understand, to let her and the *Fenris* stay and fight. "The *Ran* can—" She never got to finish what she was about to say.

"The *Ran* does not have a functional jump drive and is about to be engaged in her own battle. And before you say it, we both know that the *Krulak* would never survive a running fight to the hyperlimit. That leaves the *Fenris* as our only hope for getting the word out."

"Sir, I can't just leave," she said again. "Please, sir, don't make me leave another fleet behind." Alex was pleading now. Greg had been right; this was Ross 128 all over again, and she did not know if she would be able to survive it a second time.

"No, Alex. You are going to leave us behind and get home. If you stay, not only will this fleet be lost, but the Home Fleet will be caught completely off guard. There is no doubt about it—we have been sold out here. The Sally's in-system jumps were too damn accurate for them not to have been given the exact deployment of the fleet. If we've been betrayed here, the Home Fleet in Sol might be compromised as well, and they need to be warned. I'm going to implement your plan with one change. *We're* going to hit the Sallys and get their attention, and you're going to punch out of here."

"Sir, I—" Energy torpedoes impacting starboard amidships interrupted her argument. Energy torpedoes meant that they were in the range of a least a light cruiser. She cast a quick glance at her panel and saw that Greg had updated it for her; they had drawn the fire of not one but a pair of light cruisers on the outskirts of the attacking fleet.

"You have your orders, Captain McLaughlin," Stevens barked at her, and Alex straightened in her chair as years of military service took over.

"Sir, yes, sir!" Admiral Stevens' voice softened as he consoled her.

"Alex, don't worry about us. Remember what I said. We're going to make the bastard work for it, and we're going to take a hell of a lot of them with us, too. Hopefully enough to give Earth time to prepare. Now, go." He was smiling sadly now, knowing not only what he was asking of her but also what he was committing his fleet to.

"Good luck, sir. I'll see you in the halls." The screams and sounds of rending metal coming from the *Asgard* kept her from returning his smile, though she tried.

"I'll save you a bench—just don't be in a rush to fill it. *Asgard* out." The connection was cut, and she sat there for a moment longer until the ship rocked under another impact.

"Come to a heading of two zero zero mark one eight zero, and get those Valkyries back on board, now!" The command crew jumped into action, and her mind began working furiously on how to get the *Fenris* clear of all of those enemy fighters. "Commander Martin, reconfig starboard laser mounts for sweeping. When that's done, prepare to fire a single missile into those fighters. We're going to splash them all." A wicked grin spread across her face as a plan formed.

"Break right!" Digger shouted into his mask as he felt the Valkyrie roll onto its wingtip and pull sharply to the right as laser fire pulsed through the space they'd just occupied. "That was too close."

"Amen to that." Barbie continued the turn she had started at Digger's shout and came up on the tail of a Sally fighter. She squeezed the trigger on the control stick. Twin bolts of laser fire flashed out from *Valkyrie One*, and the fighter was transformed into a ball of fire. "Got 'em. *Valkyrie Three*, you've got three bandits on your tail. Pull up—I'm on them." *Valkyrie Three* began to climb, but it was too late. Three pairs of missiles followed him though his maneuver and caught up with him. *Valkyrie Three* disappeared, and Barbie let out a howl of rage. She had known Lieutenant Sheppard since flight school; they had been close friends. She let that rage take her and her Valkyrie into a downward spiral as she opened fire on the trio of fighters. First one, then another flashed out of existence, and she flew through the fireballs as the third fighter broke off and was lost in the spinning dogfight that was taking place in space around them.

Flight 127 had been reduced to five remaining Valkyries—four, now that *Valkyrie Three* was gone. They were facing over ten times their number. The only thing allowing them to survive as long as they had was the fact that the Xan-Sskarns could not freely fire on them without risking hitting their companions. That, and because after almost two years of constant battle, the remaining pilots of Flight 127 were some of the best combat fliers in the fleet.

"Valkyrie Flight 127, break off and return to base. Prepare for combat landings." The CAG's voice broke over the squadron battle net.

"Negative, CAG, cannot disengage, we're right in the middle of one hell of a knife fight right now." Barbie was trying to shake a Sally fighter that was intent on removing them from existence. "*Valkyrie Seven*, break, break, break. You've got missiles incoming."

"Thanks, boss," *Valkyrie Seven* said as he juked to port and released countermeasures, evading the incoming missiles. His move brought him up on the tail of a Sally fighter, and his finger squeezed the trigger before thought caught up with action. Another ball of fire blossomed in space.

"I say again, Valkyrie Flight 127, you are to disengage. Now!" Kaufman broke into the net again.

"I think he's serious, boss," Digger called from the rear of the fighter. "Missiles incoming, break left, releasing countermeasures."

"I don't give a fuck," she snarled as she went through evasive maneuvers. She had lost too many friends today to simply break off. "I say again, cannot disengage."

"Damn it, Barbie! Break off now! We're leaving, and the captain's cooking up something special for the Sallys. Now, get your ass back here or get left behind."

"Shit! All Valkyries, we are to break off and return to the *Fenris* immediately. Combat landings. Be careful, and I'll see you on deck," she announced over the squadron battle net. Barbie knew that breaking off contact in the middle of a dogfight was difficult at best and suicide at worst. With the odds stacked against them, it would be closer to worst. She spun to the left at Digger's yell, and as she leveled out she saw that she was near the edge of the swirling mass of fighters. "Digger, where is everyone else?"

"They just got *Valkyrie Nine*, and *Six* is already making a run for the *Fenris*. *Valkyrie Eleven* is still scrapping with two Sallys, but is maneuvering to the edge. Feel free to head on home."

"Roger that. Keep your eyes open as we disengage. Those Sallys are going to jump all over us as soon as they see us turn tail." She yanked the stick back, and her Valkyrie pulled into a tight loop, ending with her nose pointed toward the *Fenris*. She rammed the throttle forward, and they shot ahead, accelerating to full engagement speed. Landing was going to be rough, but she'd been ordered to perform a combat landing and that meant blasting in at full throttle, then slamming on the retros, and hoping like hell that she stopped before she hit the bay wall. She saw the *Fenris* grow rapidly as they closed. Her Valkyrie was tossed sideways as several missiles detonated off the starboard wing. She'd known they were going to draw fire as they broke for home, but that had been too close.

"Tower, this is *Valkyrie One*. I'm on approach and coming in hot, so clear the road." She hated combat landings, but it was either that, reengage the Xan-Sskarns, or walk home. Given those choices, she'd take the landing.

As she maneuvered on to her final approach vector, a single missile tore from the *Fenris'* starboard broadside and raced past her. A second later, a full spread of laser fire followed it. She gripped the stick tighter as her Valkyrie bucked and kicked as if caught in a maelstrom. As she blinked to clear her eyes of the spots the lasers had left on her vision, she looked down at her lidar display. Over ninety percent of the remaining enemy fighters vanished in that instant, vaporized out of existence. It took her a moment to realize what had just happened. The captain had sent a missile into the middle of the Sally formation, but because of the proximity to the *Fenris*, the warhead would not arm, so she had detonated it with their own lasers. She smiled. Unorthodox? Maybe. Dangerous? Most definitely. But highly effective. Barbie pushed that thought from her mind as she fired the retro thrusters full and was slammed forward, her fighter shedding speed quickly, then touching down on the deck of the landing bay. Retro thrusters still wide open, they stopped less than one meter from the bulkhead. She killed the forward thrust and taxied them over to the side of the landing bay, making room for *Valkyrie Eleven*, which was screaming in on approach right behind her.

"That was one hell of trick the captain pulled out of the bag.

I've never even heard of that one before. What about you, Digger?" She didn't get a response, and an icy hand closed around her heart. That last missile barrage.

"Digger?

"Digger!?"

"Touchdown. The last Valkyrie is on the deck, ma'am," Bennard called from his station as Alex continued to study the projection. She wiped her hand across her eyes and lifted her head; Greg saw that despite the sadness in her eyes, Alex had a determined look on her face.

"Helm, bring us up to full power and maintain current heading." They needed to make it to the hyperlimit as quickly as possible if they were going to escape to warn Earth.

Commander Samuels once again brought the *Fenris* up to maximum military power. Alex turned her concentration to scanning as another torpedo impacted them.

"Ensign Green, what've we got left?"

"We have eight Sally fighters left, but it looks like they're disengaging. We're still in range of those two light cruisers, but we're outside of beam range. At our current heading and speed, we will be clear of their engagement envelope in thirteen minutes."

"Thirteen minutes, roger. Keep an eye on the rest of them. If they figure out that we're trying to make a break for it, you can bet your ass that they'll sure as hell try and stop us. Helm, keep our starboard side to the cruisers. Guns, continue sweeping until we are clear of missile range, and maintain your fire, rotating targets." She watched her display a moment longer, seeing the flashes of the battle they were rapidly leaving behind. It looked as if it had intensified in the last few minutes, and that meant that the admiral had begun to get the Xan-Sskarns' attention; as she watched, icons begin to pulse then vanish from the projection. Hitting a button on her chair, she opened a connection to the engineering net.

"Heron, I need everything you can give me, and I need it now. And spin up the jump engines."

"Bringing the jump engines on line now. But, Captain, the engines are at one hundred percent now, and the drive envelope is still showing fluctuations."

"I know the engines are at one hundred percent. I want more. Remove the safety locks on the reactors." Alex was not in the mood to argue prudence with her chief engineer.

"Removing the safety locks would be dangerous, ma'am. The *Fenris* has taken a beating, and even if the engines are at one hundred percent now, there may be damage in the subsystems we haven't found yet. I would not recommend it at this time."

"Your recommendations are noted. Now remove the safety locks."

"Captain, I—" Heron began to argue, but never got to finish as Alex roared into the mike.

"God damn it, Commander Denton! This is not open for debate. Admiral Stevens and the rest of the fleet are buying us escape time with their *lives,* and we are not going to waste one second of it. Remove those fucking safety locks, and remove them now! I don't care if you have to melt the reactors down to slag, just get us to the hyperlimit ahead of the Sallys. Now, you have your orders, Commander—carry them out."

"Aye, aye, ma'am. Removing safety locks now." Alex could hear the resignation in her engineer's voice and felt a momentary pang of regret for the way she'd just spoken to one of her oldest friends, but they needed that extra speed. That regret disappeared with the icon of the *Asgard.* No, they would not waste one precious second of the time the admiral had bought them.

"We're answering one hundred twenty-three percent on particle concentration, ma'am," Commander Samuels informed her several minutes later as the *Fenris'* speed leveled out. Her earpiece came to life, and she heard Commander Denton's voice.

"Captain, I've removed most of the safety locks. The bottles were starting to become unstable, and if I had removed any more, we would be running the risk losing containment. I'm sorry, ma'am—that's the best I could do." Her voice was a dull monotone.

"Thanks, Heron." Alex's voice was soft, and her use of her engineer's nickname carried an unspoken apology. "Great job. No one could've done better. Keep a close eye on things down there—this is going to be a bitch of a ride."

"Yes, ma'am." Alex cut the line to engineering and sat back in her chair. The *Fenris* had finally passed beyond the range of the light cruisers chasing her.

"Commander Martin, reconfigure starboard mounts from missile defense to engagement."

"Reconfiguring now, ma'am. Estimated time to completion is sixty seconds."

"Thank you. Commander Samuels, time to hyperlimit at current speed," Alex called out over the open net, allowing her crew to know how much longer this nightmare was going to continue.

"We will be zero-zero at the jump limit in six point three hours, ma'am." Alex shook her head. Zero-zero at the jump limit meant that the *Fenris* would be totally motionless prior to initiating a jump, which was standard procedure. But that also meant that they would soon reach a turnover point where they would have to begin to decelerate, and decelerating would allow the Xan-Sskarns to close on them again.

"Negative on zero-zero, helm. Recalculate. No turnover—we're hitting the wall, and we are *not* slowing down." There was a stunned silence on the command deck at that announcement. Hitting the wall was almost as dangerous as jumping in-system.

"Ah, yes, ma'am. New ETA at current speed is two point one hours, mark." Commander Samuels' voice wavered slightly. Jump calculations needed to be very precise, and with their current speed, the complexity of the calculations increased by an order of magnitude. His hands shook slightly as he began plotting their jump back to the Sol system.

"Alex, are you sure about this?" Greg asked over their private net. "We're already redlining the reactors, plus we're shot full of holes. Hitting the wall, especially at this speed, might be pushing our luck."

"Greg, look at the display." She waved her hand at the projection. "Those cruisers that are chasing us have backup, and they're pouring on the speed." As they both watched, they saw what appeared to be two destroyer squadrons on a high-speed interception course with the *Fenris*. "If we go for a zero-zero jump, those ships will be on top of us almost two hours before we reach the limit. We'd never survive the encounter. No, we hit the wall running full out, and we'll just have to hope that she holds together. The admiral wanted us to warn Earth, and that is exactly what I intend to do."

"Yes, ma'am," Greg replied, but he did not sound defeated. She knew he was only playing devil's advocate, like any good XO, and he was one of the best. Alex began to order a stand down from battle stations when Ensign Green once again broke into her thoughts.

"Status change! Captain, a Sally battleship and her escorts just jumped in."

●   ●   ●

The xan-liarn pacing back and forth across the command center of the kisnan *Swift Current* ran a talon along one of the three stripes adorning his muzzle, tracing it down his heavily muscled neck, waiting. The pale yellow light filling the compartment was quickly replaced by the dim green lighting of combat stations as the ship secured from fold operations.

"Ki-Tesh, what is the status of my squadron?" the xan-liarn demanded in a guttural voice of the Xan-Sskarn operating the communications position.

"Squadron all present and at combat stations, Xan-Liarn."

He did not bother to acknowledge the information given by his subordinate, but instead turned to his second-in-command.

"Is the *Swift Current* ready for battle, Ki-Xarn?" The quiet, lisp-like hiss of his question was more civil than his demand of the communications officer; etiquette and protocol dictated this. His second-in-command's muzzle was marked with the same three stripes as his own, making the ki-xarn the closest thing to an equal the xan-liarn would find within his squadron.

"We have secured from fold operations, and all combat stations report ready, Xan-Liarn."

"Excellent." Flaring his nostrils and picking up the slightly damp, musky odor of excitement, the xan-liarn ran a talon down his neck once again. "When those pathetic Dry-Skins attempt to flee like a pack of frightened hatchlings, they shall be ours."

"What's their heading?" Alex asked quickly. She was afraid that she knew the answer even before Green told her. If she hadn't believed the admiral's statement that someone had sold them out, the sudden arrival of the Xan-Sskarn battleship would have changed her mind. That battleship was on a reciprocal heading for any Earth ship that might be trying to escape the system and jump to Sol. They weren't moving to intercept the *Fenris* yet, but that wouldn't last for long. Either the distortions from the residual jump energy would clear, and they would pick up the *Fenris* themselves on their long-range sensors, or they would receive the messages their companions were no doubt sending, telling them of the *Fenris'* attempt to escape. Whichever happened first, the outcome would be the same. The *Fenris* would have no choice but to engage the Sally battleship group if she wished to exit the system on a heading to Sol.

"They're maneuvering toward us now, Captain, coming in on our starboard side. Ninety minutes to engagement range," Ensign Green informed Alex as soon as his sensors reported the change. That would put the *Fenris* under enemy fire for twenty-seven minutes before she could make the jump to Sol. The only good news was that the position the Xan-Sskarns were starting from was not an exact reciprocal and would not put them on a direct interception course; they would be coming in at a steep angle relative to the *Fenris*. The difference in their vectors would keep the range open enough for the Xan-Sskarns to be able to engage with missiles and torpedoes only, and Alex was thankful for that. Xan-Sskarn battleships mounted hellishly powerful lasers and she had no desire to be on the receiving end of the damage they could dish out.

"XO, stand down from general quarters, sixty minutes, then we're back to work." She wanted her crew to have a chance to relax, and she needed a break as well. She released her harness, stood up, stretched, then began to pace around the command deck, looking over displays and murmuring words of encouragement. A steward entered arrived on the lift, carrying a tray, and Alex grabbed a bottle of water from it, drinking deeply, trying to clear her mind now that the immediate threat was over and adrenaline levels in her bloodstream were dropping. She desperately wanted a cigarette, and her hand moved of its own accord to her breast, stopping as it encountered a row of ribbons. She blinked twice in confusion and looked down, startled to realize that she was still in her dress uniform. No wonder she was feeling so spent—except for a short catnap on the shuttle ride back to the *Fenris*, she had been awake for almost twenty-four hours. She saw Greg pass by the steward, grab two cups of coffee, and head toward her. Handing her a cup as he reached her, he spoke up.

"Yeah, I just noticed it, too." He indicated his once-pristine white uniform. "Thanks to those harnesses, it's going to take weeks to get the creases out of it, and I don't even want to think about the blood." She looked over his and then her uniform and could see what he meant. She put her water down and swallowed half the contents of the cup and grimaced. The coffee was bitter, but strong, and just what she needed. She continued her rounds on the command deck, working her way through three cups of coffee in the process. The haze was just beginning to lift from her mind as Greg broke in over their net.

"Ten minutes to engagement range, ma'am."

"Thanks. Bring us back up to general quarters." She moved to her command chair and began to strap herself down as alarms called everyone back to their stations.

"All battle stations manned and ready, Captain," Greg reported to her ninety seconds later.

"Commander Samuels, maintain a continual monitoring of our jump calculations. Any changes in ship status, and I want them updated immediately."

"Understood, ma'am." Alex looked down at the projection, watching the time and distance count down. At one minute until engagement range, she spoke up again.

"Commander Martin, prepare your drones. Launch at thirty seconds out."

"Yes, ma'am." His hands began to move across his board as he programmed the first pair of drones and then waited as the time counted down. "Drones away."

Thirty seconds later, the first of the Xan-Sskarn missiles began to home in on the *Fenris*. As they closed, the point-defense net began to clear them from space. The range was great enough that point defense was able to track and destroy all of the first three waves of incoming missiles. First a missile, then an energy torpedo managed to weave past the defense net, and the *Fenris* once again began to bleed vapor from hull breaches.

The *Fenris* had not been silent during this onslaught. Her missile tubes continued to launch wave after wave of missiles back at the enemy. This exchange continued for several minutes before the Xan-Sskarns inflicted major damage as a salvo of four energy torpedoes impacted along the starboard bow, rocking the ship and vaporizing entire sections of armor.

"Damage report." Alex could see their acceleration as well as their volume of fire beginning to drop.

"The entire bow has been stripped down to the frame, and we've lost contact with everything forward of beam forty, including the hangar bay. Multiple fires are being reported throughout the ship. Engineering reports that the drive envelope is beginning to become unstable and maximum speed is down to one hundred eight percent. Reactor three's in emergency shutdown, and reactor one's mag bottle is showing signs of imminent containment loss." Greg finished his recital of the damages and looked up at her. Alex could see the hopeless look on his face, and she smiled at him. Hopeless or not, the *Fenris* was not going down without a fight.

"Guns, deploy our mines, two groups. First group set for delayed proximity detonation twenty seconds, second group proximity detonation, no delay."

"Yes, ma'am!" Commander Martin shouted back. Deploying the mines for delayed detonation would ensure that they were in the middle of the Sally formation when they exploded. The second wave would go up right in their faces. Unless they wanted to attempt to break off their pursuit, they would have no choice but to sail right through the middle of them. Mines tumbled from the sides of the *Fenris*, oriented themselves, and, with a large burst of energy, set themselves directly toward the Xan-Sskarns. "Mines deployed."

It would be several long minutes before the Xan-Sskarns entered the minefield that had just sprung up in front of them. All the while, the long-range duel continued. The *Fenris* had fallen to one hundred one percent acceleration when a pair of missiles detonated amidships topside. Explosions ripped through the command deck. Lieutenant McKeenan's head and chest disappeared as his console erupted in his face, and Commander Martin slumped in his chair, pieces of Lieutenant McKeenan's console, and Lieutenant McKeenan, embedded in his head and neck. Petty Officer Conrad was shrieking in pain, her left arm severed above the elbow by a piece of shrapnel from the exploding overhead. As blood loss caused the sensor tech to lose consciousness, Alex could hear several more moans of pain from around the command deck. Her XO was already on his way over to the weapons console, ignoring the gory mess that covered it, as Ensign Green attended to his tech. She was shocked by the familiarity of this situation, realizing that she had been here before. At Ross 128, with her ship being blown apart around her, half the command crew dead or too wounded to function, Greg had sat calmly at a blood-drenched tactical station, awaiting her orders. She heard herself issuing the same order she had during that battle.

"Rapid fire, all tubes, cascade launch. Run them dry!" Greg also seemed to be reliving the same battle, as the new firing solution was locked in and in effect before she even finished issuing the order. Missiles blasted from the tubes, one after another, moving down the ship. By the time the last tube had fired, the first tube was reloaded and launching. A continuous flow of missiles streaked from the *Fenris*, blurring into one steady stream of fire on the Xan-Sskarns' sensor displays, making them easier to intercept but much harder to track, as the sensors read them as one long target. Typically, this was a tactic to be used against a single opponent or a formation of light ships where their point-defense nets were not as tightly concentrated as larger formations. They were two minutes from the jump limit when the ship was once again rocked by an explosion. This time, Commander Samuels was killed as a support strut broke free from the overhead, swinging down and caving in the side of his head. Several more consoles exploded, sending shards of metal and plastic spinning through the air, cutting down several more people on the command deck. The *Fenris* was now ninety seconds from the jump limit, and there was no one updating their jump program. Alex ripped at her harness, freeing herself from her chair, and raced across command to the navigation station, slipping in the gore covering the deck. She reached the console at sixty seconds from the jump limit and began to update the program, not even noticing that her hands were covered in blood that was not her own.

"Greg, status?" She had to shout to be heard over the alarms and sparks erupting from consoles.

"I can't raise anyone. Internal comms are down, and so are internal sensors," he shouted back as his hands continued to update targeting solutions. Fifteen seconds from the jump limit, his hand slapped down one final time, and the last of the *Fenris*' missiles shot from the remaining missile tubes. "That's it, Alex. I'm dry."

"Ten seconds to jump!" Alex shouted across to him.

"Incoming energy torpedoes!" They were both shocked to hear Ensign Green's voice coming out from the smoke-filled command deck. "Point defense is down. Impact in five seconds." Alex looked at her countdown; seven seconds to jump. Two damn seconds—that's all they needed. Just two more seconds, and the *Fenris* would be able to escape this death trap.

The torpedoes impacted, and the *Fenris* rocked once more. Someone shouted her name, and then something heavy collided with her, knocking her off her feet. But she didn't notice. Alex's eyes were transfixed, staring at the painfully beautiful, delicate flames that danced over the command deck, directly at her.

Chapter Thirteen

FOLKVANG STATION
OCTOBER 8, 2197
0920Z
LUNAR POLAR ORBIT, SOL

Petty Officer Third Class Brian Phelps arrived in Folkvang station's operations center and headed directly toward the coffee. His almost fanatical love of coffee had earned him the nickname Chief in tech school, when an instructor said that he drank more coffee than any three navy chiefs he knew. A demon with all types of sensor equipment, the pimply faced nineteen-year-old had only two loves: coffee and his job.

Sitting down at his station with a large mug of coffee, Phelps looked over at the woman who had become one of his few friends and greeted her. "Morning, Lisa."

"Morning, Chief. How's the coffee this morning?" she asked, smiling sweetly at him as she teased him.

"Just like mom used to make. You know, you should really give it a chance. It'll put hair on your chest."

"Yeah, and guys just love the hairy chest."

"Huh?" He glanced up from his console and looked at her, puzzled. Lisa rolled her eyes at his total lack of comprehension.

"Nothing. Anyway, I'll stick with my tea, thank you very much."

"Suit yourself—more for me. So, what's on the agenda for today?" Phelps turned back to his panels, focusing on his job now that his repertoire of pleasantries was exhausted.

"Looks to be nothing much outside of the norm. No training exercises today, but then I'm not too surprised by that. Every time they schedule an exercise and try to surprise us, you and I pick 'em up, and gunnery tracks them in and picks them off. I think they finally gave up on us and are concentrating on the other shifts now." She sounded rather smug.

"Well, let's get to work, then," Phelps said cheerfully at that thought and began almost lovingly to manipulate his boards. Shaking her head and smiling, Lisa turned to her own station. They sat in companionable silence, listening to the humming and chirping emanating from their respective readouts.

They both began to run their overlapping sensor sweeps, monitoring and recording over a wide range of spectrums. Information was relayed to their consoles from Folkvang's own sensor suites as well as all of the sensor platforms seeded throughout the system. They were on the lookout for a wide variety of objects and readings: Xan-Sskarn drones, unauthorized communication waves, stealthed enemy vessels, and, most importantly, space-fold phenomena.

Umeko Hoshiko and Terrance Muxlo were not the first scientists to theorize folding space or FTL travel, but they were the first to combine Werner Heisenberg's uncertainty principle with an innovative and truly unique drive design. By starting with Heisenberg's principle, they discovered the possibility of determining, with a high degree of accuracy, where a jump would take a ship, but the means to achieve that jump still needed to be figured out. Hoshiko and Muxlo's unique drive design took care of that problem. Utilizing not one but two quantumly entangled jump engines, the Heisenberg Umeko Muxlo Dimensional Drive was created, and FTL became a reality. The first engine opened a jump point where the generating ship was, the second opened a point at the desired destination at the same instant, light years away, and the ship simply translated between the two. Due to the egglike shape of the drives, coupled with their tongue-twisting name, they were christened with a new, shorter name by fleet engineers: the Humpty.

Space folds not only required a great deal of power to generate jump points; they released a large amount of energy across both the visible and nonvisible spectrum during the translation between those points. They could be the easiest disturbance to detect, or they could be nearly impossible to read. The difference came from the location of the event in relation to a sensor platform. That's what made detecting them such a tricky and complicated task, and such a challenge to people like Petty Officer Phelps. Xan-Sskarn scout-ship standard doctrine called for them to jump up to a light-month out from the target system, and the residual energy from a jump that far out of a system was almost impossible to detect among the background energy of the universe. Needle in a haystack would be a gross understatement.

Jerking up in his chair, Phelps let his coffee mug fall to the deck as his sensors began to shrill a warning at him.

Modern sensor and communication satellites were not restricted by the conventions of transmission lag. Powered by a large onboard reactor with a life span measured in years, opening and maintaining a microscopic jump portal was relatively simple. Satellite transmissions were energy with no mass, and this lack of mass, coupled with the extremely short distances that a signal had to travel in-system, meant that the effects of local gravity wells were negligible. However, even without mass, transmissions were still affected by gravity over interstellar distances. The constant motion of planetary bodies and the consequent change in a system's gravity fields made anything beyond transmitting across a solar system nigh impossible. The expense of the satellites as well as the need to maintain the secrecy of their functioning dictated that they only be deployed in secure systems.

"New contact!" Phelps shouted into his mike, alerting everyone in the operations center. "Sensors report a single point source." Chief of the Watch Maxwell rushed over to Phelps' station.

"Good catch, Chief. What've you got?"

"Jesus, Chief, a blind man could've seen that translation. It looks like a single ship came across the wall at full military power. I've never seen anything like it." He didn't even look up from his readouts, but continued reporting as more information scrolled by. "My birds are having a hard time cutting through the distortions, but I'm reading massive power fluctuations and an expanding debris field."

"An expanding debris field?" Chief Maxwell asked, frowning.

"That makes about as much sense as a ship coming across the wall at full power. Are your sensors reading any explosions aboard the ship? Maybe the debris came from that."

"Negative. I would have to say the explosion took place immediately prior to jump. If that's the case, I'm surprised they even made it through the jump. Wait one." His hand pressed the earbud of his headset deeper into his ear. "I'm picking up something now from another bird, beyond the distortion field. It's an IFF signal. Signal reads as USS *Fenris*. She's one of ours."

"Brown, punch up data on the *Fenris*. Find out who she is and where she is supposed to be," Maxwell snapped, and Lisa moved to comply with his orders. He then reached past Phelps and cut himself into the watch officer's net. "Lieutenant, we've got something here you need to see."

An officious-looking lieutenant bustled over to the chief and his two techs and distractedly addressed the group while reading a pad.

"Okay, what've you got for me?"

Chief Maxwell looked up from Phelps' displays to the seemingly oblivious lieutenant.

"Sir, Phelps here has picked up a ship crossing the wall at max speed. IFF ID's her as the *Fenris*, and she's showing signs of heavy battle damage."

"The *Fenris*? What have you got on her?"

"Petty Officer Brown, what did you find on the *Fenris*?" Maxwell asked Lisa.

"Coming up now, Chief." Lisa began reading the information aloud, "Okay, here we go. USS *Fenris*, a heavy cruiser under the independent command of Captain Alexandra McLaughlin, currently attached to Admiral Stevens' battle group."

"Admiral Stevens? Aren't he and his battle group assigned to Groombridge 34?" The lieutenant had finally looked up from his pad at Lisa's litany, a quizzical look on his face.

"Here it is. Yes, sir. Admiral Stevens' battle group is assigned to the front lines, at Groombridge 34," Lisa replied.

"So what you're all telling me is that what we've got here is a ship, assigned to Admiral Stevens' battle group, showing up here showing signs of battle damage. Is that correct?" the lieutenant demanded of the three enlisted personnel in front of him.

"Yes, sir, that's what it looks like," Maxwell answered for the group.

"Run a reciprocal on her course and tell me where she came from."

"Aye, sir." Maxwell tapped Phelps on the shoulder, indicating he should begin the calculations.

"Got it, LT," Phelps called out as the final equations ran themselves out. "Reciprocal plotting shows an eighty-seven point four probability that the origin of her jump was Groombridge 34."

"Eighty-seven point four, huh? That's good enough for me. Patch me through to CIC, Chief."

"Yes, sir." Maxwell tapped some more commands into Phelps' panel then turned to the lieutenant. "CIC on the line for you, sir."

"Commander Easly, this is Lieutenant Ford in tracking. We've got something you need to see." He listened to his earpiece for a moment then replied to whatever he heard. "Yes, ma'am, sensor readings are on the way up to you now." He nodded to Phelps, who nodded back and began compiling his readings and forwarding them up to CIC. Phelps gave Ford a thumbs-up when all the information was sent.

"Data dump complete, ma'am. You should have it all, and we will continue a constant track and update you as the situation changes." He listened to the reply before responding and cutting the connection. "Yes, ma'am, I'll pass that along. Ford out." Turning to the team in front of him, he spoke again. "The commander passes on her compliments for the quick catch and rapid response from you three. Keep up the good work, and let me know if anything new develops."

"Yes, sir, we will," Chief Maxwell answered for the three of them.

"Very good. Carry on." And with that, the lieutenant moved back to his command console.

"Keep that up, Chief, and you'll be one in rank as well as name sooner than you think. You, too, Brown." Maxwell smiled down at the two blushing petty officers in front of him. "Now, you heard the LT. Keep it up, and let me know if anything develops as well."

"Aye, aye, Chief," they both responded quickly and spun back to their stations, trying to wring as much information from them as possible.

CIC had turned into a frantic hive of energy with arrival of the sensor readings from Lieutenant Ford's watch section. Admiral Sean Rachere, commanding Folkvang station, continued to stare at the "Eyes Only" pad he had been given when he first stepped into CIC, reading and rereading the pad over and over again. He kept coming back to the line "USS *Fenris*, Captain Alexandra McLaughlin, commanding." Slowly, a smile formed on his face. Rachere, a man of slightly less than average height, with short-cropped dark brown hair and dull, lifeless brown eyes, stood up from his command chair. His hand reached up to stroke his completely nonregulation goatee—it was good to be an admiral after all—and he turned toward the operations officer.

"Lieutenant Commander Milo, the *Fenris* still refuses our hails?" Rachere asked his comm officer perfunctorily.

"I don't know about refusing our hails, sir. She's heavily damaged. But the only transmission we've received is the encrypted recording from the emergency lifeboat. I don't think anyone's on board the lifeboat—they probably didn't even launch it. The transmission lag is dropping too fast in relation to the maximum speed of a lifeboat."

Rachere turned to the watch officer. "Commander Easly, contact bay three and have them prepare a fast courier. Tell the crew to plot an intercept course with the *Fenris*," Admiral Rachere ordered. "Tell them we will launch as soon as I arrive."

"As soon as *you* arrive, sir?" Commander Easly sounded shocked. "I don't understand."

"What part don't you understand, Commander? I am going to be aboard that courier when it meets up with the *Fenris*," he barked back at her. His face flushed slightly, hiding the light spattering of freckles that covered it. "Also, contact the master-at-arms. I want a squad of MPs on board as well, and I want them there before I arrive."

"Ah, yes, sir. I'll inform the courier-boat captain to expect your arrival and will have the MPs there before you arrive, sir." She sounded perplexed by the admiral's odd orders but moved to obey as he stood up and began to head for the hatch.

"Very good, Commander. Also alert Admiral Reynolds that she will be in command while I'm off-station."

"Yes, sir. Sir, shouldn't we send a larger ship to assist the *Fenris*? With that much damage, she'll have wounded on board, and her environmental systems may be nonfunctional." The admiral turned and looked back at the commander with a strange look in his eyes and an equally strange smile on his face. Easly stepped back.

"You have your orders, Commander. Carry them out." He turned back toward the hatch.

"Aye, aye, sir," she called to his retreating back. She could see a ten-centimeter scar running down the right side of the back of his head, and she smiled to herself, speculating how he had gotten it. *Probably by being the officious, pompous prick that he is, and someone putting him in his place.* That cheerful thought stayed with her as she turned back to her console and continued issuing orders.

And what is it with men and facial hair? They're always stroking it like it was a pet or something. Disgusting.

And just what the hell did that pad say?

Lieutenant Web, captain of the fast courier, hull number 254, ran though his checklist with his copilot.

"Particle Drive?"

"Particle Drive, check," Ensign Coburn called off as he switched the drive to standby. Fast courier ships were the smallest ships to mount Particle Drives, but at the expense of weapons and armor. This was considered an acceptable trade-off in a ship designed for operations behind the front lines. The crews of the dozens of courier boats that had been lost to Xan-Sskarn fast attack frigates would argue that point—if the dead could complain.

"Reaction thrusters?" Lieutenant Web continued the litany.

"Reaction thrusters, check."

"Environmental?"

"Ah, Cap, did anyone tell you about MPs coming along on this trip?" Coburn asked as he saw the squad of marines forming up in the bay next to their craft.

"MPs?" Web craned his neck to look past his copilot to see for himself. "No. No one told me about any damn marines on my boat. All I got was an order for an emergency launch, and that we would have a passenger. Nothing more than that."

"Well, your passenger has arrived, Lieutenant, so you had best be prepared to launch," said a voice from the hatch leading to the flight deck behind them.

"We are. And while you're on my boat, you will refer to me as—" Lieutenant Web began waspishly only to freeze in mid-snarl when he turned and saw the owner of the voice.

"Yes, Lieutenant, I'll refer to you as what?" Admiral Rachere inquired, staring at the shocked face staring back at him.

"Ah, you'll refer to me any way you please, Admiral. Please

excuse my rudeness—emergency launches always put me on edge," Lieutenant Web said apologetically.

"That's right, I will. You are forgiven, *Captain*. Emergency launches are stressful, but I would like to think that I have a good reason to order it." Admiral Rachere settled into the flight engineer's chair and began strapping himself down. Lieutenant Web could hear the thump of boots as the marines boarded his ship and settled down in the passenger compartment.

"Of course, sir. Okay, Coburn, looks like the marines are all tucked in. Let's go."

"Roger that, Skipper. Thrusters are coming on line now. She's all yours."

"Thanks." He nodded to his copilot and dialed up flight control. "Tower, this is *Courier 254*, request permission to launch."

"*Courier 254*, this is the tower, your flight path is clear and you are clear to launch," a seemingly disinterested voice replied.

"Roger, tower. *Courier 254* launching now." Web eased the throttle forward and felt himself being pushed back into his chair as the lights of the landing bay streaked by. Seconds later, the inky blackness of space surrounded Lieutenant Web and his ship. "Ensign Coburn, please bring the Particle Drive on line and set coordinates for intercept with the *Fenris*."

"Yes, sir, P-Drive coming up now. Coordinates locked in. Fifteen seconds to full drive envelope."

"Thank you, Ensign." Lieutenant Web turned his head and looked over his shoulder at the admiral behind him. "ETA to the *Fenris*, assuming she holds current speed and heading, is two hours forty-seven minutes." Web watched as the admiral checked his watch then smiled.

"Very good, Captain," Admiral Rachere said. Then, after a moment's pause, he spoke again, softly. "I've waited this long—I can wait another three hours."

Though the admiral's last statement was very low, Web still caught it.

"Excuse me, sir?" His voice quizzical.

"Oh, nothing, Captain," the admiral replied and settled back into his chair with a look of satisfaction on his face. "Nothing at all." Unnerved by the admiral's expression and tone, Lieutenant Web turned back to his controls. He would be glad when this particular flight was over.

Chapter Fourteen

USS *FENRIS*
OCTOBER 8, 2197
0925Z
SOL

Alex awoke to darkness, facedown on the deck. A heavy weight across her back pressed her down, and as she tried to move, a wave of pain flared through her body causing her to gasp out. As the pain subsided, she tried to ascertain her situation. Twisting her head around, she fought down the nausea even that small movement caused and surveyed her surroundings. The dim red lights of emergency lighting glowed feebly, diffused by the smoke filling the command deck, but there was enough light to allow her to see. She felt more than heard the footsteps of someone approaching her.

"Captain McLaughlin?" the voice coughed out, raw but undeniably Ensign Green's. "Ma'am, are you alright?" There was deep concern and a tinge of fear in his voice.

"Still alive, Ensign. Don't know about alright, though." Alex barely recognized her own voice. It sounded to her as if she had been gargling razor blades. The acrid smoke that filled the compartment was choking her. With the weight across her back, she could not get a full breath. "Get this weight off my back, and I'll let you know."

"Ah, of course, Captain, just give me a sec." The voice had an odd quality that Alex could not quite understand. That is, until she felt the weight shift off her and she rolled onto her back. As the blinding pain subsided, she understood all too well. Commander Greg Higgins' blackened and burned face was mere centimeters from hers. She began to remember. A shout, something heavy hitting her, flames, and then blackness.

"Oh, God," she whispered. "Greg!"

"Captain?" Green called out softly. Alex could hear the desperation in his voice but could not take her gaze off of her friend's disfigured face. "Captain, are you alright?"

Alex knew she had duties, knew she had obligations to what was left of her ship and crew, but just could not get past the face next to hers. It took a moment for her to realize that she was looking at Greg's face though only one eye. She fought down a wave of panic as she tried to lift her right arm to probe her face and find out why. The pain, worse than before, caused her to gasp and inhale a lungful of smoke, which in turn caused a spasm of coughing to wrack her body, setting every nerve ending in her body afire. Broken ribs grated together as she fought to stay conscious and get her body under control. Once she could concentrate on something more than the pain, she again tried to move her arm, this time very slowly. The pain that lanced through her body was bad, but not incapacitating. She gently felt the side of her face and could feel the swelling keeping her eye shut. She managed to take her gaze off of her friend's face and look up at Ensign Green. The concern on his face was evident. Her crew was decimated, her ship shot full of holes and falling apart around her. Two crews, two ships, two lost battles. Tears flowed from her one good eye, running down her soot-streaked face. *There is no time for crying.* She fought down that pain as well and tried to get her emotions under control. *You are an officer, and you have a job to do, so* do it.

"Battered, bruised, and beat to hell, Ensign, but raring to go." She forced a smile onto her face for his benefit. "What's our status?"

"Well, first off, Commander Higgins is alive, but barely." She could hear the relief in his voice at her revival. "We need to get him and the others to sick bay, but the lift is jammed and internal comms are down. I've got Chief Mendez trying to get comms back now."

"Good work, Ensign. What else?" She gasped out in pain as she tried to sit up. Green reached out to steady her as he continued his report.

"Engines are off line, but we're running near full out with the momentum we carried over the wall. Most of my sensors are burnt out, but from what I could see, we're home. I'm effectively blind beyond a few thousand kilometers, though. I have no idea as to the status of weapons—both primary and auxiliary panels are slag. That's all I can tell you at this time. I haven't had a chance to take a closer look at anything, I...." He faltered and stopped.

"You were looking after the wounded. I understand, and it was the right thing." She gave him a real smile now. "Help me up. Then get back to the wounded. I'll take care of the DC net from my chair, assuming any of the panels are working."

"Yes, ma'am." He put his arm around her and slowly rose to his feet, bringing her with him, then began to move slowly toward the command chair. Alex let out a hiss of pain with each step. She was sweating and shaking by the time they reached her chair. Ensign Green helped ease her down into it, then stepped back to look at her, the worried expression back on his face.

"Thanks, I'm fine," she rasped out to him and could see him hesitate to move on. "Really, I'm fine. Carry on, and I'll do the same." She tried to wink, but was reminded, painfully, that her right eye was swollen shut. So she decided to begin checking her panels and waited until he had moved off before leaning back into her chair, trying to get her mind to focus on something more than the pain. It took her a moment to realize that most of her panels were indeed working, and she could ascertain the status of her ship. It was worse than she had feared. Engines were definitely down, and there were only three surviving energy mounts. Missile tubes did not really matter, as she had ordered Greg to launch everything they had. With her mind turning to Greg, her good eye did the same. She could see him lying there on the deck. Ensign Green was bent over him, trying to do something that would help ease the commander's suffering. She wrenched her mind back to her duties and continued to pull up more information. Primary environmental was off line, but secondary systems functioned, barely. External communications were nonexistent—not even the short-range emitters and receivers were operational; for all intents and purposes, they were silenced.

She continued to read and saw that Ensign Green was correct: sensors, too, were effectively nonfunctional. She winced as she began to absently stroke her chin, contemplating their situation. The *Fenris* was blind, mute, and crippled. Structural integrity was so bad, she was half-afraid that the relief ship that should be heading their way would send the remains of her ship spinning apart into space with the impact of their docking.

Alex stopped stroking her chin when she suddenly realized that her hand was sticky with blood. She beckoned a med kit–carrying petty officer over.

"I'm sorry, ma'am. I didn't know you were in this bad shape," he began as he set his kit on the deck and opened it.

"I'm fine," she rasped out. "There are others who need you more than I do. I just want something to wipe my hands off with." She held out her hands, indicating the gore covering them.

"No problem, ma'am. Me and Jones did what we could for everyone, but we're no corpsmen. We need to get these folks to sick bay, or at the very least get a real corpsman up here to them." He shrugged his shoulders while glancing around, then turned his attention back to Alex. "So, let me get you cleaned up a bit and see about stopping that bleeding."

"Bleeding?" Alex, so covered in blood, did not even realize that some of it was her own.

"Yes, ma'am. You've got a nasty cut above your right eye, but I won't know about anything else until I get some of that blood cleaned up." He applied saline to some gauze, then reached out to Alex's hands and began wiping them off. "Okay. Now, I'm sorry, ma'am, but this is going to hurt." He replaced the soiled gauze with a clean piece and moved his hand toward her face, but stopped short, hesitant.

"That's okay, Sebastian." She could see his surprise that she knew his first name. "Just go ahead and do it. I think this face can take a bit more abuse." She tried to smile, but grimaced instead as he began his ministrations. As he cleared the blood clotting her nostrils, the smell of burning plastic and charred flesh assaulted her. She nearly gagged at the stench, which caused the petty officer to jerk his hand back.

"Sorry, ma'am. I'm trying my best, but I really don't know what I'm doing. Last first-aid class I had was boot camp." He gave her a wan, apologetic smile.

"You're doing fine—just a momentary shock. Please, continue." He followed her orders, finished cleaning the soot and blood from her face, put a pair of butterfly bandages across the gash above her right eye, and stepped back.

"There you go, ma'am. Best I can do with what we've got." He bent to gather up his kit. As he stood again, he nodded to Alex and then withdrew back to his station.

Alex felt a little better, but was still in pain and exhausted. She surveyed her command deck, and her spirits fell at what she saw. Too many of her command crew were dead or wounded, still seated at their stations or sprawled across the deck. She knew that this scene was being repeated throughout the ship. Alex continued to check the status of her ship from what she could pull from her panels. Lost in thought as a litany of destruction scrolled by on her screens, she did not notice the person coming up on her blind side.

"Ma'am?" a soft Hispanic-accented voice said in her right ear, causing Alex to jump, then gasp in pain. Alex turned her head to face the speaker and saw Chief Mendez standing beside her command chair.

"Yes, Chief, what have you got for me?" she said wearily as the pain subsided. Mendez looked up from the data pad she was carrying and saw her captain's face wincing as she took stock of the damage.

"The battle nets are a total write-off, but I've got partial internal comms back on line. Nothing fancy—only one channel at a time." The small dark-skinned woman looked down shamefacedly. "Sorry, ma'am. It's the best I can do with what I've got up here. Most of the comm station is just gone." Her head came up, and Alex could see the tears forming in her soft brown eyes.

"Good job, Chief." Alex tried to put a soothing tone in her voice, but her smoke-seared throat turned it into a harsh rasp. "Best news I've heard all day. Now, I know it's asking the impossible, but see what you can do about external comms." She gave the weary chief a small smile and nodded her approval as Mendez smiled back before heading back to her station.

Now that she had limited communications, she punched up a connection to her chief engineer. "Heron?" Alex half whispered into her mike, afraid she would not get an answer from her oldest friend. Static hissed on the channel a moment before a raw voice came over the earpiece.

"Alex, is that you?"

"Yeah, it's me." The relief in her voice was evident. "How are things down there?"

"Well, ma'am, it ain't pretty. Reactor three is out of commission—mag bottle is fused shut. Reactor one went critical just before we jumped, but the emergency ejection system kicked it out before total containment loss. Took most of the reactor room's staff with it as well." Heron's cool litany changed with her last statement, and Alex could hear the bitterness in her voice. "Reactor two's in emergency shutdown, but we're trying to restart now. Hull integrity is not good, but I think she'll hold together long enough for a relief ship to get to us. Weapons are pretty much gone, but I'm guessing we're home, so we won't need them at the moment. Environmental is in bad shape, but backups are working. We have fires throughout the ship, but I've got teams chasing them down now. Also, the galley that Dr. Swartz commandeered for additional space is cut off. It's still airtight, but the passageway is open to space. Two teams are there now, trying to get emergency patches in place. The flight deck is open to vacuum, and I have not been able to get anyone to it to check for survivors or assess the damage. There's just too much damage in the bow that's blocking our way, but we're working on that. That's all I have now. My teams are still reporting in, but it's hell having to communicate with runners."

"Very well, Commander." Thank God she had agreed to the doctor's request for emergency generators for the galley, or everyone in there would be dead right now. "Get that passageway sealed, and get the reactor back on line—we're going like a bat out of hell, and we need to slow down to make lunar orbit. Also, the lift to the command deck is out of commission, and the entrance to the service passage is buried in debris. So I need the lift repaired ASAP. We've got wounded up here, and we need to get them some help." She began to rub her chin again as she continued to issue orders. "Next, I want you to personally find a lifeboat with a working transmitter. I know they are normally just used for automated beacons, but those transmitters are powerful, so I want you to swap out the standard beacon and send a transmission on a continual loop, but do not launch the lifeboat." Alex began to copy and encrypt Admiral Stevens' assessment of what happened at Groombridge 34 while she continued to speak. "See what you can do about external comms and sensors—we're flying blind up here. We only have the one channel for internal comms right now, so I am handing it over to you for damage-control coordination, and I've just sent you the message I want transmitted. Any questions?"

"No, ma'am. I'll take care of it and keep you updated as I can. Engineering out." The line cut back to static as Alex ran the damage assessment over again in her mind, seeing not only the present but also another time and place. Feeling fatigue and the ghosts of her past pulling at her, she ignored them both. The *Fenris* and her crew were hurt, and hurt bad, with all of the damage not even known yet. She was surprised that any of them had even survived to make it to the wall. She yearned to know the status of her wounded, but knew that this was not the time to disturb the medical staff. Her battle might be over, but theirs would continue for hours to come.

The lift hatch groaned open and two blood-spattered corpsmen rushed onto the command deck, immediately setting to work attending to the wounded. Following them out of the lift, a slower-moving Commander Denton stepped onto the command deck. The chief engineer looked around wearily, taking in the chaos and destruction surrounding her before stepping down toward the captain. Her torn and scorched hazard suit hung open, the hood thrown back. Even while wearing the suit, she had managed to singe her hair and smudge streaks of soot across her face. But as bad as she knew she looked, she thought that Alex looked worse, her face pale and sweating, twisted into an ugly grimace. Heron knew from that quick glance that her friend was in extreme pain. As she stepped up beside the command chair, her gaze fell on the blackened figure of Commander Higgins lying on the deck, a corpsman bent over him, hands frantically trying to save his life. Breath catching in her throat, she turned her sorrowful gaze back to her captain. Greg Higgins was a friend of hers, but he was nowhere near as close a friend to her as he was to the captain. Now that Heron stood beside her friend, she could see that the pain disfiguring Alex's face was not entirely caused by her physical injuries. Heron set a comforting hand on her friend's shoulder, speaking softly.

"Captain?"

"What?" Alex said distractedly, seemingly startled by both the voice and physical contact, and turned her head. "Oh, Heron, how'd you get up here?" Heron watched Alex's one good eye staring at her owlishly, wide and uncomprehending.

"I've got some of the lifts working again, and brought a med team with me on the way up here, ma'am," she explained patiently, gesturing toward the corpsman kneeling beside Commander Higgins. Alex was definitely not tracking at the moment, and Heron couldn't tell if it was from the shock and pain of her injuries, if she was stunned by their current situation, or if she was lost in thought, trying to figure out what they were going to do next. She hoped it was the latter. But regardless of the reason, having the captain sitting in the middle of this kind of situation and looking to the world as if she had spaced out, well, that fell under the heading of "a very bad thing." She shook Alex lightly, hoping to snap her back to the here and now.

Alex, feeling herself being shaken, wondered if the *Fenris* had fallen under attack yet again. Adrenaline spiked in her system at that thought, and she bolted straight up in her command chair. The sudden action elicited a hiss of pain from her lips. As reality came crashing back down on her, Alex's unfocused gaze sharpened, and she finally saw the engineer standing in front of her.

"Heron!" She half shouted, startling Commander Denton back a step. "Oh, thank God you're here—that means the lifts are working again. We need to get the wounded down to sick bay, now. Some of them are in a bad way. Including Greg."

"I saw, ma'am." Heron nodded, a flash of relief flowing across her face as Alex came back to the land of the living. "There are corpsmen here now, and litter bearers are on the way up here to start transferring the wounded down to sick bay."

"Good. What's our status? Did you get reactor two up and running? Do we have any power, besides emergency batteries?"

"Yes, ma'am. Reactor two is up and running, but only at twenty percent, and that's pushing it. The mag bottle has microfractures running along the surface, and the stability is iffy at best." Sliding out of her command chair at that report, Alex began limping her way over to the navigation console with Heron in tow, listening to the engineer's report. Raising her hand to cut the engineer off when she got to the blood-soaked chair of the navigation station, she stood staring down at it for a handful of heartbeats. Even though she could vaguely remember sitting at this very station, updating jump calculations for their escape with her hands covered in Lieutenant Commander Samuels' blood, she could not force herself into that seat again. Shivering once, she leaned forward past the chair, laying her hands on the sticky console. Setting the P-Drive to the best speed possible with her stiffly moving fingers, she ordered the *Fenris* to begin to slow its mad rush into the heart of the Sol system. Stepping back, absently wiping her hands on her stained uniform jacket, she looked around at what remained of her command deck, searching. Looking over Heron's shoulder, her gaze settled on what she was looking for, and she called out.

"Sebastian."

Reaching for his med kit, the petty officer looked up from the sensor console he was helping Ensign Green attempt to repair. Seeing the captain looking intently at him with her one good eye, he rose wearily to his feet, kit in hand.

"Ma'am?" He looked exhausted, but determined.

"Could you come here for a moment, please? I have a job for you." Alex watched as Sebastian picked his way across the deck, stepping over bits of burnt metal, plastic, and, unfortunately, flesh, to stop in front of her. "I need you to wipe down this station then remain here and keep an eye on our course and speed. We're flying blind, and I need someone to make sure we don't veer off course or overexert the engines. Thanks for volunteering." She managed a weak smile at that.

"Not a problem, ma'am. I'm on it," Sebastian said as he braced to attention, returning her smile. Pulling bottles and gauze from his kit while stepping past both women, he looked down, face blanching. Alex waited until he had settled into his grim task before turning to face Heron.

"Now, Commander, please continue. How are the rest of your efforts going?" she asked, beginning to walk back to her command chair. Standing, even for that short amount of time, was causing her injuries to flare to a new level of pain.

"Well, Captain, it took a bit of work, but we've finally got the passageway to the galley sealed off and repressurized." They stopped their slow trek across the command deck as half a dozen battle-weary ratings burst from the lift, moving toward the injured at the directions of the attending corpsmen. Under their watchful eyes, the ratings lifted the wounded onto their stretchers and began moving back toward the hatch with their precious cargo. With the first of the wounded being evacuated from the carnage pit of the command deck, the exhausted corpsmen shuffled on to new patients. There would be no relaxing for them for quite some time.

"Good, good," Alex said as they finally reached the command chair. She lowered herself into it, feeling a twinge of pain from broken ribs grating together. "What's the status of our air locks? Please tell me we have at least one functioning."

"Well, ma'am, there I can give you some good news," Heron said, her face wearing a slight smile. "We've got two functioning air locks, both starboard side aft, which is good, 'cause that's the only part of the ship I can be sure of structural integrity."

"What about the landing bay? Any chances of landing shuttles there, and, if so, can we reach the hangar deck?"

"We can land maybe one shuttle, but that's all, and it won't do us any good."

"Explain," Alex said while punching information from her chief engineer's report into her panels, building as complete a picture as she could. The information would be vital for the crew of the relief ship. Knowing not only where they could go, and the best routes to get there, but where they would need to concentrate their efforts for search and rescues would be vitally important for recovering any of her people who might be trapped.

"The hangar deck is completely cut off as of right now. We have no communication with anyone that might still be in there. Plus, our remaining Valkyries are still sitting in the landing bay, the lifts are not working, and we have no way to clear them out of the way to land any rescue shuttles." Heron concluded her report while Alex's hands continued to update her information.

"Okay, here is what I need from your DC teams right now," Alex began, looking up directly into Heron's eyes. "First, get to that hangar deck. We need to find out what the situation is there. And once you're there, find some way of getting those Valkyries back inside. Second, I need paths from our working air locks to our wounded cleared and marked. We're going to want to move them as soon as possible, and I want it done as quickly and efficiently as possible. Finally, I need external comms up. I don't care what kind it is, but I need to alert command as to the situation." Finishing, Alex continued to stare into her friend's eyes, waiting for confirmation that her orders were understood.

"Understood. With your permission, Captain, I'll get right on it." Watching her friend standing at attention in front of her, Alex was grateful for her presence on the *Fenris*. There was no better engineer that she knew of.

"Very good, Commander," Alex said just as formally. "Permission granted. Carry on."

"Carry on, aye, aye, ma'am." A large toothy smile split the engineer's face as she responded, did an about-face, and marched to the comms panel, intent on getting the job done.

Watching the retreating back of her chief engineer, Alex could not discern the reason for the look of relief that had passed over Heron's face at her orders. She watched as Heron murmured orders into her headset while settling into the chair at the communications console and pulling tools from her suit pockets. Alex snapped back from her reverie at Ensign Green's shout.

"New contact!"

Turning to the ensign, her voice rasped out across the command deck. "Type and status?"

"Unknown," Green shouted back, bent over his panel and trying to coax information from it.

"What can you tell me?" she asked after watching him work with his damaged console for a few moments.

"I'm reading a power emission, so it's a ship of some sort. It also looks to be on an intercept course with us. I would have to estimate course and speed match in approximately twenty minutes. Assuming that's what they are going for." His hands continuing to massage his board and nodding at what he saw, Ensign Green looked up at his captain. "I can't get a mass reading or an IFF signal, though from its heading I would say it's one of ours. But beyond that, I just can't tell. Sorry, ma'am, it's the best I can do with what's left of my sensors."

"That's alright, Ensign. Good work." Turning back toward Heron, she began issuing orders. "Heron, seeing as how you have the only working channel right now, I need you to get someone to both air locks. Tell whoever greets our visitors to lead them to sick bay on the double. Also pass on that I will await the damage control officer here in command." She couldn't think of anything else at the moment.

"Roger that, ma'am. I'll pull two of Captain Mathews' marines from the damage-control teams and have them meet the relief ship, and I'll also have my crews put a move on clearing a path for them."

"Good. Get on that right away."

"Yes, ma'am." Reaching up, Heron touched her earpiece then began to pass on the captain's orders.

Alex leaned back in her chair, stroking her chin. Hopefully the relief ship would be able to handle all the casualties.

Chapter Fifteen

COURIER 254
OCTOBER 8, 2197
1202Z
SOL

Lieutenant Web, captain of *Courier 254*, was keeping a close eye on his instruments. His sensors indicated that the ship they were closing with was showing obvious signs of battle damage. Keeping that in mind, along with their spectacular entrance to the Sol system, he was not going to take any chances of missing something because of residual jump interference. Normally that would not be an issue this long after translation, but with the amount of energy that had been released on the *Fenris'* arrival, he knew that lingering interference was a possibility. That being the case, he had no desire to fly into a piece of debris that might be speeding along in front of his target. Or, worst-case scenario, anything that might have followed the *Fenris* through her jump with less than friendly intentions.

"Time to intercept USS *Fenris*?" he asked very formally. That's how you did it when you had an admiral not only riding on your boat, but sitting directly behind you. The ensign sitting in the co-pilot's chair and monitoring their course, along with performing a dozen other tasks involved with maintaining the smooth running of the ship, turned to his captain.

"Sir, time to intercept USS *Fenris*, maintaining current course and speed, is ten minutes," Ensign Coburn said, pausing for a moment. "Mark."

"Very good, Ensign. Keep me updated if anything changes."

"Aye, aye, sir." With that, Ensign Coburn returned his entire focus to his instruments. Calling over his shoulder, Lieutenant Web began to update his passenger.

"Admiral, time to intercept—" he managed to get out before being interrupted.

"I heard him, *Captain*," came a waspish and sarcastic reply from behind him.

"Ah, yes, sir. Sorry, sir." Actually, Lieutenant Web did not feel sorry at all. In fact, he was becoming more and more pissed off at his passenger. Admiral or no, this was his boat, and there was such a thing as common military courtesy. But Admiral Sean Rachere had apparently missed that class at OCS. Only the fact that Lieutenant Web had *not* missed that particular class kept him from snapping and telling the admiral something he was sure he had *not* heard before. Well, that and keeping an eye on his forward sensors. No matter how much of an asshole the admiral was, Web would take him over a catastrophic hull breach any day.

Several minutes passed, the only sounds breaking the silence coming from the instrument panels. Quite suddenly that silence was broken, causing Lieutenant Web and Admiral Rachere to jump.

"Holy shit!" Ensign Coburn shouted in a totally unprofessional manner, pointing at an object looming in the distance but growing steadily. Lieutenant Web, opening his mouth to reprimand the ensign, lifted his head to see what he was pointing at. The reprimand died on his lips.

"Jesus Christ," he whispered to himself, understanding now what had caused his copilot's outburst.

"Yes," hissed a voice from between them. Out of the corner of his eye, Web could see Admiral Rachere leaning forward, a smile on his face and a glint in his eyes. Feeling his skin crawl, the lieutenant suppressed a shudder at the admiral's obvious glee at seeing the object they were rapidly closing on.

"Ensign, find me a functional air lock and let's get docked,"

Web snapped, his nerves, already stressed from this trip, frazzled at the sight outside the armor-plast viewport.

"Yes, sir." The ensign's reply came back quiet and small.

Sparing one more glance before turning back to his sensors and preparing for maneuvering, Lieutenant Web let his eyes settle on the scorched, mangled, and horribly disfigured object that was the *Fenris*.

Admiral Rachere fought against the smile that continued to tug at his lips. Schooling his face once again, he reached out and opened a channel to the passenger compartment.

"Marines," he began without preamble. "Gear up and get ready. We will be docking with the *Fenris* momentarily, and I want you all ready to go when we arrive. I don't want to waste any time."

"Yes, sir," said a voice through the small speaker by his head. "Sir, if I may ask, what exactly is it that we will be doing when we arrive?"

"Don't concern yourself with that, Sergeant." Rachere, feeling his annoyance rise at having to deal with insignificant questions, embraced it, used it, let it color his expression, hiding his true excitement. "Just be ready to follow my orders to the letter. Instantly. Are we clear on that, Sergeant?"

"Yes, sir. We'll be ready." If the sergeant had more to say, the admiral did not hear it, having cut the channel as soon as he got his acknowledgment.

"All hands, prepare for docking maneuvers," he heard that arrogant little pissant of a pilot say. Well, he was going to ruin one officer today; it would not take much more effort to ruin a second one while he was at it. The admiral was still debating whether or not to expend the energy on getting the pilot reassigned to a dead-end position when he felt the ship rock slightly.

"Excuse me, sir," the pilot said as he stepped by him on his way back to the passenger compartment, where the ship's air lock was located. Standing and following the lieutenant, Admiral Rachere watched as he performed the necessary checks to ensure that they were firmly attached to the *Fenris*. This would normally be the flight engineer's job, but he had grounded the engineer on Folkvang station to commandeer his seat. "Hard seal. We've got green lights across the board. Confirm."

"Confirm, reading all green and a hard seal up here, sir," came Ensign Coburn's voice from the small speaker in the panel that Lieutenant Web had just spoken into.

"Roger that. I'm cracking the hatch now." Admiral Rachere watched impatiently as the lieutenant opened the air lock hatch. Hearing *Fenris'* outer air lock cycle open, he began to step forward, but a wave of smoke and the stench of burnt metal forced him back, coughing. He waved off the lieutenant coming over to assist him and stood straight. His nostrils acclimated to the smoke quickly, and he felt his confidence and conviction return full force as he stepped forward. Hearing the pilot and marines following him, he stepped from the air lock onto the *Fenris.*

A young marine stood there, looking battered and dazed in his filthy hazard suit. The admiral waited for his entourage to join him in the small bay before turning his gaze to the still-stunned marine.

"Well?" Contempt dripped from his voice; he planned to savor every possible moment of joy aboard the *Fenris.*

"Well what?" the marine responded, obviously lost.

He vaguely wondered what they were teaching them nowadays. He pushed that thought aside and turned his full attention onto the unsuspecting marine.

"I believe that's 'Well what, sir?'"

"Uh, yes, sir. Sorry, sir. Well what, sir?"

Suppressing a laugh at this poor marine's apparent confusion and discomfort, he decided to explain the situation.

"Well, where is my greeting? My 'Welcome aboard, Admiral'?" Blinking owlishly for a moment, the marine was obviously trying to figure something out.

"Yes, sir," he said at last. "Good afternoon, Admiral. Welcome aboard." Rachere could hear the tone in the marine's voice. The hope that, with the pleasantries taken care of, things would proceed in a way he expected them to. They wouldn't.

Rachere stood patiently, waiting for the marine to break the silence between them. He could hear the lieutenant and MPs behind him shifting nervously and sensed their discomfort.

"Excuse me, sir?" The marine finally broke the silence. Rachere just continued to gaze at him. "Sir, where are the medical teams? I'm to escort them to sick bay immediately. And I have a message for the damage control officer. Is he with you, sir?"

"I'll tell you what, marine," he finally said after watching the marine shift from foot to foot uncomfortably. "How about a few less questions and a lot more shut the hell up? Hmm?" It took all of his control not to laugh at the slack-jawed expression on the marine's face. This game was over. "Sergeant!"

"Sir." Came the immediate response.

"Restrain this man and leave him here with the lieutenant, then follow me." Pivoting around, he glared at the befuddled officer in question. "Lieutenant, you will stay here with the ship and keep an eye on our young guest, is that clear?" Mouth working soundlessly for a moment, Web finally found his voice.

"Yes, sir. May I ask why, sir?"

"You may not," Rachere bit back at a stunned Web. Yes, he decided, he could spend the energy on taking care of this lieutenant. He waited until he saw that his MPs had shackled the shocked marine. "Ready, Sergeant?"

"Yes, sir, we're ready." His voice was unsure, but he kept any comments he might have to himself.

"Good. Then let's go," he said and started marching down the passageway, MPs trotting to catch up. After a few minutes, he reached a working lift shaft and loaded himself and his MPs on board. He punched the destination in. Trying to keep the smile off his face as he watched the location display, he could feel his heart rate speeding up as excitement coursed through him the closer they came to the command deck. Feeling the lift beginning to decelerate, he tugged his uniform into place and tried to get his breathing under control. This was what he had been waiting for, and it was his at last.

The lift doors parted, and he stepped out onto the command deck, his MPs following him. He could see the destruction around him, and the stares of the men and women present, and he ignored them all, focusing on one single person. Let them wonder why an admiral was on board, and how he had gotten there, he thought. They would know soon enough. His gaze never leaving the face of his target, he stepped down and crossed the command deck, vaguely noting that she looked much different than her file photo, injuries or no. He cast that thought aside as irrelevant and, stopping less than a meter from his prey, spoke, clearly and loudly, his exuberant voice filling the entire compartment.

"Captain Alexandra McLaughlin, it is my distinct pleasure to place you under arrest."

■ ■ ■

"Arrest?" Alex croaked. Sitting there, stunned by what she had just heard, she couldn't think of anything else to say. An admiral she did not know had just marched onto her command deck, coming right up to her and telling her she was under arrest. And all she could do was sit there and stare, her mind refusing to work. She felt lost, as if waiting for something, but she could not put her finger on it. After a moment, it occurred to her; she was waiting to hear Greg say something smart. Smart and totally inappropriate, of course. The admiral forgotten for the moment, she felt a pang of grief for her friend. Forcing her mind back to the current situation, she furiously dug through her memories to try and determine why this was happening. She came up with nothing. "Can this day get *any* worse?"

She did not realize she had said it out loud until she heard a snigger from Heron. Snapping out of her mental file rummaging, her head whipped up to see her friend smiling and the unknown admiral slowly turning a dangerous shade of red. Best to find out what was going on and how to fix it before her guest had an aneurysm.

"Arrest?" she repeated, her voice firmer now. "What are the charges?"

"The charges, Captain McLaughlin, are cowardice in the face of the enemy, desertion in a time of war, and treason." Admiral Rachere was smiling malevolently as he finished. "Now, get up from that chair. You are coming with me." His voice, condescending now, set her on edge. Holding a tight leash on her temper, she managed to grind out a response.

"Admiral, I don't know who you are or why you came aboard *my* ship, but you wasted a ride on a relief ship." She could feel her grip on her temper slipping, and she did not care. "This is my ship, and regulations state that you have no standing here, nor are you in a position to give me orders on it. I see no charge sheet, nor have I seen any kind of proof of your authority to carry out any arrest order. In short, Admiral, you will stand aside and let me get on with seeing to the immediate needs of my ship and crew. You are welcome to try to bring me up on charges some other time, but frankly, right now, I don't have time for you." She turned to Commander Denton, preparing to assign her to coordinating the damage-control teams from the relief ship, but one look at her panels showed that the only people to board her ship were the admiral and his MPs. She turned to the admiral, who was now an alarming shade of purple, and questioned him. "Where are the teams from the relief ship?" Ignoring her question, the admiral continued their argument.

"McLaughlin, I think you will find that I have all the authority I need to carry out any kind of arrest I wish." He drew himself up to his full, unimpressive height, and said, "I am Admiral Sean Rachere, commanding officer of Folkvang station. And as such, I am hereby relieving you of command and taking you into custody." His color was returning to normal as he spoke, full of his own importance. Alex could see that his complexion was the pale, pasty white of someone who spent too much time aboard ship. She decided he could do with a bit more color. Smiling, she opened her mouth to say something that would definitely change his color to something more interesting. As well as give his heart a bit of a workout. She never got the chance, as he raised his voice to talk over her.

"Before you bring up the chain of command, let me point out to you that you have an independent command, and, as such, when you arrived in-system without your commanding officer, you were automatically placed under my command." His self-satisfied smirk began to annoy Alex, and, balancing on the edge of outright insubordination and violence, she managed to keep her temper . . . barely.

"I'm still acting under orders from Admiral Stevens and must first complete our misson," Alex ground out through gritted teeth.

"And those are?"

"I need to report the destruction of the fleet at Groomsbridge 34, and . . ." Alex hesitated on the last. While she knew she could trust her command crew implicitly, there were too many other people on deck. If Stevens was right about a traitor, it'd be best to keep the knowledge of that information from leaking.

"And?" The officious prick dangled it in the air like irresistible bait.

"And . . . some highly sensitive information. Fine—I'll come with you, and we can straighten this out later," she said, capitulating for the sake of her crew. "Just get those medical and damage-control teams off the relief ship and get them working." Rising from her command chair, she turned toward Heron, preparing to turn command over to her as the next senior officer aboard.

"I didn't come on a relief ship, Captain," a snide voice said behind her.

"What?" Alex turned to face the admiral, not liking where this was heading.

"I said I didn't arrive on a relief ship. I came via a courier boat."

"Fine. I don't really give a damn how the hell you got here—get that relief ship docked and those crews moving." She could feel her temper rising, and holding it in check was becoming a serious effort.

"But there is no relief ship, Captain." The admiral's voice, dripping with malevolence, brought all conversation on the command deck to a halt.

"Say that again?" she whispered, seeing nothing but the smirk on the admiral's face and hearing her heart pounding in her chest. Only one phrase stood between sanity and her complete downward spiral into a killing rage.

"There is no relief ship, Captain McLaughlin. We don't treat with traitors. Or their crews."

That was the phrase.

"You Rat Fuck SON OF A BITCH!" Alex screamed at the top of her lungs, launching herself at the admiral, left hand extended and reaching for his throat as the right groped at the holster on her hip. Admiral Rachere stumbled back from the unexpected fury that had just erupted in front of him and was attempting to reach him, worry and uncertainty etched on his face for the first time since he had received word that the *Fenris* was in-system.

Bones grated together, and blood began to flow from her head, but Alex felt none of it. She did not feel Heron trying to hold her back; she was only vaguely aware of something slowing her. All she could feel was the hatred and rage pounding in her brain. The man standing in front of her was putting her crew at risk, and she could not allow that. *Would* not allow it. He had to be stopped, and if it meant killing him, and anyone who stood in her way, then so be it.

"Alex, no!" Heron shouted, trying to break through to her friend, all the while holding her back from committing murder. "Green, get over here and help me!"

Ensign Green bounded over at Heron's order and wrapped his

powerful arms around his captain, trying not to hurt her in the process of restraining her, even as the shocked MPs finally moved to protect the admiral.

Alex continued to struggle, her one good eye locked onto the man she intended to kill. She had to save her crew. Nerve endings already inflamed from heavy trauma overloaded as fresh damage was inflicted. The fresh, overwhelming pain pulled Alex out of her rage, the pain overriding everything else in her body. The self-preservation instinct of her hindbrain calmed her, allowing her to take in the situation.

She saw the admiral standing in front of her, a look of abject fear on his face with the realization of how close to death he had come. The MPs surrounding him, uncertain as to what to do, placed hands on pistol butts. The huge arms wrapped around her, pinning her arms to her side, were unmistakably Ensign Green's. And standing off to one side, Heron massaged the knuckles of one hand with the other. Alex snorted at that, thinking she must have really lost her temper this time, if Heron had to *punch* her to snap her out of it.

Putting the individual images together, she decided she must not have lost her temper. She must have lost her mind. Funny, that thought did not bother her as much as she thought it would. *But then again, do crazy people know they are crazy?* She began to laugh at that thought, and seeing the expressions on the faces surrounding her, she laughed harder.

"Okay, Green, you can let me go now," she said as she stopped laughing. She could feel his reluctance to release her, so she let herself relax, allowing him to read her body language. "Really, I'm okay now."

She felt his massive arms slacken their hold on her, and as her arms were freed, she raised the right one to probe at her overabused eye. Hissing in pain at the movement, she looked at her chief engineer.

"Nice punch."

"Yeah, well, next time I'll let Green do it," Heron said, shaking her hand. "That hurt."

"Tell me about it," Alex said as she tried to smile past the pain that radiated from what seemed to be every part of her body.

"Admiral," she said, turning back to him. "I don't know what kind of game you're playing at, or why, but I will make you a deal." She kept her one good eye locked onto his. "You get a relief ship here immediately, and I will surrender myself into your custody. But I will tell you this—if even one single member of my crew sustains an injury or dies because of your actions here, I swear to *Christ* that the last thing you see while lying in a pool of your own blood will be my face staring down at you. Do we have a deal?" she ended with a snarl.

"Captain, you are in no position to bargain," Admiral Rachere said, regaining his composure. "Especially not after that little display. I think we can add attempted murder to the charges, don't you? Sergeant, take her into custody now."

Alex could see the sergeant pause, looking around the command deck, a sheen of sweat appearing on his face.

"What are you waiting for, Sergeant? Arrest her," the admiral barked, clearly trying to reestablish some form of authority.

"Actually, Admiral, I think I am in a very nice position to bargain, and the sergeant here has seen it as well." Alex, ignoring the pain, forced a smile onto her face as she looked from the admiral to the sergeant then back again.

"What the hell are you babbling about now?" he snapped, casting his gaze about the command deck, trying to see what she could possibly be talking about.

"Why don't you tell him, Sergeant?" she said as sweetly as possible, just to annoy the admiral. *What the hell,* Alex figured. *In for a bullet, in for a barrage.* "I think he has heard enough bad news from me today." The sergeant swallowed before replying.

"It's the crew, sir."

"What about the crew?"

"They're armed. Every damn one of them is armed, sir."

The admiral looked around again, and this time Alex could see comprehension dawning in eyes, just as the worry returned to his face. Every single member of her crew present on the command deck was armed with a heavy flechette pistol, and over half had them drawn. While they were not directly pointed at the small group of visitors clustered together, they were not exactly pointed away, either. Those who did not have them drawn had hands resting on them, clearly ready to use them if the situation warranted.

"This is mutiny!" the admiral, clearly panicking now, squeaked out past his dry lips.

"Well, sir, I am the captain of this ship, and it seems to me that none of those weapons are pointed at me. So this is clearly not a mutiny. What this could be, mind you, is a response to a hostile boarding action. In which case, I think you and your MPs are about to join us in having a very bad day." Speaking calmly now, she wanted to make her point crystal clear. What she was offering him was a very simple and elegant equation. She would get what her crew needed, or he would die. "On the other hand, if you were here on my command deck to, say, inform me that a relief ship was inbound at max speed, well, this situation might just be an unfortunate misunderstanding."

"I see. So either I get you a relief ship, or I get dead, is that it?" he said, the slight tremor belying the arrogant façade he was trying to project. "That's blackmail, Captain."

"Actually, it's extortion, but let's not quibble over semantics." Alex continued to stare at the admiral. "So, tell me, Admiral, what exactly are you doing on my command deck?"

The question hung in the air between them. Live or die, the decision was his now, and she could see that he knew it.

Admiral Rachere stared back into the eyes of the defiant captain standing across from him. He knew that he had lost control but could not quite figure out when that had happened. Everything had been going so well; he'd had her right where he wanted her, hadn't he? So why was he the one standing here with an ultimatum to answer? He came to a quick decision. He would give the captain her relief ship. So much the better for her to be in his debt as well as being forced to pay for past sins.

"Very well, Captain," he heard himself say, blushing at the quaver he heard in his voice. "You have your relief ship. Sergeant, contact Lieutenant Web. Have him contact Folkvang station and get a relief ship to rendezvous with the *Fenris* as quickly as possible."

"Yes, sir!" the sergeant snapped, sounding grateful and relieved.

"Now, Captain, if you would be so kind as to join me on my ship, there are some things you and I need to discuss." He stepped aside and gestured toward the lift, inviting her on. The gall of having to do it this way burned in his throat, but he swallowed it. As long as he got her, that was all that mattered in the end.

He watched as Captain McLaughlin, turning to the commander standing beside her, unbuckled her holster and handed it over.

"Take care of that for me, would you, Heron?"

"Yes, ma'am."

"And get our people home."

"I will, Alex. I swear it."

"Very well. Commander, you have the con," McLaughlin snapped out formally.

"I have the con. Aye, ma'am." The commander's response came just as formally.

Rachere watched this byplay disinterestedly. He did not care about the ship or crew at all, beyond using them as a weapon to hurt her. And he had accomplished that, albeit almost at the cost of his life. But now that that situation had passed, the incident added one more nail in her coffin.

"Come along, Captain. We don't want to keep anyone from their duties, do we?" he sneered, twisting the knife in her.

"No, Admiral, we don't." Her voice was cold and emotionless.

He watched her hold her head up and march to the lift, limping slightly, trying to appear as if still in command. Following her onto the lift, he gave her that moment. He turned to face the still-motionless crew assembled on the command deck and let them see the triumphant smile spreading across his face. Regardless of the circumstances, he knew he had gotten what he had come for, and from the hateful stares of the crew, he could tell they knew it, too.

Chapter Sixteen

The high commander did not look up from his displays, continuing to enter data into them, planning for the next step in the offensive against the Dry-Skins, trusting in his guards to maintain his security as his subordinate approached the command throne.

"By your leave, High Commander," Si'Lasa said, dropping to one knee.

Seeming to have not heard the vice commander's request, the high commander unhurriedly entered the last of his data. Done at last, he raised his head to watch the top of his friend's bowed head for a moment longer before breaking his silence.

"Rise, Vice Commander, and give me your report. What is the status of the Swarm?"

"We have suffered many losses, both in ships and in lives. The Dry-Skins, for all their faults, fought like a cornered *tavark*. It will be many tides before all of our losses are fully known, and even more before we are able to repair them."

"Yet we are victorious, Vice Commander. We have defeated their

163

largest swarm outside of their home system. This is something to rejoice in." The high commander inhaled deeply, picking up the scent of disappointment and regret emanating from his friend. "Why do you despair?"

"Yes, High Commander, you are correct. We are victorious—but the cost was too high."

"Too high?"

"Yes. We will not be able to pursue the Dry-Skins back to their home system with sufficient strength to overcome them at this time, and reports from the kisnan that was assigned to intercept any ship attempting to flee show that one ship managed to escape our talons. They will not fail to prepare for our attack."

"No, you are correct—they will not. Yet all is not lost," he reassured Si'Lasa. "I have a plan that I believe will give us our final victory over the Dry-Skins, and much sooner than you would seem to think possible."

"I trust in your leadership, High Commander. I always have, and if there is a Xan-Sskarn that can perform this task, it is you," Si'Lasa told his superior, sounding relieved. "Might I know your plan, so that I can begin to prepare the Swarm?"

"Not yet, my friend. I still must discuss it with the Swarm Masters. Your task will be to oversee the repair of our Swarm and to integrate the reinforcements the Swarm Masters will undoubtedly send us." Saying this, the high commander rose from the command throne to approach Si'Lasa, laying a hand on his shoulder and staring directly into his eyes. "Do this, and with the Supreme One's blessings we shall once again be victorious."

Bowing his head once more, Si'Lasa spoke in a confident voice.

"It shall be as you command, High Commander, and with your leadership we shall remove the threat of the Dry-Skins from our people. I will not fail you."

Chapter Seventeen

NAVAL ANNEX, WASHINGTON DC, TERRA
OCTOBER 8, 2197
1930Z
SOL

"Destroyed?" asked a shocked voice.

"Yes, sir," responded a deep voice.

"Are you sure?"

"I believe so, sir. My office has been trying to compile and correlate all the information for the past several hours." The man speaking wore the uniform of a full admiral and continued to stare at the man sitting across from him. Though appearing to be a man once muscular, he obviously was slowly going to seed as age caught up with him. Pale, with dark eyes, his hair, which had been lightly flecked with gray only a few short years ago, was now totally white. Despite all of this, the steel in him was still evident.

"How long ago?" the shocked voice asked.

"Over ten hours, at least," the admiral answered him flatly. He knew what question was coming next and braced himself for the response his answer would bring, knowing it would be explosive. The kind of explosion that started an avalanche. He was not looking forward to the forthcoming inevitable conversation at all.

"Why am I only hearing of this now?"

Yes, that was the question the admiral had been expecting, and he gave his answer.

"He did *what?!*" shouted the man behind the desk, his voice echoing around the handsomely appointed office, and the admiral sitting across from him winced as the avalanche began. The Secretary of War was well known to have a vicious temper and a tendency to collect heads.

"As I said, Mr. Secretary," Admiral Greco, Chief of Naval Operations, said in a placating voice, "it *appears* that Admiral Rachere boarded the *Fenris* shortly after her translation into the system and proceeded to place her captain, Captain McLaughlin, under arrest, keeping this information from reaching us for several additional hours."

"What the hell was that man thinking?" Secretary Lapinski asked, leaning back in his chair and mopping at his balding head with a handkerchief. Admiral Greco watched as the secretary's face grew redder and redder. Greco looked down at the pad gripped in his hands and knew that he should report the rest of the information he had, but he hesitated. He was at a loss as to how to explain what he had read—he did not understand it himself.

"Richard, you know, you never were that good of a poker player. I can see you're holding something back. What is it? Did Rachere have reason to do what he did?"

"Well, there is more, Mr. Secretary, a lot more, and it is very confusing. I have several reports here from members of the *Fenris*' crew, the crew of *Courier 254*, personnel aboard Folkvang station, and the admiral himself." Glancing down at the pad once more, he hoped that the information within had miraculously changed from what he had seen a moment before. Of course it hadn't, and his knuckles turned white as he gripped the pad even tighter and brought his head up to lock eyes with the secretary. Well, if Secretary Lipinski wanted to kill the messenger, then so be it. In thirty-five years, he had never once shirked his duty, and he was not about to start.

"Before we get into the specific reports, I wanted to point out that the 'how' of the destruction of Admiral Stevens' fleet at Groomsbridge 34 led the admiral to believe, and I'm afraid I must concur, that there is a traitor or traitors in our midst who gave away our fleet maneuvers at Groomsbridge 34 to the enemy.

"In light of this theory, we have already begun adjusting our defensive positioning here in Sol system and alerted what few ships we still have remaining out-system. Obviously, security has been tightened on all fleet maneuvers, but until we catch the traitor or traitors, whatever our moves, we have to assume the Sallys might be aware of them." Admiral Greco paused, having finished summarizing the most important news.

Secretary Lipinski leaned back, closing his eyes and locking his hands together over his ample belly. Sitting motionless like this, most would think that he had fallen asleep, but Admiral Greco was not fooled. The secretary was digesting and assimilating this new information, and the meeting would not proceed until this task was complete. After a long pause, the secretary's eyes opened, and he spoke. "And does this have anything to do with Admiral Rachere and Captain McLaughlin?"

"Okay, Mr. Secretary, please keep in mind that all of the reports I have, naturally, are trying to paint a picture in the best light possible from their point of view." Admiral Greco waited for the secretary to nod his understanding before continuing. This was one shitstorm that was going to take a great deal of skill to navigate.

"Out of all the reports I have, I believe that of the captain of *Courier Boat 254*, Lieutenant Web, is the most unbiased."

"But not totally?" asked the secretary, leaning back in his chair.

"No, not totally. Reading between the lines, I believe that Lieutenant Web does not much care for Admiral Rachere. I had my adjutant do a quick records search, and it appears that neither of them has served together—granted, they could have run across each other without being posted to the same command," he added when he saw Lipinski open his mouth to speak. "But, given what I know of Rachere, both personally and professionally, I think he just pissed Web off."

"I see. So, am I given to understand that you don't particularly care for Admiral Rachere yourself?" Admiral Greco watched the secretary's eyes stare at him levelly for a moment, clearly demanding an answer. He felt his expression change as he tried to find a way to answer that question without it sounding too judgmental. "Richard," the secretary said, "I can see you have an opinion. Just give it to me. I know you well enough to know that, no matter what your personal feelings, you will give me a professional, unbiased report. I've met Captain McLaughlin before, but not that admiral. I've my own opinions of only one of the two central figures to this little drama. I trust I know you well enough to know that my opinion would probably be similar if not the same as yours. Now, if you don't mind?"

"Very well, Mr. Secretary," Admiral Greco said, letting his face fall back into a neutral mask. "I don't like Admiral Rachere. He is pompous, full of himself, and quite frankly an arrogant bastard. He doesn't have much, if any, tactical or strategic instinct. While he earned his flag at the end of the Dragon Wars, I believe that he got to his present rank by a series of commanders who like his kind, and by his cultivation of political connections. There have also been a few reports of occasional mood swings and odd behavioral patterns, but nothing that ever warranted investigation." He paused in his report. He knew that speaking of one of his subordinates in this manner was not befitting a senior officer, even if the secretary had asked, and he felt he should say something positive, if only to assuage his own conscience. "Still, the admiral does have some things going in his favor. He is a superb organizer and systems administrator. He is a very talented bureaucratic commander, and while in command of Folkvang station he has increased its efficiency by seven percent. Granted, that does not sound like much, but with the amount of traffic and supplies that go though the station on a daily basis, that is an impressive figure." He paused for a moment, wondering if there was anything else he could or should say.

"I hear a 'but' lurking in there somewhere, Richard," Secretary Lipinski said.

"Well, I was only going to add that while Admiral Rachere's record on-station is impressive as it stands, should the situation aboard ever change—meaning, being engaged in direct, active hostilities, or even in support of them—then I think that his nitpicking, anal attention to detail will be a hindrance, not an asset. Given the news of the destruction of Admiral Stevens' fleet, and the change it has on the scope of the war, that is something that needs to be kept in mind." Admiral Greco wondered, orders or no, if he should have been so candid. But after reading the reports on the current situation, he could not help it. Admiral Rachere's actions had been totally contrary to standard operating procedures and seemed to be almost vindictive in nature.

"I see," Secretary Lipinski said and leaned back again, hands locked over his belly. "Very well, Admiral, let me hear the rest of it. From the beginning."

Admiral Greco began his formal report, keeping his voice level and dispassionate. "At approximately zero nine twenty zulu this morning, the heavy cruiser USS *Fenris* translated in-system. All indications from sensor logs aboard Folkvang station pointed to massive damage to the *Fenris*. That, along with the *Fenris*' acceleration curve, led to the conclusion that the *Fenris* had been damaged in combat."

"Acceleration curve?" said Secretary Lipinski questioningly.

"Yes, sir. The *Fenris* had translated in-system at maximum military power." Admiral Greco's voice held an incredulous tone as he added, "In short sir, she hit the wall at a flat-out run." He watched Lipinski's reaction to this news, and was surprised to see that the secretary had it without so much as an eye twitch. But then again, the secretary had never been a military man himself, so he might not be aware of the ramifications of that last statement, and right now was not the time to enlighten him.

"Upon receipt of this news, Admiral Rachere proceeded to order a courier boat to intercept the *Fenris*. Lieutenant Web's *Courier 254* was the boat that drew the assignment. Leaving his XO, Admiral Reynolds, in command of the station, Admiral Rachere then proceeded to board *254* with a squad of MPs. I should at this time point out that Admiral Rachere ordered a courier boat to intercept with the *Fenris*, and only a courier boat. A relief ship was not dispatched. As a matter of fact, it was expressly denied." *That* got the secretary's attention. Admiral Greco had spent enough time working with the secretary to recognize the tightening around his eyes as not a good thing. He knew that it was only going to get worse, but like someone enthralled by a hovercar accident, Greco could not help getting a slight perverse satisfaction from the secretary's reactions.

"While this was occurring, the *Fenris* herself was headed in-system, and from the report of the chief engineer, one Commander Denton, it was a miracle that the *Fenris* was still in one piece. A majority of their primary systems, and several of their secondary systems, were off-line or outright destroyed, including communications. They had no way to tell us what had happened. But reports from members of the command-deck crew, as well as Commander Denton, show that Captain McLaughlin was intent on getting external communications reestablished to contact High Command. Needless to say, casualties were extensive." Pausing for a moment to lick his lips, Admiral Greco continued at the secretary's nod.

"Drawing from Lieutenant Web's report, during the entire flight of *254*, it appeared that Admiral Rachere was very eager to get to Captain McLaughlin and did not seem to care at all for any damage the *Fenris* may have sustained. While, of course, it is not explicitly stated in his report, I believe that Lieutenant Web was under the impression that the admiral was harboring some sort of vendetta against the captain." Greco saw the secretary's eyes flick back and forth as he tried to place the players in the morbid play. He understood the secretary's momentary confusion. He had felt the same on first reading all the information amassed. When Lipinski's eyes stopped moving, Admiral Greco continued without prompting.

"What occurred next seems to support Lieutenant Web's insinuation about the admiral. Upon boarding the *Fenris,* the admiral proceeded to order his MPs to arrest the marine guide stationed at the air lock." At that, the secretary interrupted. His nonmilitary background required that he have some things explained that a seasoned officer would consider common knowledge.

"Guide?" asked Lipinski. "That seems odd. Certainly you wouldn't expect an honor guard given the circumstances, but wouldn't an admiral be expected to be at least familiar enough with a ship of the fleet to be able to find his own way around?"

"Under normal circumstances, yes, sir, he would," Greco answered tolerantly. "However, please keep in mind that the *Fenris* had been in heavy combat and taken significant damage. Under those circumstances, the interior layout of a ship can and will be radically changed. A guide is often necessary to ensure that relief-ship personnel can reach their destinations as quickly as possible. Also, remember, Captain McLaughlin was not expecting the admiral, but a relief ship."

"I see. Please continue."

"As I said, sir, after his arrival, Admiral Rachere had the marine guide placed under arrest by his MPs and then proceeded to the command deck. Also, Lieutenant Web's report is very explicit in stating that the admiral taunted the marine before his arrest," Admiral Greco said, then cast his eyes down to his pad to make sure he had his facts correct. He satisfied himself as to the accuracy of his report and picked up where he had left off.

"After detaining the marine, the admiral headed to the command deck with his MPs, leaving Lieutenant Web with his ship. I am now relying on the reports of the MPs, command-deck crew, Commander Denton, and Admiral Rachere. I have tried to take"—he paused trying to think of the right word—"an 'average,' if you will, of the reports in question, to try and get a feel for what really happened. I think my staff and I have come to a fairly accurate conclusion, though we will probably never really know. The command deck was smashed, and the surveillance systems were off-line."

"Yes, I understand. I'm sure your staff has come to a close approximation of the actual occurrences," Secretary Lipinski said. Admiral Greco could see that the muscles of his jaw were bulging as he tried to keep his temper in check.

"This is what we think happened, sir," Admiral Greco quickly continued. He referred to his pad one last time then locked eyes with the secretary. "Admiral Rachere entered the command deck and attempted to place Captain McLaughlin under arrest. Understandably, the captain was more than a bit confused. She apparently decided to go along with the admiral as long as she thought a relief ship was on the way. Upon Admiral Rachere's statement that not only was there *not* a relief ship enroute, but that he considered her and her crew to be traitors, she verbally assaulted the admiral and made a very great effort to physically assault him as well. The reports are split here as to the actual events. Admiral Rachere and his MPs seem to think that McLaughlin was trying to kill him, and the crew seems to think that their captain was merely trying to strike the admiral." Closing his eyes for a moment, Admiral Greco could picture the situation in his mind, and what his own reactions would be if he were in McLaughlin's position at that time and place. Not surprised by what he saw himself doing, he went on.

"Putting her actual intents aside for the moment, the only reason she did not succeed in getting to the admiral was that members of her own crew restrained her. Commander Denton even admits to punching her, despite McLaughlin's injuries, which included severe scalp lacerations, one eye swollen shut, several burns, and two broken ribs." Both men twisted their faces in sympathetic pain at the list of Captain McLaughlin's injuries. "While the captain was restrained, the admiral once again tried to place her under arrest. Once again, the two groups of reports diverge significantly. The admiral's group seems to be under the impression that the captain and her crew threatened to shoot them where they stood—all of them. The crew's reports say that Captain McLaughlin reasoned with the admiral and traded herself for a relief ship."

"I see. But that still does not tell me why the information about Admiral Stevens was delayed for so long." Lipinski's voice carried a hard edge, letting Greco know that he had best be coming to the end of his report, and that it had best contain the information he wanted.

"It's actually quite simple, Mr. Secretary," Admiral Greco said. He was not being condescending or sarcastic, just stating fact. "When Captain McLaughlin surrendered to Admiral Rachere, he immediately withdrew from the *Fenris*. The relief ship that Captain McLaughlin had secured via her deal with the admiral was still several hours away, and the *Fenris*' communications were still down. And knowing Admiral Rachere as I do"—he raised his hands in a gesture of futility—"he probably kept Captain McLaughlin sequestered from any contact or did not allow her to speak. So you see, sir, even though the *Fenris* had been in-system for several hours, they had yet to be able to tell anyone what had happened. Only with the arrival of the relief ship was the information able to be passed on. And once I received it, I, of course, forwarded it to you. Also, knowing that you would be briefing the president immediately, I took that time to find out why this information was so late in coming, when the information provided showed that we should have had it hours sooner. Once I had a preliminary report, I reported here, and, well, Mr. Secretary, you know the rest."

Secretary Lipinski abruptly stood up from his desk and began to pace behind it. After several passes of his chair, he stopped directly behind it and stared out the window. Admiral Greco could hear him softly speaking, repeating himself.

"What the hell was that man thinking?" Finally he seemed to reach a decision as he stood even straighter and spun about. "Admiral Greco."

"Yes, Mr. Secretary?"

"Relieve Admiral Rachere for cause. Immediately," Lipinski snapped out.

"I'm sorry, Mr. Secretary, but I cannot do that," Greco said, expecting that the secretary would not take his answer well. He was not disappointed.

"Excuse me?" Lipinski said through clenched teeth. "You may be the CNO, but *I* am still the Secretary of War. You report to me. When I give you an order, you will God damn well obey it. Is that clear?" Admiral Greco understood quite well, but some orders could not be obeyed, despite the secretary's penchant for taking the professional head off of anyone who disobeyed his orders. And this was one such order that could not be obeyed.

"I am quite aware of who you are, Mr. Secretary, and I am quite aware of who I am as well," Admiral Greco ground out in a harsh voice, the implied insult from the secretary coloring his response. As if he would ever forget his duty, or the chain of command. "As Chief of Naval Operations, it is my responsibility to know, understand, and enforce naval regulations. And knowing naval regulations as I do, I can tell you, Mr. Secretary, that you cannot relieve Admiral Rachere for cause."

"And why not?" Lipinski demanded.

"Because, sir, he has broken no regulations—no serious ones, anyway—and therefore there is no reason or cause for having him relieved."

"Excuse me?" Lipinski said again. He seemed to deflate before the admiral's eyes.

"Sir, believe me." Greco let his anger go. He knew that both of them were upset at the situation, not at each other. "There is nothing I would like more right now than to relieve that idiot, but legally I can't. As I said, he hasn't broken any regs that would allow for his relief."

"How is that possible?" Lipinski's voice sounded incredulous.

"Well, sir, it's complicated." Greco sighed and began to massage his temples. "Admiral Rachere is the commanding officer of Folkvang station. As such, any relief ship that is to be dispatched within the Sol system is at his discretion. Also, as Captain McLaughlin holds an independent command, when she returned to Sol alone, she was immediately placed within Folkvang's TO&E. Being an independent command only means that she gets orders to go out on her own, not part of a battle group or only peripherally associated with one, as she was with Admiral Stevens. She still needs to report to some-one, so when she got home, she became part of Folkvang's chain of command." Greco sighed again, the situation weighing heavily on him. "So you see, sir, Admiral Rachere didn't do anything 'technically' wrong, or at least nothing that we can relieve him for. Oh, morally, ethically, and professionally he was wrong, and the rest of the fleet is going to know that. But legally, no one can touch him."

"Are you telling me that there is no regulation regarding the dispatching of relief or support ships for damaged vessels? How in the hell is that possible?" Lipinski's agitation began to return.

"To be frank, sir, we've never needed one before," Greco said, disheartedly.

"And now?"

"Now? Prior to my arrival here I sent a priority-one flash message to all ships and commands, clearly stating that any damaged ship should receive immediate and unconditional aid of the type commensurate with the level needed. I hated having to add that last part, but if I hadn't, people like Admiral Rachere would send out a single shuttle and say that they had rendered aid within the letter of the regulation. In fact, I hated having to issue the order at all, and I would have never thought I would need to. It disgusts me that it's needed."

"Do you think that your order will be enough?"

"I think it will be more than enough, as this is the first time I have ever even heard of a situation like this. However, I am not the kind of man to do things by halves. My office is preparing a formal regulation that I expect to be signed off on by the judge advocate tomorrow, and it should be in effect by the day after. This *will* not happen again, not without someone paying for it." Admiral Greco's voice was laced with venom.

"I totally agree," Lipinski said, nodding his head. "What I want to know is how we can make someone pay for it now. Not only for what happened with the *Fenris* but for the withholding of vital information, unintentional or not. This whole situation is inexcusable, and it seems to me it's Admiral Rachere's fault. Nothing you've told me seems to justify his arrest of Captain McLaughlin—unless there was something more you needed to report?" Admiral Greco saw the secretary stare levelly at him, and he returned the stare just as intently.

"No, sir, I have told you everything that I know, or that I can surmise," Greco answered quietly but clearly. Paging through the information on his pad one last time, he looked back up at the secretary. "I can find no reason for Admiral Rachere ordering Captain McLaughlin's arrest, let alone enforcing that order himself. Nothing other than a vague reference to her being a traitor, and, having examined her record, I find that accusation to be laughable."

"Having met Captain McLaughlin and seen her record as well"—Lipinski nodded to Greco in support of his assessment—"I have to agree that the idea of Captain McLaughlin being a traitor is preposterous. But I can't help wondering why he would make that statement without first getting a formal charge issued."

"I couldn't say, sir, but it is puzzling. And I agree with you— someone should be punished. But who? And we don't have much time to figure it out. With Admiral Stevens' death and the destruction of his fleet, you can sure as hell bet the Sallys aren't going to just sit back and take a break. We need to clear this up fast, 'cause knowing the rumor mill, this will be all over the system by tomorrow night, and with someone like McLaughlin, who many consider a hero, and the commanding officer of something as strategically important as Folkvang station, well, we need to know what the problem is or was and get it corrected fast before everyone starts focusing on it and picking sides. We can ill afford to have the fleet split over this, and have them doubting High Command."

"I agree, Admiral, but how do we proceed? As you said, some of your report is summarization, and some of it guesswork. How do you propose to find out what actually happened? There is also the concern about possible traitors and, of course, our primary responsibility—the defense of this system. A board of inquiry would be too long, and a court martial would take even longer. If the Sallys won't wait for long before acting on the advantage of Admiral Stevens' death, we don't have time for either. Yet even with their altercation not being the highest priority, we can't just sweep this under the rug."

"Well, sir, first, I have already issued orders to Admiral Tanner and to planetary defense informing them of the likelihood of a Xan-Sskarn attack and to prepare accordingly. Second, I have informed counter intelligence of the possibility of traitorous activity within the fleet or the government, and they are beginning an investigation as we speak. Finally, I have a plan on how to deal with McLaughlin and Rachere." Admiral Greco leaned back in his chair, the first evidence of relief since his entrance into the secretary's office crossing his face. It appeared that the secretary was going to leave this in his hands, and not try to take charge. Which, seeing as how they were *his* officers and therefore his responsibility, was as it should be. But he had been a bit concerned.

"And that plan would be?" Secretary Lipinski asked as he resumed his chair, leaning forward with his elbows on the desk, waiting expectantly.

"Well, first I am going to get the both of them in my office."

"Then?"

"Then, Mr. Secretary"—Admiral Greco, actually smiling now, let Secretary Lipinski in on his master plan—"then I'm going to ask them what *actually* happened."

Chapter Eighteen

QUANTICO, VIRGINIA, TERRA
OCTOBER 8, 2197
2112Z
SOL

Pain.
Hate.
Death.
Alex felt them. Felt them all directed at her. Confused, she began looking around. She saw herself strapped into her chair on the command deck, but it was blurry, as if she were looking at it underwater. The structure kept shifting. One moment it was the *Fenris*, the next it was the *Gna*, then back again. Shaking her head, she tried to focus. Yes, she needed to focus; her crew needed her. As if summoned by her thought, her crew appeared, seated at their stations, apparently oblivious to her presence. They, too, were out of focus, morphing between faces she knew so well. Faces she had thought never to see again. Then they began to transform with each change. Uniforms became blacker, as if burnt; faces grew paler; movements became stilted. Then the blood began to appear: first in small, isolated patches, then blossoming into large splotches, as if her crew were a canvas being painted with

broad strokes. Alex tried to turn her gaze away, but no matter where she looked, the same scene was played out. Unable to look anymore, she squeezed her eyes shut. Then the voices began.

"Captain McLaughlin," The hollow sound echoed in her head. She could not differentiate between voices, yet somehow she knew each one, remembered hearing it in better times. Happier times. Living times. *"Why?"*

"Why? I don't understand," Alex choked out, tears streaming down her face.

"You left us behind."

"No, I didn't want to. It was my duty..." She fell silent at this. It sounded hollow even to her. Duty or no, she knew. She knew. They were right. She had left them behind.

"What of your duty to us? You were our captain, yet we are alone. We died, yet you still live." She could hear the voices clearly now. So very clearly, friends she had known. Friends she had loved. Friends she had abandoned.

"I'm sorry. Oh, God, please forgive me." She wept openly now, her shoulders slumped in defeat. "What can I do? What do you want?"

"You belong with us."

"Yes," her voice whispered back, her head down and eyes still clenched shut.

"Join us, Captain McLaughlin," the voice whispered in her ear. Looking up, her tears gone, she opened her eyes and looked out upon her dead. They stood before her, an endless sea of horribly mutilated, bloody faces, each with accusation in their eyes. They beckoned to her. Join them. Do not leave them behind again. Her hands began to work at the buckle, trying to release herself.

"Yes," she breathed dreamily as the straps began to fall from her.

"Captain McLaughlin." They called to her, waiting for her. The last strap fell away.

"Captain McLaughlin." She began to rise as their hands reached for her, pulling her, bringing her home.

"Captain McLaughlin." Home, yes, never to leave. Her crew needed her, and she would not fail them again. She felt the hands grip her tighter, like they would never let her go.

"Captain McLaughlin! Wake up!" the parade-ground voice snapped, loud enough to wake the dead.

Alex jerked awake. The howls of her dead still echoed in her head as she tried to sit up. She couldn't, and looking down, she could see why. She was strapped to the bed. What she could not figure out was *why* she was strapped to the bed, or, for that matter, what bed it was. Nor did she recognize the room. The single overhead light cast dark shadows on the gray painted walls. Letting her gaze sweep the room, she saw a toilet, sink, desk, chair, and bars. So, she was in a cell. That certainly did not bode well, but with consciousness came remembrance. Threatening an admiral, no matter how much he deserved it, was certainly reason enough for her to be here. Though she still could not figure out the reason for the restraints. Her gaze finally rested on the owner of the voice that had brought her back. A marine corporal stood at the bars, looking in at her, concern on his face. Upon closer examination, she could see his sidearm and the MP brassard on his left arm. So, he was her jailer.

"Captain McLaughlin, are you okay?" his voice, much softer now, held the same concern she'd seen in his face.

"Well, Corporal," she said, her voice still harsh and rasping, "if you define 'okay' as being strapped to a bunk and locked in a cell with no idea as to how you got there, then I'm just peachy." She tried to make light of her situation, but the restraining straps around her arms and legs felt too much like the hands that had been pulling at her. She shivered at the thought, though she could not tell if it was from relief or regret.

"Well, ma'am, the restraints were for your own safety." He reached down and pulled a communicator from his belt. "She's awake," he said into the device.

"My own safety?" she asked. That didn't sound good, and she said so.

"Oh, it's not 'cause you were going crazy or being difficult. The doc just thought it would be a good idea. You were pretty banged up when you got here, and the doc patched you up, then gave you something for the pain. He said that between the injuries and the meds, you might have some pretty vivid dreams, and that he wanted you restrained so you didn't hurt yourself more if you started thrashing about. And it's a good thing he did. It looked like you were having one hell of a nightmare."

"You have no idea, Corporal," she said, letting her head fall back on the pillow. *And I hope you never do*, she thought to herself.

"So, now that I am awake, would you please unstrap me?" she asked the overhead lights. Turning to face the guard just hurt too damn much right now.

"Well, ma'am, I'd be happy to, just as soon as someone comes down here to join me." She could hear the amusement in his voice. Alex laughed at this.

"Corporal, I am flattered that you think you need backup to deal with one beat-up little captain. But let me assure you right now—I think I'd have a hard enough time battling with gravity, let alone an armed marine."

"Oh, it's not because I am worried about what you might try to do, Captain," he said in a tone that was not arrogant, just factual. "I could deal with anything you might try. But regulations do not permit me to enter a prisoner's cell without another person in attendance, except in the event of an emergency. Regardless of their condition."

"I see. Well, I hope your backup arrives really soon." Her voice held a little aggravation.

"Why, is something wrong?" The concern was back in his voice. "Do I need to get the doc back down here?"

"No, it's just that I've got this itch on the end of my nose, and it's driving me crazy." Alex was twitching her nose as she said this in a futile attempt to stop the discomfort. She heard the guard laugh at that.

"Well, you're in luck, ma'am. Here he comes now." With that, she turned her head slightly to see him begin punching buttons on the face of the cell door. After what seemed to be an overly long and complex code, the door began to slide open as another marine arrived. Once the door was fully opened, the corporal entered her cell and knelt beside her bunk.

"Okay, now let's get these off you." He began to unfasten her restraints. As her right arm was freed, she began to move it up toward her nose, which incidentally moved it in the direction of the marine leaning over her.

"Freeze!" the second guard shouted, hand dropping to the butt of his sidearm.

"Relax, Frank, she's just trying to scratch her nose," the corporal called over his shoulder. Then he looked down at Alex. "All the same, ma'am, I'd appreciate it if you kept your arms and legs still while I finished this. Don't want any misunderstandings."

"Gotcha."

"Right, that's got it." The corporal stood up as the last strap loosed around her ankle. He backed toward the cell entrance and, once he was through, pressed a button. The door slid shut. Alex had been scratching at her nose the whole time.

The itch taken care of, Alex finally got a chance to remove the sheets covering her. She was still sweat-soaked from her nightmare, and the feel of the cold air on her damp clothes made her shudder again. She also noticed she was in a hospital gown, and there was nothing else to wear in sight. *Oh, well, not like I'm going anywhere anyway.*

Wincing in pain, she forced herself into a sitting position. Then, after a moment's rest, she stood, wavering slightly. Still under the marines' watchful eyes, she shuffled over toward the sink. Stopping in front of it and grabbing the sides to help support herself, she looked into the mirror and began to take stock of her injuries.

What looked back at her was not pretty. The entire right side of her face was a mass of bruises and scratches. The swelling had gone down enough that she could see out of her right eye now. She still had a pair of butterfly bandages on her scalp, but she guessed that they were fresh, not what a rushed petty officer had applied. Her hair, which she had always worn long, was lopsided, burned and seared short, so it fell just above collar length. Supporting herself with only her right arm now, she ran her left hand over her right side. Feeling the bandages under the gown, she assumed that her ribs had been ministered to as well. She took a last look at her face before turning back toward the bunk. Deciding that lying down was not what she wanted to do right now, she headed for the chair at the desk instead.

Lowering herself into it, she let her mind wander. Treason, desertion, cowardice, attempted murder, and assault. *Yep, you've really done it this time, Alex. You really need to do something about your temper.* Then she remember why she had done what she had done, and she allowed herself a small smile. If it had saved her crew, then it had been worth it, and she'd happily pay the price for it. *Just like you were ready to pay the price for your other crew.* The thought surfaced in her mind, and she pushed it down but knew it would never go away. And she wasn't sure if she wanted it to.

Coming back to the here and now, she looked up at the corporal.

"So, are you supposed to stay there staring at me the whole time I'm here?"

"No, ma'am," the corporal said, standing back from the cell door, arms behind his back, relaxed. "The doc said to keep an eye on you for the first half hour or so after you woke up in case anything happened, and I figured if something did happen, it would be easier to deal with if I was here, rather than seeing it on the monitor and having to run down here." He pointed up at the camera behind him aimed down into her cell.

"Well, I appreciate it, Corporal." she said, trying to smile without it looking like some sort of grimace. "And seeing as how I have you for the next twenty minutes or so, do you mind if I ask you some questions?"

"Not at all, ma'am. Ask away."

"How long was I out?"

"Couldn't tell you," he said. "You were out when you got here. You've been here for the last three hours."

"Okay, fair enough. So, where is here, exactly?"

"You're dirtside. Quantico, to be specific." Dirtside, and in the brig closest to Navy High Command . . . and, coincidentally, to the Judge Advocate General's offices as well. The situation was not getting any better.

"Well, that explains a lot." She saw that he didn't quite see how that explained anything to her, but he just nodded. "Don't suppose you know the status of my ship and crew?" He shook his head.

"Can I have my uniform back now? I'd like to get out of this gown."

"'Fraid not, ma'am." He actually sounded sorry to her.

"Well, can I at least have my cigarettes?" Alex asked. She was alone, in pain, with a lot on her mind, and more than a little bit scared. All of which had her fiending for nicotine something fierce.

"Sorry to say, ma'am, that you didn't have any cigarettes on you when you arrived—just a few cigars. Regardless, though, it's against regs to smoke in a government facility." Alex snorted at that.

"Are you kidding me?" she asked incredulously. "Corporal, I'm in here because some idiot has charged me with treason, desertion, attempted murder, and a whole slew of other charges. Do you think I can get into any more trouble by smoking a cigar in here?"

"Probably not, ma'am. But you still can't have them." He smiled as he said this, taking any heat there might have been out of his words. She yawned back in return.

"Can I have some coffee, then? I'm beat." She stifled another yawn.

"That would be the DermaGen and QuickKnit the doc gave you, ma'am. Really takes it out of you." Alex nodded her understanding. Dermal regenerators and quick-knit bone reconstructors might speed healing, but they burned a body's resources just as fast. Now that she thought about it, she was ravenously hungry. She started to open her mouth to ask when she could get something to eat, but the guard seemed to be expecting the question.

"Chow's on its way now, ma'am, and coffee." He was still smiling. For a jailer, and a marine, he was rather nice. She smiled back.

Alex was working on her third cup of coffee when she heard someone coming down the passageway toward her cell. The corporal had left soon after her food had arrived, allowing her to eat in private. Sitting back in the chair, sipping at her coffee, she could see that he was back, and that he was not alone. A lieutenant commander was with him.

"Captain McLaughlin?" the lieutenant commander asked, and continued on at her nod. "I am Lieutenant Commander Painter, adjutant to Admiral Greco. You will come with me, please."

"Where are we going?" Alex asked, still sitting calmly at the desk, sipping her coffee.

"I am to bring you to the admiral's office." He seemed to be affronted by the question.

"I see. And what does the Chief of Naval Operations want with a lowly captain?" She had still not moved, but her eyes caught the small smile on the corporal's face. Apparently she was not the only one around here who did not like the lieutenant commander's whiny, officious attitude.

"That does not concern you," Painter snapped, obviously not accustomed to having his commands ignored.

"Well, I would like something to wear, if you don't mind." She smiled sweetly at the officer, knowing it would just irritate him more but unable to resist the temptation. What the hell? She was already in trouble, so in for a bullet, in for a barrage, as her father always said. "I'm sure the admiral would not want me reporting to his office in a hospital gown. It's bad enough I am going to have to do it in chains." She added this last sourly.

"Get her something to wear," Painter snarled over his shoulder at the corporal. "She needs to be at least somewhat presentable for her meeting with Admiral Greco and Admiral Rachere." Turning back to face her, he gave her a condescending look and said, "You need not fear, Captain, you will not be in chains. In fact, you will not even be under arrest. Now, I suggest you keep your questions to yourself so that I can deliver you to the admiral's office without any more delay."

At the mention of Admiral Rachere's name, a surge of hate flowed into her body. So strong was this wave of hatred that she did not register the rest of what Painter had said at first.

"As you were, Corporal," Alex snapped, stopping the guard mid-sentence as he spoke into his communicator.

"Captain McLaughlin—" Painter began, but she did not let him finish.

"Silence," she said, the bite of command evident in her voice. Being the adjutant to the highest-ranking naval officer apparently gave the man delusions of his own importance. Now, that would not do at all. Alex knew that she should keep her mouth shut and just do what she was told, but she couldn't. Something about the officer standing in front of her irritated her to no end, and situation be damned, she was not going to put up with it. He had said she was not under arrest, and that changed things considerably.

"Now, Corporal, I would like my uniform please. Have it sent down immediately." Her voice was calm, but commanding.

"Yes, ma'am." The corporal could see the shift in power immediately, and acted accordingly, issuing orders into his communicator. "Respectfully, ma'am, I don't think that your current uniform is appropriate for a meeting with the CNO. If you will give me an hour, I can find you a new uniform."

"Thank you for your concern, Corporal." Her eyes held his while she continued. "But I think my current uniform is appropriate for a meeting with the CNO and Admiral Rachere. More than appropriate." A puzzled frown crossed his face, but he said nothing to her. Instead he spoke quietly into his communicator.

"Painter, do you know the status of my crew?"

Lieutenant Commander Painter shook his head, then began to

protest again, but she silenced him with a glance. Several long moments later, another marine hurried down the hall carrying a bundle in his arms. Handing it to the corporal, he turned to go but stopped when he saw Alex. Her command presence was a physical thing, and the marine could feel the effect. Even out of uniform, here stood an officer worth following.

Alex saw the look the second marine was giving her, and the corporal as well. She hated it. She had seen that look too many times before, on faces she would never forget but would only ever see again in her dreams. She shook herself back to the situation at hand, taking her uniform from the corporal. She had a duty to perform, and she would do it, no matter what the cost to her soul.

All three men stood looking at her expectantly. She finally had to say something.

"If you gentlemen don't mind, I'd like a little privacy to change." They said nothing as their faces flushed. Then they moved a short distance down the passageway. Alex changed into her uniform as quickly as her injuries would allow. When she was finished, she again stood in front of the mirror, taking an account of herself.

Her dress uniform, once pristine white, was now blackened and scorched. Blood stained her shoulder boards and ribbons. But somehow, the top ribbon, the sky-blue one with the stars on it, still looked brand-new. She smiled at how capricious the universe could be, and how perverse. The rips and tears in both her blouse and trousers seemed appropriate, considering the damage to the rest of her uniform. Yes, this was indeed the appropriate uniform to wear to her meeting. Let Admiral Greco see what she had looked like, how damaged both she and her ship had been, when Admiral Rachere marched onto her command deck. Let him see what Rachere had abandoned in his own weird vendetta.

She snarled at the thought of Rachere again and turned to head out of the cell. She was certain that the admiral's actions had been personally motivated, but she could not determine what she had ever done to him to warrant his wrath. Regardless, he had threatened her ship and crew, and she would see that he paid for it. Yes, one way or another, he would pay.

Striding down the passageway, she could see the corporal and lieutenant commander waiting. The other marine must have headed back to his post. Stopping in front of the marine, she spoke.

"Corporal, you are a credit to the service, and to that uniform.

Thank you for your concern, and keep up the good work," she said very formally. Alex could see his eyes travel from her eyes, down to her ribbons, then back again. He snapped to parade-ground attention.

"Thank you, ma'am. It was an honor to meet you." She gave him a small smile and nodded, then turned to the officer beside him.

"Let's go, Painter. The admirals await." The deliberate omission of his rank was not lost on any of them.

Chapter Nineteen

NAVAL ANNEX, WASHINGTON DC, TERRA
OCTOBER 8, 2197
2245Z
SOL

Captain Alexandra McLaughlin stood outside the door lead-
ing to the Chief of Naval Operation's inner office. Lieutenant
Commander Painter, standing beside her, reached for the handle.
Turning it, he pushed the door open and preceded her inside.
She knew that he hated and resented what tradition dictated he
do next, but, to his credit, he did his duty. Begrudgingly.

"Attention on deck," he ground out through clenched teeth.
Alex stood in the doorway and watched as both the CNO and
Admiral Rachere came to attention. Normally Alex hated this
tradition—having a room come to attention as she entered it, all
because of the Medal. But not this time. This time she wanted
it clear that she had proven herself to her nation. Proven it in
combat, in a trial by fire that had cost her more than her own
blood, more than these men could ever know. There would be
no question of her loyalty and dedication in this room, not now,
not ever.

"As you were," she said softly as she stepped into the room

and marched up to the CNO's desk, pointedly ignoring Admiral Rachere on her way past him. Stopping several paces away from the desk, she came to attention. The sole source of light in the huge office was coming from the lamp on the corner of his desk, and she stood in the pool of light as if it were a spot light.

"Sir, Captain McLaughlin reporting as ordered." Alex remained at attention while she waited for Admiral Greco's response. Eyes fixed on a point above his head, she could not see the shocked look on his face as he took in the state of both her uniform and her face. Nor did she see the accusatory look he shot at Admiral Rachere. Had she seen it, she would have been pleased to see that this meeting was starting off just the way she had wished it to.

"At ease, Captain," Admiral Greco finally said, his voice hushed as he continued to stare at Alex. "Please, sit."

Alex lowered herself into the indicated chair, face tightening in a grimace of pain as she did so.

"Captain, are you okay?" Greco's voice held real concern. "We can postpone this meeting until tomorrow if you need more time to rest." Alex, unaware of the conversation that had taken place between the CNO and the Secretary of War, did not know how quickly both men wanted this situation resolved. She would not have cared even if she had. She wanted the situation resolved now, and she would not see it delayed one moment longer.

"I'm fine, sir," she said, still ignoring Admiral Rachere even though military courtesy dictated that she at least acknowledge his presence. "I wish to proceed without delay."

"If you are sure?" He waited for her nod before continuing. "Then, can I offer you anything to drink?" She could see that while the admiral wanted to move on, he was slightly hesitant to do so, as if, once the peace were breached, it would be impossible to regain. "Coffee, tea, or perhaps something stronger?"

"I'm fine, sir," Alex repeated; there was no pretense of civility in her voice or posture. She had come for a fight and wanted to get to it.

"Very well." Sighing, Admiral Greco began. "I believe you both understand why you are here, but to set the record straight, Admiral Rachere, you are here because of your actions or lack thereof in regard to the USS *Fenris* and her crew upon their emergence in this system." Admiral Rachere inhaled deeply though his nostrils but said nothing. Turning to face her, Admiral Greco continued.

"Captain McLaughlin, you are here to answer for your actions in relation to Admiral Rachere. Are we all clear on that?" Both officers ground out an acknowledgment. The reminder of each other's actions brought the tension up in the room.

"I have spoken with the Secretary of War, and we both agree that this situation needs to be resolved quickly and fairly. We can ill afford to be at loggerheads now. With the destruction of Admiral Stevens' fleet, this system is exposed, and we must keep our focus on preparations for a possible Xan-Sskarn attack." Alex felt her head nod in agreement with the CNO's assessment.

"So I have asked you both here to find out exactly what occurred, and what we can do to rectify it." Alex watched him toy with a pad on his desk before he turned to face Admiral Rachere. "Admiral, can you please explain why you failed to dispatch a relief ship to aid the *Fenris* when all indications pointed to damage, and why you proceeded to board her and place Captain McLaughlin under arrest for treason?"

"Admiral Greco," Rachere began in a silky-smooth voice. "While I do agree with the assessment that the *Fenris* did enter this system apparently damaged, I had received no information indicating that she was due to return. Given the emergency communication from Admiral Stevens, however garbled, as well as the captain's past record, I assumed that she had abandoned Admiral Stevens' fleet in the face of the enemy and run for home."

"What!?" Alex snapped up in her chair, all pain forgotten as a spike of adrenaline flooded her system. The smarmy smile that he turned on her goaded her even more. She could tell that he was trying to push into losing her temper again, and unfortunately it was working. "How dare you even suggest—"

"Captain!" Admiral Greco's voice cut across her, pulling her attention from Rachere. Admiral Rachere continued as if he had not been interrupted.

"As commanding officer of Folkvang station, it is up to me to determine whether or not a relief ship should be dispatched, and in my opinion, given lack of evidence to the contrary, I had no choice but to believe that Captain McLaughlin had turned traitor. One escape *might* be considered miraculous, but two? No, two escapes are not miraculous, but traitorous. It was obvious."

During Rachere's calm explanation, Alex's fingers were gripping the arms of her chair hard enough to begin to tear the two-hundred-year-old leather. Only a supreme effort of will was keeping her seated and not hurtling toward Rachere.

"So, what you are saying, Admiral Rachere," Admiral Greco began, the look on his face clearly wondering what kind of perverse logic could have led Rachere to draw the conclusions he had, "is that because the *Fenris* arrived in system alone, you determined that not only Captain McLaughlin but her entire crew had turned traitor?" Holding out a placating hand toward Alex, he kept his gaze on Rachere.

"Of course not, sir. But as much as it pained me, I did believe that a majority of the crew was behind her, as there would be no way for her to bring the *Fenris* home alone."

"I see." Alex could tell from Admiral Greco's tone that he did not understand; she did not, either. "And once you boarded the *Fenris*? Can you please explain why you attempted to remove Captain McLaughlin from command without even asking her what the situation was?"

"Yes, sir." His honeyed voice once again filled the room as he cast another smug gaze toward Alex. More leather tore under her fingers.

"Operating under the belief that most if not all of the crew of the *Fenris* had turned traitor, I had hoped to remove the head from the body, as it were, by removing Captain McLaughlin from the ship as quickly as possible. Thereby hopefully allowing the crew to see the error of their ways. At which time I would have immediately given the orders to dispatch a relief ship. But without knowing the status of the crew, I could not in good conscience send a ship out to the *Fenris*, not knowing if it would be fired upon, or even taken over. So I made the decision to see for myself that the situation was safe before ordering good men and women into harm's way. Also, regulations state that I am not to give aid and comfort to the enemy, and traitors, sir, are considered the enemy."

"And the reason why you never asked the captain why she was back in Sol, obviously battle damaged?"

"I never got the chance, sir." The pleasure in his voice was unmistakable. Alex could see that he had guided the conversation in this direction for the express purpose of painting her in the worst possible light.

"Explain."

"When I first attempted to place Captain McLaughlin under arrest, she laughed then ordered me off her command deck. After I explained the situation regarding the relief ship to her, she physically and verbally assaulted me, and it is my sincere belief that were it not for members of her own crew, I would quite possibly be dead now. She then proceeded to threaten my life." Pausing here, he smirked at her, twisting the knife even more. "I should point out at this time, sir, that Commander Denton, the chief engineer, did in fact *punch* Captain McLaughlin at this time, while she was physically restrained by another member of her crew. While I have no plans to bring charges against the commander, I believe an investigation is warranted."

"You know God damn well, that—" Alex began, only to be cut off by Admiral Greco once more.

"Anything else?" Greco asked, his tone indicating that he knew that there was. Nodding, Admiral Rachere continued.

"After my second attempt to arrest the captain, she attempted to bargain with me, and, failing that, she and her crew threatened both my life and the lives of the MPs with me." Rachere shook his head in disappointment. "Finally, seeing that no other course was open to me, I agreed to dispatch a relief ship if McLaughlin would stand down. The only reason I capitulated was that it appeared to me that the remaining senior officer, Commander Denton, was not supporting Captain McLaughlin's actions. She did punch her, after all." Finishing his statement, Rachere leaned back in his chair, a content smile playing about his lips.

"And knowing what you know now about Admiral Stevens' final order to Captain McLaughlin? What would your response have been?"

"I would, of course, have dispatched relief ships immediately and contacted High Command."

Seeing red and still tearing at the arms of her chair, Alex missed what Admiral Greco said. Finally he turned his attention to her, and she could see his hope that she could say something that would mitigate what Rachere had just said. Unfortunately, what Rachere had said, at least the portions involving her actions after his boarding, was fairly accurate. But that was not the same as entirely accurate.

"Captain McLaughlin, I am well aware that you are no traitor or deserter. A copy of Admiral Stevens' final order to you was forwarded to my office, and I know you were directed to return to Sol as quickly as possible. Right now, I am trying to determine what occurred when you arrived." His gaze stayed locked on Alex's eyes, and he asked the question. "Does what Admiral Rachere just reported coincide with your recollections of the incident?"

They say that discretion is the better part of valor, and most times they are right. Today *is not most times. Fuck discretion,* she thouht.

"Would I say that the admiral is lying through his teeth?" Alex snarled. "No, sir. Would I say he is dancing on the razor's edge of the truth? Oh, yes, sir." Now it was Rachere's turn to clutch the arms of his chair and try to interrupt, with about as much success as she had had.

"Admiral Rachere, you have had your say. It's the captain's turn now," Greco said pointedly. "Please proceed, Captain."

"Yes, sir." Alex collected her thoughts for a moment then began to speak. "After returning to Sol, to say my ship and crew were in bad shape would be an understatement. Frankly, I was surprised that we had survived our translation. Once we reached Sol and were finally no longer under fire, I devoted the entire efforts of the crew to damage control. Including, I might add, external communications, so as to report the situation. I am sure the admiral has seen the reports as to the status of the *Fenris*?" She waited for Admiral Greco's nod of assent before continuing. "Then you know there was no way for us to inform anyone as to our or the fleet's situation. After several hours, we were finally boarded by what I thought was a relief party. It was in fact Admiral Rachere and his MPs." She cast a hateful glance toward Admiral Rachere.

"And after Admiral Rachere arrived on the command deck?" Admiral Greco prompted, seeing that Alex was content to sit and stare murder at the admiral.

"After the admiral arrived on the command deck, he marched right up to me, stepping over injured crew members, to place me under arrest," she ground out through clenched teeth. "Of all the things that I had expected, an admiral marching onto my command deck and placing me under arrest was not one of them. I admit I did not handle it well, thinking it was some kind of sick joke. Then, when he persisted, I informed the admiral that the *Fenris* was my ship and that if he was not going to assist in damage control, he could leave. He then repeated that I was under arrest, and I decided that it was not the time to argue about the absurdity of that. I told him that I would gladly go with him, just to get his damage-control and medical teams moving to assist my crew. That was when I found out that not only did he believe me and my entire crew to be traitors, but that there was no relief ship." Alex was seething now, the entire scene playing out in her mind again.

"At this time, did you attempt to assault the admiral?" Admiral Greco asked expectantly.

"No, sir."

"Good. Now please—" The admiral did not get to finish, as Alex completed the answer to his question.

"I tried to kill him. Sir." She was smiling back at Admiral Greco now, and was not surprised to see him sit up straight and stare at her open-mouthed as her statement registered. "Ensign Green's and Commander Denton's interference is the only reason that Admiral Rachere is sitting here now."

"Then his statement about you watching him in a pool of his own blood?" he asked hesitantly.

"A girl's got to have goals," she said back lightly, looking down at her nails then staring at Admiral Rachere. She could see him pale a bit, realizing that she truly did want to kill him, regardless of the circumstances or repercussions. She smiled as sweat began to appear on his upper lip and he cast his glance about the office, looking for escape routes.

"Captain, I find your casual attitude to be disturbing," Admiral Greco finally said, trying to regain his composure.

"I'm sorry, sir, but you asked, and I am duty bound to answer as truthfully as possible."

"Is there any reason why you are openly admitting to all of this?"

"Yes, there is, sir." Alex turned her gaze on Admiral Greco now. "I think that my actions were not only appropriate, but justified."

"How in the hell do you think you can justify—" Admiral Rachere tried to interrupt again.

"Admiral Rachere!" Greco half shouted, determined not to let the situation get out of control. When the admiral closed his mouth with a snap, Greco turned back to Alex. "He does have a point, Captain. How can you believe that your actions were justified?"

"Well, sir, at no time did Admiral Rachere express any interest or concern in the status of my crew, or for the reason why I was in-system and shot to hell. What he did seem interested in was pursuing some sort of personal vendetta against me by goading and pushing me into a reaction. I freely admit that I lost my temper, and that I did indeed try to assault the admiral. But not only did he know damn well what he was doing, he was doing it on purpose, and I could see it in his face that he wanted the reaction he got."

"Personal vendetta?" Admiral Greco asked, his interest sparked by this new development. If this was indeed personal, things changed significantly.

"Yes, sir, though I confess I have no idea what it could be." Alex's voice was as puzzled as her expression. "I had never met the admiral before he walked onto my command deck." It was true that she did not know what the admiral had against her, but she was about to find out.

"Admiral Rachere, do you have a response to this? I should tell you, several of the reports I have received seem to support the same theory. That you have some sort of personal grudge against Captain McLaughlin."

"I cannot attest to the contents of the reports you have received, Admiral, but I harbor no ill will against the captain, present circumstances excepted, of course." Alex could see that he was still sweating, and she was pretty sure it was not because of the threat on his life. It was time to push, and push hard.

"Bullshit! You and I both know you have something against me," Alex hurled at him. She saw Admiral Greco open his mouth to cut her off, but it was too late. She had goaded Rachere into a response, and she was not going to stop until she had what she wanted.

"You don't know what you are talking about, *Captain*."

"Try again. There is no way you could put two and two together and get four, let alone determine my complicity in some sort of traitorous activity, unless it served your personal interests."

"How dare you!"

"How dare I what? Point out that if your brainwaves dipped any lower it would be legal to harvest your organs? Or that you have an agenda that you are willing to do anything to achieve, even sacrifice the lives of good men and women?"

"I have no such agenda. And you have no right to accuse me of sacrificing the lives of good men and women when you have abandoned so many behind you."

"I have abandoned no one!" Alex shouted, leaping to her feet.

Anger and guilt had pushed all thoughts of goading the admiral into a confession aside. Thankfully she did not have to try any longer. Admiral Rachere was on his feet now as well, and Admiral Greco was speeding around his desk to impose himself between the two of them before they came to blows.

"You abandoned my son!" Admiral Rachere's shout shocked them all into silence and immobility.

"Your son?" Alex breathed out, collapsing back into her chair, ignoring the pain the action caused.

"Yes, my son." Admiral Rachere fell into his chair as well, looking defeated and deflated.

"I didn't know you had a son," Admiral Greco said, returning to his own chair.

Alex looked between the two men, and then inward toward herself. The mood in the room had changed, and so had her feelings. She was still furious at the admiral—not for his actions, now that she understood them, but because he had given her yet another ghost to answer to.

"His mother and I divorced years ago, and he took her name when he entered the Academy," Rachere said quietly, tears welling in his eyes. "When he graduated, he was accepted into flight school." Alex looked up and could see him staring at her now, and she knew what was coming next.

"He was so proud to serve," he continued in a cold, hard voice. "When he was assigned to Admiral Wentworth's fleet, he could not believe his luck. He was going to help save humanity, and I couldn't have been more proud of him. Then you came back." His finger pointed accusingly at Alex. "You came back, but he didn't."

"Sean," Admiral Greco said quietly. "She was not the only one to come back from Ross 128."

"I know that!" he shouted at the admiral. "But she is the only one who left him behind."

"What?" Alex said.

"I've reviewed the *Gna*'s logs, the ones that survived." The hatred was returning to his voice now, and Alex could feel hers returning as well. "Your sensor records clearly show that on your exit of the system, you passed several Valkyries still engaged, but failed to retrieve them. You didn't even try!"

"There was no way I could have retrieved them," Alex whispered back. "We were redlining the reactors, and there was no way to slow down in time to even attempt retrieval." She hated herself for what she was about to add, but she could not leave it unsaid. "And even if there had been a way to slow enough to retrieve them, I would not have done it. The Xan-Sskarns were too close behind, and they were gaining. I had to balance the lives of a few Valkyrie pilots against the lives of the crews of three ships. I had no choice, and I have hated myself since then."

"No choice? Hated yourself?" Rachere said mockingly. "I don't give a fuck about that. I want you to hurt. Hurt like I did, like I do. Your self-pity means nothing to me."

"So, you did it on purpose, then, for no other reason than revenge?" Admiral Greco said quietly.

"Of course I did. I'd read her record and asked questions. Alexandra McLaughlin is fanatical about the welfare of her crew, and I knew the best way to hurt her would be to hurt them. When the *Fenris* jumped in-system wounded and crippled, I saw my opportunity, and I took it."

Alex was livid, once again, teetering on the edge of violence. Suspecting the admiral of attacking her through her crew was one thing. Knowing it for a fact was entirely different. She wanted vengeance for her crew, and watched Admiral Greco rubbing his temples, waiting for him to dispense it. Finally, his fingers stopped and it appeared he had reached a decision.

"I have the defense of this system to oversee, a possible traitor in our midst, and this mess between the two of you to deal with, and I don't have the time for you two. So this is what I am going to do, and I will not listen to one word of argument. If I ever hear of this again, I will personally see to it that the remainder of your natural lives is a living hell. Am I clear?" The steel in his voice was unmistakable.

"Yes, sir."

"Yes, sir."

"Very well, Admiral Rachere, you will return to your command and resume your duties. You will receive a reprimand for the delay of vital information. As there was no additional loss of life aboard the *Fenris* due to your actions, there will be no other action taken against you. You will, however, seek out counseling, and I will expect regular reports on your progress. And if you set even one toe out of line again, that will be the end of you. Do you understand?" Alex watched as Admiral Rachere nodded his head in acceptance, unable to speak.

A slap on the wrist. A God damn, fucking slap on the wrist for endangering the lives of her crew for his own petty gains. She ground her teeth together, waiting for her own punishment. She felt sure that it would be significantly worse than Rachere's, and if it was too disproportionate, she would damn well make sure everyone knew what really happened, and damn her career.

"As for you, Captain McLaughlin, while it is obvious to me now that you were pushed into your reactions and that your casual attitude about them now is, in my opinion, sheer bravado, the fact that you could be manipulated so easily shows me that you too are harboring demons that need exorcising. Therefore, you will undergo a full psychological evaluation prior to the assumption of your new command. Should you not pass with flying colors, not only will you be denied a new command, I will down-check you and have you beached until such time as you *do* pass. Do you understand?"

Now it was her turn to nod wordlessly as the admiral continued speaking. Not only did she, too, get a slap on the wrist—she apparently was getting a pat on the back as well. A new command. Usually a captain knew long ahead of time before actually reporting to a new command. She could not help but wonder if this was in part a bribe for her silence. She pondered that thought for a while before she saw that Admiral Greco had stopped talking and was looking intently at her.

"Sir?" she said hesitantly, hoping she had not been spaced out for too long.

"I asked how you were doing, Captain." She looked around as if to find the answer written somewhere for her to read off and saw that she and the admiral were alone in the office.

"I'm fine, sir," she said, stifling a yawn, "just really tired."

"I'm not surprised. It's been a long day for you." He seemed tired himself.

"Yes, sir, it has."

"I've had my aide arrange for quarters for you during your stay dirtside, and to have your gear shipped down from the *Fenris*."

"Assuming I have any gear left. We took quite a pounding, sir." She tried to keep the melancholy tone out of her voice but could see by the way the admiral looked at her that she had failed.

"Yes, I know. I've seen the video from Folkvang station. You did one hell of a job getting her home at all."

"Thank you, sir. We tried. How is my crew? You said there was no further loss of life?"

"That's right, Captain. Relief crews moved in quickly, and your entire crew has stood down. Every single crew member that made it to Sol system is expected to recover. But there will be time enough for this later, after you have submitted your full report." He tried to sound upbeat, but failed miserably. Tonight was just not the night for jocularity.

"I'll have it to you as soon as possible, sir." She knew that she would be sending it directly to him, not via her chain of command, which, as far as she knew, still included Admiral Rachere. Thinking of him, and of what he had done, she felt the anger burning in her again.

"I look forward to it. Now, as I said, I've had quarters arranged for you, and I'll have a new uniform delivered tomorrow morning." She looked down and grimaced at herself.

"I'd appreciate that, sir." She stood, swaying slightly, and heard the door open behind her. The admiral must have summoned his adjutant when she was not looking, but she took his presence as a dismissal. "Good night, sir."

"Good night, Captain." She was just passing though the doorway when he called out to her. "Captain McLaughlin, one last question."

"Sir?"

"After everything that you have heard tonight, are you still harboring any thoughts of vengeance against Admiral Rachere?" His voice floated out to her from the darkness of the office.

Yes, I am.

"No, sir, of course not," she said as she pulled the door shut.

Chapter Twenty

NAVAL ANNEX, WASHINGTON DC, TERRA
OCTOBER 11, 2197
0930Z
SOL

"So, McLaughlin passed her psych eval?" Secretary Lipinski asked.

"Yes, Mr. Secretary, she did, but I had no doubt that she would," Admiral Greco said.

"If you had no doubts, why did you order it, then?"

"I ordered it before I remembered she used to be a Loki pilot."

"I know that's a very intense job, but what does that have to do with passing a psych exam?"

"Well, Loki pilots are required to undergo intense psychological testing prior to even being accepted as a candidate. The job is almost a suicidal one, but unfortunately necessary. With that and the expense of a Loki itself, we can't afford to have anyone who isn't one hundred percent stable behind the stick. That's one reason Loki pilots are limited to ten active missions and no more than that. Going out and painting yourself as a huge target is nerve-wracking, and it's all too easy to lose touch with reality. Thus, in addition to the original psych eval, they are subjected to one after each active mission. So it's no surprise that Captain McLaughlin passed. She's had more than her fair share."

"Do you think that is the only reason she passed? Because she has experience with evaluations?" Lipinski seemed concerned now, as if there were a walking time bomb out there.

"That and the fact that she looks like she does." Greco smiled at that, and saw Lipinski nodding in agreement.

"I know what you mean. She looks like a little girl, and her injuries only support the fact that she was the victim. I have no doubt that Captain McLaughlin is not above using that, or anything else for that matter, to help her reach her goals," Secretary Lipinski said lightly, not noticing Admiral Greco's wince at the use of the word "goals." He remembered all too clearly the last time he heard that word used in such a light manner, and it was not a pleasant memory.

"I agree, sir."

"Are you having second thoughts about the new command? Do you think that she is still too traumatized?" Lipinski asked him intently.

"No, she is still the best choice available for the position with the loss of Captain Chapman." Captain Chapman, commanding officer of the USS *Asgard*, was due for a new command, and his XO was due for a command of his own. Chapman's loss with the destruction of the *Asgard*, and the loss of a several other, more senior officers, had left the list of available, experienced captains very short. "Of course, there are still officers senior to her still in-system, but with the current situation, it would be unwise to disrupt any ship's command structure. That being the case, McLaughlin is who we need. Besides, with her record, I have no doubt that she will be able to handle the additional responsibility. Plus, her XO is an outstanding officer and very experienced. I am also assigning a majority of the *Fenris'* remaining crew to her new command, so she should settle in quickly."

"Okay, I can understand that, but what about any lingering trauma? Is she going to hold up or collapse when it hits the fan?"

"Oh, I don't doubt that there is some lingering trauma there," Admiral Greco said, waving the thought aside with his hand. "You can't see what she has seen and not be affected by it. But even if she did manage to put one over on the shrinks, I'm sure she'll do her duty. She always has."

"It's your call, Richard. I just want to be sure that you're sure. Now that we have put that unpleasantness behind us, what is the status of our defenses and Counter Intelligence's investigation? I have to brief the President in half an hour, and I don't want to tell him everything is coming up roses and have it turn around and bite me on the ass later." Lipinski held Admiral Greco with his stare until Greco nodded.

"I'm sure about Captain McLaughlin. There won't be a problem. The system's defense network has been put on alert, Admiral Tanner is preparing a new deployment plan for the fleet, and Counter Intel is still looking."

"What about transferring the crew of the *Fenris* with McLaughlin? Are you sure that's wise? You're not worried about putting a traitor in the heart of our fleet?"

"Sir, while I am in agreement with Admiral Stevens' assessment, the odds of the traitor having been on the *Fenris*, then living through that battle, and then being in a healthy enough condition to be reassigned are virtually nonexistent." Admiral Greco paused before finishing. "You can give the President my word on that, and I'll take any blame should it turn out otherwise."

"Very well, Admiral. Thank you for your report, and keep me informed." Admiral Greco knew a dismissal when he heard one. Heading for the door, he was glad that he had not divulged the specifics of his conversation with Admiral Rachere and Captain McLaughlin. Lipinski would down-check her immediately, but that would be the wrong response. He knew that things were going to go from bad to worse any day now, and they needed someone like McLaughlin on the front lines. Trauma or no.

Dressed in a new uniform, Alex entered the outer office of the Chief of Naval Operations. Her space-black uniform was unadorned except for rank tabs and her black-skull Loki wings. Lieutenant Commander Painter was not in the office, and none of the other staff had ever seen her in uniform, so the flow of work merely paused to see who had intruded in their little world and to stare at the mass of bruises that still decorated the right side of her face. Oblivious to their looks, Alex walked over to a chair in the small waiting area and took a seat, not saying anything. She felt almost no pain from any of her wounds, thanks to the wonders of modern medicine. Wondering for a moment at how life must have been before the advent of DermaGen, QuickKnit, and the host of other pharmaceuticals that she took for granted, she could not imagine having to spend weeks or even months recuperating from the injuries she had sustained, instead of days. She hoped Greg and the rest of the crew were recovering as well.

She let her eyes close and felt a wave of weariness wash over her. Still tiring easily from the medication she was taking to mend her, she found that she had a tendency to slide into a light sleep if she sat still for too long. She knew that this would pass in a few more days, but until it did, she found the entire situation to be highly annoying. She felt her head begin to dip, and she tried to fight it, to stand up and stay awake, but to no avail.

Alex felt herself being shaken and opened her eyes.

"Are you well, Captain?" Painter's voice was as condescending as she remembered.

"Yes, I'm fine, Lieutenant Commander," she said, though her accelerated heartbeat and the last vestiges of a bad dream floating in her mind said otherwise. "Just fine. Is the admiral ready to see me?"

"Yes, ma'am. If you will follow me, please."

"I'm pretty sure I can find my way to the door by myself, Painter, but thank you anyway." She stood, clasping her beret in her left hand as she patted his shoulder and marched past him, ignoring the stares of the staff. Stopping at the open doorway, she knocked, waiting for permission to enter.

"Come," came the deep baritone of Admiral Greco.

Alex marched into the inner office. Seeing the admiral begin to rise to attention, she stopped him.

"Please, sir, don't. I'm not wearing it." She was slightly embarrassed. She knew she had used the Medal as a club a few nights past, to make a statement, but today it seemed somehow wrong to have the Chief of Naval Operations snapping to just for her. Her request did not have any effect. Admiral Greco came to parade-ground attention behind his desk. She sighed, feeling her face flushing.

"At ease." She watched as the admiral relaxed, smiling at her as he retook his seat.

"Please have a seat, Captain," he said, pointing at the same chair she had occupied two nights before. The armrests were

still damaged from her hands. "Tell me, why are you not wearing your awards?"

"Sir, regulations state that I have the choice of wearing all, none,
or just personal awards in uniform. I choose to wear none—it
just makes life easier." She hated the stares she got wearing them,
then the inevitable questions, dredging up memories she did not
want to remember.

"I see. Well, that is your prerogative, of course." His voice and
look seemed to indicate he understood. "Now, the reason I called
you here today was to discuss your new command."

"Yes, sir." Her flat tone belied her interest. It usually took some
time to bounce back and compose herself after what she had
come to call "The Dream," but she had not had the chance this
time. The admiral's quizzical glance and cocked head worried her.
She needed to assuage his concerns before he down-checked her;
besides, they were only dreams, and she was stronger than them.
"I'm sorry, sir. I'm still not fully recovered from the meds, and
they're really wiping me out. Please, go on."

"Very well," he continued, seemingly accepting her explanation
for her apathetic demeanor. "As I said, I invited you here to discuss
your new ship. It's unlike anything you have commanded before.
Matter of fact, it's unlike anything anyone has ever commanded."
Passing her a data pad sitting on his desk, he waited for her to
glance over the first few pages. Alex could feel the excitement
and interest building inside her with each line she read. When
she got to the dimensions of her new command, she snapped her
head up, mouth gaping.

"Two kilometers long?" she said disbelievingly.

"That's right." Admiral Greco smiled, clearly enjoying this.

"But that's huge. And this weapons load-out is an obscene
amount of firepower. My God, you could take on a full Sally
carrier group and come out on top."

"That's the point, Captain."

"Of course it is, sir. It's just overwhelming. I mean, I've heard
about this project, of course, but I didn't think it would be on
such a grand scale." She breathed, shaking her head, still having
difficulty getting her mind around the size and power of her
new command.

"Well, I was just as shocked when the design team brought this
to me. But we are hoping that this will give us the edge we need.

Two more keels were laid for her sister ships several months ago, and they should launch in approximately five weeks."

"So she's ready to sail now?" She held up the pad, indicating her new ship. "Her shakedown cruise is complete?"

"Yes, she's had her trials and is ready for action." He gave a short laugh. "Which is a good thing, because Admiral Tanner has been inquiring almost daily as to the status of his new flagship. Are you familiar with Admiral Tanner?"

"Yes, sir. He was the Valkyrie squadron commander during my midshipman's cruise. He was the one who recommended me for Loki training after graduation." She smiled at the memory.

"Well, I'm glad you remember him, because he remembers you and is looking forward to having you captain for him."

"Yes, sir." She did not know what else to say, but felt that she had to say something.

"Now, before I have your orders cut, I wanted to speak to you about one last thing." The admiral's tone was very serious now.

"My psych eval." It was not a question.

"Yes. I've read the doctor's reports, and you checked out just fine. But when I ordered the evaluation, I forgot you were a Loki pilot." The unasked question hung between them.

"And you wanted to know if I just told the shrinks what they wanted to hear, is that it, sir?" She asked the question for him.

"Yes, I do," he told her frankly.

"No, sir, I didn't." He kept staring at her, and she returned his gaze levelly. After several long minutes, he seemed to find what he was looking for in her eyes.

"Very well, Captain. Now, let's get into the specifics of your orders." Alex let her mind wander as the admiral began discussing her new duties, knowing from past experience that she would be able to recall this briefing with crystal clarity later. Right now she was thinking about her answer to the admiral's question. She had been honest in her response to him; she had not told the shrinks just what they wanted to hear. She just hadn't told them *everything* they had wanted to hear. She knew that it had been a very fine line that she hadn't crossed. Her reverie was interrupted with the admiral's next words.

"Finally, I want to be very specific as to your primary orders."

"Yes, sir."

"Your orders are to ensure the survival of the human race, by whatever means necessary. That is your mandate, as well as the mandate of the entire Home Fleet. I want every single member of the fleet to know it. We are not fighting to preserve our way of life, but to ensure the survival of our species."

"I'm sure the fleet understands what's at stake sir, and we won't fail, not so long as at least one of us is still alive."

"I have no doubt, Captain," Admiral Greco said approvingly. "Now, I think you need to go and get prepared to take command of your new ship. You launch in three days. Good hunting, Captain."

"Yes, sir. Thank you, sir," Alex acknowledged as she rose. Then, bracing to attention, she did an about-face and headed toward the door. Still clutching the pad in her hand, she glanced down at it and read the name of her new command. Snorting derisively, she shook her head and muttered to herself, "The universe is sure one hell of a twisted place."

Captain Alexandra McLaughlin stood still, staring out the porthole of the shuttle. Despite her outside calm, her mind was racing. She knew she was about to take command of the most powerful warship in the entire fleet and felt apprehensive. She still heard the voices of her dead every time she went to sleep, calling for her to join them. Alex closed her eyes and took a deep breath, pushing the dark thoughts to the back of her mind.

They're only dreams, for God's sake. In a few days, you'll put all that behind you and move on. You've done it before, so get your shit together and grow up!

Alex was pulled out of her ruminations by the voice of the shuttle pilot requesting permission to land. As the shuttle began its final approach, she got her first real look at her new command. Even having read the full details on her new ship, she could not get over how huge it was. Heavily armored, bristling with weapon emplacements, it looked like some sort of killer leviathan. She turned and sat down, strapping herself in as the shuttle began to head into the port-side landing bay.

Several minutes later, the hatch of her shuttle cycled open, and the sound of a bosun's pipes, announcing her presence, greeted her. Stepping down onto the hangar deck, she headed toward the commander standing at the head of the side party. Immaculately turned out in full-dress uniform, he stood stiffly at attention, saluting, awaiting her approach. She marched directly up to him, her space-black uniform contrasting with the sea of white of the assembled crew's dress uniforms. She had not had the time or opportunity to replace her dress uniform.

Stopping in front of the commander, she returned his salute and spoke, very formally. "Request permission to come aboard, Commander."

"Permission granted, Captain," he said just as formally. Alex cast her eyes about the hangar deck, seeing hundreds of her new crew assembled there to greet her, and behind them, in the shadows, she could see the eyes of her ghosts, her fallen warriors. Alex felt a cold chill run down her spine as the commander continued his welcome.

"Captain McLaughlin, welcome aboard the battle carrier *Valhalla*."

Yes, the universe was definitely a twisted place.

Chapter Twenty-one

USS *VALHALLA*
OCTOBER 13, 2197
0730Z
SOL

    Lance Corporal Alan Lewis, fresh from Marine Reconnaissance School and reporting to his first ship-based command, marched down the passageway, carrying an overstuffed duffel in each hand, eager to report in. His eyes, always thoughtful and intelligent, now held a new intensity, and after three months of long days and arduous physical labor, his features looked as if they had been planed down, leaving a strikingly handsome, chiseled face. The only detraction from his features was a nose that looked like it had been broken some time in the past, but that only added character.

    Following the directions he had been given upon boarding, he made his way unerringly toward the battalion's area of the ship. Turning the corner and seeing the Marine Corps emblem emblazoned on the hatch at the end of the passageway, he increased his pace. Reaching the hatch and dropping the bag from his right hand, he reached out to punch the Open button, cycling the hatch to allow him to enter. Grabbing his duffel again, he stepped through the hatch and into what was known aboard ship as Marine Country.

Marines might be a department of the navy, but the corps was an entity unto itself. They had their own customs and traditions, and they most definitely had a very unique perspective on the world in which they lived. Some would say the whole lot of them were crazy; others would say suicidally brave. Both would be right. So, to make life much easier for all parties concerned, the marines maintained their own section of the ship and tended not to mingle with the navy. The navy was, of course, more than happy to return the favor.

With the hatch cycling shut behind him, Alan looked around the compartment and, spotting the desk with the marine seated behind it, stepped toward it. Reaching the desk, he could see that the marine was a woman, a very beautiful woman.

"Lance Corporal Lewis, reporting for duty," he said, dropping his bags and standing at attention.

"At ease, marine," said a drawling voice. Looking down, Alan could see that she had been reading a manual of some sort prior to his interruption. He felt vaguely uncomfortable as she set her pad down and slowly ran a critical eye up and down him. His discomfort increased when she finally stopped and let her gaze rest on his face, eyes locked on his. Her sea-foam green eyes seemed to be boring into his mind, as if reading everything there. Finally, she spoke again.

"Orders?"

"Here, Corporal." Digging into his breast pocket, he drew out a chip, dropped it into her hand, and watched as she inserted it into her console. Standing still, he waited for her to finish reading.

"This can't be right," she said, more to herself than to him. Then, looking up, she directed her next statement directly at him. "This here says you were Intel before you went to Recon School."

"Yes, Corporal." After that first day, the intense pace of training had formed the trainee platoon into a tight-knit unit. He may have been Intel before he got there, but by the time he graduated, to his classmates, he was Recon, and that was all that mattered. However, he'd been warned, by instructors and classmates alike, that he would have to deal with this kind of problem eventually once he got out to the fleet. He just hadn't thought it would be within the first minute of his arrival.

"How the hell did an Intel weenie get a slot at Recon School? That's an infantry position. Always has been." She seemed to be eyeing him more closely now.

"Well, Corporal, Recon is actually not a primary MOS, so anyone can apply for a slot."

The Marine Corps had once tried to make their special forces a primary military occupational specialty, thinking that it would draw more desperately needed personnel to a very understrength, but very necessary, occupation. Unfortunately, while this did get the bodies Recon needed, it didn't work out as planned. More time and money was spent per class, but roughly only the same number of graduates was produced. After several such cycles, it was decided to go back to the old way of doing things. Any marine, regardless of their primary MOS, could apply for a slot at Reconnaissance School as long as they met the minimum requirements to attend. The requirements included the recommendation of a current Recon Marine. Recon Marines, the corps' special forces, were combat units and, as such, typically deployed from infantry commands. Thus, Recon Marines tended to deal almost exclusively with the infantry. The infantry, in turn, had the most exposure to Recon, which ensured that a majority of the recommendations were given to them. This had continued until it became the norm for the only Recon applicants to be members of the infantry. The norm, but not the regulation. Anyone could apply.

"I'm aware of the fact that anyone can apply, Lewis. I'm Recon myself. Corporal Tracy Clark, third fire-team leader." She held out her hand, and he shook it. "Now, I seem to remember that when I was still regular infantry, Recon tended to only mingle with the infantry, and then only rarely. I can't imagine that has changed much in the past couple of years." She lifted one pale eyebrow, beckoning his response.

"It hasn't," he said, watching her bob her head in agreement.

"I thought not." She leaned forward now, intently curious. "So, I would like to know how you happened to get a slot."

Sighing, he felt his shoulders slump. He had told this story all too often in the past months.

"You want the short version, or the long version?"

"Oh, the short version will do for now. I still need to get you checked in." She rocked back in her chair, obviously settling in for a story.

"Okay, the short version." He hoped that this time it would be sufficient, but somehow he knew it wouldn't be. "I was home."

"That's it?"

"That's it."

"You were home?"

"Yes."

"Well, I'll say this much for you, Lewis," she said with a laugh. "You don't disappoint. When you said short, you meant short."

"Thanks." He smiled back at her.

"Tell you what, Lewis." Leaning forward, she began to enter information into her console, processing him into his new command. "Why don't you tell me the long version while I finish checking you in. Then, when my relief gets here, I'll get you settled in. Mine is the only fire team that's short a body, so it looks like you and I are going to be spending a lot of time together."

Feeling himself blush at her last comment, he saw her smirk, apparently enjoying herself. Still smiling, Alan cleared his throat and began.

"The long version..."

"Well, Lewis, I can't tell if you are the luckiest or unluckiest son of a bitch alive, but we'll have plenty of time to find out, I'm sure," Corporal Clark said. Some time during Lewis' narrative, they had left the quarterdeck and headed toward third fire team's compartment.

"Thanks, I think."

"No problem. That's what a good fire-team leader is for—keeping her troops' morale up." She laughed again, and Alan liked the sound of it. Her smile was infectious, and her eyes piercing. Just a few centimeters taller than he was, she was greyhound lean, with the smooth, confident grace of an experienced killer. Short dirty-blond hair framed a beautiful face. She could easily pass as a vid star, but shallow, flighty people did not survive Marine Reconnaissance training.

"Well, here we are—home sweet home."

Opening a blank hatch, she ushered him inside the compartment. A pair of bunk beds on opposite bulkheads showed that the entire fire team lived together. A small area beyond the beds contained a table and four chairs. Beyond that he could see the head though a partially closed hatch.

"This one's yours." Tracy indicated the top bunk, closest to the head. "And here's your wall locker. Keyed to one two three four right now. You're welcome to set it to anything you like." The locker stood to one side of the bunks; the other occupant's locker was on the other end. Alan opened the locker and, after dumping the duffel he carried unceremoniously on the bottom, took the one she had been carrying for him and dropped it on top of the first.

Looking around the compartment, taking everything in, he noticed Corporal Clark watching him intently.

"I know it's not much, but it's home," she said.

"Where is everybody, Corporal?" Alan asked her, still examining the compartment.

"Call me Tracy. We're pretty informal in Recon." She pulled out a chair and sat at the table, indicating the chair across from her. She waited for him to sit before continuing.

"As for where everybody is, that's easy. Some of the battalion is dirtside. Most of the rest are on-station."

"How come?"

"Well, the Old Man gave the battalion a seventy-two-hour liberty. We're shipping out today, and everybody's taking the opportunity to get in as much fun as possible. I don't expect to see many people until around fifteen hundred."

"Why fifteen hundred?"

"There's a formation at sixteen hundred."

"Okay, I can understand people wanting to go dirtside. I remember seeing something about a shuttle run between Folkvang and Andrews every Monday, Wednesday, and Friday. But why is everyone else aboard station? Don't they have pretty much the same things there as they do here?"

"God, I can tell you've never been on-ship before." Laughing again and looking into his eyes, she waited until she had his attention before passing on this little tidbit of wisdom. "Yes, the facilities are the same—hell, this is a new ship and the facilities are probably better—but the station is not the ship. We're going to be stuck in this tin can for a long time. No need to stare at the bulkheads any more than necessary. Savvy?"

"Makes sense to me."

"Okay, now that we've got your gear stowed, let's go. I'll show you around your new home."

"Yes, Corporal," Alan said stiffly. Her casual humor and seeming devil-may-care attitude made him nervous, and he wondered how he was supposed to act. Tracy apparently saw his discomfort, and she burst out laughing, slapping the table as she stood.

"Tracy," she reminded him. "Once you get settled and loosen up a bit, I think you're going to fit right in with this fire team."

"Let me ask you something, Tracy," Alan started timorously, trying to shake his nervousness as they stepped through the hatch and began to walk down the passageway. "If everyone is out enjoying their time off, why aren't you? Not that I don't appreciate what you're doing."

"Well, Alan, lets just say our estimable squad leader, Lieutenant Dietz, does not seem to have a sense of humor as developed as mine—though he does seem to have vindictive streak a kilometer wide. He took the entire squad down to Georgetown for a unit party." She looked at Alan, shaking her head ruefully. "While I'm confined to the ship for the duration of our stay in port."

"What did you do?"

"Do you want the long version or the short version?"

"The long version, of course."

"Well, Lance Corporal Lewis, this is what happened," she began as they continued down the passageway. Alan could not help but laugh as her story unfolded, but he began worrying about fitting in. His new fire-team leader apparently had limitless energy, boundless enthusiasm, and a very questionable sense of humor. Regardless of whether or not he fit in, it looked as if he had managed, once again, to get himself in the middle of what seemed to be developing into a very interesting situation.

"The story of my life," he sighed as Tracy continued to regale him with stories of her "humorous" activities.

Chapter Twenty-two

USS *VALHALLA*
OCTOBER 13, 2197
0845Z
SOL

Newly promoted Commander Elaine "Barbie" Grant, former squadron commander of Valkyrie Flight 127, assigned USS *Fenris*, now wing commander of Valkyrie Wing 115, assigned USS *Valhalla*, strode across the hangar deck toward her waiting fighter.

Seeing a figure dressed in flight gear standing beside it, she quickened her pace. The man must have sensed her approach, because he turned to face her as she drew up behind him. Dressed in flight gear, it was difficult for her to determine what kind of build he had, but he was the same height as she. Helmet tucked under one arm and with his other hand on his hip, he stood there cockily. Jet-black hair, obviously pushing the grooming standards, dark brown eyes, and a pencil-thin mustache only added to his demeanor. All and all, she thought he looked like the stereotypical hotshot flier. She was not impressed.

"Ah, Commander Grant, how nice to meet you. I'm Commander Socha, your new RIO," he said, cheerfully extending his hand, seemingly oblivious to the glare she directed at him. Hesitating for a moment, then letting his hand drop when she did not accept it, he continued to smile. "Not much for conversation, are you?"

"You're not supposed to be here." she accused him.

"I am assuming you were expecting Lieutenant Eichinger." He waited for her nod before continuing. "Yes, well, the CAG decided that you've had enough time to torture potential candidates. You've gone through, what, three in two days, I believe?"

"Something like that."

"There you have it. Oh, and don't get your hopes up that I'll be number four. I guarantee you there is nothing you can do in this bird that I can't handle. You won't get me puking my guts up like your last victim."

"You think so, do you?" she said in a mildly interested voice.

"Most certainly. This is the latest model Valkyrie, equipped with all the latest systems available." Still smiling, Socha turned toward the waiting Valkyrie and patted the fuselage. When he turned back, his smile had become an evil grin. "I was on one of the flight teams that helped test it. You may push the envelope, Commander, but I defined the envelope. So, like I said, your auditions are over. Now it's time to have some fun."

"This is not fun."

"Of course it is. It's flying, and flying is always fun. Hell, it's even better than sex," he exclaimed, spreading his arms, voice cheery once again. "Sure, there are some risks involved, but that just adds a little spice."

Dropping her helmet and reaching out, Barbie grabbed the front of Socha's flight harness and hurled him up again the plane.

"Are you out of your fucking mind?!" she shouted at him incredulously. "This is not a fucking game."

"Really?" Socha's innocent voice only angered her more. Not believing what she was hearing, Barbie shook him, trying to knock some sense into the man.

"God damn it, this is serious!"

"Dangerous?"

"Yes!" Veins standing out on her neck as she yelled at the man in her grip.

"People can die?"

"Yes! People can die!" Barbie's shouts could be heard above the din of the hangar deck.

"Like Digger?" Socha asked softly.

●   ●   ●

Commander David Socha stared into the face of the woman who held him pinned up against the side of a Valkyrie. Watching as her expression changed from white-hot anger to confusion and sorrow, he felt a swelling of sympathy for the woman whose walls he had just shattered.

"Digger?" she said, and Socha could feel her grip on his harness loosen as she stumbled back almost as if he had punched her. Which, in a way, he had.

"Yes, Digger." He kept his voice soft and level.

Socha and the CAG had met in flight school and had developed a deep friendship. Each had owed the other innumerable favors, so when his old friend had approached him about the problems his wing commander was having, he agreed to help. He would have helped in any case, regardless of their friendship. He knew what the young woman in front of him was going through; he had been there himself.

"What do you know about it?" Her anger was clearly returning.

"I know he is dead, and I know that you miss him." Hating himself for it, he continued, knowing that he would be setting her off again, "And you need to get over it."

Yes, that definitely set her off.

"Get over it?! He was my best friend." Her voice echoed around the hangar deck. "I flew with him for years. I was closer to him than to any other person in my life, and you expect me to just get over it?" Socha watched as tears began to stream down her face. A good sign.

"Yes, I do. Because you don't have a choice."

"What the hell is that supposed to mean?"

"You're the wing commander. You've got responsibilities, and you can't let your personal feelings get in the way of that."

"I'm not. I'm doing my job." The accusation in her voice was unmistakable.

"Really? What do you call three RIOs in two days?" He saw he had made his point when the look of guilt flashed across her face. Hanging her head, she spoke so softly that he almost missed it.

"I'm sorry."

"Barbie." he began, and, not getting a response, he tried a different approach. "Elaine, look at me."

Barbie raised her head to look him in the face. He could see the shame and grief plainly evident beneath the tears.

"You're the best pilot in the fleet, and we need you. Not some soulless automaton just going through the motions. You."

"I want to," she sobbed, "but I just... I can't..." Her mouth worked soundlessly as Socha watched her search for the words.

"I know."

"What should I do?"

"Well, the first thing you should do is cancel this morning's flight." he said, bending down and retrieving their helmets. "You're in no condition to fly right now, and besides, you don't need to audition any more RIOs, do you?"

"I guess not." Giving him a small smile.

"Then"—handing her helmet to her, then putting his arm around her shoulders, he began to walk toward the hatch of First Squadron's ready room—"What do you say we get out of this flight gear, find something to drink, and toast Digger and the rest of our fallen comrades?"

"I think I'd like that."

"And after that"—his voice taking on a cold and vicious edge—"we kill every Xan-Sskarn that crosses our path."

Chapter Twenty-three

Captain Alexandra McLaughlin sat at the head of a long conference table, looking at the assembled officers seated around it. Unlike her previous commands, it looked as if the designers of the *Valhalla* had actually taken into account that the captain of a ship might like to be able gather all of her senior staff in the ward room at one time without the room becoming claustrophobic.

Quiet, individual conversations took place as the last of the chairs filled, and Alex took this time to survey her new command staff.

Seated in her customary position to the right of her captain, Commander Grace "Heron" Denton sat quietly, reading a pad. Craning her neck slightly, Alex could see that her oldest friend was once again firmly engrossed with a technical manual. Alex had been relieved when she received the news that Heron had been assigned as the *Valhalla*'s chief engineer. Normally that position would have been filled weeks, if not months ago, and it had been; however, High Command thought that the man's experience would be of greater use overseeing the completion of

217

one of the *Valhalla*'s sister ships and hopefully speeding it up. So Commander Denton had fallen into the position, being the most qualified candidate available. Taking a closer look at her friend, she could see the dark circles under her eyes and slight slump of her shoulders. Obviously, events aboard the *Fenris*, along with her rush to learn as much as possible about the ship she was expected to keep flying, had taken their toll. She made a mental note to talk to her and get her to take a break.

Next to Heron, Alex's new senior tactical officer sat sipping coffee, occasionally trying to engage the officer sitting next to him in conversation. Having read his file did not stop her from being shocked at his stature. While Commander Michael Fain might be only a few centimeters taller and a few kilos heavier than she, he did not have the look of a teenager that she possessed. Three years her junior, he could easily pass for fifteen years her senior. Stark white hair and a deeply lined, gaunt face made him appear fragile until Alex saw the glint in his eyes.

Normally Alex did not put too much stock in file facts. Too many officers, in her opinion, were sycophants and ass-kissers and had received their excellent fitness reports because of these skills rather than for a more-than-adequate performance of their duties.

Looking into Commander Fain's eyes, she did not doubt the veracity of his file when it noted him as being a devilishly effective tactical officer. Alex could not put her finger on it, but despite his appearance, something about the man screamed predator.

The target of Commander Fain's attempt at conversation was a powerfully built lieutenant junior grade. His dark skin only a few shades lighter than the uniform jacket he wore, Emanuel Green possessed the same laconic attitude he had aboard the *Fenris*, but the haunted look was new. Happy that her recommendation for his early promotion was approved, Alex knew that he deserved it, and more. She had taken him into battles before, but never into a bloodbath like the one they had barely survived. He had per-formed admirably, and while he wore the expression of someone who had seen too much in a short period of time, the set of his jaw clearly showed that his animosity toward the Xan-Sskarns had grown exponentially. The hate radiating from him was almost a physical thing, and Alex felt concerned that it might slip from a dedicated focus to a dangerous obsession. But then, she did not have room to talk when it came to obsessions.

Compared to Green, the man seated beside him seemed to be a nonentity. Alex's new senior medical officer, Commander John Stratis, sat chatting with the officer seated across from him, twirling the stylus of his pad idly in his fingers. From what she had read of his file, he did not seem to be the kind of man who put much stock in military decorum, and his present mode of dress attested to that. With a white dress shirt, open at the collar, under a white medical lab coat, he seemed oblivious to the fact that he stood out. He did not even have any rank or rating tabs on his abbreviated uniform; the only badge that he did wear was the symbol of his profession, a caduceus, embroidered in red on the chest pocket of his coat. Taking a closer look at him, Alex saw a man who appeared to avoid the gym until just prior to his annual PFT. His thinning long, plain brown hair, shot though with gray, was slicked back, and he sported anachronistic eyeglasses behind which muddy brown eyes resided—he appeared to be nothing more than a dumpy, middle-aged man. His complexion, still darkly tanned, told her that he had just come from a dirtside command. Alex's eyes, drawn once again to the stylus dancing in nimble fingers, came to the conclusion that this man spent more time practicing his profession than practicing being a naval officer. Having never been under his care, she couldn't attest to his competency as a doctor or as a surgeon, but she hoped for the sake of her crew, and for his as well, that he was as good as his record indicated.

Alex had sent more than one incompetent medical officer packing with a fitness report almost guaranteed to get them dismissed from the medical field, let alone the navy. She would have felt more comfortable with Dr. Swartz remaining on as her SMO. The good doctor, however, refused to have her patients from the *Fenris* under anyone else's care but her own. Which is where Dr. Stratis and his unknown level of competency came in; only time would allow him to show his worth, and they did not have much time.

Dr. Stratis' conversation partner was the *Valhalla's* communications officer, Lieutenant Commander Lea Albers. One hundred sixty-five centimeters tall and weighing in at sixty-six kilos, with chin-length hair and hazel eyes, Lea looked like nothing more than an average woman with a stocky build and a long face. Slightly bucked teeth and heavily lidded eyes, along with her stature, gave the impression of a slow, unimaginative person. That is, until one listened to the constant flow of speech she seemed unable to contain. Her appearance fell away in the listener's mind, and the image was replaced with a highly intelligent, well-spoken, professional officer.

From what Alex could see, Lea could maintain several fast-paced conversations simultaneously and knew exactly where she was in each at any given moment. Lea's record, stating that she was a preeminent communications specialist, with an innate ability to find and track any type of signal, was another that Alex would take with a grain of salt until she could form her own opinion. Though she did not have a problem believing the section in her new comm officer's bio that the woman had a tendency to maintain a running dialog with anyone within earshot. Alex grinned at that, thinking that Lea and Greg would get along swimmingly, until, with a pang of regret she remembered that Greg was still dirtside, confined to a critical-care unit. Her smile vanished in an instant. Maybe it was a good thing Doc Swartz was staying behind.

Another officer whom Lea had engaged in conversation—a separate conversation, Alex noted—was a tall blond officer with intent gray eyes. Jeffrey Tucholski, chief navigation officer, tried to get a word in edgewise but seemed to be limited to short, very short, answers or statements. He looked as if he didn't mind the situation, and Alex guessed that the lieutenant commander had served with Albers before and was used to it. Closing her eyes for a moment, Alex reviewed his fitness reports in her head, just as she had done for all the other new faces around the table. Of all the evals she had read on her new command staff, Tucholski's was by far the easiest for Alex to believe. Even more so than Commander Fain's. Average officer, not overly assertive or imaginative, content to let others take the lead, unimposing. In short, the perfect mathematician. Which, for all intents and purposes, was the job definition of a navigation officer. Alex recalled his academy math scores, and the attached solutions to several extremely difficult navigational exercises he had faced throughout his career; they were all within the top zero point five percentile. Hard evidence proving his competency. She only wished it were possible to provide such evidence for all officers.

The last two officers seated to her left were both old faces: Commander Grant and Commander Kaufman. Alex noted that Barbie looked both better and worse than when she had met with the pilot two days ago to inform her of her promotion and new position. Gone was the soulless look in her eyes, along with the rigid tenseness Grant had adopted after the death of her RIO in their last battle. The puffy red eyes and flushed face, as if she had been crying, were new, but despite these new additions Alex could see that Barbie was more relaxed, and some of her old confidence had returned. The brilliant smile and easy demeanor were still missing, and she still had a slightly haunted look about her, but Alex knew it was only a matter of time before Barbie returned to her old self.

Commander Kaufman, on the other hand, looked nothing but worse than the last time Alex had seen him in the *Fenris'* galley. Still bandaged, missing the last two fingers of his left hand, and sporting a limp from a still-healing broken femur, Alex could not tell if he had begged, bribed, or bullied his way out of Folkvang's sick bay, but she was not going to look into the situation too closely. She wanted and needed her CAG's experience and leadership down in *Valhalla's* hangar decks.

The only person missing from this meeting was the marine battalion commander, Colonel Douglas Hendrix. Alex had received his message that he and his XO would be dirtside conferring with Marine High Command and would be returning aboard on the fifteen-hundred shuttle.

Thinking of executive officers brought Alex's mind to the man sitting at the foot of the table, directly across from her. Commander Anthony Ruggs, her new XO. Alex had never served with him before, but his reputation had preceded him; she knew him to be an outstanding officer and a trusted, proven leader. Though not as tall as Greg, Tony, as he liked to be called, still towered over her at one hundred seventy-six centimeters. Alex guessed he massed somewhere in the neighborhood of eighty-five kilos. He wasn't overly muscled, but it was obvious that he kept himself in shape. He had an open face, dominated by both an aquiline nose and a bushy gray mustache. His hair, matching his mustache, was mostly gray, flecked with black, and stood out in stark contrast to his dark complexion. Whereas Dr. Stratis' skin tone was obviously the result of long-term solar exposure, it was just as readily evident that Tony's was due to his Mediterranean ancestry. What Alex noticed most about her new XO was his eyes. She remembered her first impression of them when she had initially boarded, thinking they were a soft, sleepy brown. After he had escorted her to the command deck and she had officially taken command of the *Valhalla*, she had spoken with him at length. During that conversation, Alex was held enthralled by how intent his gaze was, and she saw both great compassion and great intelligence there. She knew then that he was not a man to underestimate, and that his reputation was well-deserved.

Alex coughed lightly and cleared her throat to get everyone's attention. It was time to start this meeting.

"Okay, ladies and gentlemen, let's make this fast, as we still have a lot to do before we launch this afternoon," Alex said, getting the meeting rolling. She pulled her cigarette case from her jacket pocket and extracted one. "Smoke 'em if you got 'em." She then offered the case to Commander Kaufman, who took one with a nod of thanks. Alex heard Dr. Stratis tsking as he watched not only Alex and Kaufman, but Tony as well, blow smoke before settling down.

"Let me start off by saying that I'm sorry, but there is no time for pleasantries right now. Normally I like to start off my first staff meeting by getting to know all of my officers, but we're racing against the clock. We are to rendezvous with Admiral Tanner's Home Fleet ASAP so he can transfer his flag from the carrier *Heimdall* to the *Valhalla*, and to that end we are scheduled to launch at eighteen hundred today. So let's dive right in," Alex said in a matter-of-fact voice, the tone of command unmistakable.

"Heron, status report."

Heron had placed her data pad on the table during Alex's opening comments. Now she retrieved it, double-checking her answers before replying.

"Well, Captain, looks to me like the yard did one hell of a job putting her together. I've gone over the reports of my predecessor and can't find any of the usual post-trial-run repairs or problems that typically turn up. All engines are on line, the Humptys are good to go, and the P-Drive is fully functional. All in all, she looks ready to run to me."

"Good to hear." Alex nodded toward her friend and then turned her gaze on to her tactical officer. "Commander Fain, weapon status, please."

"Yes, ma'am," Fain answered in a raspy voice, and, sitting up straighter in his chair, he closed his eyes for a moment, recalling the information Alex had requested.

"All energy mounts are fully functional and have only a minimal amount of wear on the focusing lenses. Basically, only what accrued during *Valhalla*'s gunnery trials. Also, we are the first ship to have the newest model of focusing servos, giving us an additional thousand-kilometer range on our energy mounts. Unfortunately, even with the increased range, distance and jamming still leave missiles as our long-range weapon of choice, but the first Xan-Sskarn we meet that are foolish enough to get within our new energy envelope will get a nasty surprise." A ghost of a smile appeared on his face before he continued. "Missile and KEW launchers are at one hundred percent. PDLs and PDGs are all tied into the point-defense computer, and diagnostics on that are all in the green." He opened his eyes, and Alex felt his gaze lock onto her.

"We are armed to the teeth, and my crews and I are ready to dish out a world of hurt," Fain growled.

Yes, definitely a predator, Alex thought, then pulled herself away from his cold, dead gaze, glancing down at her pad and the list of questions she had prepared.

"With this heavy a weapons load-out, what is the status of consumables?"

"All magazines are completely stocked, and as I am sure the captain is aware, the *Valhalla* carries several manufacturing plants that are capable of an impressive range of output, including ordnance for both the launchers and the PDGs." A rare smile crossed the commander's face.

"Which, I must say, is a great relief to me, ma'am. Because you are right—we *are* packing a massive weapons load-out, and if we didn't have the capability of rearming ourselves, we would burn through all of our on-board magazines in any kind of prolonged engagement, and I hate having to wait on tenders."

"It's a relief to me as well, Commander." Alex returned his smile. "And I know what you mean—I don't like waiting on tenders any more than you do. I always feel vulnerable during a reload."

"Ensi—" Alex began, then caught herself. "Sorry, I mean, *Lieutenant* Green, how are your sensors? You going to be able to find some Sallys for Commander Fain to play with?" Alex knew how best to address her questions or concerns to her former crew members to set them at ease. If it had not been for his dark complexion, Alex was sure that he would be blushing furiously. As it was, a grin found its way onto the lieutenant's face as he looked down at the table top.

"I don't think I'll have a problem finding playmates for the commander." Green's deep baritone filled the wardroom as he tried to fit into his surroundings. Alex could see that he was well aware of the fact that he was the most junior officer present by a wide margin and was making a conscious effort not to be intimidated by it.

"The *Valhalla*'s sensor suite is light-years ahead of the *Fenris*." Green looked around guiltily as what he had just said registered.

The face of every member of the *Fenris*' crew around the table closed as each of them turned their thoughts inward to memories that haunted them.

Alex was the first to shake herself out of this retrospection. She had had quite a bit of practice in the last few days. She saw Lieutenant Junior Grade Green open his mouth in what she suspected was an apology, and Alex knew that no matter what he said, it would only make the situation more uncomfortable. So, she decided to spare him the embarrassment.

"Thank you, Emanuel," Alex said as she watched Green close his mouth, a sheepish expression still on his face. *Oh, well,* she thought to herself, *we've all tasted our fair share of boot leather. It comes with growing up.*

"Doctor, how are things down in sick bay?"

"Thankfully quiet, ma'am." Stratis was still leaning back in his chair, twirling his stylus, seeming oblivious to the stares his casual attitude drew from the other assembled officers.

"Though," he continued, "I would like to see both yourself and Commander Kaufman down in my neck of the woods as quickly as you can manage it. You both have suffered severe trauma, and I want to make sure that whoever put you back together again knew what he was doing."

Alex was not quite sure what to make of the doctor's statement. It made sense that he would want to check up on both her and Kaufman's injuries, but the way he had presented his request left her wondering if he was speaking from bravado, or, like some of her own past observations, experience in dealing with somewhat dubious medical practitioners.

"I'll be sure to stop by as soon as my duties permit." Alex felt safe in that response. While she knew how to treat with her former crew, she was still feeling her way with the new and didn't want to start things off on the wrong foot by rubbing someone the wrong way.

"Which, of course, means I'll see you sometime six months from now." The doctor's smile was infectious, and Alex felt herself responding in kind. She was starting to like this man and was getting the feeling that he *was* as good as his records indicated.

"I see you've dealt with reticent captains before, Doctor," Alex said.

"One or two," Stratis responded. Sitting up, stylus halting its twirling, his smile vanished as he continued in a brisk, professional tone. "Seriously, though, Captain, I would feel much better if I could see how you are recovering from your injuries. Commander Kaufman as well."

"Very well, Doctor, as soon as my duties permit," Alex replied just as professionally. "Commander Kaufman as well." She could see the grimace on the CAG's face at that, but he kept any comments to himself and just nodded his assent to the doctor.

"Thank you, Captain," Stratis said, leaning back in his chair, his stylus beginning to dance in his hands once more.

"Lieutenant Commander Albers, if you please." Alex turned her attention to the other side of the table.

"Oh, communications is just fine, Captain. I've got a small variance in one of the phased arrays, but I have two of my techs and one of Commander Denton's engineering crew looking at it right now. They should have the jitter tracked down and taken care of soon. Other than that, everything is looking good." Lea's words seemed almost to run together.

Alex stared at the young woman as she continued to recite the status of her department, amazed not only at how fast the woman was speaking but at the fact that it appeared that Lea had yet to take a breath.

"*Thank you*, Commander," Alex said forcefully, realizing that if she did not interrupt, her communications officer would happily report the status of every single circuit of the *Valhalla*'s entire communication network. Then she would no doubt move on to every one of her communication techs. Alex was grateful to see that her interruption of Lea's litany had not seemed to upset the young woman. Lea had simply beamed a very toothy smile at her and settled back into her chair with a content look on her face.

"My turn, I believe, Captain?" Jeffrey Tucholski asked, seeming to break with his evaluations by showing some initiative and speaking up. But it seemed to be a short-lived personality change, as he remained silent, staring at Alex, obviously waiting.

"Yes, Commander," Alex finally said, realizing that Tucholski was not going to say anything more until he was asked, "it is indeed. Proceed."

"Yes, ma'am." He cleared his throat and leaned forward, resting his forearms on the table. "Currently, all navigation systems check out at one hundred percent. I have full response from both the Particle Drive as well as the Heisenberg Umeko Muxlo Dimensional Drive."

Alex was surprised to hear the full name of the jump engines used. She couldn't even recall the last time she'd heard the proper name for them. From the looks of the rest of the staff, they were surprised as well, all except Lea Albers. Alex surmised that the reason for that was that Lea lived to hear as many long, complex words spoken as possible. Even if she was not the one using them. She gave a mental chuckle at that, while continuing to watch Tucholski.

He had paused in his report, and it took Alex a moment to realize that he was waiting for her to tell him to continue. She was definitely going to have to do something about this young man's initiative and self-confidence, but now was not the time for that.

"Please continue, Commander."

"Yes, ma'am." He cleared his throat again, as if starting over from the beginning. Thankfully that was not that case, as he had a tendency to speak slowly and deliberately. The antithesis of his bouncy friend, Lea.

"I have several course plots for our rendezvous with Admiral Tanner on my board at this time, all of which are constantly updating as we speak. I have nothing else to report at this time, ma'am," Tucholski ended formally.

At least he's thorough, Alex thought. *Multiple, updating course plots are a pain in the ass to maintain for any long period of time, especially with all of those different variables. Just thinking about it gives me a headache, but Tucholski seems to love it. Well, more power to him. As long as he gets me where I want to go as quickly as possible, he can crunch as many numbers as he wants.*

"Barbie?" Alex asked, turning her attention to her new wing commander.

"Well, Skipper, I've got ten full squadrons down on the hangar decks. One hundred forty Valkyries, and all of them the new variant," Barbie said proudly.

"Ten squadrons—that's a big step up. You up to the challenge?" Alex knew that Barbie was, but it was more important that Barbie think that she was equal to the task. Alex shouldn't have worried.

"Oh, it's a bit overwhelming, but I'm sure I'll manage. Besides, I've got some damn good flight teams down there." Talking about her people seemed to light the fires in her eyes, lifting her one step closer to her old self.

"How do you have your squadrons bedded down?"

"I conferred with Hangman here"—Barbie nodded her head toward Commander Kaufman—"and we decided to go with odd squadrons port, even starboard, and subdivide the wing into two flights, Alpha and Bravo."

Alex, while not a Valkyrie pilot herself, knew fighter doctrine well enough to understand the reasoning behind the split. All of fleet's ships of the line carried Valkyries, and one could not command such a ship without knowing how to deploy those Valkyries correctly. So she knew that splitting the wing into two flights would allow her to run fighter ops round the clock, with each flight taking shifts, or, in a worst-case scenario, should either flight deck or even the flight itself be taken out of commission, viable command cohesion would be maintained.

"Anything else?"

"No, ma'am. I've checked on all my birds, and they're all fully functional. My pilots are ready to ride." She turned her gaze to Commander Fain and Lieutenant Green. "I just hope that when you two boys find your playmates, you don't forget to invite me to the party."

That elicited a bark of laughter from Fain, but Green only smiled, obviously still embarrassed by his *faux pas* earlier in the meeting. The rest of the assembled officers laughed lightly as well.

"Okay people, settle down," Alex said as she chuckled herself, checking the time on her pad. "We're almost finished here, and the sooner we wrap this up, the sooner we can adjourn for lunch."

The laughter died down quickly as all eyes turned toward Commander Kaufman.

"Well, CAG, looks like you have everyone's undivided attention," Alex told Kaufman. "So, what have you got for us?"

"Yes, ma'am." Kaufman winced in pain as he tried to sit up straighter in his chair. "You all heard what Barbie had to say regarding the Valkyrie wing, so that takes care of that. As for the rest, well, down in the bays I've got a handful of shuttles, enough assault boats to land the entire battalion in one flight, and five Lokis. Plus full flight crews for all of my birds, so I'm sitting pretty. No double shifts for anyone, at least not right now."

He looked down at his mangled hand as he said the last, and Alex's gaze followed his. They both knew, as did every one else in the compartment, that, unfortunately, the circumstances that had Kaufman's department and the rest of theirs at full manning would not last for long once the war caught up with them again.

Alex looked around the table and nodded, satisfied with the individual department reports she had just received. All that was left now was to hear the overall ship status, and for that she turned her gaze on the man seated at the far end of the table.

"Commander Ruggs, how are things proceeding for today's launch?"

"Everything seems to be going fine, ma'am." Commander Ruggs held up his pad and began to scroll through the information there, reading off the important highlights to his captain.

"We have about fifty personnel on-station for various reasons. Otherwise we are fully manned, and all sections report full operational status. Our supplies are almost finished loading and should be complete within the next hour. As Commander Fain indicated, all weapon magazines are fully stocked, and the armory is fully equipped as well. With the exception of the marine battalion, the *Valhalla* could be ready to launch within the next sixty minutes." Tony set his pad down as he finished his recital.

"Very good." Alex smiled across at him. "Status of the battalion?"

"As you know, both the CO and the XO are dirtside for a briefing. However, as to the rest of the battalion, Colonel Hendrix issued a seventy-two-hour liberty, so a vast majority of the battalion is not on-ship at the moment. Most are on the station, but approximately twenty percent of the unit is dirtside. They should be returning on today's shuttle, and I know that the colonel has an afternoon formation scheduled, so we should have his manning reports within minutes of formation's end." Tony chuckled now. "And I wouldn't worry too much as to the contents of that report. Colonel Hendrix runs a tight ship, and if even one of his marines is missing, well, he will wish that he had dropped on the Sally home world rather than face the colonel's wrath."

"That bad, huh?" Alex asked. She had never served with, or even met, her marine counterpart.

"From the talk I have heard from his junior officers in the club, even worse. He takes his job very, very seriously, and he expects the same from his people. If he doesn't get it, they find themselves transferred to another unit before they know what's happening. Hell, I've had to vet two transfer orders in the last month, as he found some weak links while training."

"Well, sounds like he's got things under control down in Marine Country. As long as he's there when we need him, he can run his unit any way he pleases." Alex leaned back in her chair and extinguished her cigarette. "I know for a fact that the Corps does not hand out battalion commands capriciously, especially detached commands aboard ship, so if Hendrix has command, he knows what he's doing."

Alex sipped the last of her coffee and watched her staff over the rim of the cup. She could see them begin to shift in their seats, obviously ready for the meeting to be concluded and to head back to work. She had the makings of an outstanding command crew, and she knew that it would not take much for her and Tony to mold them into such. Her only concern lay with her new XO. She didn't know him well enough yet to know if the two of them would gel and be able to function as efficiently as she hoped. She didn't think that there would be any issues, not with an officer with his reputation, but one could never tell. Alex decided it was time to get started, and to find out.

"Thank you, ladies and gentlemen." She set her cup down and sat up straight in her chair, eyes intent and face set in a serious mien. "That was a very complete and thorough status update. You've all done a great job. Now I would like to invite you all down to the galley for lunch, and to see if we can all get to know one another a bit better in less official surroundings. Unless anyone has any objections?"

Alex added the last as a polite courtesy, not expecting any. Woe be it to any officer who could not attend to a captain's *request* for their company at a meal. Especially when it was this specific captain. Her reputation had preceded her as well.

"Very well, then." She pushed her chair back and began to rise. The rest of the officers in the room, the doctor included, shot to rigid attention before she had completed her motion. Alex felt a flush of pleasure at that. The speed with which her crew had moved showed her that she already had their respect, and that they were already beginning to merge into one entity. The majority of the battle for a cohesive, confident command staff won, all that remained was to smooth down the rough edges, and her lunch invitation seemed a good way in which to begin.

"Dismissed."

All of her officers broke into movement at her words and began to move toward the hatch, conversations beginning almost immediately. All but one. Commander Tony ·Ruggs stood next to his chair, looking at her. Lieutenant Green was the last officer to leave the compartment, and when the hatch cycled shut, the *Valhalla*'s executive officer spoke.

"Captain, request permission to speak freely."

Tony watched as a shocked expression passed over his captain's bruised face, and an uncomfortable feeling began to develop in the pit of his stomach. He wasn't looking forward to this discussion, but he knew it had to be done. His duty demanded it of him.

"Of course, Commander. Always." Alex recovered from her surprise and moved toward him.

Tony saw that she stopped at the chair next to his and indicated his own seat as she took hers. Now it was his turn to be shocked; he had not expected the captain to come and sit next to him, as if this were going to be just any other conversation. He didn't doubt that even though she might not suspect the topic, she had to know that it was likely to be unpleasant.

"Thank you, ma'am," Tony said as he resumed his seat and watched as she settled more comfortably into her own, an open, inviting look on her face despite the quizzical glance she directed toward him.

"So, what's on your mind, Tony?" Her tone was not demanding, and Tony could see that she was going to wait for him to get his thoughts in order before beginning.

"Well, to be frank, ma'am, I'm concerned about the ... I'm not quite sure how to say it." He paused, searching for the right word to use in this delicate situation.

"Go ahead, Commander. Just tell me what you have on your mind. I promise not to bite your head off."

"Yes, ma'am. I'm concerned about the effectiveness of some of the crew."

"And by some of the crew, you mean the members that transferred aboard from the *Fenris*." It was not a question.

"Yes."

"I see. Why?" Her tone held no venom or rancor, and Tony was grateful for that. This was difficult enough as it stood.

"Well, let me first say that I have no doubt, no doubt whatsoever, as to the competency, dedication, or bravery of any man or woman from the *Fenris*. As far as I am concerned, they have all proven themselves in the most difficult situation I can possibly imagine, and I am honored to serve with any of you."

He watched as Alex took that in, and she seemed to give the feeling that she had picked up on something, though she gave no physical signs of it.

"I am sure they would be flattered to hear that, Commander. They have indeed passed through the fire and proven their worth. We both agree on that, so tell me what exactly is the source of your concern." Though still not hostile, Alex was clearly not fully open and inviting anymore, either.

"Please, ma'am, understand that I mean no disrespect." How to say what needed to be said, but in such a way as not to alienate his captain had Tony in a bind. "It's hard to explain."

"Try."

Alex's voice was flatly neutral now. Tony could see that he was dangerously close to setting her off, and he did not doubt that rumors of his new captain's temper were *not* greatly exaggerated. But then again, his reputation had been earned as well.

"Okay. I've spent time with several of the *Fenris*' crew since they have come on board—Commander Denton, Commander Grant, and Lieutenant Green in particular."

"I had gathered as much." Alex's voice was slightly warmer. "I see that everyone on board is wearing their sidearm. I figured that someone had told you about my standing order."

"Yes, ma'am. Commander Denton."

"Good." Tony watched as her expression closed again. "I'm sorry, Commander. You were saying?"

"After talking with them, and others from the *Fenris*, I observed that while every single one of you is performing outstandingly, there seems to be a heavy aura of sorrow surrounding you." He sought Alex's eyes with his own and held her gaze. "I know there hasn't been time to recover from that kind of experience, let alone mourn your friends. And I know how that can haunt a crew."

Tony cocked an eyebrow at the way Alex reacted when he said the word "haunt." She jerked in her seat as if she had been punched.

"Commander Ruggs," Alex started, then stopped for a moment before beginning again. "Tony, I noticed that twice you switched from referring to the *Fenris*' crew as 'them' to 'you.' I take it you are including me in your concerns? I would appreciate an honest answer, Commander. You have my word that it won't go beyond this compartment."

"Yes, ma'am, I am," Tony answered directly, without hesitation.

"You do realize that I have been cleared by the shrinks dirtside as fit for command?" she asked, obviously playing devil's advocate.

His only response was to drop his gaze to the black skull and wings pinned to the left breast of her jacket. He looked back up into her eyes and saw a small smirk, just the upturn of the right corner of her mouth, appear for a fleeting moment. He found that he was not surprised when she did not try to defend herself. Here sat a woman who was honest enough in her self-assessment to realize that she was not perfect, that she had flaws, and worked to correct them. Her right hand stroked her chin in what he was sure was an unconscious action while she thought for a moment.

"Let me reassure you, Commander"—her voice held no anger, Tony noted with interest, only the unmistakable inflection of command—"that I am confident in the abilities of *every* member of this crew, and I will give each of them the benefit of the doubt. However, if *anyone* aboard this ship performs to less than the best of their abilities, I will relieve them immediately. Am I understood?"

Tony caught all the nuances of that statement, and he understood them quite clearly. Captain McLaughlin would not play favorites among her crew, but, on the other hand, neither would she tolerate any prejudices. He would be expected to extend the same benefit of the doubt to the crew of the *Fenris* as she was to the crew of the *Valhalla*. He also understood that if he didn't, he could very well find *himself* relieved of duty.

"Perfectly, ma'am. Please understand it was never my intention to insult you or any member of the *Fenris*." Tony watched her relax now, and felt better for it. "I am sure you will do what you have done in the past."

"And what's that, Commander?" The light tremor was evident in her voice once more.

"Perform your duty to your crew, just like you have always done." Tony had meant for that to be a reassurance of his confidence in her abilities. It clearly was not taken as such. He watched as the blood drained from her face, leaving her paper white, and her breath came in shallow rasps as her eyes lost focus, as if seeing something only she could see.

"Captain?" he said worriedly and watched her shake herself back to lucidity. "Are you alright?"

"What? Oh, fine, just fine. Still get a twinge from the ribs now and then. They're not quite fully healed yet." She gave him a reassuring look.

"Of course, I understand. Been there myself a few times." Tony decided to play along with her explanation. It was plain that there was something else going on, but if she didn't want to talk about it, then there was nothing he could do about it, as long as it did not interfere with her performance. If it did, then he bloody well *would* do something about it.

"I'm glad you brought this up now, Commander, and not later. I would have hated for us to have been working at cross-purposes, especially in light of the current situation. We can ill afford anything other than a unified front." She began to rise as she spoke, clearly indicating this conversation was over. "I hope that your concerns about the crew have been addressed?"

"Yes, ma'am, they have. Thank you."

"Good. Now let's get down to the galley. I am sure everyone is wondering where we got off to."

"After you, Captain." Tony stepped aside and indicated that she should precede him out of the compartment.

"Thank you, Commander." Alex dipped her head in his direction and started off. Tony followed her through the hatch, where she could not see the doubt crossing his face.

Yes, my doubts about the crew have been taken care of, Captain McLaughlin. But I am starting to have some doubts about you.

Chapter Twenty-four

USS *VALHALLA*
OCTOBER 13, 2197
1100Z
SOL

    Corporal Clark and Lance Corporal Lewis continued to trek through the *Valhalla*'s passageways, Clark pointing out different areas and what took place in some of the more interesting parts of the ship.

"Tracy, just how long have you been on this ship?" Lewis asked after a particularly involved explanation of the contents of several compartments they had just passed on their way toward the hangar deck.

"Oh, I'd say about three or four weeks. Why?" Clark said, still pointing out items of interest. Or things *she* found interesting, anyway. Lewis thought that he could have gone a lifetime without knowing the intimate details of a waste-reclamation unit.

"Well, it's just that you seem to know where everything is, and how it all works. Just kind of surprising is all."

"Well, Alan,"—she turned one of her fabulous smiles on him, making his heart beat just a bit faster as she explained—"first off, I'm Recon, just like you are. Now, remember one of our jobs is to be pathfinders. So, keeping that in mind, I decided to find out where everything on the ship was. I figured I might as well get the lay of the land. You never know when it can come in handy."

"Like, say, if we were ever boarded?"

"Exactly."

"Okay, I can understand that, but how did you do it in only a few weeks? This place is huge." Lewis waved his hands around, indicating the ship as a whole.

"We're on-ship, Alan." The way she said it made it clear that this should be answer enough. It wasn't.

"Yeah, I kind of noticed that." After spending several long hours together with the corporal, he felt comfortable enough to let his somewhat sarcastic sense of humor out.

Alan took several more steps before he realized that Tracy had stopped in the middle of the passageway. He stood to one side as a pair of ratings walked by, then made his way back to her side.

"Remember what I said about staring at the same bulkheads day in and day out?" Tracy asked him as she took his arm and led him to one side of the passageway. Alan felt an almost electrical tingle where she had touched him.

"Yeah...," Alan said, knowing that what Tracy had said should mean something to him, but all he could think about was her hand on his arm. Closing his eyes and shaking his head, he pushed the thoughts of Tracy from his mind and concentrated on Corporal Clark and what she had said.

Opening his eyes, he could see she was watching him intently, clearly waiting to see if he could deduce what she was implying. With his mind functioning on something other than hormones, the answer came to him almost immediately.

"Got it." Alan smiled triumphantly. "You're saying that there's not much else to do on ship other than wander around and poke your nose into everything."

"Right in one. I knew there was a reason I liked you." Her smile was dangerously close to causing Alan another hormone imbalance. Taking a deep breath, he forced it away.

Alan tried to concentrate only on what Tracy was saying.

"Now, as to why I know what all the stuff *in* those compartments does, well, I figured what's the point in knowing what's where, if I didn't know how it worked, so I just asked someone that was there."

"Hmm, and of course they just told you."

"Of course." She turned a winsome smile on him and batted her eyes. "I can be very persuasive when I need to be."

Alan tried to think of something, anything, to say, but all he could manage was to gape open-mouthed at her and feel his face flush. Thankfully, that appeared to be an appropriate answer, as Tracy just laughed and winked at him before starting to move down the passageway again.

He'd just caught up to her at an intersection and began to fall in step with her when five people came around the corner and forced each of them to opposite sides of the passageway.

The three men and two women, oblivious to their presence, continued their conversation, marching past them. All five were dressed in identical black flight suits, though the suits looked different from those of the other pilots he'd seen. They seemed bulkier and perhaps a bit more rigid, but Alan wasn't sure, not having spent much time around Valkyrie riders or assault-boat pilots.

It took him a moment to realize that he had not seen any gold or silver wings on their chests, though they all wore the same unit patch: a fanged skull with elongated canines, sprouting long, sleek black wings from each side and wearing what looked to be a torn and tattered black-and-white jester's hat. Emblazoned underneath the skull along the outside edge of the patch, in archaic gothic lettering, were the words The Dead Jokers.

"Who the FUCK was that?" Alan asked.

"Oh, those were Dead Jokers," Tracy said, once again making it sound as if that should answer everything. He decided to head this one off before it started.

"Tracy, I've never been on-ship, remember? And I don't recall Dead Jokers being brought up as a topic of discussion either in my old unit or Recon school. So, please, just tell me who the hell they are."

"Have you ever heard of Lokis?"

"Yeah, we touched on them briefly at Intel school. Didn't go into too much depth, though. They're some kind of EW ship, right?"

"Sort of, though they are more than a space-based Electronic Warfare platform. Anyway, Loki pilots are always referred to as Dead Jokers." Tracy watched Alan digest this information, waiting for the inevitable follow-up questions.

"All of them are Dead Jokers, every Loki pilot in the fleet?"

"Yes."

"But doesn't that get confusing? How do they tell each other apart when they're all out there?" Alan asked quizzically.

"Well, it all has to do with how the Lokis are deployed," Tracy said after a moment's thought.

"Okay, I can buy that, assuming you tell me how they are deployed—if you *know*, that is." The challenge in his voice was unmistakable. Tracy smiled at it.

"Lance Corporal Lewis, I know all about Dead Jokers and the Lokis they pilot, more so than most people." Alan watched a slight blush make its way onto her cheeks. "Let me tell you all about it."

Alan stood beside her as she leaned against the bulkhead and crossed her arms as a far-away look settled on her face. He listened intently as she began to speak.

"Do you know *who* Loki was? In the classical sense?" Tracy asked.

"Yeah, I think I remember him from school. Norse god of mischief and trickery, right?"

"Yeah, that's him, but what most people don't remember is that he was also very, very cunning. Couple that with his other talents, and, well, you can see why the other gods had him chained up."

"So, he was kind of like you, then, huh?" Alan quipped.

"Do you want to hear this or not?" Tracy said, fixing him with a stare until he lowered his eyes and nodded his assent.

"Now, a Loki—I'm talking about the ship, now—is pretty much the modern-day electronic version of that ancient god. Its one and only mission is to go out there"—she waved her hands expansively—"and fuck with the enemy. First it was the Asian Compact during the Dragon War, now it's the Xan-Sskarns. And the Lokis do a fantastic job at it."

She looked back over at Alan to see if he was with her, and when she saw he'd assimilated everything so far, she continued.

"Now, you may ask, 'What job are they supposed to do?' and that's a good question. Here's the answer. They go out and squash, mangle, and generally tie in knots every single communications and sensor wavelength that tries to get past them. How they do that is simple. The Loki is roughly the size of an assault shuttle, and, excluding a *very* large power plant, and a heavily shielded cockpit, every single square millimeter of that craft is packed full of electronics. Everything and anything you can possibly think of to trash a signal, and probably stuff you couldn't. They broadcast their interference in what can best be described as a ball of chaos up to ten kilometers in diameter. The field can be varied in strength, as well as size, which is a good thing, as a Loki itself does not necessarily have to be in the center of the disturbance. Can you guess what kind of effect that ball has on the enemy?" Her gaze was focused on the far bulkhead, but not really seeing it; her eyes were looking into the past.

"I'd say it pisses them off something fierce."

"That, my friend, would be an understatement." Voice thick with emotion, she went on. "When Lokis come into play, the Sallys do their God damned best to find them and kill them. And from what I've heard, they're getting as many as they're missing. A fifty-fifty chance of not coming back every time they go out, and a ten-mission tour. I'm not even going to go into the math about the probabilities on that, but I'm sure you can see that the odds of making it through ten missions are not good."

"Jesus!"

"Yeah, and you want to hear something even better?" Tears were forming in her eyes.

"What?" Alan asked out of morbid curiosity, unable to stop himself.

"A Loki pilot, a Dead Joker, is a volunteer. All of them are. Plus, they can quit at any time, except during a mission. Even five seconds prior to launching, they can just up and quit and walk away. No repercussions, no recriminations. Keeping that in mind, how many of them do you think have walked away since this war started? How many do you think have turned in their wings?"

"I don't know," Alan whispered.

"None! Not a single fucking one of them has walked away from a mission. No matter what the incentive, every single one of them has climbed into that God damned cockpit without a backward glance." Tracy's voice, brimming with anger and regret, echoed down the passageway.

Alan stood at her side, silent, watching as she got her emotions under control.

"As for where the unit name, Dead Jokers, comes from, well, that's the sickest part of the whole damn story." Tracy gave a short bark of mirthless laughter, the tears still in her eyes but refusing to fall. "No one knows where the term came from originally. All they know is it started sometime in the Dragon War. But if you ask anyone wearing those fucking black wings, every single one of them will tell you what their name means, and why all of them are called the same thing."

Rubbing the heels of her hands into her eyes, and drawing her forearm across her nose, she continued.

"They all have the same name, because, well, what's the point of having different names when you can't talk to anyone anyway? They get their orders, get a set of coordinates to fly out to, and just turn into a big hole in space. The name itself, they all wear it so proudly, comes from the simple fact that, hey, with that much interference, there is no possible way for anyone to get a missile lock, or even a target lock for guns. The ship itself is space black, and unless it's silhouetted against a planet, it's damn near invisible. So the Sallys need to be right on top of it before they even have a chance of hitting it with guns. Missiles are totally out of the question—they just go spinning off into space. The Sallys open up with their guns at point-blank range, and poof, no more Loki. But that little plane is packing so much power and equipment on board that when it goes, it goes with a vengeance. Over ninety-five percent of ships that kill a Loki are killed themselves in the subsequent explosion. The Loki and its pilot have the last laugh, even in death. Hence the name, the Dead Jokers."

"Sounds like you have to pretty insane to be a Loki pilot," Alan observed.

"You would think so, wouldn't you? But actually it's just the opposite. You have to be very sane to be one." Tracy turned her face toward Alan as she spoke, and, seeing the confusion there, she continued.

"Every single candidate—and believe me, there is no shortage of volunteers—has to undergo some serious psychiatric examinations. If they don't meet an exact standard, they aren't accepted. And, from what I was told, it's a pretty high standard." Tracy's eyes took on a far-away look again.

"Roughly, you need to be dedicated, highly motivated, patriotic to the point of fanaticism, but not suicidal. They don't want any heroes in those cockpits. The planes are just too damn expensive, and too damn important to allow that. So it's a delicate balance. And after each mission, they all undergo a full battery of both psychological and physiological exams. Basically, they want to see if anything has shaken loose."

"After each mission?"

"Yeah, you see, these folks go out there painting themselves as one huge fucking target, trying to do a very dangerous job. The brass wants to make sure that they don't start wigging out on them after basically attempting suicide. And, too, they want to make sure that those pilots don't fall prey to their own reputation and go seeking for a way to go out in a blaze of glory."

"I guess that makes sense—the psych evals, anyway. But why a physical, too?"

"You were Intel, you tell me. How does a signal jammer work?" Tracy watched as Alan thought for a very short moment before answering.

"Radiation."

"That's right, radiation. Those babies pump out all kinds of radiation, and, well, you know what that can do to a person." She grimaced at the thought.

"I thought you said the cockpit was shielded."

"It is, heavily. Plus, did you see their flight suits? Same thing for them. Yet, despite all the shielding, there can still be problems. One in twelve of the male pilots becomes sterile before the end of his tour, and one in fifty, men and women alike, develop some kind of tumor."

"God damn, is there any upside to that job?" Alan asked incredulously.

"Well, both men and women make a genetic donation before beginning flight training, and they get free medical for insemination purposes for the rest of their lives, regardless of military status. Plus, any Dead Joker who finishes their ten missions earns a spot in the academy for any of their kids who want it." Smiling, she added, "Oh, and they get triple hazardous-duty pay."

"Still sounds like a rough job, even with the perks."

Tracy watched him shake his head in denial, not quite accepting what he had heard.

"You're right, it is a rough job, and it takes a special kind of man to do it." The sad, wistful look returning to her face.

"I'm beginning to see that." Alan spoke softly, the source of her knowledge obvious. "He must have been one hell of a man."

"He was."

* * *

Alan kept up a stream of light conversation as he and Tracy continued their exploration of the ship. He was glad to see that Tracy was returning to the cheerful, exuberant woman that he had first met.

"So, do you want to get some chow?" he asked as he checked his watch, stomach rumbling.

"Sounds like a plan. I'm getting kind of hungry myself."

They began to retrace their route, heading back toward Marine Country, Tracy once again regaling him with explanations of the ship's different systems. After a short while, Alan felt safe asking the question that had been nagging at him since hearing her story.

"Hey, Tracy, can I ask you a personal question?" His voice was hesitant; he did not want to bring back unpleasant memories.

"Sure, what's on your mind?"

"Your friend, the Loki pilot, wasn't he an officer?"

"Yes, he was." Her smile was genuine now, not bittersweet. "And you want to know how a navy officer ended up in a relationship with an enlisted marine."

"I'm sorry, I didn't mean to pry. Just forget I asked." Alan blushed furiously as he realized just how personal his question was.

"No, it's okay. It all comes down to the old saying about working hard and playing hard. The brass allows a wider interpretation of some of the regulations, mostly regarding personal conduct, for personnel assigned to extremely hazardous duty. And both Dead Jokers and Marine Recon fall under that heading."

Alan made a sound expressing his understanding. Tracy resumed her dialogue, and Alan turned his mind inward while they continued down the passageway. An uncomfortable feeling settled in his stomach as his thoughts turned toward Tracy and what she had just revealed to him.

Chapter Twenty-five

The traitor paced up and down the length of her quarters. The other three ratings who shared the room with her were on duty, allowing her to vent her frustrations.

"God damn that woman. What in the hell was she thinking? She could have gotten us killed, or, more importantly, gotten me killed."

Jennifer Pratt, who was twenty-seven years old, of average height, and had mid-length red hair that was obviously not natural, pale algae-green eyes, and teeth that were overly large for her mouth, stopped her pacing to slam her fist against the bulkhead.

"It was a perfect plan. The Sallys surprise the fleet, we're obviously going to lose, and the only logical course of action is to retreat, but what does that crazy bitch do? She decides to attack." Jennifer resumed her pacing, continuing her ranting.

"I mean, what the hell was she thinking? And of course, once she *does* finally decide to leave, what happens? We get attacked, and I end up in sickbay. Then, as if that wasn't bad enough, we

243

get home, barely, and I think I'm safe, but no—I get assigned to *her* ship again."

Sitting down on her bunk, she held her head in her hands, breathing hard, trying to gain control of her emotions.

"And what a ship. Guaranteed to draw every single enemy ship within a light-year like bees to honey. I can't even get dirtside what with the rush to get us ready to launch. Out of the frying pan and racing toward the fire."

Bolting to her feet, she began to pace again.

"All I wanted was to get home, get out of this lost cause. So what if me getting out means that other people have to die? What have they ever done for me? Then, when the Xan-Sskarns finally take over the damn planet, I would get my reward for handing them their victory. Seriously, if they are going to turn us all into chattel, why shouldn't I make sure that I am at the top? Now what the hell am I going to do? How am I going to turn this situation to my advantage? Or, at the very least, get the hell off this ship?"

Leaning against the bulkhead and rubbing her eyes, she sighed.

"I can't even get any kind of message to the Sallys to tell them what I've done, or that I'm still willing to help them, for the right price. And even if I do, how do I make sure I am not on this ship when the crazy bitch gets it destroyed?" Jennifer's eyes snapped open as she continued to rant. "On top of everything else, the rumor mill says that an investigation is underway to find me. The only thing that I have going for me is the fact that looking for one person in the whole fleet will take time. I need to use that time to figure out my next move."

Jennifer halted her diatribe as the hatch opened and one of her roommates came into the compartment.

Where are they? What are they planning? And, more importantly, how can I turn their next move to my advantage?

Pushing those thoughts from her mind, lest anything show on her face, she smiled at the newcomer.

"Hey, Monica, how go things down on the hangar deck?"

"Busy as hell, but we'll be ready for whatever the Sallys throw at us," Monica said, flopping down on her bunk, obviously exhausted. "What about you? How's engineering shaping up?"

"Oh, I think it's safe to say that the next time we run into the Sallys, I'll be ready for them," Jennifer said, not looking at Monica.

Her mind began running through different scenarios, trying to find a way to turn her statement into a reality.

"What is the status of the Swarm?" the high commander asked the figure kneeling before him.

"The Swarm is recovering quickly, High Commander. Repairs and replacements have us at seventy-seven percent combat capable," Vice Commander Si'Lasa said with head bowed.

"And the items I requested from the Swarm Masters, have they arrived?"

"Yes, they have."

The high commander did not miss the tone of uncertainty in his subordinate's voice.

"You have concerns about my plan, Si'Lasa?" he queried while indicating that his old friend should rise.

Staring intently at his subordinate, the high commander felt his own apprehension return. While he had held overall command of the last battle with the Dry-Skins, and it had been a great victory, his vice commander had held tactical command of the Swarm's flagship. And Si'Lasa had performed admirably, destroying or crippling more Dry-Skin ships than any other ship commander. Si'Lasa's popularity with the Swarm and with the Swarm Masters was rising rapidly.

The scent of confidence and self-assurance did not completely mask the doubts and misgivings emanating from his vice. He would need to be even more vigilant when around his old friend, but he could not forget his duty to the Swarm and to his people, even in the face of possible assassination. With that in mind, he began to lay out the plan he had devised, and the reasoning behind it.

After divulging the complexities, even the portions he had kept secret from all but the Swarm Masters, he both saw and felt his vice commander begin to relax with understanding.

"This is a very audacious course you have set for us, High Commander," Si'Lasa finally said after he had time to digest all that he had heard.

"You do not approve?"

"It is not for me to approve or disapprove. You are the high commander, and you have the full support of the Swarm Masters. I am, and have always been, loyal to you and your command.

You have led this Swarm from victory to victory, and even if I do not fully understand your plans, I never question them."

"That is kind of you to say, old friend," he said after a few moments of silence. "But I sense you still have your doubts."

"Not doubts, High Commander, merely concerns."

"Please share them with me."

"As you command," Si'Lasa intoned before beginning. "In our last encounter with the Dry-Skins, even with surprise and superior numbers, the Swarm took tremendous damage. Even with the replacements sent by the Swarm Masters, we are still not at full battle readiness. The Dry-Skins will have the advantage should we assault their home system. Both in numbers and in fixed defenses. Surprise will not mitigate that."

"I believe that I have addressed that concern," the high commander reminded him.

"Yes, you have, but that action depends on the veracity of the information you have regarding the Dry-Skins' deployment. From where does the information come, and can it be trusted? It was a bold gamble, trusting the information that Tesh Na'Leash brought us last time."

"Very true, it was, and indeed the information I am relying on was provided once more by Na'Leash. But this time I am fully confident in the information that he has brought me," he assured Si'Lasa.

The Xan-Sskarns had more than a dozen Ssi-Nans deployed in the Sol system. It took several dozen tides to replace each ship, as they translated into the Dry-Skins' home system far enough away to avoid detection and proceeded in-system under normal power. Their mission to track the movement of the Dry-Skin Home Fleet and the status of the system's fixed defenses lasted for several hundred tides before they began to exfiltrate. The process was long, slow, and tedious, but necessary to ensure the continued secrecy of their surveillance.

The surveillance provided very accurate information that was unfortunately several dozen tides out of date.

The high commander needed to have more up-to-date information for his new battle plan to succeed. Thus he sent for the tesh who had brought him news of the Dry-Skin fleet at Groombridge 34. That news provided vital intelligence allowing for the success of his last plan. He had a new mission for that tesh and

his crew—a mission which, while only slightly dangerous or difficult, was highly important to the fruition of his plans, because
it would once more bring information that would allow for the
destruction of the Dry-Skins.

Tesh Na'Leash began his mission, jumping into the Sol system
at a distance that was barely far enough out to be undetectable
but well within communication range of the Ssi-Nans currently
keeping the Dry-Skins under surveillance.

After accepting the intelligence from the first Ssi-Nan, Tesh
Na'Leash repeated the process. Na'Leash and his crew maintained
a furious pace, pushing themselves and their ship to the limits
of their endurance. With the last transmission recorded, they
jumped back to their Swarm, bringing with them a complete,
updated picture of the Dry-Skin defenses.

"I understand now. I, too, trust the information brought to us
by Tesh Na'Leash. He is an exceptional Ssi-Nan commander, and
I do not doubt that he would not have returned to the Swarm
without completing his mission," Si'Lasa stated, his voice placating. "Please forgive my concerns."

"There is nothing to forgive, my old friend. You were concerned
for the safety of this Swarm. There is no shame in that." The high
commander watched his subordinate indicate his thanks and that
he had no more concerns which needed to be addressed. "Will
the Swarm be ready when the time comes?"

"Yes, High Commander. I will see to it personally."

"Excellent. With you by my side, I do not doubt that we will
be victorious."

"You flatter me," Si'Lasa said, bowing his head. "When do we
attack?"

"Soon, Vice Commander," the high commander hissed, leaning
back into his command throne, rows of razor-sharp teeth exposed
in a frightening parody of a human smile.

"Very soon."

Admiral Elliot Tanner, the wizened old man commanding
Home Fleet, stood with his hands on the rail running around the
pit housing the flag deck's projector, his eyes intently following
the information presented before him. Flanking him, *Heimdall's*
commanding officer, Captain Ryan Ash, stood, hands clasped

behind his back, splitting his attention between the admiral and the projection.

The projector was currently displaying the whole of the Sol system, including all current assets, both fixed and mobile, and their status and location. Ash easily picked out the few lone light codes denoting the pickets Admiral Tanner had deployed around the system, right at the wall. Along with the individual green outlines of the picket ships was a much larger symbol representing the bulk of Home Fleet.

The admiral whispered a command to the chief standing at the control panel, and the holographic image dissolved. Then, after a moment, it coalesced into a view of a much smaller area of space. The three areas in which Home Fleet currently resided.

Ash could understand what he was watching, but what he couldn't understand was why he was watching it.

"Captain, I think we could use a bit more fighter cover. Please inform all carriers to launch an additional ten percent of their Valkyries. And I want the escort frigates to push out a few thousand more kilometers to give us a better screen and more sensor coverage," Admiral Tanner's rasping voice said, though he never took his attention away from the projection. "What do you think?"

Ash didn't have a problem passing on the admiral's orders to the other captains of Home Fleet. While normally these orders would be passed on by the admiral's chief of staff, the officer in question was currently preparing for the upcoming flag transfer to the *Valhalla*.

What Ash did have a problem with was passing on orders that, in his professional opinion, made absolutely no sense. Granted, he knew he was not the military genius the admiral was rumored to be, but neither was he tactically or strategically inept. He kept his opinion to himself as he acknowledged his understanding of the admiral's orders.

"I think that will be all for the moment, Captain." Admiral Tanner finally turned his attention from the projection to the man standing with him. "I'll be preparing for the transfer, but also keeping an eye on things from my workstation. I don't envision any problems in the next few hours, but if you need me for anything, don't hesitate to contact me. Understood?"

"Understood, sir," Ash said as he extended his hand. "Sir, it's been an honor to carry your flag. I'll be sorry to see you go."

Taking the proffered hand, Admiral Tanner smiled at his flag captain.

"Captain, it has been a privilege."

With that, the admiral turned his back on Ash and headed for the hatch. Just as the admiral reached it, the *Heimdall*'s executive officer stepped into the compartment, immediately stepping to one side as the admiral stepped through the hatch, exchanging greetings with Commander Washington as he exited.

"What is it, Tyrone?" Ash asked his XO as he came up beside him.

"Nothing, sir. Just came down to see if there was anything you might need a hand with. I'm sure that with the admiral's staff tied up at the moment, their duties have all devolved onto you." The tall commander smiled, white teeth flashing in his dark face.

"Well, XO, as a matter of fact, I have some orders to pass on to some of the fleet." Ash explained the nature of the admiral's orders.

"Sir, I don't mean to say anything against the admiral, but I just can't fathom the reason for those orders."

"What you really mean to say, Commander Washington, is that these orders make no fucking sense," Ash said quietly, his voice carrying no farther than the two of them.

"Yes, sir," Commander Washington replied.

"Well, as you can guess, I agree with you. I mean, I can understand why he would be worried after what happened at Groombridge 34. Having the fleet spread across the system would invite defeat in detail. But this..." Ash waved his hand toward the projection, and both officers turned their gaze to it, watching the small holographic ships of the fleet slowly drift across the display while much smaller icons representing the Valkyries on patrol darted between their larger sister ships.

What had both officers concerned was their current deployment. The entirety of Home Fleet, sans the half-dozen ships assigned to picket duty, was deployed in one large formation. They were well dispersed but still within spitting distance of each other, in astronomical terms. While the current deployment did in fact address the issue of the possibility of the fleet being defeated in detail, it brought up a host of other concerns for the two experienced officers.

"Well, you may see the reasoning behind the admiral's orders, but I still find it unnerving," Commander Washington told his captain, voice still low.

"What would you do if it were up to you, Tyrone?" Captain Ash clearly wanted a second opinion to match against his own ideas.

"I'd keep with the admiral's train of thought and not have the fleet scattered to the winds, but I *would* break it into three or four task forces and station them at a few key points. Mars, Terra, with the rest on constant patrol, and have the pickets strengthened and set to cover beyond the wall. If the Sallys try to sneak in, they're going to do it from far enough out that we won't see them coming until they're right on top of us." His analysis finished, Commander Washington fell into a relaxed parade rest, waiting for his captain's response.

"Well, Tyrone, you've clearly read my mind once again. That's exactly what I'd do, with a few modifications." Ash turned away from the projection to gaze at his XO. "I would detach a few of the destroyers and frigates from each of the task forces, have them parallel the main body, but farther out, giving us a bigger picture. But that's just a matter of preference. Either way, close deployment or dispersal has its advantages."

"I can see that, sir." Captain Ash shook himself then tugged his uniform jacket down. It was time to get back to work.

"Well, Commander, while I would enjoy standing here debating tactics with you, I have some orders to pass on."

"Yes, sir." Commander Washington braced to attention as his captain began to follow the admiral's path out of the compartment. But before he could reach the hatch, Tyrone called out.

"Captain?"

"Yes, Commander?" Ash said, stopping and turning to face his XO.

"I just thought of something. What if the Sallys managed to jump into the middle of us? Our responses would be severely limited while the fleet tried to get clear of each other's field of fire."

Captain Ryan Ash gave his XO a wry smile, turned on his heel, and continued on his way toward the hatch, calling his response over his shoulder.

"That thought hadn't so much as *crossed* my mind, Commander, but rather ran screaming in incoherent terror over it."

Chapter Twenty-six

HOME FLEET
OCTOBER 13, 2197
1313Z
BEYOND PLUTO ORBIT, SOL

"SENSOR CONTACT!" bellowed from nearly one hundred throats simultaneously. "MULTIPLE POINT SOURCES!"

Heads snapped up throughout Home Fleet as the information registered. To the credit of the captains of the fleet, the responses were almost universal, varying only on the order in which they were issued.

"Location?"

"Sound general quarters!"

Regardless of which order was shouted first, the responses were the same. Alarms howled throughout ships as crews were called to their battle stations, followed by a voice giving the same bad news.

"Multiple point sources—too many to localize."

Sensor officers turned to the task of trying to glean more information from their equipment to determine just what, where, and how many of the intruders there were.

Had any sensor suites within Home Fleet been able to penetrate the massive distortion field generated by multiple folds, the resulting information would have caused even the most seasoned personnel to blanch.

What: thermonuclear warheads ranging in yield from one thousand to fifteen hundred megatons.

Where: interspersed within the main body of Home Fleet. Many within meters of ship hulls, some materializing within the ships themselves.

Number: one hundred thirty-six. All of which arrived in the Sol system within mere moments of each other.

Fifteen seconds after the last warhead arrived, Admiral Tanner's Home Fleet was consumed as a new star was born.

Brian "Chief" Phelps, customary coffee cup firmly clenched in his hand, kept a watchful eye on his boards. He and his partner, Petty Officer Lisa Brown, had had an eventful week following the excitement of the *Fenris'* unexpected arrival in-system with the news of the destruction of Admiral Stevens' fleet. Drill after drill, diagnostics, and extended shifts all geared toward making sure that they, along with the rest of Folkvang station and its crew, were as ready as possible for any possible Xan-Sskarn incursion into Sol.

All of that training was about to pay off as for the second time in a week alarms screamed for attention from the boards in front of the two sensor techs. This time Petty Officer Phelps managed to hang on to his cup as he snapped forward, shouting into his mike, unknowingly repeating dozens of voices.

"Sensor contact! Multiple point sources!"

Lisa had just begun to analyze the incoming information when it suddenly stopped.

"What the hell?" she exclaimed in a disgusted voice as she began to run diagnostics on her boards. "Chief, my board's just fried, and I've lost the feed. What've you got?"

"I don't think it's your board, Lisa. My feed just went dead, too."

As they were discussing the situation, the watch chief rushed up to their stations, stopping between them and bending forward to look at their boards himself.

"What've you got?" Chief Maxwell asked them.

"I don't know, Chief. I was reading massive fold events from multiple sources when my board just went dead." Phelps indicated his silent board. "Same thing for Lisa."

"Brown?"

"It's like he said, Chief. I was reading fold events, then there was what looked like a huge spike of energy, then nothing. It happened so fast that I really couldn't get a read on what it was."

"Okay, I want you to cancel the diagnostics and play back the records." Chief Maxwell rose back up, waving his hand to get the attention of the watch officer, Lieutenant Ford. "Phelps, you try to get a read on what happened from another satellite."

"Time lag is going to play hell with what I can get, Chief. I won't be able to do a true active search."

"I know, but it's better than nothing. Now get on it before we miss anything."

"Aye, Chief," Phelps said. Turning back to his board, he called up the satellites closest to the disturbance and tried to gather any information he could.

Lieutenant Ford arrived as Brown pulled up what little information she had. Chief Maxwell brought the officer up to speed on the current situation, and when he finished, he indicated that Brown should begin the playback.

The playback took exactly seventeen seconds.

"Oh, fuck," Chief Maxwell whispered as he registered what he saw. A moment later, Lieutenant Ford turned pale, all the blood draining from his face as he, too, began to comprehend.

Petty Officer Phelps, completely engrossed in his work, failed to notice the reactions of his companions. His efforts were finally rewarded as he began to pull readings from another sensor satellite.

"Chief, I've got something," Phelps said, not looking up as more information began to scroll by on his screen. "Looks like—"

He didn't get the chance to finish, as Maxwell interrupted him. "The results of a large nuclear detonation."

"Yeah, that's right." He sounded a little confused. "How did you..."

The looks on their faces stopped his first question, but a second one came in its place.

"What?"

"Son, between Brown's records and your current feed, I would have to say that we have just been witness to the largest nuclear detonation created by a sentient species in history." Chief Maxwell's voice was still a whisper. "I'm willing to bet that if you went up to the observation deck in approximately five hours, you would be able to see the light from that explosion."

"But an explosion that size," Phelps started. His mind raced, assimilating what he had just heard with what he knew. He did not like the path his mind had started down.

"Admiral Tanner...Home Fleet...," Brown breathed as she, too, began to understand the repercussions of what Chief Maxwell had just said.

"Gone." Maxwell's voice was flat and unemotional.

"Some of them," Phelps began, but Maxwell cut him off.

"No, they're all gone, or they will be shortly."

"How can you be so sure, Chief?" Brown asked.

"With a detonation that size, if the blast didn't kill them outright, the radiation burst will."

They all fell silent at this as Chief Maxwell moved to confer with the lieutenant.

While the three of them had been discussing the fate of Admiral Tanner and Home Fleet, Lieutenant Ford had been busy passing their information up the chain of command. His voice was clear, but with a slight waver in it.

Ford was still speaking into his mike when alarms began to echo throughout the station.

The high-pitched wail of Brian's boards demanding his attention was nearly lost in the din of the station's call to battle stations. Turning his attention back to his readouts, Brian saw something that caused his blood to run cold.

"Chief!" Brian screamed into his mike this time, the tremor of fear in his voice readily apparent. "New contact, multiple fold events!"

The lieutenant and the chief seemed to teleport to his side, both of them staring intently at his readouts.

"Multiple fold events this soon after what just happened can mean only one thing, sir," Chief Maxwell said to Lieutenant Ford.

"I know, Chief." Ford's voice was as quiet as Maxwell's had been. Touching his earpiece, Ford was once again connected to Commander Easly in CIC. "Commander, the Xan-Sskarns have entered the system."

■ ■ ■

Captain Alexandra McLaughlin sat at her desk in the small office located just off the command deck reviewing readiness reports. Sipping coffee, she took her time scrolling though the data displayed on her screen. As she made her way through the reports, Alex came to the conclusion that she had taken command of a superb crew.

Leaning back from the screen and rubbing her eyes, she took a moment to stretch the kinks out of her shoulders. Then, lighting a cigarette, she turned back to her reading when the admittance chime to her office sounded.

"Come."

As the hatch began to cycle open with a soft hush, Commander Tony Ruggs stepped into the office.

"Captain, Folkvang station has just gone to general quarters," Tony reported in clipped tones, the concern evident on his face.

Alex came quickly to her feet, stabbing out her cigarette as she moved from behind the desk.

"Sound general quarters, Commander," Alex heard herself say as she strode toward the command deck, watching her XO lift his hand to his earbud.

"General quarters, general quarters, all hands man your battle stations." Tony's calm voice, emanating from speakers throughout the ship, was quickly replaced by the ululating wail of the alarms announcing to the crew that the war had just caught up with them.

Alex settled into her command chair, picking up her earpiece and inserting it before she began to secure her harness. As the last buckle clicked into place, she reached up and touched the earbud, cutting her into the battle net.

"Commander Ruggs, I have the con." Her voice was calm and assured as she took command.

"You have the con. Aye, ma'am." Tony's voice was just as calm as hers had been.

Alex took the time to arrange her display panels before she cut back into the net.

"Status?"

"Ma'am, all stations report manned and ready," Tony answered.

"Very well, Commander. I believe we can do without the alarms now." She smiled at him, waiting to see his nod of understanding before turning her attention to her communications officer.

"Commander Albers, what are you getting from the station?"

"Ma'am, from what I'm hearing over their general net, Home Fleet has been destroyed and the Sallys have entered the system." Lea's voice was hushed, her speech slow and deliberate, the shock of what she had heard and reported affecting her normally exuberant personality.

Thankfully, Lea had had the presence of mind to cut over to the command staff net. Alex didn't know what kind of effect an announcement like that would have on her crew, but she knew that it would not be good. The gasps and hisses from her staff attested to that. If they were shocked, she knew that the crew would be even more so.

"Lieutenant Green, can you confirm this?" Alex was the first to shake herself out of her disbelief. There was a job to be done, and it was time to get to it.

"I can't go active while we're still in dock, ma'am, but I can get the same telemetry that the station is receiving via the docking umbilicals," Green responded after only a brief moment of hesitation.

"Do it," Alex snapped, then turned her attention back to Lea. "Commander Albers, sound the recall. Get all of our people back on board, now. Then I want you to open a channel to High Command. Specifically, I want to talk to the CNO."

"Yes, ma'am. I'm on it." Albers seemed to be bouncing back from the shock, her voice coming across the net in a rush.

"CAG," Alex called to the Commander Kaufman, still on the command staff net.

"Kaufman." His voice sounded winded.

He must have had to run to the tower, and with his leg still healing, I'm sure that wasn't a pleasant journey, Alex thought, smiling at how quickly her friend had responded despite his injuries.

"Get the Valkyries lined up, but don't move them into the tubes yet, and don't launch the alert fighters. We'll worry about getting them out and dancing once we're clear of the station."

"Roger that, ma'am."

"Commander Fain, weapons status?" Alex changed nets from the CAG to her tactical officer without a moment's hesitation.

"I've got fish in the tubes. All energy mounts are charged," Fain reported. Then, glancing at Lieutenant Amy Gardner's board, he reported the status of the junior tactical officer as well. "PDLs and PDGs are all in the green and standing by for tasking. ECM programs are loaded and ready for implementation." He gave a nod of approval to his subordinate before turning his eyes to his captain.

"Excellent, Guns." Alex complimented the commander without looking up from her boards. She began to inquire as to the status of engineering when Lieutenant Commander Albers' voice sounded in her earpiece.

"Captain, the recall is sounded, but I am unable to contact dirtside. Something is wrong with the transmitters. I can't contact anyone, but I can still receive."

"What?!" Alex burst out. Not being able to communicate was a severe handicap.

"I don't know what the problem is, ma'am. I had active channels earlier this morning, but now I've got nothing but dead air. Yet all my diagnostics are coming back in the green."

"Can you patch in going through Folkvang?"

"Sorry, ma'am." Lea's voice was small and depressed. "We've got access to their local nets via the umbilicals, but I can't tap into their transmitters."

"Commander Ruggs!" Alex barked, "Get hold of Heron and get a team to track down the problem. I want those transmitters up, and I want them up now."

Alex barely registered his response as Lieutenant Green's strangled voice came across the net.

"Captain?"

"What've you got, Lieutenant?"

"I've just received the telemetry from Folkvang's sensors, ma'am."

Alex turned to face her sensor officer, the look on his face making her break out in a cold sweat.

"Can you confirm the status of Home Fleet?" Alex found herself whispering back, afraid to hear the answer.

"If these readings are accurate, and I don't doubt that they are, then Folkvang's report is correct. Home Fleet is gone."

"How?" The question came out before she could stop it.

"Thermonuclear explosion, most likely from multiple warheads. Readings indicate that it was bigger than anything previously recorded, by several orders of magnitude."

"Jesus!" Tony's voice broke the stunned silence on the staff net, igniting a flurry of questions. Alex stepped on it, hard.

"Enough!" When silence was restored, she continued. "It's

happened, and there is nothing we can do to change it, but that doesn't mean there is nothing we can do about it. Clear?"

The assents coming back across the net were confident, the edge of panic a moment before gone before it could take root.

"Now, Commander Ruggs, begin preparations for immediate departure."

"Aye, ma'am. Preparing for immediate departure," Tony called back. He turned his attention to his own boards and began to issue orders quietly into his mike.

Alex paused and cast her gaze around the command deck, gauging the response of the personnel around her. While there was fear and uncertainty written upon their faces, their eyes were intent, and they were clearly under control.

Unbidden, her last meeting with Admiral Greco played across her mind. His final orders echoed in her ears.

Your orders are to ensure the survival of the human race, by whatever means necessary.

The current situation brought home the full ramifications of that order. She knew what she had to do.

Her ghosts wailed in protest.

Please, God, don't let me fail them.

She sat back into her command chair, radiating an air of calm, not letting her worries and fears show on her face.

"Commander Tucholski, begin plotting us a course out of the system, away from the incoming Sallys." She heard the gasps from some of her crew, but ignored them and went on. "Go for zero-zero at the jump limit."

"Aye, aye, Captain," Tucholski called back to her. If her orders bothered him at all, he didn't let it show as he turned to his boards and began to lay in their course.

"Captain, I've got Folkvang's CO on the net, *demanding* to speak to you," Commander Albers said. "Sorry, ma'am—his words, not mine." She looked sheepishly at Alex.

"Very well, patch him through," Alex said, making a mental bet with herself as to the reason behind Rachere's call.

"Admiral Rachere for you, Captain."

"Thank you, Commander." Alex reached down to one of her panels and typed in a quick command to begin recording their conversation. "Admiral Rachere, what can I do for you?"

"Captain McLaughlin, you will prepare for my arrival. I am

assuming command of the *Valhalla*." Rachere's voice was confident; he obviously assumed he would be obeyed without question.

Alex smiled grimly; she had won her bet.

What the hell can that man be thinking? Does he seriously think that I'm just going to turn my ship over to him because he said so? I was wrong about him. He's not stupid—he's insane.

"Oh, I don't think so, Admiral," Alex said sweetly into her mike.

"Captain, that was not a request." An edge was apparent in his voice.

"I'm sure it wasn't, Admiral, but that does not change the fact that you will get command of this ship when hell freezes over."

"Captain, with the death of Admiral Tanner, I am the senior officer in-system, and as such, it is my duty to take command."

Alex could picture the admiral's face slowly turning crimson.

"With all due *respect,* Admiral, you are not the senior officer in the system. Admiral Greco is, and I have my orders directly from him."

"McLaughlin, do I need to remind you about what has just happened, what is happening right now, even as we speak?" Rachere asked, exasperated.

"Yes, please do. And could you go slow?" Sarcasm dripped from her voice. Before Rachere could begin again, Alex continued on.

"Admiral, you said it was your duty to take command of the *Valhalla*, but what of your duty to Folkvang station?"

"This station is lost, Captain, and you know it."

"That may be, sir, but that does not change the fact that you have a duty to perform."

"Don't talk to me about duty, Captain. I've seen what your concept of duty is, and it disgusts me."

She was about to give Rachere the last few meters of rope with which to hang himself.

"I see." Alex's voice was light and cheerful, knowing that it would irritate the admiral even more. "Well, sir, the last time we met, you had accused me of desertion in the face of the enemy. Your feelings in that regard were plainly evident as you tried to get not only myself but my entire crew drawn up on charges. We both know that the charges you tried to bring had no basis in fact. Yet here you are, clearly abandoning your command at the first sign of trouble."

Alex could hear spluttering noises coming over the net, the admiral at a loss for words.

Lieutenant Green's voice snapped Alex's attention back to the current situation.

"New contact, multiple incoming!"

"Report!"

"Station sensors are reporting a Sally carrier group fifteen light-minutes out, accelerating hard toward the station."

With the new arrivals, the time for games was past.

"Commander Albers," Alex said, opening a channel to her communications officer.

"Yes, ma'am?" With a fresh burst of adrenaline in her system due to Green's last announcement, Lea's response came so quickly as to be nearly incomprehensible.

"Take this recording." Alex touched her panel again, stopping the recording. A few more strokes of her finger had the file on its way to Lea's console. "I want you to send it to Folkvang's executive officer, with my compliments. Highest possible priority."

The venom in her voice was not missed by Albers. Nor was it missed by Admiral Rachere, whom Alex had deliberately left on the line. Alex cut Albers out of the net, leaving her alone with Rachere's protests.

She was ignoring them.

"XO, status of launch preparations?"

"We're good to go, Captain," Tony said, staring at his captain, wondering what was *really* going on. He continued to watch as she once again cut him out of the net to murmur quietly into her mike.

"You know, Sean—you don't mind if I call you Sean, do you?"

An inarticulate gurgle answered her.

"I'll take that as a yes. Now, as I was saying, Sean, locked in the brig, stripped of your rank, waiting for the Sallys to come for you, it might not be a pool of your own blood, but I think it will do rather nicely. I do wish your crew the best of luck in their fight. I've done everything I can for them by getting you out of the way. I do appreciate your facilitating that."

Alex set Rachere's connection to receive only before reestablishing her own connection to the command-staff battle net.

"Commander Ruggs?" Alex called out formally.

"Yes, ma'am?"

"Seal the locks and blow the tubes. We're leaving."

Chapter Twenty-seven

ASSAULT SHUTTLE FOUR
OCTOBER 13, 2197
1827Z
MARS, SOL

Captain Stewart Optika, Commanding Officer, Bravo Company, Twelfth Battalion, assigned USS *Valhalla*, felt the pressure pushing him into his seat increase. He and his marines were at the mercy of the fates, strapped into their chairs in the belly of the assault shuttle racing toward the planet. The rest of his company was just as helpless, riding in Bravo Company's two other shuttles.

The pressure on Optika and his marines passed one g and continued to increase. With nothing to see but the blackness of space displayed on the monitors strategically placed within the troop bay, Optika allowed his mind to replay the last few hours, and how they had led to his current situation: leading an undermanned company on a combat drop onto a planet with little planning and no intel on the size and disposition of the opposition's force.

"Captain Optika reporting as ordered," the burly marine said as he stopped at the foot of the conference table, standing at attention. He felt the eyes of the three officers seated at the far end of the table taking in his appearance.

One hundred ninety centimeters and weighing close to one hundred twenty-four kilos, heavily muscled, bald with bright green eyes, he would have been described as ruggedly handsome were it not for the scars crisscrossing the right side of his face. The aftermath of a close encounter with a burst from a Xan-Sskarn flechette rifle.

He watched as the two flanking officers read the ribbons on his chest. Added together with his stature and the mangled remains of his face, the awe and slightly intimidated look that came across their faces was something he had come to expect.

Switching his attention to the diminutive captain seated at the head of the table, he saw something he did *not* expect. Respect. Respect and understanding.

So, she's someone who has been face-to-face with death, spit in his eye, and walked away. Not unscathed, though. You never walk away unscathed, and she knows it.

"Captain Optika, please, have a seat," the officer at the head of the table said, waving her hand toward the chair he was standing beside.

"Thank you, ma'am."

"From what I understand, you know both Commander Ruggs and Lieutenant Commander Tucholski. I'm Captain Alexandra McLaughlin, and you are Captain Stewart Optika, the ranking officer of Twelfth Battalion on board. Is that correct?"

"Yes, ma'am. Both the Old Man and the XO were dirtside when we launched." His voice was slightly bitter.

"I know, and I'm sorry, but there were no other options." Captain McLaughlin gave him a wan smile by way of apology before continuing. "Can you give me a manning report on the battalion?"

"Generally, ma'am." He cleared his throat as he shifted uncomfortably in his seat. A marine officer was supposed to know where all his marines were at all times, and Optika didn't. There were extenuating circumstances, but Optika was still embarrassed.

"I know that approximately one hundred marines were dirtside, with a majority of the rest being on-station when the alert was sounded. I believe that most, if not all, of the personnel aboard Folkvang were able to make it aboard before we left, but I cannot be one hundred percent positive." He didn't want to seem to be making excuses, but he could tell by the look on the captain's face that some sort of explanation was in order.

"The battalion is still manning their battle stations, and it is difficult to get a full head count with the unit scattered throughout the ship, ma'am."

"I thought as much," McLaughlin said, nodding, obviously not holding him responsible for the lack of an accurate count. "We are about to secure from general quarters, Captain, and when we do, I will need you to get an accurate report as quickly as possible."

"Understood, ma'am." Optika dipped his head in acknowledgment. "Once we secure, I'll have the battalion fall in and get a full manning status."

"Good. You have thirty minutes, Captain." McLaughlin stared at him, making sure she had his attention.

If she didn't with that, she definitely had Optika's complete attention with her next statement.

"Then I want you back here with whomever you need to plan a company-level planetary assault and extraction mission on a Xan-Sskarn–held facility."

Optika felt his jaw drop.

"Thirty minutes, Captain."

Understanding that this meeting was over, Captain Optika rose to his feet, coming to attention.

"Yes, ma'am."

"Dismissed, Captain."

Exactly twenty-eight minutes had elapsed since Captain Optika was last in the wardroom. This time however, he had not arrived alone. With him was Twelfth Battalion's senior SNCO, Sergeant Major Martin Creech, and his three platoon leaders, First Lieutenants Marshal Rook and Sandra Luthi, and Second Lieutenant Fred Burnette. Also accompanying him were the only Recon Marines on board, Corporal Tracy Clark and Lance Corporal Alan Lewis.

"I have the information you requested, ma'am," Optika told Captain McLaughlin after he had reported and taken his seat.

"Thank you, Captain." She smiled at him. "How bad is it?"

"Ninety-six marines, all of them dirtside, including Colonel Hendrix and Major Fishman. All marine personnel aboard station were able to make it back on board before the locks were sealed, ma'am."

"How do the numbers break down?"

"Eighteen in my company, Bravo, thirty-four in Alpha, and twenty-five in Charlie." Though Optika held a pad with the information, he recited from memory. "The final nineteen are from the headquarters unit."

"Damn, twenty percent," McLaughlin said, eyes closed, doing the math in her head.

Optika then felt her deep blue eyes staring intently at him.

"How does this affect the operational status of the battalion?"

"Ah, I'm not sure, ma'am," he began. "I'm not a battalion commander and—"

He did not get a chance to finish.

"You are now, Captain." Her quiet comment brought him upright in his chair. He could see that he was not alone in his surprise. With the exception of Sergeant Major Creech, all of the marines around the table were just as surprised as Captain Optika.

"But, ma'am," he began again, only to be cut off once more.

"There are no buts about it, Captain. You are the ranking officer on board the *Valhalla*, and we are out of contact with High Command and are unlikely to reestablish contact within the foreseeable future. With that in mind, Captain, who *else* is going to assume command?"

Optika's gaze unconsciously moved to Creech. The sergeant major caught the motion.

"Oh, no, sir," Creech said firmly, shaking his head. "Not a chance. An old salt like me has no business trying to run a battalion. The job's yours, sir, and you'll do just fine."

A small smile split Optika's face as he listened to the grizzled sergeant major. Creech might be right about his abilities, but that didn't stop the cold feeling of dread spreading through his body.

"Besides, sir, we all know that NCOs are the backbone of the corps, and I don't plan on going anywhere anytime soon. Plus, the battalion still has a viable chain of command—most of the officers and senior NCOs are still present. It won't be as difficult as you may think. Trust me." The last was said with wink and a smile.

"Thanks, Top." Turning his attention back to Captain McLaughlin, Optika continued on. "Sorry about that, ma'am." He actually felt himself blush under her amused gaze.

"Not a problem, Captain. I didn't think the full weight of the situation had occurred to you yet."

"You're right about that, ma'am."

"So, back to my question." McLaughlin's voice took on a serious tone as her face adopted a matching mien. "Do you have an idea of how the current manning situation will affect the operational status of the battalion?"

"No, ma'am, I don't." He took a deep breath before continuing. "However, I can tell you that from the numbers it looks like both Bravo and Charlie companies will be relatively unaffected by our losses. Alpha will need a bit of restructuring before it's fully combat ready, but that should not be too difficult to accomplish, though they will need some time to train up afterward."

"That's the best news I have heard all day, Captain. Thank you."

Optika felt himself blushing again.

"Now, Captain, down to business."

"Yes, ma'am," he said, ready to get to work himself.

"We have received a distress call from a top-secret military research facility on Mars," Captain McLaughlin began, "and have changed our course to come to their aid. Unfortunately, a communications malfunction prohibits us from contacting them to let them know we are coming"

Captain Optika and the rest of his ad-hoc staff began to enter information into their pads, even though the information would be available for download after the briefing had concluded.

"It is imperative that the research and materials located on that base do not fall into the Xan-Sskarns' claws."

Lieutenant Luthi stirred in her chair, and Optika could see that she had something she wanted to say. During one of their own mission briefs, everyone would be expected to voice their questions, concerns, and comments. Here it was clear that his platoon leaders did not know the protocols in this situation.

"Lieutenant, do you have a question?" he asked, interrupting Alex himself rather than having her do it.

"Please, Lieutenant, speak freely." McLaughlin turned her smile at the young woman. "That goes for the rest of you, too."

"Yes, ma'am," Lieutenant Luthi said in a quiet voice. Optika still couldn't understand, even after the two years they had served together, how someone as quiet and unimposing as Sandra could transform into a whirling dervish of death and destruction when she took her marines in harm's way.

"I was just wondering—if it's so important to keep this base's information from the Sallys, why don't we just take it out with a kinetic strike from orbit?"

Optika nodded his head in agreement with his lieutenant's question, and he saw the rest of the marines around the table were thinking along the same lines. Why should they risk a planetary assault when the mission could be accomplished with no more difficulty than pushing a button?

"Well, Lieutenant, that thought had occurred to me, but I've decided that I want the information from that base, too," McLaughlin replied.

When Luthi didn't respond, McLaughlin leaned back and began stroking her chin, then spoke again, trying a different approach.

"Let me ask you this—what's the best way to end a conflict?"

Optika could see that she was directing the question to all of them, and he felt as if he were back at infantry school and this was a tactical question that had been assigned him. Before he could formulate an answer, a cocky voice cut across the silence.

"Peace through superior firepower?"

Nine pairs of eyes turned to face the speaker.

Corporal Tracy Clark sat calmly under the scrutiny, though she kept her eyes carefully averted from theirs.

"Corporal Clark," Optika snapped, "now is not the time for frivolity." He had heard of her peculiar sense of humor from her squad leader.

"Actually, Captain, she is correct, or at least partially," McLaughlin said, the amusement evident in her voice.

"That's a marine answer if I ever heard one." This came from the officer seated to the captain's left, Commander Ruggs, the *Valhalla*'s XO.

Commander Ruggs' comment set them all to chuckling, dispelling the air of tension that had begun to develop around the marine end of the table.

Optika shot Clark a warning glance, and he was satisfied to see a slight flush appear on her cheeks. Having silently reined in his subordinate, he turned his attention back to what McLaughlin was saying.

"As I was saying, the corporal is partially correct—superior power. And knowledge is power, which brings me back to you, Lieutenant Luthi. This facility is engaged in weapons research. Weapons that could give us a significant edge against the Xan-Sskarns. I want that research, to use it myself to help defeat the Xan-Sskarns. And should there not be any information of immediate use in the facility's computer core, well, the scientists themselves should be able to produce the weapons we need to ensure *peace*."

Optika did not miss her emphasis on the last word, and by the looks on the faces around the table, neither had anyone else.

"We understand, Captain," he told McLaughlin, speaking for all of the marines present. He had no doubts that they were in agreement with him, that Captain McLaughlin was right. "We'll get you that data, and the scientists to go with it."

Something in his tone registered with McLaughlin, and she fixed him with that penetrating gaze once more.

"Captain, while I appreciate your dedication, I want you to understand that I do not mean to spend your lives on a lost cause." Her tone was reassuring. "If you tell me it can't be done, or if, when you get there, the mission goes south, you will withdraw and we will go with plan B."

"Plan B?"

"Yes, we go with Lieutenant Luthi's original train of thought and use kinetic strikes to turn that facility into the biggest crater on the surface of Mars." The feral smile she gave him would have made any marine proud.

Chuckling, Optika gave her a smile of his own.

"Well, ma'am, why don't we see what we can do about a plan A?"

She didn't say anything as she turned to face the XO.

Commander Ruggs took his cue from her and rose to his feet, entering a command into his pad as he did so.

Optika leaned in with everyone else as the lights in the wardroom dimmed and a holographic display sprang to life.

"Ladies and gentlemen, this is the research facility Hugin," Commander Ruggs said.

Optika began to formulate a plan of action as the commander continued his briefing.

"The Hugin's distress call indicated that a Xan-Sskarn force of indeterminate size was on a heading directly toward them and would reach them in approximately four hours. That was just over an hour ago. The *Valhalla* is currently moving at maximum speed toward Mars. Even so, our calculations indicate that we will not be able to put a strike force on the ground until approximately sixty minutes after the Xan-Sskarns arrive. Our only hope is that the fixed defenses and marine detachment stationed there can hold them off until your arrival. Failing that, Captain, you and your company will have to go in and dig them out. Remember—you are not there to retake the facility. This is an extraction mission only."

Commander Ruggs continued the briefing, highlighting areas of the station as he spoke. After another ten minutes, the XO had finished. His attention, and the attention of the other naval officers, turned to Optika.

Showtime.

"Thank you, Commander." Optika dipped his head toward the XO as he stood. "I wish we had more information about the enemy's strength and deployment, but at least you've given us a good lay of the land. Better than we usually have."

There were several chuckles from the assembled marines, and a snort from Clark. Marines normally performed drops on hostile planets or boarding actions on enemy vessels. Neither of which allowed for much in the way of detailed knowledge of their surroundings. It was up to Recon Marines, like Corporal Clark, to go out and get those details.

"Keeping that in mind, I think I've come up with plan of attack."

"Very well, Captain, please proceed," Captain McLaughlin called out from the shadows at the end of the table.

"Okay, making the assumption that the Sallys will be in the facility when we land, there are a few things we can do."

"Excuse me, Captain," interjected Commander Ruggs. "Why are you assuming that the Xan-Sskarns will have breached the facility before your arrival?"

"Sir, the detachment stationed there consists of only twenty-five marines. The Sallys have to have an idea of what they can find in the facility, or else they would not be attacking it." Commander Ruggs nodded his understanding, but Clark interrupted again.

"How could they know that, sir?"

Optika cast another withering glare in her direction. "That's not our concern right now. We can assume that since they are moving to attack the base with an assault carrier, they intend to take the base, not destroy it, and they will use sufficient force to ensure their capture of the facility while still being able to retrieve what they came for."

Optika felt a brief moment of pity pass through him at the thought of what those twenty-five marines were about to face.

"The detachment commander has drawn the same conclusions I have, I'm sure. And I don't doubt that in the time he has before they arrive, he will have more than a few surprises ready for the Sallys. After those surprises have been spent, the enemy will force their way into the facility, which actually will be to the defenders' advantage, for a while. The Sallys won't be able to assault en masse, and the marines will be able to mount a very effective resistance at these choke points." He highlighted several different areas of the facility.

"However, eventually numbers will tell," Optika whispered as he cleared his highlighting. "And when that happens, Hugin will be theirs. I just hope they can keep the Sallys busy long enough for us to get there with time enough to stop them from accomplishing their mission."

"What do you think the chances are of that happening, Captain?" Commander Ruggs asked, with nothing more than a hope for reassurance in his voice.

"Sir, they are *marines*." He rose to his full height. "They will die to a man before they give that facility to the Sallys. I wouldn't be surprised to find them still holding out by the time we get there."

Commander Ruggs opened his mouth, possibly to point out that the odds of that being the case were almost nonexistent, but the hard looks on all seven of the marines' faces stopped him.

"Now, as I was saying, I've come up with a plan that takes all of that into account."

All eyes in the room focused on Captain Optika again as he began lay out the bare bones of his plan.

"What about the information in the computer core, Captain?" McLaughlin asked after he had finished outlining his battle plan.

"That's what Lewis and Clark will be retrieving, ma'am."

There were chuckles from the naval officers and two of the marine lieutenants. McLaughlin must have seen the confused look on his face.

"I take it you are not much into history, Captain."

Optika wasn't sure what that had to do with the current situation, but he decided to answer anyway.

"Not really, ma'am, with the exception of military history." He didn't understand what was so amusing and said so.

"Oh, there's nothing to worry about, Captain. Please continue."

He did so, making a mental note to himself to find out what was so funny, but not right now.

"There's not much more, ma'am. Clark and her team will extract the information from the core then make their way back to the hangar. Once there, we make our extraction and rendezvous with the *Valhalla*."

"Very well, Captain. It sounds like you have things well in hand," McLaughlin said as she and Commander Ruggs stood. "Lieutenant Commander Tucholski here"—she patted the navigation officer on the shoulder—"has already calculated your insertion profile, and he'll work out a rendezvous plan as well while the rest of you hammer out the details. As for the assault carrier, the *Valhalla* is more than its match. It'll be disabled or destroyed before you leave the ship. Any questions before I let you get to it?"

"No, ma'am. We'll get it done." Optika came to attention.

"I'm sure you will, Captain. Just keep in mind that you have exactly"—she looked over Tucholski's shoulder at his pad—"two hours and seventeen minutes to flesh out your plan, brief your marines, and board the shuttles before launch."

That wasn't much time, but he knew that complaining about it wouldn't give him any more. There was only one thing left to say.

"Not a problem, ma'am. We'll be ready."

Captain Optika was jerked out of his ruminations as the shuttle hit atmosphere traveling at close to two thousand kilometers per hour. Normally, as a battalion commander, he would not be leading a company-level assault, but with the rapid reorganization of the battalion, he deemed it safer to remain in command of his original company. Optika trusted his XO to run the company, but with the new chain of command in place for only a few hours, it would make things smoother and keep confusion to a minimum with him still running the show. The pilots rode the turbulence as the shuttles bucked and groaned, rapidly closing on the surface. At the last possible moment, the shuttle began its braking maneuver in the simple and expedient method of simply reversing thrust—with the throttles wide open.

Optika and the rest strained at their harnesses as they were thrown forward. Blood rushed to his face, giving him the feeling that his face was about to burst. He tried to concentrate on what little intelligence they had, but his mind continued to drift back to something he had once been told by an instructor during his assault training.

Unless an assault shuttle explodes upon reentry, it can plow into the ground traveling at unbelievably high speeds and still possibly be salvageable—once the remains of the passengers are sponged out of it, that is.

Optika smiled. No matter how many drops he'd done over the years, it always came back to him when they hit the atmosphere.

As the shuttle leveled out at one hundred meters above the surface, Optika reviewed their current status. He glanced at the monitors and saw *Shuttle Five* on his port side, *Shuttle Six* starboard. Their speed was one thousand kilometers per hour and falling. Glancing at the display projected on the inside of his helmet, he could see that they were rapidly coming up on their jump-off point. In fact, they had less than a minute until touchdown. Time to get to work.

"Lock and load, marines!" He had to shout over the company net to be heard. The sound of their flight, while not deafening, was uncomfortably loud. Optika listened as his platoon leaders passed the order on. Keeping an eye on his countdown, Optika followed his own order and inserted a magazine into his pulse rifle and cycled the power up, charging the capacitors, then moved on to his pistol when was finished.

The shuttles went subsonic and continued to decelerate as he counted down the last five seconds over the net. Feeling the shuttle's skids hit the ground in a bone-rattling impact, Captain Stewart Optika slapped the quick release on his harness and sprang to his feet, shouting.

"Everybody out of the boats! Move, move, move!"

Following his marines out the shuttle, he jumped to the ground, watching as they raced to form a perimeter.

The assault had begun.

Chapter Twenty-eight

HUGIN RESEARCH FACILITY
OCTOBER 13, 2197
1915Z
MARS, SOL

Bravo Company was deployed along a slight ridge in a two-hundred-meter arc with First and Second Platoons on the line, and Third Platoon to the rear. Captain Optika had stationed himself within First Platoon, keeping himself from being in the center of the formation. Lying prone, gazing at the carnage beneath him, he could see that he had been right about the facility's marine detachment. They definitely had laid out a warm welcome for the Xan-Sskarns. There were dozens of bodies. Some of the Xan-Sskarns, mostly those directly in front of the main entrance, had been so badly torn apart as to make it impossible to identify individual bodies.

"This is Bravo Actual," Optika called over the company's command net, his call sign identifying him as Bravo Company Commander. "Report."

"This is One Actual. We're in position," Lieutenant Rook reported.

"Two Actual, in position," came Lieutenant Burnette.

"Three Actual, ready to roll," Luthi said from behind him, the anxious tone in her voice unmistakable.

"Acknowledged, wait one," Optika told his platoon commanders. He wanted to wait for Corporal Clark to get into position before moving.

While he waited, he took the time to inspect the marines around him. Each of them was outfitted in combat suits and gear identical to his own.

First was a form-fitting bodysuit of semihardened synthetic material that provided protection in a variety of environments without sacrificing mobility. The suit was coated with a skin of what marines called "mimic material." The official name was a long and complex number-and-letter combination that once heard was promptly forgotten. Whatever the name, it was the effect that was important. It could be set to mimic a variety of colors and patterns. The selection was by no means limitless; the current coloring was proof of that. The suits were set to a swirling red and ochre pattern—while not a perfect match to their surroundings, it was close enough to make them difficult to see.

Worn over the suit was an outer layering of hardened armor. A full combination torso and groin piece provided protection to vital areas, while smaller individual pieces covered arms and legs. The armor was also coated in mimic material.

Air supply, helmet, combat harness, and pistol belt completed the outfit. The last two items were loaded down with the tools of war.

Each marine in the company also carried two rifles and a pistol. Normally, one or the other of the two rifles would be used, depending on the mission.

The pulse rifle, firing magnetically accelerated rounds of depleted uranium at a respectable fraction of the speed of light, was a perfect weapon for open-field engagements or inside a ship or facility where collateral damage was not a concern. Pulse-rifle rounds had a tendency to punch holes in anything they hit, including bulkheads and hulls.

For situations where shooting a structure full of holes was not an option, the flechette rifle was employed. A cloud of very small, needle-sharp metal darts was expelled from the barrel with each stroke of the trigger. While not very effective over long ranges, or against full body armor, they were horribly effective at close ranges against lightly armored or unarmored targets. A person hit at a range of ten meters by a flechette-rifle burst was turned into so much chopped meat.

Their mission called for both weapons. The pulse rifles would be used if they needed to fight their way into the facility. Once inside, the marines would switch over to the flechette rifles. They didn't want to risk hitting any of the personnel they were there to rescue, nor did they want their weapons' fire to inadvertently destroy the information they were there to retrieve. Once the civilians and data were secured, however, all bets were off, and the pulse rifles would make their presence known once again. And if it came down to fighting with their flechette pistols, they were in trouble.

After a few minutes of waiting, Optika's earpiece crackled to life.

"This is Romeo Three One. Objective in sight."

Romeo Three One—Clark was still using her original call sign, identifying her as team leader of third fire team, Recon squad. There had not been time for updating call signs for units that were missing members. They could not afford the confusion that would come from using unfamiliar identifiers.

"Roger, Romeo Three One, proceed at own discretion," he radioed back to her, letting her know that she was now on her own. "Out."

Trusting that Clark and her team would be able to handle themselves, Optika directed his attention to the situation before him.

The facility's main entrance opened directly to the west and was wide enough to allow two large surface-effect vehicles to pass through at once. The entrance was also currently closed. Optika surmised that once the Xan-Sskarns had cleared out all the traps and silenced the fixed defenses, they managed to override the door's locking mechanism. If that was the case, they had more than likely rendered it useless.

If they trashed the door mechanism, well, that's why we have breaching charges.

"One, proceed to the north. Two, south. Scouts out in front," he told his platoon commanders. "And make sure everyone treads softly. The Sallys have had time to leave *us* a few surprises."

Optika listened as his subordinates radioed back their comprehension. He took a moment to listen in on each of their platoon nets to get an idea of how they were going to deploy their marines.

Once he had assured himself that he had a good idea of where the men and women of First and Second Platoon were, he switched to Third Platoon's net.

"Three, move up to my position." He wanted his armored platoon close enough to support the advance, should it be needed.

A red-and-ochre-patterned suit of armor dropped down beside him. He couldn't see the face behind the polarized faceplate, but the black rank insignia painted on the chest told him it was Third Platoon's commander, Lieutenant Luthi. Being encased in a full suit of pseudomuscular-enhanced armor made it difficult, if not impossible, to read a person's mood, unless one knew the wearer of the suit well. Optika knew his lieutenant quite well and could tell from the way she was hunched forward, fingers drumming on the ground, that she was eager to press the attack. Cutting into her direct net, he tried to reassure her.

"Sandy, relax. Once First and Second are in position, I'll move you up and have you set the air locks and breach the doors. Then things will get interesting."

"I know, sir, but I just hate waiting, especially knowing that there might be people still alive in there."

"It grates on me, too, but we won't do anyone any good if we get ourselves chopped before we can even get inside."

His words seemed almost prophetic as he heard his First Platoon commander shout over the company net.

"Contact! Two men down, moving to engage."

"Easy there, Luthi." Optika held on to her arm, knowing that it was his presence, and not the pressure on her arm, that stopped her. If she wanted to go, there was nothing he could do to stop her. He switched to the command net.

"Two Actual, take cover and wait for orders, Three Actual, remain in position."

He listened to both officers acknowledge his orders before he cut into First Platoon's net, listening to the situation but not interrupting.

"Two-one, move your squad into position and lay down suppressing fire and try to locate the shooters," Lieutenant Rook barked, getting his marines to move and respond to the ambush. "Three-one, take your squad thirty meters to the north. Then I want a right echelon on line. Advance until you make contact. One-one, get the wounded and pull back."

There were no acknowledgments over the net, but Optika could see the platoon move to follow Rook's orders. He also saw that first squad now had four wounded, none of which seemed too serious as all four of them were mobile, albeit with assistance.

"Target!" an unidentified voice called out over the platoon's net. "Looks to be a Sally manjack."

Both humans and Xan-Sskarns shared some of the same types of weapons, and the manjack, an emplaced gun with a simple yet effective targeting system, was one of them. When the weapon's sensors detected movement, the manjack went active, seeking out the movement and opening fire, prioritizing targets based on proximity to itself. They could consist of a variety of weapons, but this particular manjack appeared to be an automatic flechette gun. Anything else would not have left survivors at such close range.

"Take it out," Rook ordered without hesitation.

There was a small crump, and a ball of smoke began to rise from the north.

"Target eliminated," an unidentified voice reported.

"Good job. Where was it?"

"Looks like the Sallys dug a small pit then put parts of their dead on and around it to hide it."

"First Actual to Second Actual." Rook contacted his fellow platoon leader to pass on the discovery.

"This is Second Actual, go ahead," Lieutenant Burnette's young voice responded.

"Have found Sally manjacks, dug in and concealed by body parts. Recommend you probe with fire."

"Roger, thanks for the warning, First. Second out."

Captain Optika watched as Lieutenant Rook's suggestion was enacted by both platoons.

Marine platoons no longer carried rocket launchers in this day and age. After all, a pulse-rifle round traveling at a significant fraction of the speed of light delivered more destructive power in the form of kinetic energy when it impacted than any portable rocket ever could.

As rifle fire flashed out from both platoons and hypervelocity rounds punched their way through the already-dead enemy, they were rewarded by more than one new explosion.

While the firing continued, Optika contacted Rook for a status on his casualties.

"Three wounded. One superficial—the other two need evac." Rook's voice lost some of its professional edge as he finished. "One dead."

"Who?"

"PFC LeBeau. He caught a burst on his right side at close range. Tore through his femoral. He bled out before the doc could patch it."

"Understood." Optika's voice took on a slightly softer tone as well. "Pull your wounded back to my position. We'll move them back to the shuttles."

"Roger, they're on the way now."

When the firing had ceased, Optika had First and Second Platoons continue on to their objectives. While they were doing that, the wounded arrived, supported by their comrades. Optika indicated that they could let the wounded rest there and the hale could return to the platoon.

"Sandy, pull two guards off the shuttles and get them to come and pick up the wounded."

"Sir, that'll leave the shuttles with only two guards left."

"I know, but it's a small risk." Optika waved a hand toward the facility. "If the Sallys were going to do something, they would have done it already. I think they're all busy inside."

"Yeah, I'm sure they are." Hate laced her voice. There was a moment's silence before she came back to him. "They're on their way in now, sir. ETA two minutes."

Optika was still impressed with how quickly something as cumbersome-looking as combat armor could move.

"Good. It looks like First and Second are in position, so when they get here, we'll move up."

"Roger that, sir."

He half listened in as Lieutenant Luthi got her platoon ready to move, the bulk of his attention on what was about to come.

This was the easy part, and we were damn lucky to get off as light as we did. But once we breach those doors, things are going to get much, much worse.

Moving up with her Third Platoon, Lieutenant Luthi was relieved that the journey was uneventful. It appeared that the marine detachment had kept the Sallys busy long enough to ensure that they didn't have the time to set any more traps for the company. She only hoped that there were some still resisting inside the facility.

"Three Actual, place your charges and get those locks in place," Optika ordered over the net. "First Actual, Second Actual, keep an eye on our flanks. I don't like it when things go this smoothly."

She signaled an affirmative.

Luthi watched as the charges were placed on three different

locations of the facility's entrance door. The long, thick, ropelike substance was formed into an oval, large enough for an armored marine to walk through without having to duck, on the door. The breaching charges in place, more members of Third Platoon moved forward to assemble the portable air locks. They were trapezoidal and made of transparent plastic. The air-lock door at the base was large enough to accommodate one fire team at a time, or two armored marines. The top of the trapezoid was attached to the facility door by use of a molecular adhesive.

Once the locks were assembled and attached to the facility door, two armored marines moved into the newly created room between the facility door and the air lock, while two more remained in the air-lock entrance. Once all the marines were in place, detonators were inserted into the charges.

The charges were composed of a unique explosive compound that wouldn't detonate until it reached an *extremely* high temperature. The charges were designed to breach the hull of an enemy ship, and they would make short work of the facility door. So when the detonators fired, the charges began a chemical chain reaction and began to heat. As the heat rapidly rose, the metal of the door bubbled and melted. The charges had nearly burned their way through when the temperature reached critical. The resulting explosion was directed inward by the charge, and the newly cut metal was blown forcefully into the room behind it.

Before the echo of clanging metal ended, the first two marines in the body of the air locks were through the opening, spreading out with weapons sweeping from side to side, looking for targets. As more of Third Platoon entered the facility, they began to search the small car park that was between the inner and outer doors.

Lieutenant Luthi entered the car park with the middle wave of her platoon and took her platoon sergeant's report stating that the area was secure.

"Good job, Staff Sergeant." She looked around to see just how many of her people were now inside. When sufficient numbers of her platoon were present, she moved on to the next part of the plan.

"Three-five, take one and secure that hatch." She pointed at the hatch in the south corner of the car park. "I'm going to take two and secure the other. Wait for my signal, then secure the corridor on the other side."

"Roger that, One," said Five. Staff Sergeant Duska called for first squad to join him and began to move off toward his objective when they were all assembled.

"Three, secure this room. Two, on me."

When the last member of second squad trotted over, Luthi headed for the hatch in the north corner.

Both hatches opened onto the same corridor running along the inner wall of the car park. If the schematics she'd studied were accurate, there were no other openings other than the intersections five meters up and down the corridor past the hatches.

Reaching her objective, she pointed to first squad's first fire-team leader and indicated that she and her team would be the ones going though first.

Sergeant Galvin and her fire team moved into position with two members on the left of the hatch—one crouching and the other standing behind him ready to press the hatch release—and the other two crouching on the right.

"Two-one in position," Galvin said.

"One-three, in position." First Squad's third fire team was going to be leading the squad through the south-side hatch.

Luthi took one last look around the car park, seeing her third squad, minus the fire team guarding the shuttles, spread out behind first and second squad, putting themselves in position to support them should it be needed. Members of Second Platoon began to enter, and she knew that she had to move her platoon out before it became too crowded in the park, and thus unsafe. Turning back around, she gave the order.

"Go!"

Both hatches began to cycle open, and the first marines crouched on the right-hand side reacted in unison, throwing flash-bang grenades into the corridor before the hatch stopped its movement. Three seconds after the hatches began to move, a loud bang and bright light flashed in the corridors, and, right on its heels, the fire team at the hatch raced through, securing the area immediately beyond.

A soft cough came from the south hatch, and two more came from the north.

"Clear."

"Clear."

Both entry teams reported, and the rest of the squads began to move swiftly through the hatches. As Luthi came though behind the last fire team, she saw two dead Xan-Sskarns, their blood covering the bulkheads and deck, victims of point-blank flechette fire.

"Bravo Actual, this is Three Actual, entrance corridor secure."

"Understood, Three Actual, wait one." Captain Optika entered the car park along with the bulk of Second Platoon. When the final members of Second arrived, he ordered Lieutenant Burnette to relieve Third Platoon, releasing Luthi to complete her part of the mission.

"Good hunting, Three," he said over Third Platoon's net. A chorus of various acknowledgments came back. "Bravo Actual out."

Optika turned his attention to his own part of the mission. All of Second Platoon had passed through the car park and was now in the corridor, pushing out only far enough to make room for First Platoon to join them. When Lieutenant Rook stepped through the cut opening, he knew it was time to begin.

"First Actual and Second Actual, this is Bravo Actual," Optika began. "Second, you will pull your squads back and cover the northern end of the corridor as First moves in to relieve you. First, maintain cover of the southern end. We'll hold those positions until we get word where the civilians are."

He waited for their responses before continuing.

"I want you both to keep your platoons sharp. Those Lokis let the Valkyries get awfully close before they torched that Sally carrier, but the ones on the ground probably suspect we're comin'. And they sure as hell will know it when Three reaches the command center. Bravo Actual out."

Lieutenant Luthi tried to flatten herself against the bulkhead, a difficult task when wearing combat armor. Enemy fire flashed around her, missing by centimeters, gouging out sections of the bulkhead she was currently trying to become one with.

Third Platoon was caught in a crossfire just short of their first objective. She held her flechette rifle close to her body, pointing it down the corridor as she pulled the trigger and swung the barrel back and forth. She was rewarded with a fountain of blood erupting from one of the Xan-Sskarns holding the far intersection. This fire fight was delaying them; they needed to be moving.

If they didn't make it to the control room quickly enough to get the information about the civilians' location to the captain, he could find himself decisively engaged and unable to act on it.

One of her marines was trying to advance along the opposite bulkhead. He had just come even with her position when he bounced away from the wall and began to jerk as if electrocuted—the normal response of a combat-armored marine when hit with a penetrator round. The round entered from one side of the armor, but did not exit the other side. Instead, it caromed around the inside, shredding the flesh and bone of the wearer.

He was the third marine she had lost since this ambush was sprung. Third Platoon controlled one intersection and two stretches of corridor that extended from it in opposite directions. The two corridors that extended from their intersection, perpendicular to the corridor, were held by the Xan-Sskarns, as was everything else, and they were using it to their advantage, pouring fire into the platoon.

Lieutenant Luthi made a quick decision. If there were this many Xan-Sskarn here, then the chances of there being anyone else around were negligible. With that in mind, she shouted her order over the platoon net.

"All hands! Concussion grenades, now." She reached down to the pouch attached to the waist of her suit and withdrew her own grenade. Thumbing the activator while cocking her arm, she threw it down the passageway. The enhanced strength from her suit turned the grenade into a missile as it hurtled into the intersection. She gave a small smile of satisfaction as she watched it punch through the throat of a Xan-Sskarn who had moved into the grenade's path.

Less than a heartbeat later, her grenade was joined by a dozen more, and she knew the scene was being repeated in four different directions. Detonation came seconds later as the nearly thirty grenades exploded almost simultaneously, sending a shockwave moving down the corridor past her. Her armor handled the concussion without difficulty.

"Up and at 'em!" she yelled over the net. They needed to exploit the opening they'd just created.

She and the first fire team to enter the Xan-Sskarn–held intersection looked around to see if there were any Xan-Sskarn survivors. There weren't. The concussive shockwave that had simply buffeted her armor had pulped the eleven Xan-Sskarns holding the position.

"Okay, this is where we split up." She connected to her three squad leaders. "Two, Three, you go and secure the hangar and make sure we have a ride out of here. I'll take One and head to the control room. If you run into heavy opposition, do you what you need to. I don't think there are any survivors in the area."

She waited for their assent before using hand signals to start them all moving again. The hangar team continued through the intersection they had just taken, while Luthi and the rest of first squad turned to the right and raced forward. The command center was just ahead.

Lieutenant Rook ducked his head down behind the makeshift barrier his platoon had placed across the entrance to the corridor he was defending. Flechette rounds pinged off the bulkhead and the workbench barricade. The workbench, like the rest of the materials used in the barricades around First and Second Platoons' perimeter, had come from the car park. Rook was glad that the captain had thought to reinforce the perimeter, even though they weren't expected to be in position for long. Things never had a way of going right when the enemy was involved. They didn't seem to want to play by your rules. Case in point: the ambush of Third Platoon and the consequent delay that had allowed the Sallys to bring troops against the rest of the company.

"Well, crying about it won't do me any good, but this will," he muttered to himself, popping his head and shoulders above the barricade and loosing a burst of flechette fire at the advancing Xan-Sskarns. He was happy to see that one of them had dropped, clutching at its arm, before he ducked back down as their response came flying back at him.

It took Rook a moment to realize what he had seen during his brief exposure.

"Bravo Actual, this is First Actual."

"This is Bravo Actual, go First." Captain Optika sounded like he was a busy as Rook was.

Well, the captain is about to become even more busy, but, hey, that's what they pay him the big money for.

"I've got the Sallys setting up what looks to be a heavy flechette cannon at the other end of this corridor, and this barricade won't hold up long under that kind of firepower."

"Understood, First. See what you can do to slow them down."

The strain in Optika's voice was clearly evident. Rook knew as well as the captain did that if the Xan-Sskarns got the cannon up and running before the marines made their breakout, they would have to fall back into the car park, and that would scrub the mission.

"Roger, Bravo, I'll see what I can do." Rook broke his connection to his company commander and opened one to the squad with him in the barricaded intersection.

"Okay, listen up people. One-one, I want continuous fire down this corridor—keep them down. One-two and One-three, I want you to keep your eyes open. If the Sallys are bringing up any more of their big guns, I want to know about it."

He let the fire-team leaders get their marines into place as he took stock of the rest of his platoon. Second squad was spaced out along the corridor, and third was still in the car park, watching their backs. If they stayed here much longer, he would have to start rotating squads as ammunition ran low and casualties ran high.

Rook came up beside One-one and took another quick glance to check the Xan-Sskarns' progress. So far, it looked as if his marines were succeeding in keeping them pinned down, but he knew it wouldn't last.

One of his marines pitched back, head nearly severed by a lucky hit to the gap between his torso armor and helmet, spraying Rook and the rest of One-one with blood. Another went down, this time from One-three, clutching the mangled remains of her left arm.

He listened in on Second Platoon long enough to find out that they were in the same situation as his platoon.

Shouts for corpsmen rang out over the net.

Hurry up, Luthi. We can't stay here much longer.

The Xan-Sskarn standing in front of the hatch leading to the control room burst apart in a shower of gore as Lieutenant Luthi walked a burst up its chest and into its face. The combat-armored marines of Third Platoon carried the same type of weapons as the rest of the company, the only difference being the size. Theirs were much bigger. And in this case, size did matter. A normal flechette rifle wouldn't have been able to penetrate the body armor the Xan-Sskarn guard had been wearing.

This thought brought a grim smile to her face as she stepped through the remains of her victim and dove into the command center. Coming up onto one knee, she snapped the butt of her rifle into her shoulder and scanned a section of the room. The fire team following her in did the same.

"Clear," she said, getting to her feet. The rest of the entry team followed suit.

"LT, you better see this," her squad leader said softly, beckoning her over.

Luthi walked around the first row of consoles and down into the recession in the deck where the second row was. Lying in the recession were the mutilated remains of eight marines. She looked around again, not seeing any Xan-Sskarn bodies; their comrades must have removed them. Looking back at the carnage at her feet, she saw dozens of spent rifle magazines and several drawn pistols. These marines had not gone down without a fight, nor had they simply stopped when the ammunition ran out. One of them held the haft of a broken combat knife in her hand.

She felt the anger begin to boil in her blood at the sight before her, but she kept it out of her voice as she got her team moving.

"Spread out. See if you can find out whether or not the scientists are still alive, and, if so, where they're at."

The fire team began to move, going from console to console, finding most of them smashed beyond any hope of repair. Finally someone found what they were looking for.

"Got 'em!" a voice called out.

"Where?" Luthi barked as she sped to the speaker's side, looking at the console herself.

"They're in the galley." The marine at the console began to switch between different camera views. "Looks like they've got the doors barricaded and sealed, and—Jesus Christ!"

Luthi saw what had caused the outburst.

There were still marines down there, and they were still fighting.

Captain Optika was about to order a withdrawal. Lieutenant Rook had reported the flechette cannon had finally been set up and had managed two bursts. What was left of the lieutenant's barricade would not stand up to a third. Fortunately, his marines had managed to take out the shooter, but it was only a matter of time before that third burst came, and, when it did, the Xan-Sskarns would have his two platoons in a shooting gallery.

He had just connected to the company net to issue the order when Lieutenant Luthi's voice burst out.

"Third Actual to Bravo Actual, found 'em."

"Where?" Optika asked back, not worrying about radio discipline.

"They're in the galley, and, sir, there's still a couple of marines down there putting up a hell of a fight. I recommend you hurry."

"Understood. What about the rest?" Luthi's mission to the control room had not only been to find the civilians.

"Looks like the guys here took care of it for us, sir." Lieutenant Luthi's voice hovered somewhere between respect and sorrow. "All hatches are in local control only, the environmental board is slag, and the power-distribution board is in even worse shape."

"Good work," Optika said, relieved. "Rejoin the rest of your platoon. Then I want you to establish a perimeter around the hangar. After that, get the shuttles moving and bring them in. I want to be able to load as soon as we get there."

"Roger, Bravo Actual. We'll take care of it."

"Carry on. Bravo Actual out."

Their extraction taken care of, now all he needed to do was get to the galley, rescue nearly one hundred fifty civilians, drag them through a Xan-Sskarn–held facility, load them onto shuttles, and blast out of here.

But first he needed to get out of this corridor, and to that end he opened a channel to his two other platoon commanders.

"First Actual, Second Actual, this is Bravo Actual. We've located the scientists and remaining marines. They're still holding out, so listen up. We're about to break out of here and go and get them." Optika began to issue the orders that would allow them to do just that.

"Get your wounded ready to move. Second, we'll be moving through your position—the civilians are in the galley. Just follow the signs. First, when Second begins to move, I want you to perform a fighting withdrawal. But leave a few surprises behind for the Sallys to play with. Questions?"

There was only one, and it was like an icy hand clenching around his heart.

"The dead?" Lieutenant Rook asked.

"Leave them." He hated saying it, hated doing it even more,

but they simply did not have the time or manpower to carry the dead and the wounded and maintain what was likely to be a running firefight throughout the facility. "Redistribute their ammo and disable their weapons. I'm sorry."

It sounded hollow, even to him, but he had other concerns. The living took precedence over the dead.

"Understood, Bravo." Rook's voice was tight with anger. Not at Optika, but at the Xan-Sskarn for putting him in this situation. Burnette's voice was just as emotional.

"Two minutes, gentlemen," Optika said as he started a countdown timer, watching as it began to tick away the seconds on his helmet's display. "Second, I want you to lead off with flash-bangs, then hit them with everything you've got and keep moving. Gentlemen, this facility's marines put up one hell of a fight, and still are. There were only twenty-five of them. Let's go and show the Sallys what a *company* of pissed-off marines can do. One minute."

Optika watched as the ammunition from the dead and incapacitated was redistributed, and as the wounded were prepared for movement. He didn't doubt that he would probably lose several of them before they reached the shuttles, but he would not leave them behind for the Sallys. He might have to leave his dead behind, but he would never leave his living.

The last few seconds of his timer counted down. When it reached zero, he shouted, "Go!"

He watched as grenades were thrown down the corridor, and he could hear the increase in the fire from First Platoon behind him. The grenades detonated, and before he could say anything, Lieutenant Burnette had his lead fire teams up and racing down the corridor, slowing down only long enough to put a burst of fire in any Xan-Sskarn they passed.

The rest of Second Platoon began to move out, and, as the last fire teams began to move, Optika called to Lieutenant Rook.

"First Actual, begin your withdrawal." He didn't wait for a response as he began to follow the last members of Second Platoon.

When he reached the next intersection, he stopped and knelt with the fire team providing cover. Lieutenant Burnette had his marines performing a fighting withdrawal. The first team to reach an intersection set up to cover the rest of the platoon as it came through. When the last marine passed, they would begin their own withdrawal. This was repeated at each intersection.

He knew this kind of maneuver could leave his platoons spread out too far, but with the galley being only a dozen intersections away, Optika was confident they would be able to make the journey without having to worry about exposing themselves too much.

First Platoon's first fire team had reached the intersection and exchanged places with the current team. He could see that Lieutenant Rook had things well in hand. Leaving the lieutenant to oversee the end of the withdrawal, Optika moved to catch up to the lead elements.

Lieutenant Burnette moved down the corridor at a fast pace. He did not want to break into a run and spread things out too much, but he did not want to lose the momentum they had. He began to think about what he was going to do if the captain was not in the lead when they encountered the Xan-Sskarn. As he rounded the last corner, he didn't have time to worry about it anymore.

Crowding the passageway in front of him were over twenty Xan-Sskarns bunched together, apparently trying to enter a side passage all at the same time. Burnette's finger tightened on the trigger of his rifle even before his mind could fully comprehend what he was seeing. Thousands of tiny projectiles flashed out of the barrel of his rifle, impacting the Xan-Sskarns closest to him. Flesh and bone parted in a spray of blood as the first of the enemy began to fall. Burnette's rifle, firing on full auto, had already expended its magazine by the time the next member of the lead team entered the passageway, opening fire without hesitation.

Reaching for another magazine, Burnette moved forward again. As more marines entered the passageway, the air filled with hundreds of thousands of flechettes, and the Xan-Sskarns had nowhere to hide from them. But neither did the marines.

The last half-dozen Xan-Sskarns, having been protected by their comrade's bodies, had time to refocus their attention on their attackers and bring their own weapons to bear.

Three more marines went down before the last of the Xan-Sskarns fell. Two dead, one wounded.

Using hand signals, Burnette directed his marines to spread out and cover the corridor as he moved toward the side passage that the Xan-Sskarns had been so intent on entering. What he saw there almost made him vomit.

The passageway was one point five meters wide, and it was packed from side to side and almost half a meter deep with shredded Xan-Sskarn bodies. He had just begun to pick his way toward the hatch at the end of the short passageway when the captain arrived.

"Looks like they earned their way into the Halls," Burnette whispered over a private channel.

"And then some, Lieutenant," Optika whispered back. "And then some."

Burnette had finally managed to make his way the ten meters to the hatch. The last meter had been mercifully clear of bodies, except for two marines and one Xan-Sskarn behind a pockmarked barricade. He bent down to examine the marines' bodies in the vain hope that they might still be alive when one of them, his body half covered by the Xan-Sskarns, gasped as his eyes flew open.

"Holy fuck!" Burnette jumped back, startled. Recovering immediately, he dropped to his knees and began to try and move the dead Xan-Sskarn while shouting for help.

"Corpsman up! On the double—I've got a live one here!"

At Lieutenant Burnette's shout, Captain Optika began to slog his way through the dead Xan-Sskarns as quickly as he could. He could hear someone following him and assumed it was the corpsman.

When he reached Burnette, he saw that the lieutenant had a pressure bandage pressed over the marine's stomach. It was almost black with blood. He put his hands beside the lieutenant's, then turned his head toward him.

"Lieutenant, get through that hatch," Optika growled. "There's got to be a surgeon in there somewhere. Find him and get him out here. Now!"

"Yes, sir!" Burnette had already started moving before the captain finished his order.

The corpsman arrived and took over for the captain, working rapidly. Optika moved up to the marine's head and cradled it in his lap as he watched the marine's lips move.

"Civilians," he whispered, almost too softly for the receptors in his helmet to pick up. "Have to protect the civilians."

"You've done that, son." Optika's voice was thick. "You just save your energy and let the doc here patch you up."

He looked at the corpsman and saw him shaking his head.

"It's his liver, sir. The Xan-Sskarn ripped most of it out with its talons," the corpsman said over the net, not wanting the marine to hear. "There's nothing I can do."

Optika looked over his shoulder at the hatch, willing a doctor to walk though it.

"Xan-Sskarns!" the marine shouted, blood beginning to flow from his mouth. "Can't let them get the civilians. Gotta stop them. Gotta..."

"You did, marine—you saved them." Tears ran down the captain's face. "You just sleep. We'll take it from here. You've done the corps proud, marine."

The dying man smiled up at him upon hearing that.

"Semper Fi..." His voice fell off as the last breath left his body.

The hatch opened, and Lieutenant Burnette came through, dragging a middle-aged-looking man by the collar of his lab coat. Behind the two of them was a severe-looking woman.

"There he is," Burnette said over his helmet speakers. "Help him."

The man pulled away from the lieutenant and began to kneel down.

"It's too late, sir," the corpsman said, shaking his head as he stood.

"Who's in charge here?" came a shrill voice.

"That would be me, ma'am." Optika came slowly to his feet and faced her. "Captain Stewart Optika."

"Well, *Captain*, I wish to register a complaint about your subordinate here." She stabbed her finger toward the lieutenant as she spoke. "He just came bursting in, scaring us half to death, then started demanding a surgeon. He was very rude and very vulgar, and I want him dealt with."

Optika stood, staring at the woman standing there with her dark hair in a bun, her clothes immaculate, as if she had just gotten dressed, and clean-looking except for a single smudge of dirt on her cheek. He looked from her down to the bodies at his feet. He saw the Xan-Sskarn, a combat knife buried in its throat. He saw two marines, both having died protecting her. He lifted his gaze and looked out at the mounds of Xan-Sskarn bodies those two had piled up in what they almost certainly believed was a vain hope, but never once giving up. He turned back to her.

"Fuck your complaint."

Chapter Twenty-nine

HUGIN RESEARCH FACILITY
OCTOBER 13, 2197
1925Z
MARS, SOL

"Well, isn't that just downright nice of him," Corporal Tracy Clark, Marine Recon team leader, said after cutting off from the command net and back into Recon's net.

"What's nice of who?" asked Lance Corporal Alan Lewis, the second and only other member of the team.

"Oh, the captain. He said we could proceed at my discretion."

"You know, Tracy, I've known you for all of twelve hours, and I must say, out of all the adjectives I can think of to describe you, 'discreet' is not one of them."

"Why, Lance Corporal Lewis, I am shocked that you would think that about your fire-team leader." Her voice was heavy with indignation.

Alan snorted.

"So, when do we go in?" he asked after a few minutes. "It's getting friggin' cold sittin' around out here."

"Things'll be plenty hot once we go inside. I'd say in another couple of minutes or so. We'll wait for Bravo to get the Sally's attention—then we can pop the door and get in without anyone the wiser."

"Sounds good to me."

They both fell silent as they maintained their observation of the small hatch they were going to use to enter the facility.

Tracy saw a pillar of smoke begin to rise from the direction of the company. Nudging Alan's elbow, she pointed.

"Looks like that's our cue."

They rose together, heading toward the hatch at a run as more smoke lifted from the company's position. They hit the outer wall of the facility at the same time, one on either side of the hatch.

Alan tried the panel, and after a few attempts turned to Tracy.

"It's dead."

"Override it."

She watched as Alan slung his pack off his back and rummaged through it for a moment before coming up with a small black box. He attached it to the wall, just beside the control panel. Opening both the panel and the box, he took leads from one and attached them to the other. After eight or nine connections, the panel's lights turned green, and the hatch cycled open.

"Grab it and let's go," she told him and stepped through the hatch and into the air lock. Alan disconnected the leads, pulled the black box off the wall, and followed her in.

Tracy looked over her shoulder to make sure that Alan was in the lock before she keyed the sequence that would let them enter the facility proper. The outer hatch closed, and she could hear the hiss of air being pumped into the small compartment. She pressed herself up against the bulkhead and saw that Alan was doing the same opposite her. They were not expecting company when the inner hatch opened, but there was no need to silhouette themselves.

A tone sounded as the pressure equalized. The inner hatch opened, and they both waited a handful of heartbeats before moving.

She pointed at Alan and raised one finger, then at herself and raised two. He would go through first, then her. Holding up three fingers now, she slowly began to fold them back into her fist. When the last one fell, they moved.

They both went through the hatch in a dive, rolling up onto their knees back-to-back, weapons pointed outward, seeking targets.

"Clear," she whispered.

"Clear," Alan responded, just as quietly.

Tracy took a moment to orient herself. Being a Recon Marine, she was accustomed to having to move quickly and assuredly in any kind of environment, so it had taken her only ten minutes back on the *Valhalla* to decide on primary and secondary routes to their objective, and to memorize them. She carried the complete facility schematics on her pad, but she wouldn't need them as long as they didn't have to take too many detours.

"Okay, the core is that way, two levels down." She pointed down the passageway she was covering with her rifle. "Let's go."

She rose to her feet and took a step forward before stopping and half turning to face Alan.

"Oh, and Alan?"

She waited until he was looking at her.

"Yeah?"

She held a finger up to the faceplate of her helmet, where her mouth would be.

"Shhhhh!"

Alan leaned out around the corner of the intersection and quickly looked both ways. When he didn't see anything, he beckoned to Tracy, waving his hand forward, indicating that she was clear to cross the open area. As she began to dash across to the other side of the intersection, he dropped to one knee, turning to face behind him as he went down. He covered their rear for the few short seconds it would take for his team leader to make it across. When he judged that enough time had passed, he looked behind him and saw her waving him onward.

They leapfrogged down corridors and through mechanical areas of the facility for what seemed like forever to Alan, though a look at elapsed mission time showed that it had only been fifteen minutes.

The two of them had managed to make it down to the computer-core level without being detected, but he didn't think that they would remain undetected much longer. They were entering the outer areas of the research labs themselves, and if the Xan-Sskarn were here for the same thing they were, they would be running into each other very soon.

He sprinted over to Tracy, and the two of them continued their silent way deeper into the facility. The passageway ended at a hatch, and they took positions to either side of it and prepared to go into the room, just like they had every other room they had entered.

Alan watched, and, as her last finger dropped, the hatch began to open. Bolting through, he came up, searching his side of the room, knowing that she was behind him doing the same. They had just finished their scrutiny of what looked to be a large lounge when she spoke.

"I don't like the looks of this room."

Alan dove for the floor behind a bank of computer consoles, weapon extended before him, looking for signs of anything out of place.

"I don't see anything—what've you got?" he breathed quietly, still searching.

"Oh, it's nothing like that. I just think it's tacky in here."

He got to his feet and stared at her through his faceplate.

"Don't *do* that. Christ, you almost gave me a heart attack."

"Mmm?" She seemed distracted as she slowly turned in place, taking in the whole room. "Oh, sorry about that. But really, why is it that the eggheads always have such ugly looking stuff? I mean, look at those paintings, and the furniture. It's as if the smarter you get, the worse your taste gets."

"Well, Corporal Art Critic, can we please get moving?" Alan began moving toward the hatch on the far side of the room. "This place is giving me the creeps."

"Me, too, Alan. Me, too."

Alan couldn't tell if she meant the room's decor or the eerily silent facility they were moving through. He thought it better not to ask.

They positioned themselves at the hatch as before, and, just as before, Alan watched as Tracy counted down from three. The hatch opened, and they went through it the same as before. What was different this time was the Xan-Sskarn three meters in front of Alan, bringing a flechette rifle to bear.

"Contact!" he shouted, stroking the trigger twice and feeling the slight recoil in his shoulder as the Xan-Sskarn in front of him came apart under the impact of multiple flechette bursts. Alan saw two more coming around the corner, weapons leveled.

He stroked the trigger again and watched his target drop as he heard Tracy's own contact report. A burst of flechettes chewed their way into the deck directly in front of him. His response was more accurate, and another Xan-Sskarn hit the deck, dead.

He waited for several long moments as Tracy dispatched her own targets. Finally, he heard her announce that her area was secure. He responded in kind.

"Clear."

"Okay Alan, let's get out of here before any more show up," Tracy said, still covering her section of the corridor. "We're almost there, and I expect that we'll have a few more run-ins like this, so stay sharp."

He looked at the broken remains of the Xan-Sskarn directly in front of him.

"You don't have to tell me twice," he said as he put a fresh magazine in his rifle.

Tracy led them down the corridor to a hatch labeled Metallurgy Lab, and stopped in front of it.

"We cut through the lab here, then through the biology lab," she outlined to Alan. "After that, a couple more corridors, and we're there."

She stepped to the side, and they began the room-entry ritual again. This time there were no unexpected surprises waiting for them. She began to creep along the length of the lab, while Alan paralleled her on the other side of the counter that ran the length of the room.

At the hatch leading to the biology lab she stopped, ready to key the hatch open. Before she began the countdown, Alan held up his hand.

"What?" she whispered, even though they were on a secure net.

"I hear something," Alan said, pointing at the hatch.

"What's it sound like?" She didn't hear it herself, but that didn't mean there was nothing there to hear. It was always better to be cautious than careless.

"Don't know. Sounds kind of like howling or screaming."

They dialed up the audio feed, and a cacophony of noises overwhelmed them. It sounded like all the animals in a zoo had become raving lunatics. They quickly dialed the feed back down.

"Well, there's nothing we can do about it. We either go through here or double back and take the long way around." Tracy knew that the final decision was hers, but she still wanted his input.

"I say we go. We know something's there, so we won't be totally surprised by it, and it's faster. Besides, we can always withdraw if we have to."

"Okay, here we go."

She leaned back into position and waited for him to do the same before she began her countdown.

When she dove through the hatch, she found that she had not prepared herself enough.

The center of the biology lab looked like a vision from hell. Blood ran off of the four examination tables to pool on the floor. Carcasses and hunks of meat that had once been organs littered the room. The noise was deafening as half a dozen Xan-Sskarns stood around each table, calmly dissecting the lab animals. While they were still alive.

Tracy felt her stomach roil and almost vomited. She was thankful she couldn't smell anything, or she would have, and that distraction could land her on one of those tables. As it was, she still paused, shocked by the scene before her.

The first cough of Alan's rifle brought her back, and she began servicing targets. None of the Xan-Sskarns in the lab were armed, and ten of them were down before the rest knew they were under attack. The blood and screams in the air masked their deaths from the others at first. Seven seconds later, all of the Xan-Sskarns were down, and Tracy watched as Alan fired four more bursts, one at each table. The room fell silent save for the dripping of blood.

As she watched Alan, she noted that his combat suit was a deeper red than it had been when they were outside. Looking down, she could see hers was as well. The short, sharp, one-sided firefight had coated them in blood as much as it had the room—all but their faceplates. The nonstick surface of the plate resisted all types of substances. In the case of liquids, even the slightest gravitational pull would cause it to run off, leaving the wearer with a clear view.

Too bad the rest of the suit's not like that. It'll be a bitch to clean when we get back. But given a choice between ease of cleaning and camouflage, I know what I'll take any day.

Pushing that worry aside for the time, she made her way carefully across the lab, trying not to step on anything that might have once been living, and failing at it. She slipped twice and managed to catch herself both times before she saw how Alan was traversing the room. He was merely sliding his feet along, as if ice-skating. Wondering why she hadn't thought of that, she followed his example.

The rest of their journey to the computer core was uneventful until they reached the final passageway. The sight of the bloody remains of the four marines behind a broken barricade sent a spike of adrenaline into her system. These were the first human bodies they had seen since they entered the facility.

If they were there, that meant that the Xan-Sskarns had reached the computer core first. All that remained was to see if they were still in there with the data she and Alan had come for.

She slung her rifle diagonally across her back, crisscrossing it with her pulse rifle, and drew her flechette pistol. It operated in the same manner as the rifle, though was not as powerful and thus less likely to damage any of the equipment on the other side of the hatch. From what she had seen of the schematics, the computer core was not an overly large room, and the pistol would be more than adequate if there were any Xan-Sskarns still inside.

Waiting for Alan to draw his pistol, she stepped over the bodies and positioned herself in her customary spot on the side of the hatch. When Alan joined her, she began her countdown.

They burst into the room, startling the five Xan-Sskarns there. Their first bursts took down one of the enemy each. Before either of them could switch targets, the Xan-Sskarns recovered from their shock and charged them, closing the distance in a few steps.

The Xan-Sskarn closest to Alan stopped just short of him and, lifting itself up onto its left leg, did a parody of a pirouette, bringing its thickly muscled tail sailing around to impact with Alan's chest, hurling him three meters across the room and slamming him up against the bulkhead.

Tracy had enough time to watch her partner slide down the bulkhead to the deck before the lead Xan-Sskarn reached her. Desperately trying to bring her pistol around, she was a fraction of a second too slow as the Xan-Sskarn reached out with both of its powerful arms and grabbed her on either side of her chest. Talons dug into the armor she wore as he hefted her over his head, and, like his companion, spun in place and threw her in the direction opposite to Alan.

Managing to twist her body in the air, she bounded off the wall and landed in a crouch. Somewhere during her short flight, she had lost her pistol and there was no way she would be able to unsling one of her rifles before they were on her. Reaching up to her combat harness, she wrapped her hand around the vibro-knife sheathed there and drew it, thumbing the activation stud as she did so.

A soft, deadly purring filled the room as all three Xan-Sskarns advanced on her, slowly this time.

All of them. Either Alan is dead, or I'm the more serious threat. Either way, it's not good.

Rising up from her crouch to a fighting stance, she stared at her assailants calmly as she switched on her external speakers. They might not understand the words, but she hoped they would understand the meaning.

"Come on, you rat bastards, let's dance!"

"That hurt," Alan moaned to himself, trying to sit up. Groaning, he made his way to a sitting position, thankful for the armor he wore. He knew that if it weren't for that, he would, at the very least, have multiple broken ribs, but more than likely he would be dead.

He heard Tracy's shouted invitation and snapped to full alertness, adrenaline kicking in. He saw three Xan-Sskarns closing on her, spreading out, the better to attack her from all sides at once.

Looking about him, he didn't see his pistol, nor did he want to use a rifle for fear of hitting his fire-team leader. With that thought, he reached his left hand up to his combat harness while he dropped his right to his belt. Grasping hilts, he drew his blades, activating his vibro-knife as it cleared the sheath.

Rising silently to his feet, gripping the humming fury of a vibro-knife in his left hand, and a mono-molecular combat knife in his right, he chose his target. With a primal scream bellowing from his helmet speakers, Alan launched himself at the center Xan-Sskarn.

Startled again, all three Xan-Sskarns instinctively turned to face this new threat.

As Alan collided with the center Xan-Sskarn, he saw Tracy

launch herself at the Xan-Sskarn to her right. Impacting with his target, Alan could spare no more time on thoughts of his partner as he began to grapple.

Burying the vibro-blade into the Xan-Sskarn's side, then ripping outward, Alan sent a spray of blood across the room. His right hand hooked up, attempting to sink his combat knife into his opponent's throat.

The Xan-Sskarn's left hand shot up, blocking the upward thrust, and razor-sharp talons raked along Alan's forearm, tearing the combat suit and the flesh beneath it.

Grunting with the pain of torn flesh, Alan drew his left hand across the front of his enemy before it could be blocked. Flesh parted as his vibro-knife disemboweled the Xan-Sskarn. As it went down, Alan followed. Reversing his grip on the combat knife, then driving it through the Xan-Sskarn's eye and into its brain like a spike, he finished off his opponent.

Something raked across his back, pushing him down onto the body of his enemy. Rolling over, he saw the third Xan-Sskarn standing above him, raising its arm, preparing to rake his claws across Alan's throat.

As the arm began to fall, Alan brought his own up to block it. But instead of meeting his arm, the Xan-Sskarn met the edge of his vibro-knife. Screeching loudly, the Xan-Sskarn pulled back a bleeding stump.

Seeing his new opponent turning to flee, Alan threw himself forward, ramming the tip of his combat knife through the top of the Xan-Sskarn's foot. He followed through with his stroke, stopping only when the hilt was pressed firmly against the flesh of the foot it pierced. The blade extended from the bottom of the Xan-Sskarn's foot and was lodged between the gaps of the grating that was the computer core's deck.

Rolling to the side in an attempt to escape the blow he knew was coming from the Xan-Sskarn's uninjured arm, Alan heard a soft hiss followed by a shower of blood. Turning his head, he could see Tracy standing over the body of her own opponent, flechette rifle aimed directly at the space where the final Xan-Sskarn had been standing.

"Nice shot," he said, still lying on the deck looking up at her but making a show of checking his armor for holes.

"You're welcome."

After taking a few more moments to catch his breath, Alan stood up and surveyed the carnage they had wrought in the small room then took stock of his own condition, finally turning to face Tracy.

"Can we go home now?"

"We can go home just as soon as you find the memory module with all the data on it," Tracy told him as she went to retrieve her pistol. Picking it up, she ejected the partially spent magazine and replaced it with a fresh one, then holstered the weapon. Slinging her rifles and pack off, she dropped them to the deck and knelt beside them. Rummaging around in the pack for a moment, she came up with three bricks of what looked like black clay.

"And while you're doing that, I'm going to leave a little thank you for our wonderful hosts."

Standing up, she moved about the room, peeling strips from the backs of the blocks and sticking to them to the three largest banks of computers in the room. She found Alan's pistol in her wanderings and brought it back over to him as he worked a large flat box out of one of the computer banks.

"That it?" she asked him.

"It's the backup storage device, so it should have everything Captain McLaughlin is looking for." Alan shrugged as he set the box on the floor.

She watched as he began to divest himself of pack and rifles then paused, looking at the remains of his pack and flechette rifle.

"Looks like that Sally wanted to take a serious piece out of you, doesn't it?" Tracy asked.

Tracy reached out and took the shredded piece of cloth that was once his pack. Not much of it remained beyond the straps and the backing. It and his flechette rifle had taken the brunt of the Xan-Sskarn's stroke. There was a crease in the magazine well of the rifle, trapping the magazine.

"Well, at least it happened now, and not earlier," she told him, patting him on the back as she bent to retrieve the module.

"Meaning what?" he asked as he shecked to see if the rifle still worked.

"Now that we've got what we came for, and I'm sure the

captain's gotten the civvies squared away, well, we're free to use these babies, now, aren't we?" Tracy patted her pulse rifle.

"Good point," Alan agreed, picking up his own, inserting a magazine into the well, and charging the capacitors.

"God, this thing's heavy," she hissed, trying to work the memory module into her pack. Thirty centimeters long, twenty centimeters wide, and five centimeters deep, the module was an impressive piece of storage medium.

She emptied her pack and stuffed in the module, then quickly looked through the former contents for anything she might remotely need in the next thirty minutes. Nothing caught her eye, so she rose.

"You want me to carry that?" Alan asked her, pointing at the pack sitting at her feet.

"No, I've got it. Besides, I think your back has taken enough of a beating on my behalf."

"Are we ready to go?"

"In a minute. Here," she said, holding out her hand to him, "go put these detonators in our thank-you presents while I get hold of the captain."

Alan slung his rifle and moved off to arm the explosives.

"Bravo Actual, this is Romeo Three One," Tracy called over the command net.

"Romeo Three One, this is Bravo Actual, go ahead." Captain Optika's voice sounded harried and tired.

"Have secured objective and are preparing to exfiltrate."

"Tracy, we've got company!" Alan shouted to her from the hatch. "At least a squad, maybe more."

She looked up to see him kneeling beside the opening, leaning around to fire bursts from his pistol. She opened the Recon net, patching Alan into her conversation with Optika.

"Bravo Actual, be advised, we are meeting heavy resistance. Romeo is going to pulse weapons," she informed the captain, not waiting for permission now. "We are preparing to break out and head home. Make sure everyone knows we're coming, and that we're probably going to bring guests."

She saw Alan holster his pistol then snug the butt of his rifle into his shoulder.

"Understood, Romeo Three One. We'll be waiting, Bravo Actual out." Captain Optika signed off.

"Okay, Alan, are we ready to go?"

"You know it." She could hear the grin in his voice.

"Good." She shouldered her pack and charged her rifle. "Light 'em up."

Alan ejected the spent magazine from his pulse rifle and drew a fresh one from his belt.

"Jesus Christ! How many fuckin' Sallys are on this planet?"

Slapping the magazine into the well, he charged his rifle and brought it up to his shoulder, looking for targets. He and Tracy were once again leapfrogging down the passageways, working their way toward the hangar and their ride home. He watched as she pulled away from her position, turned, and sprinted down the corridor toward him. Just as she was halfway to him, three Xan-Sskarns came around the corner behind her, weapons leveled, preparing to fire.

"Down!" he shouted, sighting in on the middle Xan-Sskarn.

Reacting as soon as she heard his command, Tracy threw herself to the deck, and, once she cleared his line of fire, he pulled the trigger.

A stream of hypervelocity rounds cracked down the passageway, ionizing the air before impacting the lead Xan-Sskarn. The result looked as if the Xan-Sskarn had been packed full of high-yield explosives: it came apart in a mist of vaporized blood and tissue. The hypersonic shockwave of its death took its two companions with it into the afterlife.

"Clear!"

Tracy jumped to her feet and tore down the corridor toward him. When she finally drew even with him, she took up a position along the opposite bulkhead and breathed deeply.

"You know, I've been wondering the same thing," Tracy said to him, her breath already returning to normal. "Seems to me like we've taken out a company by ourselves."

"Yeah, I know, but it's probably only been about twenty-five or thirty. Seems like more, though." He saw another Xan-Sskarn come around the same corner as the earlier three, and it shared their fate.

"Fuck this!" Tracy snapped. Jerking her rifle up and thumbing the capacitor to full charge, she aimed down the corridor. Alan watched as a long stream of rounds impacted with the corner she had just left.

Hypervelocity rounds hitting flesh was one thing, but hitting solid matter was something else entirely. With a lesser charge set on the rifles, the rounds would punch through bulkheads as if they were made of rice paper. At the maximum charge, however, the kinetic impact was quite literally explosive. Alan and Tracy had both had their weapons set for a mid-level charge, but it appeared that Tracy was no longer in the mood to play.

The corner and surrounding bulkheads vanished in a cataclysmic explosion that collapsed part of the structure.

"That should slow them down some," she said.

"I hope so, 'cause I'm getting tired," Alan told her, never taking his eyes off his sector of responsibility.

"Yeah, me, too. Ready?"

"Ready." He saw her nod before taking off down the corridor, pausing at the next junction to scan for targets. Another explosion reached his ears, and he turned to look back at her. Seeing her waving, he took one more look down the corridor behind him and sprinted toward her. One more step closer to escape.

He took up a position opposite her and started to say something when he saw her put up her hand to stop him.

She must be talking with the captain.

When she turned her head to him, he asked what the new situation was.

"The captain is pulling back the perimeter as we get closer. They're engaging some Sallys, but not many. Seems like they really want us."

"Well, I've always wanted to be popular."

"Me, too, but not this much. This module is like a God damn Sally magnet," Tracy said, jerking her thumb over her back.

"How close are we?" Alan hadn't had time to check his pad for their current location. All he knew was that they were traveling in the right direction.

"Two more hops down this corridor, then a left and three more straight to the hangar." Her voice was light. "Piece of cake."

"Right," he said dubiously. "So, whose turn is it?"

"Yours."

"Of course it is."

Looking around one last time and taking a deep breath, Alan

sped off down the corridor, not even slowing as he blew apart the Xan-Sskarn that had stepped into his path.

Not willing to risk damaging their ride home, or being a contributor to the old axiom about friendly fire, they switched back to flechette rifles once they were in a direct line with the hangar. They had just made it to the last intersection when the Xan-Sskarns made their final push.

Alan had the one full magazine in his rifle and no way to replace it once it was expended. However, long months of training had built him, and every other Recon Marine, into an expert marksman. The Xan-Sskarns were mauled by his and Tracy's murderously accurate fire.

"Where the hell is the rest of the company? We could use some cover fire," Alan asked his fire-team leader as, with a short burst, he tore the throat out of a Xan-Sskarn that had looked into the corridor.

Alan knew that if they broke from what little cover they had at the corner of the intersection, they would be cut down long before they could reach the safety of the hangar.

"The captain's got most of the company and all of the civilians loaded already," Tracy told him. "There was an armored squad out here waiting for us, but apparently there's another way into the hangar that wasn't on the schematics, and the Sallys came pouring out on the deck. Looks like if they can't have the data, they're going to make sure no one can have it."

"So, we're on our own, then?" He took another Xan-Sskarn down.

Tracy had been busy as well, taking three more down as they spoke.

"No, an armored fire team is on its way now."

As if summoned by her words, four sets of combat armor came streaking down the corridor toward them.

"Tracy, go!" Alan shouted when he saw them coming, leaning out around the corner and dropping another enemy. "Get the module to the shuttle. I'm right behind you."

She nodded at him and let loose a long stream of flechettes before turning on her heel and sprinting down the corridor.

Alan fired off another burst as an armored marine moved up to take Tracy's spot. Another came up behind him and tapped his shoulder, indicating it was time for him to go as well.

Emptying the rest of his magazine at the Xan-Sskarns, he followed Tracy's example and sprinted toward the hangar and the waiting shuttles.

Tracy joined Captain Optika at the shuttle's hatch, having quickly stowed the memory drive in a secure locker. She finally saw Alan come hurtling through the hatch and onto the hangar deck and waved him over, feeling a rush of relief at his arrival.

He was slinging his rifle and drawing his pistol as he came trotting over. She crouched to one side of the shuttle's hatch, rifle pointed toward the hatch he had just come though. Alan took up a position on the other side, crouching with pistol extended, without any direction from her. She laughed to herself, thinking that they had settled into a routine already when it came to dealing with hatches.

The four armored marines came through the hatch in rapid succession, the last one stopping to close the hatch. Tracy held her breath as it cycled closed, expecting something to happen at the last possible moment, and was relieved when nothing did. The marine smashed the door control with an armored fist. The Xan-Sskarns would need to blast their way onto the hangar deck, and by the time they could manage that, the marines should all be airborne.

"Okay, everybody in the boat," Captain Optika's voice called over the general net. Both Tracy and Alan held their positions, waiting for everyone else to enter first. After the captain finally entered, Tracy opened Recon's net.

"Alan, go!"

He popped up and pulled himself into the troop compartment of the assault boat, and she followed.

She took a seat next to the captain, and Alan took one next to her.

"Looks like you had a few close calls, Corporal," Captain Optika said over Recon's net. "Both of you."

"Yes, sir, you could say that," Tracy said blandly. "I would highly discourage hand-to-hand combat with Xan-Sskarns. It's too messy."

"Among other things," Alan added, holding up his arm so the captain could see the bandages. "They don't believe in manicures."

The three of them chuckled while the shuttles lifted. Tracy kept her eyes on the monitor, and when it showed them a sufficient distance from the facility, she pulled a small box from her belt.

"That looks like a remote detonator, Corporal," the captain observed.

"Yes, sir, it is," Tracy said, her voice cheerful.

"To what?"

"Oh, just a little thank-you to the Xan-Sskarns from Alan and myself for all the hospitality they showed us."

"Well, my mother always told me to send a thank-you in a timely manner," Optika said deadpan.

"Mine, too." She laughed as she pressed the button.

In the computer core of Hugin Research Facility, three one-kilo blocks of high-yield explosives, each powerful enough to demolish a small, hardened military target, detonated. The initial concussion was enough to send a visible shudder through the base, right before a giant explosion consumed the entire facility, and every Xan-Sskarn within it.

Optika's eyes widened, and he looked at Clark and her detonator dubiously.

Clark shrugged nonchalantly and said, "The computer core was right by the base's main reactor. How often do you get a chance to blow up one of those?"

Chapter Thirty

"Attention on the flight deck," a voice echoed throughout the *Valhalla*'s port-side hangar bay. "Assault Boat Five *and* Valhalla Shuttle One, *now arriving."*

Captain Alexandra McLaughlin and her XO, Commander Tony Ruggs, stood together on the hangar deck, out of the way of the waiting flight crews and medical teams but close enough to witness all that was about to happen.

The lift closest to her finished its descent, and the hatch began to open. Against all safety regulations, the pilot of Assault Boat Five began to taxi out of the lift as soon as there was enough clearance.

With the number of wounded Optika had commed her about on board that boat, Alex had no intention of disciplining that pilot if her actions got them to the med teams even one second faster. She knew that every moment counted when it came to combat casualties.

The assault boat rolled to a stop directly in front of the waiting medical personnel, and its hatches began to open. Dr. Stratis and several med techs rushed forward to meet the marines carrying out their wounded comrades.

Alex noticed that none of them, not even the wounded, had their faceplates lifted. It wasn't until they set foot onto the hangar deck that the hale began cracking the seals on their helmets.

After one final look at the organized chaos around the assault boat, she turned her attention to the shuttle, just now finishing its taxi. As hatches opened, a few marines, their helmets still sealed as well, dropped to the deck and began to assist the civilians out.

"Commander," Alex said to her XO, "I want you to organize some quarters for our guests."

"I've already contacted the quartermaster. He's getting quarters and supplies organized and the master-at-arms is setting up escorts to see them throughout the ship and to keep them out of the way for now."

Alex absently nodded her approval, her eyes focusing on the group currently exiting the shuttle.

"Christ. Children," she whispered to herself. She had known intellectually that there would be children with the civilians—it was unavoidable—but seeing them with her own eyes made it a reality.

I don't want children on this ship, not with what we have to do. They're so young, and when you're young, it's too soon to die.

But Alex knew they were here to stay, and that she would do her utmost to see that no harm befell them. She knew the path ahead would see more ghosts added to her dreams; she didn't intend for any of them to be children.

"Tell the quartermaster that I want a nursery set up for those children in the most secure part of the ship, and I want it done tonight."

"Yes, ma'am, I'll see to it," Commander Ruggs replied, his tone clearly confused by the snarl in her order.

"Attention on the flight deck," the voice from the tower announced again. "Assault Boat Four *and* Valhalla Shuttle Two, *now arriving."*

Alex waited patiently for *Boat Four* to finish its descent into the hangar deck and taxi into place. When it finally stopped and opened its hatches, she saw three marines jump out immediately. The one in the middle turned his head, looking for something. After only a few moments, he walked directly toward her, the other two marines flanking him.

None of the three had lifted their faceplates yet, and as they closed, Alex could see the red camouflage of their combat suits was stained a much deeper red: the color of blood. Xan-Sskarn blood, while red like human blood, was a much deeper hue; however, Alex could not tell at first glance what species' blood was covering the marines. The marine in the center looked like he had walked though a knee-deep river of it and been splashed in the process. His lower legs were entirely encrusted with dried blood. The rest of his combat suit was crisscrossed in spray patterns. The other two simply looked as if they had been painted from head to toe in blood and ichor. Bits of unidentifiable hunks of meat clung to their gear and armor. The stench of rotting meat was noticeable even at this distance and grew worse as they moved closer. Xan-Sskarn blood decomposed extremely fast and emitted a distinct, horrible smell.

When they had closed to within a few steps of her, Alex felt an icy stab in her heart. The blood-covered figures, their polarized faceplates distorting the reflected images of her and Tony's faces, reminded her so strongly of the ghosts in her dreams she could hear the echoes of their howls in her mind. Only when they stopped and lifted their faceplates was the spell broken.

"Captain Optika reporting, ma'am," the center figure said, snapping his right hand up into a salute. Years of military discipline allowed Alex to respond automatically as her mind pulled itself back to reality.

"Congratulations on a mission well done, Captain."

"Thank you, ma'am." He reached out to his right, and the marine there shrugged off her pack and handed it over to him. Turning to face Alex, he held out the bloody and tattered bag. "The computer core's back-up memory module, ma'am."

Alex reached out and took hold of the straps of the bag, and when the captain released his grip, she nearly dropped it.

"Damn, that's heavy," she groaned, lowering the pack to the deck. She knew the marine had not done it on purpose; people his size and strength often forgot how much physically weaker someone of her size was.

Seeing the disconcerted look on his face, Alex began to assure him she wasn't offended, when a piercing voice interrupted her.

"Which one of you is Captain McLaughlin?"

Alex watched as a severe-looking woman in a business suit,

face flushed in what she guessed was anger, stormed over to her small cluster of people.

"That would be me, ma'am," Alex said cordially, extending her hand. "Captain Alexandra McLaughlin. And you are?"

"I am Director Sabrina Richardson, and I want to lodge a complaint, several actually, against these *people*," she wailed, pointedly ignoring Alex's hand and waving at the three marines.

Alex would not have believed it possible for Optika's face to adopt an even harder, deadlier expression if she had not seen it for herself. Letting her hand drop, she forced a smile onto her face before responding.

"Yes, ma'am. I'll be happy to listen to any complaints you might have regarding Captain Optika and his marines. Would you like to join me in my wardroom after we get your people settled, say in forty-five minutes?"

"That will be acceptable," Sabrina snapped before turning to stalk off toward the huddled group of civilians.

"What a bitch," Tony muttered when she was out of earshot.

"You have no idea, sir," Optika said in a voice like frozen helium.

"Well, it seems to me that we will all regret having the chance to find out for ourselves shortly," Alex commented. "Captain, once again, outstanding job. Get your marines settled, then report to the wardroom in forty-five minutes. I'll want to hear what happened down there."

"Yes, ma'am," Optika said as he and the two other marines—Clark and Lewis as she could see now that their faceplates were up—snapped to attention. Optika gave her a smart salute.

"Dismissed, Captain," Alex said, returning his salute.

As the marines marched away, Alex turned to face her XO.

"Tony, once you get those civilians taken care of, get us moving and heading out-system, maximum speed. Then assemble the command staff in the wardroom. There are some things we need to go over. We were lucky there was only an assault carrier in the area. I suspect that will soon change."

She didn't specify the time, trusting that he would have them there in time to hear the captain's mission report.

"Yes, ma'am. I'll have them there before Optika arrives," Tony assured her.

Alex smiled; she and the XO were beginning to mesh.

But then, combat and hardship tends to have that effect on people.

"Very good, Commander. Carry on."

Alex didn't wait for his response before she spun about and began to head toward the lift, plans and worries chasing each other around in her mind.

Alex sat alone in the darkened wardroom, absently stroking her chin and smoking a cigarette as she watched the hologram displayed before her. The representation of the Sol system and the last known location of any friendly units slowly rotated by her gaze. The green icons were depressingly few in number, and she wondered how many of them were still there.

Probably not many. Whatever Xan-Sskarn planned this attack did a damn thorough job of it.

The loss of Home Fleet brought Admiral Stevens to mind, the similarities between then and now standing out.

She had just lit another cigarette from the stub of her last when the hatch opened, pouring light into the compartment.

"Sorry, Captain, I didn't know you were here already," Commander Ruggs apologized, silhouetted by the open hatch.

"Don't worry about it, Tony. Come on in and sit down. I must've lost track of the time."

As Tony took his seat, two more officers entered the wardroom. Both of them paused for a moment to let their eyes adjust to the darkness before continuing to their seats. Alex merely nodded at their greetings, her eyes never leaving the display.

Over the next several minutes, the rest of her officers arrived and assumed their positions around the table. The only officer not in attendance was Dr. Stratis, and Alex had not expected him. He had more important things to attend to.

The last to arrive was Director Richardson, escorted by a marine private. Richardson, too, paused upon entering the wardroom, but Alex suspected it was due to uncertainty rather than any other reason.

"Please, Director, have a seat," Alex said, pointing at Dr. Stratis' empty chair.

"Thank you," the director said in a clipped voice, accepting the invitation with reluctance.

"Now, I understand you wish to file a complaint against Captain Optika and some of his marines," Alex began, looking at the director. Finding herself in a very delicate situation, she tried to keep her voice calm and even. She was going to need this woman's help in the days to come and didn't want to alienate her from the beginning. But neither was she going to sacrifice any of her marines to satisfy vanity. "Before we begin with that, let me introduce my staff."

Alex didn't give the woman time to object as she began go around the table, introducing her officers. She was pleased to see that each of them was openly polite and friendly, though Alex caught the tightening of eyes and fists from a few of them.

Once the introductions were complete, Alex leaned back in her chair and asked the director to voice her concerns.

"It's simple, Captain McLaughlin." The woman's voice was already beginning to grate on Alex's nerves. With a supreme force of will, she kept an interested look on her face while she maintained a firm grip on her temper.

"Your captain here and his marines were rude, vulgar, and almost totally barbaric in their treatment of me and my people. I don't see any reason for that kind of behavior, and I want them reprimanded for it. In fact, I don't see why they dragged us up to this ship in the first place. You will obviously have to return us to Hugin just as soon as you finish removing any alien presence there."

Alex watched Optika's face as the director went on. Not once did even a flicker of emotion pass over it. In fact, he didn't even seem to be blinking as he continued to stare straight ahead, eyes unfocused.

"I see, ma'am. I believe I can alleviate some of your concerns. First, you may not be aware of it, but the Xan-Sskarn now effectively control this system."

"Preposterous. That could never happen."

"Preposterous or not, Director, that doesn't change the fact that it *has* happened."

"How?" the director demanded.

Alex thought that the woman was looking for any piece of information she could use to argue her point, and there was no time for that. Alex decided on what she thought to be the safest course of action.

"That doesn't matter right now. What matters is that it has happened. You and your people will be safe on board the *Valhalla*.

We, your people and mine, are going to have to work together to ensure our mutual survival."

"What is that supposed to mean?"

"Exactly what I said. But now is not the time to go into it. There are more pressing matters to which we must attend." Alex gave her a look that any of her crew would have immediately recognized as a dismissal.

"Are you telling me that we are going to have to stay on this ship?" Her voice rose several octaves.

"I'm afraid so, ma'am," Alex sighed, her temper firmly under control; it was her annoyance that was now fighting to be expressed. "And before you ask, no, I don't know for how long."

"In that case, I demand that you return us to the station to collect our personal effects. And, more importantly, our research data."

"I'm afraid that's not possible, ma'am." Alex couldn't believe how someone who was supposed to be so smart could be so fucking stupid.

"Why not?"

"Because there's nothing to return to." Captain Optika's hard voice cut across the room.

"What?!" the director screeched. Alex was interested in the answer herself, but didn't say anything.

"I said, there is no facility to return to." Optika turned to face the director, and an evil grin spread across his scarred face. "It's been vaporized."

"What! H-how?" she sputtered. "Captain McLaughlin, do you know what this idiot just destroyed? Do you? There was years of irreplaceable research data down there, and now it's all gone. I *demand* to know what you plan to do about it?"

The word "demand" raised Alex's hackles, and she forced herself to remain silent for a moment before responding. She saw that she wasn't the only one affected by the director's words. The other officers around the table were now staring at her with open hostility.

All except the chief engineer, Commander Denton. She had her eyes on Alex, making sure her friend didn't repeat her actions from the week before and launch herself across the table at the infuriating woman.

"Rest assured, Director Richardson," Alex finally ground out, "that I will take the appropriate action in regard to the captain's behavior and actions."

Alex touched a control on the tables' surface, and the hatch cycled open. The marine private stepped through.

"Private, please escort Director Richardson back to her quarters."

"Yes, ma'am." The private stepped up beside the woman. "Director, if you please."

"Captain McLaughlin—" she began.

"I'm sorry, Director, but as I said earlier, there are more pressing matters that we must attend to." With that, she nodded to the marine, who took the sputtering director by the arm and guided her from the room.

Silence hung in the wardroom for several long minutes after the director's departure. Finally, Alex spoke.

"You were right, Tony."

"About what, ma'am?"

"She is a bitch."

The rest of the officers began to chuckle, then to laugh out loud—all except Captain Optika.

"Okay, Captain, first I want you to know that I don't put an ounce of consideration in the opinions or complaints of the director. The fact that every civilian was evacuated from the facility without so much as a single casualty speaks for itself." Alex smiled at the marine. "Now, that being said, can you please tell me what you meant by the facility being vaporized? I don't recall that being one of the mission objectives."

"Yes, ma'am." Optika shifted uncomfortably in his seat. "As we burned from orbit, three leveling charges were triggered. Their detonation caused the facility's reactors to lose containment."

"I see. And who do I have to thank for this?"

"I take full responsibility for it, Captain."

Alex could tell by his statement that it had *not* been his idea, but he had supported it.

"I'm sure you do, Captain, but that does not answer my question." She watched the captain return to staring at the bulkhead. She could see the conflict on his face: whether to obey his commanding officer or to protect his marines. Alex was sure what the outcome of that battle would be and decided to save the captain the agony associated with disobeying a direct order. "Whoever did it saved us a trip and a KEW. I was going to level that facility on our way out of the system anyway, Captain. So I would like to know who to thank for it."

"That would be Corporal Clark," Optika said in a voice mixed with relief and pride.

"I remember seeing her and Lewis with you on the hangar deck." She shuddered at the memory. "Looks like they ran into some serious resistance. I'm very impressed they still managed to retrieve the module."

"I didn't have time to get the full details from them, ma'am, but you're right, they did run into some serious resistance. In fact, on the shuttle they both discommended hand-to-hand combat with Xan-Sskarns, quite adamantly."

Alex joined the rest of the naval officers around the table in their shock at hearing this.

"Captain, after hearing only that much of their exploits, I hope you consider a promotion for both of them. I think they've earned it," Alex said.

"I couldn't agree more, ma'am."

"Now that that's out of the way, I would appreciate a quick overview of your mission. Specifically, why Director Richardson seems to be so pissed off at you."

"Yes, ma'am." The captain's face lost all expression again as he began to briefly describe his actions in the facility.

"And then, once we had the civilians, I performed a fighting withdrawal to the hangar bay. I had my platoons spread out, covering all possible avenues of attack while keeping the civilians in the middle. I admit to forcing them to move faster than they initially wanted to, and my choice of language was probably inappropriate, but I couldn't think of any other way to get them out safely. When we reached the hangar, I loaded them on the shuttles and deployed a perimeter, waiting for Clark and Lewis. Once they arrived, the last of the company boarded the shuttles and we burned for orbit."

The marine leaned back in his chair once he finished speaking.

"What were your casualties, Captain?" Alex asked softly.

"Nineteen dead, seven wounded, four seriously." Combat within a ship or facility was up close and extremely brutal and rarely left wounded. "Here's the list."

Alex accepted the folded slip of paper from him.

"I'm sorry for your losses, Captain. Please inform me when the memorial service will be held. I would be honored to attend."

Captain Optika only nodded.

"Very well." Alex sat forward, leaning her arms on the table, and slowly looked around at her command staff. "The reason I called you all here, besides hearing about Captain Optika's mission, was to inform you of what I intend to do about our current situation."

She waited for a moment, collecting her thoughts before continuing.

"Ladies and gentlemen, it is my intention to take the *Valhalla* out-system and carry out Admiral Greco's final order."

"What order is that, ma'am?" Tony asked interestedly.

"To ensure the survival of the human race."

"You know, Captain," Optika said after the shock of her announcement began to wear off, "I wish Corporal Clark were here."

"Why's that Captain?"

"Because she would know exactly what to say right now. I'm at a loss."

His comment broke the mood around the table, and Alex chuckled along with the others.

"From what little I've seen of the estimable corporal, I have no doubt about that," she agreed with the marine.

"Excuse me, Captain?" Barbie spoke up, seated between the marine and the CAG. "But are you saying we're going to go out and be like Adam and Eve or something like that? Make our own little world?"

Alex saw that the wing commander's concern was shared by most of the others.

"No, Barbie, I'm not planning on 'making our own little world,' as you put it. This is a warship, not a floating Garden of Eden." She gave the pilot a wan smile. "Besides, I think some of you know me well enough to realize that I definitely do *not* have the temperament to oversee the construction of a new civilization."

That elicited a few smiles from her old crew, and a few from her new as well.

"Then what, ma'am?" Commander Fain asked in his quiet, rasping voice.

"Let me ask you something, all of you." She looked around at them, waiting for their acknowledgment. "In nature, when two species come into conflict over territory and resources, do you know what happens?"

"I know, ma'am." Lieutenant Commander Albers sang out, raising her hand in the air as if she were still in school, almost squirming in her chair.

"Very well, Commander, please tell us." Alex hoped that she wouldn't regret letting Lea take center stage. It might be too hard to get it back once she got going verbally.

"Yes, ma'am." Albers took a deep breath and began. "Well, in nature, when the two species in question come into contact with each other, they begin to fight over the territory and resources they both want. This can go on for years and years, or even generations, but eventually the outcome is always the same. One of them wins."

"Well, of course one of them wins." Commander Kaufman snorted derisively. "Nobody can fight forever."

"Tell them how one side wins, Lea," Alex prompted Albers, leaning back into her chair to gauge the reactions of the faces around her when the last bit of information was revealed.

"By exterminating the other side," Albers said quickly.

Alex watched as, after a few moments, the communications officer's mind caught up with what she had just said. Eyes going wide, Lea turned to stare at her. The reactions of the rest were pretty much the same, though it was Tony who voiced what they were all thinking.

"You're talking about genocide."

"Yes, Commander, I am."

"Alex, you can't be serious," Commander Denton whispered, shock making her forget honorifics.

"I've never been so serious in my life, Heron," Alex snapped. "What other options do we have? Every peace overture has been rejected, if not outright attacked. We've lost all of the outlying systems. Or if we haven't, we will have soon enough, as there's no way for them to maintain an offensive without Sol as a base of support. So you tell me—what else can we do?"

"Nothing, I guess. It's just the thought of wiping a species from the universe. It seems wrong to me. I know there's no other option—it's either them or us."

"Heron, the idea disgusts me, too, but you're right." Alex laid her hand on Heron's arm. "It's them or us. I choose us.

"Okay, are there any more objections? Does anyone feel like they'll be unable to perform their duties in good conscience? If so, please let me know now—there won't be any recriminations." Alex fixed each of them with her deep blue eyes, trying to read their thoughts.

As each of them nodded, she felt the pressure on her chest lessen. They all agreed to follow her, to accept her reasoning, and the wave of relief that she was not alone warred with the weight of responsibility she had just assumed for herself.

"Thank you, all of you, for your trust and faith in me."

Feeling a swell of pride in her chest, Alex picked up her pad and began to scroll through the information. It was time to get started.

"CAG, Barbie, I want a full squadron of Valkyries ready to launch at a moment's notice, four-hour rotations per."

"Yes, ma'am," both replied as one.

"Captain Optika, I want you to reorganize your battalion at your discretion, but when that is finished, begin training in boarding actions, both repelling and initiating."

"Roger that, ma'am."

"Commander Tucholski, how many simultaneous jump calculations can you run?"

"Depends, ma'am," Tucholski said slowly. "If we're going for a zero-zero insertion, I can handle five at once. If we're going to be carrying any kind of delta-vee over the wall, then the number of plots drops as our velocity increases."

"Very well. When we're finished here, I want you to begin your calculations for five jump plots. Pick the destination at random, assuming we'll be heading out-system perpendicular to the Xan-Sskarns' translation point, on the same plane."

"Yes, ma'am. No problem."

"Commander Albers, have you managed to track down our transmission problem yet?"

"No, ma'am. I'm sorry." She cast her eyes downward and continued on in a morose tone. "Every time we think we've got the fault isolated, another relay goes down. It's like the glitch is staying one step ahead of us. Though I do have some good news, ma'am. Whatever the problem is, it's not affecting the battle nets. We can still talk to the shuttles or the Valkyries."

"That's something, anyway. Are you picking anything up from High Command or anyone else?"

"No, ma'am, but our receivers are working perfectly. I would guess that the Sallys have put up a jamming field around Earth."

"Keep working on getting those transmitters operational, and keep an ear out for any comms traffic."

"Yes, ma'am."

"How about your sensors, Lieutenant—everything in working order? Any bogies out there?"

"The sensors are working fine, ma'am, and there's nothing out there that I can see while we stay passive," Lieutenant Green informed her.

"Remain passive for now. I don't want to give away our position too soon."

"Aye, aye, ma'am."

"Commander Fain," she said.

"All weapon systems are in the green, Captain." Fain gave her a predatory smile. "The *Valhalla*'s ready for a fight."

"Excellent. Commander Denton?"

"The engines are purring like kittens, ma'am. The Humptys are good to go as well. Also, I've got my best diagnostician, Petty Officer Third Class Pratt, assigned to Commander Albers' techs to help in tracking down that communications problem. If anyone can track down the problem, it's her."

"Good."

She turned to face the far end of the table.

"Commander Ruggs, how's the crew handling the news?"

"Well, ma'am, it's about what I'd expect." Tony shrugged. "Most are still in shock over the destruction of Home Fleet and the fact that the Sallys are in-system. The ones that aren't, well, they're looking for a little payback. Some of the department heads have told me a few members of the crew are wondering why we're here and not out attacking the Sallys, but they think that's just reactionary talk, and I agree. Overall, I think the crew is up for whatever you decide to do, though I do suggest you plan on telling them your general intentions at some point in the near future. Give them a goal to work toward. If they just think we're running away that'll kill their morale."

"I agree with that, and I'd planned on informing the crew about my overall plan once we found a place to hole up and hammer out a few more details about it." In truth, Alex didn't have anything more than a few rough ideas, but the *Valhalla* couldn't stay in this system, and without a goal, the crew would fall apart in a very short time. She was fairly confident that she could come up with a plan, even one with a decent chance of succeeding. All she needed was time. Alex took one last look around the table before speaking again. "Once more, I just want to thank you for your support. I don't doubt that we'll have a difficult road ahead of us, but I'm just as confident that together we will be able to find our way along it. Now, you all have your assignments. Let's get to them."

As the assembled officers rose and began to move toward the hatch, she called out.

"Commander Ruggs, could I have a moment of your time, please?"

"Certainly, Captain," he said, stepping to one side of the hatch as Lieutenant Green and Commander Denton passed him, leaving him alone with Alex.

"Close the hatch."

When he had complied with her order, she indicated the chair Heron had just vacated, waiting as he took the seat and settled into it.

"I think we may have a serious problem, Tony," she began without preamble.

"What problem, ma'am?" She could see he was trying to figure out which of their current problems she was speaking of. This, unfortunately, was a new one.

"We may have a traitor on board."

"What?!" he shouted incredulously, snapping upright in his chair. "Why would you think that, ma'am?"

Alex was pleased to note that there was no disbelief in his voice, only intent curiosity.

She told him about Admiral Stevens' theory and her own observations regarding Groombridge 34.

"And that makes you think that we have a traitor on board now?"

"In and of itself, no, but add to that the fact we lost external comms the very minute we needed them most, and, well, coincidence can only explain away so much."

"That's true, but it could have been someone from Folkvang station, maybe someone on one of the courier-boat crews. Or it could actually be a coincidence."

"Possible, but if it is someone onboard the *Valhalla*, it's some-one who came over from the *Fenris*, much as it pains me to say. Until today, I would have taken a shot at any person who accused any member of that crew of treason. As a matter of fact"—she gave him a sheepish smile—"I did just that. But unfortunately, the possibility still remains."

"Okay, I can see that. What do we do about it?"

"There's not much we can do right at this moment. We can't afford to make wild accusations, or even let anyone know what I suspect. But we can't just ignore it, either. So, to that end, I want you to get with Captain Optika and have him station guards at vital and sensitive locations. You can tell him it's to make sure our civilian guests don't get into any trouble, which is the truth. Just not all of it."

"Yes, ma'am." He rose, but stopped behind his chair, gripping the back of it. "I sincerely hope that you're wrong about this, Captain."

"So do I, Tony," Alex said sadly, shaking her head. "So do I."

Chapter Thirty-one

USS *VALHALLA*
OCTOBER 14, 2197
0323Z
SOL

Alex sat in her command chair, sipping coffee and trying to chase the cobwebs from her mind.

Three hours of nightmare-infested sleep didn't do much for me. I don't feel very rested, but I do feel a bit better now, more focused.

Sometime around twenty-three hundred hours, Tony had stepped into her office and made a pointed suggestion that she might want to get some sleep. Especially if she thought that there might be trouble before they managed to make it out-system.

She took his advice and managed a quick cat nap on the couch in her office. She hoped she wouldn't make enough noise to be heard through the hatch as the dreams took hold.

Looking around the command deck, she saw that all of her crew were at their stations. She didn't catch any nasty glances directed her way and was pleased to see that they all looked somewhat refreshed. She had sent them all off to get a hot meal and some sleep a short time after their meeting.

Alex didn't know when an attack might come, nor did she

know when. She wasn't even positive that there was going to be one, but all of her instincts screamed at her that there would be. She had learned to trust her instincts years ago. *At least they'll be ready for it if it comes*, she thought, still watching her crew work.

She got up from her chair and walked over to stand behind Lieutenant Commander Tucholski, who was seated at the navigation station.

"How do we look, Jeff?" Her use of his first name and her hand on his shoulder were meant to reassure him.

"Well, ma'am," he began without looking up from his calculations, "situationwise, I've got those jump plots you wanted up and ready to go. Once we have an exact position, I'll put in the last bit of data, and we're out-system. As for how we look sensorwise, Commander Denton and I have managed to get our drive envelope and engine signatures pretty close to that of a heavy cruiser. Any Sallys come looking for an easy target are going to be in for one rude surprise."

"Very nice." She leaned in to take a closer look at the calculations on his display. "What are you working on now?"

"Oh, those are the jump plots, ma'am. I'm double-checking them now, just to make sure I didn't miss anything. Don't want to end up in the wrong place."

"Keep up the good work, Commander." She patted his shoulder one last time and moved on to the next station. She spent the next half hour working her way around the command deck, talking to her crew.

She had nearly made a full circuit of the command deck when the quiet atmosphere was broken.

"Contact!" Lieutenant Junior Grade Green's deep baritone echoed from the bulkheads.

"What have you got, Lieutenant?" Alex asked quickly, moving back to her command chair.

"Looks to be two Sally heavy cruisers," he answered her, continuing to refine his sensor data. "I think they saw us first, 'cause I didn't see them until they lit off their drives and went active."

"Well, if that's the case, I don't see any reason not to announce our presence." Alex smiled as she began to strap herself in. "You are free to go active, Lieutenant. But keep in mind, we're just a lowly little heavy cruiser trying to escape the system. Make sure you adjust your sensor strength accordingly."

"Yes, ma'am." He, too, smiled, looking forward to when they would drop their deception and show the Xan-Sskarns just what they were about to fuck with.

Those are pretty damn impressive sensors those cruisers are packing to pick us up this far out. I hope that's the case, because if my suspicions are correct, and they were waiting for us, they might have a few surprises planned for us.

"Give me a best-guess estimate as to how long until we're close enough for them to figure out that what they think they've caught really isn't a heavy cruiser."

She waited, calmly sipping coffee, while he punched commands and information into his board.

"I think we can keep them suckered for another forty-five minutes, tops."

"Thank you, Lieutenant. Keep me apprised of any changes, please."

Forty-five minutes until they were no longer able to maintain their deception. Alex felt confident in that estimate. She doubted anyone on board knew more about Xan-Sskarn sensor capabilities than Green, and that included Heron and all of their guests.

She began a countdown on one of her displays.

"Petty Officer Hurst, give me a plot centered on the Xan-Sskarn ships. Extend to include our position, plus fifty thousand kilometers," Alex called out in a firm voice. She had not yet switched to giving her orders over the battle net.

"Aye, aye ma'am. Putting it up on the projector now."

The projector at her feet hummed to life, forming a holographic sphere before her.

"Add Lieutenant Green's point of detection based on current speed and heading."

Petty Officer Hurst acknowledged the order, and Alex watched as a bright yellow line coalesced into view, bisecting the sphere.

Concentrating on the projection, Alex stroked her chin, planning her next move carefully.

"Captain, would you like to sound general quarters?" Tony's voice came quietly over her earpiece.

"Not yet, Commander," she murmured back. "I think we can let the crew get a little more rest before things start to get interesting."

"Yes, ma'am."

She could hear the resignation in his voice. Looking over at him, she gave him a small smile to reassure him that she knew what she was doing. Turning back to the projection, she continued to stare at it, wondering where the next surprise would come from.

Stroking her chin again, Alex punched a command into another of her panels.

"CAG," she called softly into her mike.

"Kaufman here," came the quick reply.

"CAG, we've got two Sally heavy cruisers on sensors, sitting right on the wall directly in front of us. I want you to prep the Lokis. I want three of them deployed in front of us, screening us. The other two I want as outriders. Let me know when they're ready for launch."

"Aye, aye, ma'am."

Alex cut the connection and continued to watch as the time until detection counted down. Ten minutes later, she heard Kaufman's voice in her earpiece.

"Lokis ready for launch, ma'am."

"Excellent, CAG. Wait one." She muted her connection and turned to face her navigation officer.

"Commander Tucholski, calculate an acceleration change that will drop our speed to seventy-five percent of maximum for a Loki, five minutes prior to Lieutenant Green's estimation of maximum Xan-Sskarn sensor range for positive identification."

Tucholski repeated her order back before turning to his board, entering in the parameters she had just given him.

"I have our new acceleration profile, ma'am."

"Time between new profile execution and the five-minute mark?" she asked, feeling her pulse quicken. She was beginning to set her pieces for the endgame.

"Coming up on one hour seventeen minutes."

"Execute new profile at that mark."

"Roger, ma'am," he said, keeping his finger poised over the execute command. His finger stabbed down as he called back to her. "New profile executed. One hour seventeen minutes until five-minute mark intersection."

Nodding her approval, Alex unmuted her connection to Commander Kaufman.

"CAG, launch the Lokis in one hour ten minutes. Have them accelerate to full speed for five minutes then cut back to seventy-five percent power. At that time, they will go active."

"Lokis, dancing vac in seventy minutes. Aye, ma'am."

Alex cut the connection and picked up her coffee, taking a sip before speaking.

"And now, people, we wait."

This time, we're not shot to hell and desperate to escape. This time, we're the ones with a surprise or two up our sleeve.

Sitting in his command chair, Ki-Xarn Pi'Hosin watched the display as his tail, extending from the opening in the back of the chair, absently swished back and forth. It seemed that the orders he had received from Vice Commander Si'Lasa were more than the paranoid supposition that Pi'Hosin had thought they were.

"It would seem that our estimable vice commander is correct once more. There is indeed a ship attempting to flee the system," he said to his command crew. "These Dry-Skins disgust me. Abandoning their home to save their own pathetic hides."

The sounds coming from the crew at their stations was a mixture of approval of their Ki-Xarn's words and loathing of the actions of their enemy.

"Tesh, send a communiqué to the *Deep Waters* and inform them that we have detected the enemy and, upon my honor, will prevent their escape," Pi'Hosin ordered his communications officer. "Then inform the ki-xarn of the *Crashing Waves* that he will support the *Dark Clouds* in our battle against the Dry-Skins, but the honor of the kill shall be ours."

"By your command, Ki-Xarn," came the hissing reply.

Exactly one hour later, Alex snapped up in her chair and broke her silence.

"Commander Ruggs, sound general quarters!"

"Aye, ma'am." Tony's voice seemed relieved. "Sounding general quarters."

Screaming alarms filled the *Valhalla*, and, throughout the ship, men and women rushed to their battle stations. It was time for some payback.

Alex let the alarms continue for another minute before silencing them.

"Commander Albers, shipwide, please," she said, connecting to the communications net.

"Shipwide, aye."

"Attention all hands, this is the captain. We are about to engage two Xan-Sskarn heavy cruisers that have foolishly placed themselves in our path. I know by now you are all aware of what has transpired here in Sol within the last day. The loss of Home Fleet, the loss of Folkvang station, the loss of ships and lives. Of friends and loved ones. I share your pain and grief, and my soul cries out for vengeance just as yours do. Some of you may be wondering why, if I share your desire, we are leaving the system. I will tell you why." Alex felt her pulse quicken, and a primal urge to rend and tear began to grow in her heart.

"I do not wish to simply kill a few Xan-Sskarn ships, nor do I wish to just kill the Xan-Sskarn that led the attack that caused the deaths of our comrades."

Her voice dropped to a growl.

"No, my friends, I wish to kill so many Xan-Sskarns that our name becomes something to fear, something that is only whispered in secret in the dark. The name *Valhalla* will become synonymous with death, and whole generations of Xan-Sskarns will curse the day they called us forth upon this galaxy. For we will become vengeance, and we shall strike down any Xan-Sskarn that crosses our path."

She didn't see the fire that burned in her crew's eyes. She didn't have to; she could feel it burning into her, feeding her fire, giving her strength.

"We cannot accomplish that here. Not now. The Xan-Sskarns have won today. They have won *their* war. *Our* war is just beginning. We will go out and wreak such death and destruction on them that they will find the cost of this victory too high to pay. But pay for it they shall. In blood."

Alex closed her eyes, and for a fleeting moment saw her ghosts before her. When she opened them again, she finally saw her new crew, their hungry eyes boring into her soul. She knew then that she would be leading most if not all of them to their deaths, but this time they would not go alone. Her voice dropped to a deadly whisper.

"And we are about to collect our first payment."

She took a deep breath before snarling out her last order.

"All hands, prepare for battle."

"Has there been any change in the Dry-Skins' profile?" Pi'Hosin demanded of the ki-tesh at the sensor station.

"No, Ki-Xarn, they remain on the same course, and there have been no unusual energy emissions or communications from them. They must see us, but have done nothing to avoid us."

These Dry-Skins make no sense. First they try to escape, but when their path is blocked, they do not try to evade conflict but continue on directly into it. Maybe there is some fight left in the hearts of these animals after all. But it will do them no good.

"Tesh," he said, turning to the communications officer again. "Inform our pilots that they will engage as planned."

"CAG!" Alex barked into her mike. "Launch the Lokis."

"Launching now, Captain." The fire was evident in his voice.

"Commander Tucholski, once those Lokis are in position and have gone active, I want you to drop the disguise."

"Drop disguise upon Loki activation. Aye, ma'am." His voice, too, was thick with emotion.

"Commander Ruggs, coordinate with Heron and prepare your damage-control teams. I want them in place and ready to go."

"Setting up DC net now, Captain." Tony's voice was different than the others had been, and when she looked into his eyes, she could see that he was finally *really* seeing her for the first time. Seeing the warrior that had led not one but two willing crews into the mouth of hell and brought them back out again. She gave him a wolfish smile before turning back to her panels.

Alex continued to issue orders, getting updates on readiness, times, and distances to engagement ranges.

"New contact! Multiple incoming," Lieutenant Green's voice practically sang out. He was finally getting the vengeance for his family he had craved for so long.

"Plot it," Alex ordered into scanning's net and watched as the new contacts resolved in the projection. Four Xan-Sskarn fighter squadrons were closing in on them: two from starboard, the other two from port. She took note of the time till intercept. As close as they were, she knew that they had to be lying doggo, waiting for them.

"They knew we were coming," Tony's voice whispered to her. "You were right—we've got a traitor on board."

"Yes, but there's nothing we can do about it now," she replied just as quietly. "Besides, if that's the only surprise they have waiting for us, well, let's just say it won't be enough to even slow us down. Not enough by a wide margin."

She saw a quizzical look on his face, and she flashed him another evil grin. Never taking her eyes off him, she tapped a command into one of her panels.

"CAG, we've got Sally fighters incoming. Port and starboard, two squadrons each. Estimate time to intercept as twelve minutes. Launch the wing."

"Yes, ma'am!" Kaufman's voice was exuberant. "Valkyrie Squadrons One through Ten launching for fighter intercept."

Alex saw the look of comprehension crossing Tony's face as she closed her connection to Kaufman. One hundred forty of the latest model Valkyries against eighty Xan-Sskarn fighters. The term "overkill" was an understatement.

"Lokis just went active," Green announced. "I'm blind."

"Reconfiguring now," Tucholski called out.

Alex looked at the projection and noted that the outlines of the Xan-Sskarn heavy cruisers were now surrounded by a pulsing purple ring indicating last *known* position.

"Getting feeds from the outriders now," Green called out again.

The outriders were Lokis as well, but unlike their three comrades in front of the *Valhalla,* they had not gone active, though they were still stealthed and almost impossible for the Xan-Sskarn to detect, especially at long range. Instead, they had flown out beyond the jamming fields and begun to parallel them. They were far enough out that they could scan both the Xan-Sskarn and the *Valhalla,* effectively becoming the *Valhalla*'s eyes while she was hidden by the jamming fields.

The projection updated again, and now not only were the Xan-Sskarn heavy cruisers upgraded to known targets, they were moving.

"Lieutenant Green, how long until the Xan-Sskarns will be unable to avoid energy range?" Alex asked, wanting to make sure the enemy would not be able to escape.

"Seventeen point three minutes at their current rate of acceleration, ma'am."

"Excellent. Commander Tucholski, maintain current heading and speed."

"Aye, ma'am."

Alex stroked her chin, a small smile playing across her lips. Seventeen minutes, then the tables would finally be turned. She spoke to the red icons of the Xan-Sskarn heavy cruisers.

"You're not the only one with surprises out here, my friends."

Barbie sat in the cockpit of her Valkyrie with her helmet on, faceplate up, and the cockpit open. She and her RIO had been sitting in the cockpit since the call to general quarters. The fighter was armed and lined up with the launch tube, ready to taxi into it and be hurled out into space. The rest of First Squadron was lined up down the bay beside her. The *Valhalla* could launch fourteen Valkyries, one full squadron, from each hangar deck at one time. With the entire wing ready and lined up, the *Valhalla* could launch all one hundred forty of her fighters in under five minutes.

"So, you never did tell me where you got your call sign from, Flynn?" Barbie said into her helmet mike. She was patched into their private channel.

"Oh, it comes from some old vid star, a couple hundred years dead, I think," Commander David Socha replied. "Some guy named Errol Flynn. He was supposedly some dashing, handsome scoundrel, and, well, the ladies at flight school seemed to think it fit."

"Oh, Lord help me," Barbie laughed. She was bouncing back to her normal self thanks to Flynn, but she still couldn't tell when he was being serious or not. She chose not this time. "I bet you picked that one out yourself as soon as you graduated, trying to get away from some horrible call sign."

"I would never do that, break with tradition like that. I'm shocked that you would think such a thing." He was laughing now, too.

She opened her mouth to say something else when the CAG's voice crackled in her helmet. She pulled her faceplate down and saw that he was talking across the squadron commander's net.

"Okay, boys and girls, listen up. We've got four Sally squadrons inbound, ETA twelve minutes. Two on each side of us. The captain wants this taken care of quick, fast, and in a hurry, so we're launching the entire wing. Alpha Flight will take the port-side bandits, Bravo the starboard. Any questions?"

Barbie didn't have any, and she doubted that any of her other squadron commanders did, either.

"All right," Kaufman's voice came back after a moment's pause. "Barbie, they're all yours."

"Roger that, Hangman. Alpha Flight will engage port-side incoming fighters. Bravo Flight will engage starboard incoming," she said formally over the net. "Valkyrie Wing 115 will comply."

She reached out and hit the control to close the cockpit, then began to check the seals of her flight gear. Once she was satisfied that everything was as it should be, she ran a practiced eye over her panels while her Valkyrie taxied into launch tube one.

"This is *Valkyrie One*-one," she said over the squadron commander's net, identifying herself as First Squadron's first Valkyrie and also as the wing commander. "All squadrons will hold at one thousand kilometers after launch and await further instructions from the flight commander."

A chorus of acknowledgments came back to her as the tube door finished sealing. Now it was time to worry just about her and Flynn until they launched; then the fate of Valkyrie Wing 115 would once more be in her hands.

"How do things look back there?" she asked Flynn over their net after verifying that everything was good on her side of the cockpit.

"Looks good. I've got green lights on all the diagnostics, weapons are hot, and I've got a positive catapult lock."

There was a momentary hissing as the air was removed from the tube, but it quickly stopped as a vacuum was established.

"This is *Valkyrie One*-one, requesting permission to launch," she said formally to the tower.

"Permission granted, *Valkyrie One*-one. Good hunting. Launching in three...two..."

Taking a deep breath and tightening her muscles, she waited for the countdown to finish and was slammed back against her chair when it did. Her Valkyrie raced down the tube and shot into space.

Pulling the stick over while stepping on the foot pedal, she banked her fighter away from the ship and headed toward the rendezvous point. She slowed her fighter to a near stop while the rest of her flight launched and formed up on her.

Checking her monitor, it looked like the flight had finished launch operations. Opening her squadron's net first, she confirmed that all of her pilots were with her, then she switched to the flight's net, calling for confirmation on the rest of the flight.

"This is *Valkyrie One*-one, reporting successful launch."

"*Valkyrie Three*-one, all present and accounted for."

"*Valkyrie Five*-one, we're all here."

This continued on until all of her squadrons reported in; the launch had been completed without incident. Switching nets once more, she verified Bravo Flight's status.

"*Valkyrie Two*-one, verify status of Bravo Flight."

"*Valkyrie Two*-one reports successful launch." The official tone of the speaker's voice dropped away as he added, "Good hunting, Barbie."

"You too, Jackal. See you back on the deck."

She only had one more report to make, and then it would be time to go to work.

"CAG, this is *Valkyrie One*-one, reporting successful launch of Wing 115."

"*Valkyrie One*-one, this is the CAG, roger that," Kaufman said. "Good luck, and good hunting."

She cut back to Alpha Flight's net.

"Okay, boys and girls, here's the plan. First, Third, and Fifth squadrons will go straight in. Seventh, you'll split your squadron—half go in from above, the other below. Ninth, you'll hold back and take care of any that get by us."

Her squadron leaders accepted her orders with a variety of answers.

"Now let's see what these new I-Coms can do in real combat. All Valkyries accelerate to full engagement speed. It's time to dance."

Barbie jerked the stick over while she reversed thrust and stomped on the right pedal, standing her Valkyrie on its left wing for a fraction of a second. Ramming the throttle forward, she sent the fighter shooting ahead, diving directly at a Xan-Sskarn fighter trying to get a lock on one of her pilots.

She squeezed the trigger on the control stick, and her cannons blazed to life, disintegrating the Xan-Sskarn ship. Letting out a howl of triumph, she continued on her flight path, racing through the expanding ball of fire she had just created.

"We've picked up a tail, Barbie," she heard Flynn say. Swinging her head around, she tried to find the target but failed.

"Where is he?"

"High on our six and coming in fast."

Barbie started to put her craft into a reverse roll that she hoped would send her assailant racing past her. She never got to finish the maneuver.

"Missile! Break right!" Flynn shouted. "Releasing countermeasures."

At Flynn's warning, she had put the Valkyrie into a tight barrel roll. Coming out of it, she saw two Xan-Sskarns were on the tail of a Valkyrie.

"Five-two, you've got a pair on your tail. Pull up—I've got them."

She watched as Five-two's Valkyrie went into a sharp climb and waited for the Xan-Sskarns to try and follow him. When they did, they flew directly into her line of fire.

"Eat this, you bastards!" she growled, attempting to impart her fury into the blast by pulling savagely on the trigger.

Her first burst flamed the left-hand fighter out of existence, but as she pulled over to get behind the right-hand one, it dove straight down, trying to execute the maneuver she had been attempting earlier. Recognizing this, Barbie pulled up into a loop of her own.

Coming out of the loop, she saw her opponent pulling out of his, leaving them both heading directly at each other. She couldn't get a lock on him before they raced past each other, inverted, with less than a meter between their cockpits.

"What the fuck was that?" Flynn's strangled voice half shouted.

Barbie didn't respond; she was already hunting for another target. Unfortunately, they were becoming hard to find; her flight was systematically blowing the Xan-Sskarn fighters out of space.

"I don't see any more bandits out here, do you?" She demanded of her RIO, her bloodlust not yet slaked.

"I see a few knife fights still going on, but they'll be over before we can get there."

"Damn!"

"Don't worry about it, boss." His voice was serious. "I have a feeling that we'll do this dance quite a bit for the foreseeable future."

"Yeah, you're probably right." She glanced at her display and saw only the green icons of her Valkyries. "We're clear out here. Let's round up the kiddies and head on back to the barn."

Alex watched the distance shrink between the *Valhalla* and the Xan-Sskarn ships. The last seconds of her timer flashed by, and it was now time for them to give the Xan-Sskarns a surprise for once.

"Commander Tucholski, take us over the top of our Lokis, one hundred kilometers above the outer edge of the jamming field," Alex called over the net. "Full military power, maintain current heading. I want to pass right between them."

While the navigation officer implemented her orders, Alex turned her attention to her communications officer.

"Commander Albers, contact our outriders, have them maintain their current heading and speed. When the jamming fields drop, have all Lokis move to rendezvous with the Valkyries and wait for further orders."

Albers acknowledged the orders, turned to her boards, and sent out the message.

"Guns," Alex said, patching into tactical's net. "Set PDLs and PDGs for maximum fire interdiction. I doubt they have any fighters left, but if they do, we'll just call Barbie in to deal with them."

She watched him nod as she continued to issue her orders.

"Prepare your drones and bring your ECM on line now. As soon as we read missile separation, deploy the drones. Don't wait for my orders."

Commander Fain finished reiterating her orders and implementing them before he asked a question.

"Targeting priority, Captain?"

"Maintain a lock on each of them right now, but hold your fire. I want to wait until we are within powered-missile range before engaging, if we can."

"Understood, ma'am."

"Captain, it looks like they've finally figured out that they've been suckered," Lieutenant Green reported. "They're heaving to and trying to run for it."

"Let them," Alex said, maliciously. "The *Valhalla*'s got the legs to chase them down. How long to powered-missile range?"

"Ten minutes, ma'am, but that's a rough estimate right now. Looks like we've scared the hell out of them. They're still accelerating. They have to be redlining their reactors to be generating that much delta-vee."

"Let me know when you have a firm time."

"Yes, ma'am."

■ ■ ■

Ki-Xarn Pi'Hosin stalked around the command center, hissing at the current situation.

What kind of ship is that? There is no record of it ever being seen before. And the power! Even if we believe only half of what our sensors recorded prior to their interference fields coming on line, two Kiras are no match for it. Fleeing from battle sickens me, but while honor dictates that I fight for the glory of the Xan-Sskarn Empire, honor also reminds me that I have a responsibility to my ship and crew not to waste their lives in a hopeless battle.

"What is the status of our engines?"

"The engineering staff reports that the engines are at maximum output, Ki-Xarn," Pi'Hosin's second-in-command reported. "Tactical calculations show that we will be unable to avoid combat."

"I can see that!" Pi'Hosin snapped out. "Can we establish a connection to the *Deep Waters*?"

"Negative, Ki-Xarn. The Dry-Skins' interference field is too powerful."

So we can not even inform the high commander of this new type of ship. So be it.

"Plot a firing solution and prepare to fire on my command."

"But we will not be within effective range for several more waves."

"I am aware of that, *Xarn*," Pi'Hosin's voice sounded resigned. "There is no other option. We must attempt to do as much damage to them as possible before they get into range, because when that happens, our lives will be in the hands of the Supreme One."

Alex was concentrating on the plot, watching vectors and times changing, when Tony interrupted her thoughts.

"I'm surprised that they let us get this close without confirming their target."

"Oh, I'm not," she said distractedly.

"Why's that?"

"They got complacent. Everything's been going their way so far—they saw no reason for it not to continue to do so. They weren't even worried when they lost contact with their fighters, assuming it had to do with the Lokis and not because they'd all been destroyed."

She leaned back into her chair, elbows on the armrests, fingers interlaced under her chin.

"And now we're going to make them pay for that complacency."

"Yes, ma'am. That we are." He gave her an evil smile of his own.

"Powered-missile range in fourteen point five minutes, mark," Green said when the Xan-Sskarns' acceleration finally leveled out. "And we'll be in beam range ten minutes after we cross the missile envelope."

"Thank you, Lieutenant."

The command deck was eerily silent for the next ten minutes as all eyes watched the distance fall.

"Vampire, vampire, vampire!" Green's shout ratcheted the tension on the command deck up a notch. "Tracking multiple missile launches from both cruisers."

"Drones away, Captain," Commander Fain reported, and Alex watched as a pair of *Valhalla*s joined the first on her plot. Not that the drones would do much good at the moment. The missiles coming in at them now would be ballistic by the time they arrived. But in four minutes, when they finally entered powered-missile range, those drones would emit their siren call, hopefully dragging many a missile to its death, away from the *Valhalla*.

Alex watched as every missile of the first salvo was intercepted and destroyed by the point-defense net. She activated the repeater display above her head, allowing her to actually "see" the point-defense net in action. The tri-barrel point-defense lasers picked off missiles at long range. Any missile that managed to run that gauntlet ran right into the teeth of the point-defense guns. The twenty-five-millimeter, six-barreled chain guns cycled at a phenomenal rate, the shells destroying the missiles before they could reach effective range.

The third and fourth waves of missiles went the way of the first two.

"We are now within powered-missile range, Captain," Lieutenant Green announced. "Ten minutes to beam range."

The missiles coming in at the *Valhalla* now would still have life on their drives and would be able to maneuver, trying to worm their way past the point-defense net. Conversely, their missiles would have the same advantage, and they had more of them.

"Commander Fain?" Alex asked softly. "Do you see that cruiser to the starboard?"

"Yes, ma'am."

"Kill it."

"Yes, ma'am." Even with the vengeful mood that she was in, the tone of her tactical officer's voice sent a chill down her spine.

That is one man I definitely *do not want to get on the wrong side of.*

Fain's fingers danced over his board then stabbed down on the launch button. Alex watched the plot as forty missiles streaked from the *Valhalla's* tubes. Twice the number of missiles that *both* Xan-Sskarn cruisers were sending back at them.

She was still concentrating on the plot, watching their second salvo of missiles streak toward the Xan-Sskarn cruiser, when she felt the ship shake.

One of the enemy's missiles had evaded the point-defense net, getting close enough to inflict damage.

Plasma roiled over the starboard midships.

"Damage report!" she cried out.

"Nothing serious, just some armor damage," Tony reassured her as two more missiles detonated.

"Still only armor damage, ma'am."

"Holy shit!" came an excited yell from Lieutenant Green.

"Lieutenant?" Alex snapped.

"Sorry, ma'am, it's just that I'm reading plumes and a massive debris field, plus a significant power drop-off in the starboard cruiser."

Alex whipped her head around to watch as the icon representing the cruiser began to pulse with estimated damage. It began to flash faster as another barrage of missiles intersected with it. She was concentrating on the plot with such intensity that she didn't even notice the rocking of the ship from another impact.

Suddenly the cruiser vanished from the projection.

One down, one to go.

"Guns..."

She never go to finish what she was about to say.

"Targeting remaining cruiser now, Captain," Fain said as the first flight of missiles leapt from the tubes, chasing after the fleeing cruiser.

The *Valhalla* rocked under another series of impacts, and she turned her head to look at Commander Ruggs.

"More armor damage," he said, reading from the damage-control panel. "And a small outer-hull breach. Inner hull undamaged. God damn, this is one tough ship."

Alex had to agree with him.

"Now entering beam range," Green advised.

"Cease fire with missiles!" she said quickly. "Commander Tucholski, bring us ninety degrees to starboard. Commander Fain, with energy mounts only, fire as we bear."

Both officers confirmed her orders.

The *Valhalla* swung her bow to the starboard while maintaining her forward vector. The maneuver took time. Time enough for two more missiles to breach the defense net.

"We just lost a PDL," Tony informed her.

Alex didn't reply as she watched her repeater display. The turn completed, eight hellishly bright beams of destruction flashed from the *Valhalla*'s flank. A heartbeat later, the last Xan-Sskarn ship came apart in an expanding sphere of fire.

Alex was sitting in her command chair, staring at the brightly colored holograph projected before her, thinking. She was supremely grateful that there had been no serious casualties on board during their battle. They had lost nine Valkyries, and she felt a stab of regret over that, but she knew it could've been much worse.

Her new crew and new ship had both performed superbly. She only hoped that the hardships ahead would not exact too high a toll on either of them.

She looked up as Commander Ruggs approached her.

"Recovery operations are almost complete, ma'am," he reported. "The last squadron is landing now. We'll be ready to jump in approximately five minutes."

"Thank you, Commander."

Turning away from him, she called out.

"Commander Tucholski, do you have your plots ready?"

"Yes, ma'am."

"Good, pick one, it doesn't matter which, and prepare for jump."

"Prepare for jump. Aye, ma'am."

She turned back and saw that Tony was still standing beside her chair, looking at her.

"Something on your mind, Tony?"

"I was just wondering if this was the best course of action." He gave a slight shrug as he said this.

"Like I said before, what other choices do we have?"

"I know. I just don't like the thought of leaving the Sallys in control here."

"Neither do I, but it won't be this way forever."

They both fell silent as they watched the lights on her status board change from green to yellow as the final Valkyries landed.

"Jump plotted, Captain," Tucholski announced.

"Thank you, Commander."

She fell silent, staring at the hologram in front of her.

"Do you think we'll ever see it again?" Tony asked quietly, lifting his chin toward the projection.

Alex continued to stare at the slowly rotating image of Earth.

"Yes, Commander, I think we will," she said just as quietly.

And when we do come back, it will be my turn to give the Xan-Sskarn nightmares.

Leaning back, she cleared her throat and spoke in a clear, confident voice.

"Jump!"

Glossary

ACM:	Air Combat Maneuvers.
Aesir:	Name of the Norse gods.
Asgard:	Home of the Norse gods.
Battle Net:	Communication frequencies used by different departments.
CAG:	Commander Air Group.
CIC:	Combat Information Center.
CO:	Commanding Officer.
DC Net:	Damage-Control Net.
Dead Jokers:	The call sign of all Loki pilots.
ECM:	Electronic Counter Measures.
EMP:	Electromagnetic Pulse.
Fenris:	Monstrous wolf destined to kill Odin.
Folkvang:	Home of Freya.
Frigga:	Wife of Odin.

FTL:	Faster than light.
Gna:	Messenger of Frigga.
Hermond:	The nimble god.
Hervor:	A warrior-maiden.
Hugin:	One of Odin's ravens, whose name means "thought."
Humpty:	Jump-drive engines whose shape resembles eggs. Also known as fold engines.
I-Com:	Inertial compensator.
IFF:	Identification friend or foe.
Ka-Shesh:	Xan-Sskarn rank equivalent to a Terran naval ensign.
KEW:	Kinetic energy weapon.
Kira:	Xan-Sskarn heavy cruiser–class ship.
Kisnan:	Xan-Sskarn battleship–class ship.
Ki-Tesh:	Xan-Sskarn rank equivalent to a Terran naval lieutenant.
Ki-Xarn:	Xan-Sskarn rank equivalent to a Terran naval commander.
Lashana:	Xan-Sskarn expletive.
Le-Kisnan:	Xan-Sskarn carrier-class ship.
Loki:	Electronic warfare plane. Norse god of mischief and trickery.
Midgard:	The Norse name for Earth.
Mjölner:	Thor's hammer.
Mustang:	Prior enlisted person who has earned their commission and become an officer.

Nan:	Xan-Sskarn frigate-class ship.
Odin:	Father and ruler of the Norse gods.
PDG:	Point-defense gun.
PDL:	Point-defense laser.
Phase Drive:	Also known as a P-Drive.
Ran:	Norse goddess of the sea.
Ring Knocker:	Fleet Academy graduate.
Ri-Nan:	Xan-Sskarn destroyer-class ship.
RIO:	Radar Intercept Officer.
Salamander:	Terran slang for the Xan-Sskarn.
Sally:	Terran slang for the Xan-Sskarn.
Sif:	Thor's wife.
Sigyn:	Wife of Loki.
Sleipnir:	Odin's steed.
Ssi-Kira:	Xan-Sskarn light cruiser–class ship.
Ssi-Nan:	Xan-Sskarn scout/courier-class ship. The smallest craft in the Xan-Sskarn navy capable of FTL travel.
Sunna:	The daughter of Mundifiore that rides a chariot of day.
Tavark:	A notoriously vicious amphibious creature native to the Xan-Sskarn home world.
Tesh:	Xan-Sskarn rank equivalent to a Terran naval lieutenant, junior grade.
Thor:	Norse god of thunder.
Uller:	Norse god of winter, also known as Ull or Ullr.

Patrick A. Vanner

Valhalla:	The hall of warriors slain in combat.
Valkyrie:	Space superiority fighter. Battle-maidens. Choosers of those fallen heroically in battle.
Vampire:	Incoming missile.
Vidar:	Norse god of vengeance, also known as the silent god.
Xanle-Kisnan:	Xan-Sskarn command ship.
Xan-Liarn:	Xan-Sskarn rank equivalent to a Terran naval captain.
Xan-Sskarn:	Alien species resembling Terran salamanders.
Xarn:	Xan-Sskarn rank equivalent to a Terran naval lieutenant commander.
XO:	Executive officer.